ACT 1

THE DIARY
OF
NOBODY'S HERO

NExT PACE →

STAGEDOOR

The vertical late evening rain wasn't making any difference to how wet the bricks were already. The old alley way, with its steps and railings, rusted old, dim and broken streetlights had fared well, being tucked between tall buildings, from the bombs that had scarred the area.

The sign reading "STAGEDOOR" (once painted with solid white brushstrokes though now faded and chipped, belied the majestic and extravagant flourishes of the front entrance) was illuminated by a dim single bulb lantern which was always lit and never seemed to break.

It had seen many people through its entrance way over the years, great and new, young and old and had been witness to huge adoring crowds, lovers' trysts, devastating failures and even murder. If only it could talk. It probably would have told you…but that's another story.

And tonight, tonight is another story. Tonight, a young lady and young man shall leave together for the first time. They're stepping into the beginning of their lives. If they knew what lay ahead, would they listen, take heed and turnabout or carry on regardless knowing that this will be different for the path is not yet made.

The door swung open and an excited couple came out, arm looped in arm, smiling, happy and laughing, oblivious to anything the wet drops could offer. Calls of "Goodnight" echoed and splashed around as more exited to go in different ways.

"See you tomorrow"

"Don't forget your cue" was shouted back which caused a ripple of amusement.

The couple momentarily paused, turned and waved, then kissed and moved on, trying to huddle from the rain under some imaginary shelter, the umbrella of love.

Out onto the main road, which was glistening with the reflection of streetlights, a taxi was hailed. It pulled up alongside the kerb, spraying unoffended droplets behind itself, carefully not wanting to ruin this precious moment. The young gentleman opened the door open for Cassie (or Cassandra to her parents), which she gladly accepted and climbed in. He leant into the window breathing in the smell of warm leather and sandalwood and passing a pound note to the driver "Hyde Park Avenue, please cabbie".

"Thank you, Darling. I'll miss you, be good".

"I'll miss you too, until tomorrow" said Robert as he waved and kissed the air goodnight.

The cab pulled away to its destination, with Cassandra smiling and sitting back in the comfort of her carriage, whilst Robert turned and started walking his way through the puddles back to his digs in Thayer Street. He could've shared the journey though he preferred to keep "the ladies honour" and love was comfort enough.

The hackney turned right at the lights and was now out of view. Cas leaned forward and slid open the small glass hatch. "Driver, Frith Street please" she said and closed the divide before any enquiry could come. Sitting back, still smiling, her clutch bag was opened and a compact and lipstick removed. Checking in the small mirror and adjusting any imperfections, Cassie wondered whether all the boys would be there tonight.

As Robert walked in his thoughts, he didn't notice the time of his steps or the cessation of heavenly drops, his face was wet with tears of his own. He was thousands of miles away, walking through his KwaZulu homeland smelling the mimosa trees that lined the track to their farm, reminding him of warm and beautiful motherly love and the hard pain of loss, hurt and rejection of its male counterpart. He had never been good enough.

Before his anger had time to rise, a rumble rolled around the dark skies above, unnoticed from the city streets, causing him to turn his collar up more and fasten his step.

"Not far to go" the buildings said, as he walked past the abundance of shop windows, selling everything he didn't need and nothing he wanted. The paths were quieter as Robert neared his digs, beckoning him in, into the land of confusion and loneliness, a place to run away from your answers and hide from the truths.

The key was already reaching out to the lock. His hand dropped away, his feet turned, a moment's hesitation and then Robert walked back into the night.

The cab pulled up to the club, its old-time windscreen wipers failing to keep with the times of the cats listening to the blows of an axe. Change and tip exchanged, Cassie stepped out of one world straight into another. The unassuming street level basement door opened with an outpour of dizzying allusive melodies, pungent with green, wet with sweat and hot 'til you drop.

Before Cas made her way to the bottom of the concrete stairs, she met Ronald and Jay heading up.

"Hey Cassie baby, what's happening"? said J, his body soaking from jamming too long on his kit.

"Yeah Cas" interjected Ronald "we thought you were on stage tonight? Didn't you meant to have that thing with Robert"?

"Oh, you know how it is. I'd much rather be here with you boys.

Is Tommy around"? she hoped.

"Yeah baby, he's on right now, can't you hear him"?

Straight away Cassandra recognised the trumpet blowing hard, bouncing around, not knowing which way the wind will blow...that's Tommy. His lips will be locked tight with his instrument, an eternal battle of expression, the sounds of his soul blasting out and filling her every corner.

"I said can't you hear him"? Jay shouted a second time.

"Oh yes, I thought it was him". She lied, speaking instinctively before her mind had chance to come out of its dream.

Ronald and Jay carried on up the stairs, goodness knows where their destination was, but she knew where they'd probably end up. The three of them were virtually inseparable, a bit like a coin having three sides, the edge keeping them together yet separated, that was Thomas.

Once through the darkened heavy smoke wall, the dim-stained lights announced an arrival to the small, wooden round tabled room. The obligatory ashtray on each surface, filled with an assortment of odds and ends, no coasters here, as no one would see the rings left by the glasses of statements or cups of warm coolness.

Cassie placed herself in position whilst casually waving at Thomas, not for his benefit, but rather to let others know that she was part of the in-crowd, the select group, someone special, someone they couldn't ever be.

Tina, "...bitch" the thought came quietly to Cassie, arrived at the table to offering the sale of cigarettes, "and everything else you have to offer" came the inward sneer followed by "you even know I don't smoke". She even had the audacity to ask "or perhaps you'd like something to drink"? With veins colder than ice "tea" came the response, sending Her away, little miss wiggle pants. Tina knew exactly what Cassandra always ordered and wanted, though treated her like any another guest.

Picking up her clutch, she pulled out a slightly crumpled Woodbine and waited for someone to notice that it needed lighting. A young, spotty attempt of a man lurched too eagerly forward, open mouth smiling, offered a ready lit match.

"Need a light doll? Barry".

Closing her eyes with a dismissive nature, cut Barry out of her life forever, after the naked flame had been accepted. One puff and it lit. The few loose sticks had been collected over time and only came out when on her own in company and was a handy tool for gaining attention. She didn't need them to hide behind, if anything they were an unwanted distraction of her desires, she didn't want anyone to ignore her, not ever, ever, ever... again.

Tommy was just finishing off his set, he'd soon be over, wanting to embrace with his lean, perspiration-soaked body. He lived for his music, "Trad. was so passe" mused Cassie over her cup tea which had materialised out of nowhere. "Robert, on the other hand, wasn't much into modern" drifted her thoughts "but he was tall, strong and good looking" she listed "...in a different kind of way. And he had a wounded vulnerableness about him" making Cassandra feel protective and motherly...

Her thoughts were cut short as Thomas gripped her shoulder with those strong fingers.

"Hi kid, great to see you made it. Where the boys"?

Cassie explained that she'd seen them on the stairs as she was coming in, though added some unnecessary, speculative ideas to pad out the interest.

Tommy explained that Jay and Ronald had probably decided not to wait for him, to go to a party. He omitted the part of them not wanting to cramp Tommo's style with Cassie, though they, in turn, didn't fully explain that heads could roll with too many queens around.

"I'll drop you off home on the way to the party if you like"? suggested Tommy, not allowing for an alternative option. He loved Cassie with as much as his aching heart would allow, yet lately…lately. "Things had been going well, pretty crazy in fact" travelled across his thoughts "Serious even, yet lately a sudden change".

Tom stood behind Cassie and took her chair as she stood, waved and called goodnight to all, which was responded to by a hail of replies and an impromptu chorus of applause. Cassie liked the attention and waved back.

They exited through the dark brown wooden door next to the stage and straight out, into the servant's entrance, the open basement area below street level and immediately and passionately kissed. Their embrace was mutual, their bodies fitting each other, meant for each other. The door shut behind them, closing off the rest of the world and, for a moment, they were the only two who existed.

AIR RAID

The air raid sirens fell silent. The slow whine down and for a moment, just a moment … everything was silent, the air and time itself seemed to stand still, as if hesitating to return to this moment. A deep tobacco cough, a baby's cry and then noise of hundreds of souls, scattered and packed over the platform and rails, scared and unknowing, came back into being.

The smell was awful. Though latrines had been erected, they could never accommodate the amount of people who had descended into the tube station for shelter. "How we don't all suffocate"? thought the 42-year-old father, whilst his young, beloved daughter clung terrified to his arm. The facilities were problem enough. Cassandra was staring at the old toothless man grinning, lying next to her, his urine-stained trousers and tatty torn jacket doing nothing to ingratiate himself on the family.

Mother, was busy sitting, looking around, never wanting to be seen as out of place, trying to stay aloof, but desperate to be noticed and acknowledged for the person who she was.

"Just ignore him" she said to Cassandra, somehow aware of her child's distress, perhaps it was hers too of this "vulgar little man".

You would consider that being underground and having tunnels that it would be cooler and well ventilated, but the mass of bodies warmed the small areas and the tunnels passed the odours around from one set of platforms to the other. Violence would erupt as neighbours clashed over the confine of space, thefts of belongings,

not matter how trivial and then... a distant thud. Far and distant... a pause of breath... everyone thinking the same thing "did you hear it"?

All too suddenly another followed another. Deep underground the population were trying to gauge which way the bombs were dropping. They were coming closer. Somebody screamed, someone shouted in reply "It ain't happened yet" but nobody laughed. The thuds and explosions were getting faster and closer together, dust and small bits of masonry shook from the ceiling.

"Daddy"? cried the now terrified young Cassie, tears wetting her face, but they weren't hers. He held her close, the Howitzers thumping deep in his memory, the screams of fallen comrades, echoing all around, reaching out again from the shadows of falling debris, unable to call out, unable to help them, frozen in his fear.

For a moment Cas didn't recognise the man she clung to, but she shared his heart and terror. She too felt the stillness that calamity brings, stuck in an unmoving pose of a mannequin model, yet whose mind can see all so clearly. Every detail etched forever. The shout of command, the deafening crash, exploding with such wanton ferocity almost made her laugh, but was instantly muffled dark grey air and choked by the deep smell of tons of newly exposed soil and rubble.

There was an instance where silence returned. A fleeting instant. Between the bomb and from when the screaming started. It was as if people were too scared to breath, in case the monster heard them and struck again. But once the screaming started, it did not stop. Some silenced but were replaced by moans, shouts of help mixed with anger at the suffering, some screams stopped on their own, silenced forever, never to give a parting kiss again.

Noises that had never been heard by her ears before filled her head, gurgling howls, the clambering of bodies climbing over the buried soul, the popping of her leg as a lady's hand grabbed her shoulder and pulled her cleanly from her part buried state.

Stunned by the overload on her senses, she stretched out to call for her parents but was already being hoisted away by the frantic activity of survivors. Cassandra could still hear this one scream, sounding closer yet further from the rest. She tried to struggle in a pair of strong, bare arms, but the pain of her leg burst through her entire body. The screaming was not fading as she was past from person to person, it joined her on her journey. It was still there when someone surrendered their dark green, tweed coat and was placed around her shaking shoulders. Now she was in the open air, the scream sounded lost and on its own. She didn't stop screaming until she finally slept, even then it would haunt her always.

ROOKS END

Tess stretched out on the flowered coloured towel, the warm

summer grass a bed of innocence below her and the safety of warm clear blue skies above. The pigeon was gently cooing in the tall old pine tree in the centre of the front lawn, reassured, as she, was that this was home, this was where she should be, comfortable, relaxed and secure.

Tess reflected that they had arrived at Great Aunt Janes the day before with the 40 mile drive up from London being the usual routine, though this time Dicky hadn't come, he was off somewhere, doing something, which tended to be the norm now. Anywhere was better than here. Mum had not succumbed to the anxiety routine before leaving, but that hadn't stopped Dad from smoking in the car, all the way up, which, like clockwork, made Eric sick at least twice. Regardless of the beautiful day, windows were firmly wound up (once, when down, some burning ash was flicked from the drivers almost finished cigarette, only to return hastily into Erics eye behind) and followed by a statement of "If we keep them shut, it'll put you off smoking forever". Unfortunately, that didn't work, to any of them.

They pulled off the small road and onto the well kempt gravel drive. On the left you could clearly see the ghosts of people in the once, often used, small timber pavilion and tennis court. Playing with gay abandon, full of smiles, white attire, Pimms and laughter drifting all the way up to the large house.

To the right, the distant ancient apple orchard that wasps attended to stood as if waiting for something never to happen. Leading to the

large double garage, that attached to the rear of the house, was a long red brick wall that hid the once resplendent Victorian garden, complete with three brick and glass houses that leant lazily against the mightier walls, supplying the house with all its vegetable needs.

The car drove up the stony road which opened into its circular loop by the black front doors with half pillars either side. The brass letterbox and lion headed knocker was as old as the house and had seen many carriages pull up for an evening of formal family entertainment. The lawns had hosted yearly cricket matches, laid on by the house for the villagers, which was held in high regard and, in more than one way, with good spirits.

Falling out of the car with his usual flare for showmanship, Eric asked his parents whether he and Tess could go and see Ruby.

"Go and say hello to Aunt Jane first" came the reply and with no moment to lose, disappeared, engulfed by the embrace of the welcoming house. The walls and floors creaked with gladness.

"Hi Aunt Jane" they shouted in unison, not waiting for a reply already thundering up the polite, red carpeted double staircase with the Laughing Cavalier hanging on the small landing, watching their every step. He smiled back at Eric knowing all the secrets the world had to offer.

Tess and Eric stopped briefly at the top on the stairs, pausing for an eternity to gaze into the small, glass fronted wooden cabinet filled with miniature furniture which had been used by salesmen of days gone by to show the select how fine the craftmanship was.

Amongst the array of tables and chairs were figures poised in work or transfixed still by human eyes, ready to start again when left

alone. There were tins of biscuits, loaves of bread, everything a house could need.

Without saying a word, except for maybe "They've moved since last time" in a magical hush, they leapt up and sped around the corner. A brief run around the floor, visiting all the rooms in one go. The warmth of the heavily wooden materials room, drawer upon drawer with fine brass handles all built in against one wall of the Sewing Room. The small front bedroom, peaceful and quiet, softly spoken, waiting on some long-forgotten sadness. Eric always needed to touch the window of this room, to say hello or feel the comfort of the lead lined panes.

On they went. "Hello bathroom" a cold, tiled yet cheerful place.

The large bedroom with three single beds, with a huge window overlooking the croquet lawn at the end, which Ruby would pull open the curtains in the morning whilst exclaiming "Rise and shine, Breakfasts almost ready".

Then came the door to the attic. If opened, the narrow wooden stairs would lead straight up. At the top to the right Great Uncle Crispin's room. The door was always open, though put too at night, if occupying the opposite room, so as not to catch glimpse of the candle that moved in its journey across time itself, none ventured in, unless in great need. To the left, was a little room with two small single beds and "the window". If the house was particularly full, and you arrived last, this would be your room…looking into Uncle Crispin's chamber. "But it had "the window" so "never mind" thought Eric.

Rather than go further and look in Aunt Janes room, they came to the corridor.

Standing in the main corridor of the first floor, almost opposite the children's room, was a gap in the wall where a door should be. It seemed as if, someone, a long time ago, had conjured a spell to create a passage way from this world to another. The first step would be over an old oak step, and a drop down of two inches, onto a soft dark fitted carpet. As you looked ahead the walls and floor twisted and turned over a short distance, ending with an ancient wooden door that was firmly locked shut. It seemed as if it never opened, but to the left wound a tight miniature staircase that beckoned you on.

Apprehension grew in the children's stomachs, not through fear, but excitement and expectation. Tess, being the eldest raised her hand of command and knocked. The slightest pause could be heard and then "Come in" in sweet softly tones.

The door was reverently opened and the prize was given. The little self-contained room for was a feast to the senses. Mrs Tiggy Winkle in the flesh. There sat Ruby. Great Aunt Janes housemaid. She was sitting in her neat armchair in front of a peaceful, glowing fire. Red coals glowing in each-others company, listening to the clack-clack of knitting needles, whilst the gentle voice on the wireless drifted through the warmth of freshly made scones. Ornaments, too many to count, of the year's untold stories, from places long since changed lay in their places only to be moved to wipe away the dust or clean the lace they sat upon.

Ruby smiled over her low rimmed glasses. And before words could exit from her visitors' lips...

"Now" she said "you should have gone and seen your Aunt first", with nothing but warmth and care in her voice. "Get along and I'll see thee later".

With no response but satisfied smiles of affection, the two young souls turned away, happy at last.

THE NIGHT

He stood in the rain. Night had fallen all around hours past and another day approached, yet could not be comprehended until he understood what had happened. For the first time since those early maternal blows had moved him from his path, he was truly in the now. Standing in all too familiar surroundings, he was and had lost. Everything in his life had grown until this point, it had followed a hazardous path made up of extreme risks and pleasures, fool-hardy escapades, many ignorant decisions, all disguised as the arrogance of maturing, yet now, now his future had ceased to exist, all love, warmth and family gone. By his own hand.

He stood in the rain. Moments passed as he waited for the door to open. He could not even bear to think of when it would. He could only feel the total emptiness he felt. Everything was gone. Stripped of all things he had worked for his entire life. All the experiences, all the places, all the people, all gone, just the clothes he wore and the rain on his face washing away the stains of tears that had flowed a short time ago.

He had already purged his self, already shocked as to how quick life can change, not just through the actions of your own or others, but also by the transition of his own soul. It was if something lived, deep down inside, always hiding, in the darkest shadows, waiting. The small dark claws gripping firmly onto existence, whilst the black sightless eyes shine malice and hate. The teeth, sharp with fear, bear themselves, not wanting to b seen for the dread of being discovered. This too had been suddenly ripped out, at last, as if some cruel irony in the playground of life, leaving an unrealised gaping chasm in the heart of a man. What had lurked and had dominion in the deep recesses was also gone.

He stood in the rain. He could not move. He had nowhere he wanted to move to.

Despair and sadness for all things were all he had, all he deserved and all he wanted. He had lost everything.

He stood in the rain. He had surrounded himself with silence. Even the rain felt intrusive yet important to the night. A light suddenly opened behind him, with a voice calling him in. He turned and followed, like an obedient dog, yet in stunned awe, climbed the stairs to a waiting alien bed.

He stood in the rain…

…and someone invited him in.

The grateful but undeserved shelter was given as a last resort, to who could not go further down except for that final step, and that was soon to be taken. Left alone in the large, spacious room, he empathised with the emptiness and cried once again.

He shed his tears for all wrongs, his soul was torn and bruised, his heart felt the weight of guilt would crush his being. Weakness enveloped him and crippled him to the floor. Watching from above, he had surely been judged, yet love still held on, a single thread, lost and, at this moment, invisible. Prostrated on the wooden planks, his pleads for forgiveness poured out of his eyes. The rain spat at the windows with contempt, happy to see him suffer, knowing of the rites he must take to truly make amends.

He stood in the rain to fall asleep in a stranger's bed, for the first time, absolutely alone, in body and spirit. Lost in a nightmare of uncertainty and guilt. Horrifying demons had been visited and vanquished. The highest mountain had been toppled and possibly destroyed and all for what? He begged for compassion even as his dreams swirled about him, pulling and throwing his memories into a pile of confusion. The one person he ached to kneel down before and plead clemency to, was the one that he had pushed the furthest away.

He stood in the rain.

CAFÉ

Cassandra sat in elegant poise at the clean, small cubicle table, with its upright pew style benches fixed to the clean tiled floor. The glass pyrex sugar pourer sat at command on the red and white checked plastic table cloth, waiting to attend to the next customer's needs.

The shush of hot foaming milk being created behind the counter filled the senses, as the light chatter of a cup meeting the saucer was ended by the arrival of Mr Spoon.

From her position of facing the window, afforded a panoramic view through the large glass frontage of the intimate Italian café, of the life outside on the common walkways, whilst allowing to be noticed by passers unknown.

This, "type of place", was not one she frequented regularly, much preferring the comfort of Lyons or on a special occasion, being taken to the Savoy or Fortnums, where one could enjoy the acknowledgement of discretion and the anonymity of grandeur.

"Roberts running late. We had agreed to meet at 12" she thought "I only turned up 5 minutes late so I didn't have to sit alone, this is so embarrassing. He should've been early" she continued to muse " He's such a square...not like To..."Cassies thought was interrupted by the door bell ringing open and in stepped Robert. His cream overcoat slung casually over his arm, he wiped his forehead with the back of his spare hand and smiled broadly. With rushing breath spoke "I'm so sorry I'm late" he gasped "the meeting at the solicitors went on longer than expected. I had to run most of the way".

This impressed Cassandra more than if he had arrived early. The importance of having a solicitor had already improved Robert's status in her Mothers eyes, and a longer meeting meant more prestige. "I doubt Tommy could spell "solisitor"" she considered.

Robert waved at Giuseppe, who sprang into gleeful action in his well-rehearsed dance of the coffee bean.

Rob leant over and pressed his lips against her cheek in a greeting kiss, yet both hoped and knew how more important that glancing gesture meant. Sitting opposite, blocking some of the public's view, Robert took hold of Cassies hand, the coolness disagreeing with the small beads of sweat that lay on his forehead, and pulled her gently forward.

"I'm sorry if I've kept you waiting" came from his handsome mouth, thought Cassandra, "just been trying to sort through the Trust" he continued. She knew what Trusts were.

"I also bumped into Veronica this morning. She's off to France in a bit, for a holiday" he said casually, whilst thanking the waitress for the drink.

Cassie had frozen to the hardest block of ice as soon as she had heard the first syllable of "that" name. Veronica was someone who distracted the advances of her conquests. Cassandra wondered why he had mentioned "this so-called accidental meeting" with such nonchalance, even when she was sure, she knew how little she regarded this "woman". "Perhaps" she pondered lightly to herself "he thinks to make me jealous. Or perhaps there was more to be concerned about". Cassie was certain that Veronica had not seen her leaving Tommie's flat the other day, "Dear Tommy," passed through her mind "what an in love fool he was" she concluded.

Cassandra sipped at her tea with casual indifference, not wanting to rise any suspicion or reveal the true nature of the complex game she wished to conceal.

"When are you going to take me out again"? she enquired "You know how madly in love with you I am, I just hate being apart from you darling".

Robert was momentarily taken aback by the fullness and casual manner of the sentence that fell on his ears. He had waited his lifetime for someone to love him as he was. Not pretending to be another character or trying to be the best a sporting hero can be, nor competing against his jealous and abusive brother for the recognition of his confident, popular yet aloof father or for the tender love of his patient, compassionate mother. He had travelled over waters of pain, endured the passage of brutalised rape and the journey of thousands of miles for this simple collection of words.

They echoed through his being, as if, at once, emptied of all pasts, to be filled now by new meaning and new beginnings.

Startled by the clear beauty he felt inside he heard himself say "Marry me".

The world stood still; all was silent. The traffic outside the window ceased to move, as too the birds caught in mid-flight, trapped in the poignant moment, the clock behind the counter hung, poised to count the next second.

The gentlest cough came from Cassandra's mouth, barely comprehending the quietest words of dedication she has ever heard. Her mind raced. She was looking at the now still lips of Roberts mouth and, as if in the slowest dream, now looked into his liquid, smiling blue eyes.

FOUR TO SIX

The young boy was playing quietly in the corner of his cool, square bedroom, content with his world of cars and Teddy Bears. He looked up out of his open window, with the built-in wardrobe door behind him, as the clear blue sky of the city let the happy Sun shine its beams for all to see and be comforted by the fresh brilliance of its heat.

He was wearing his favourite blue striped T-shirt, red and yellow lines edged each band of blue and seemed to match his little red shorts, which, he thought deeply but not longly about, might be getting a bit small for him, as the slight chubbiness of his puppy fat legs showed.

Big Ted, as usual, was overseeing the situation that lay before him. Little Ted had been run over by Speedy (another small bear, but sporting a sewn on red jumpsuit) whilst driving his large, plastic red sportscar. The smaller metal vehicles had gathered around to spectate and make helpful suggestions, though none helpful. The undersized fork lift truck made easy work of moving the gargantuan obstacle that was still keeping Little Ted pinned to the ground, and the miniature fire engine was hosing the leaping flames that might engulf the area.

A soft breeze drifted through the early afternoon, as too did the constant distant hum of the afternoon traffic, though didn't distract from the unfolding dramatic events that were taking place in front of him.

Little Ted was remarkably intact after such an experience, yet, Eric thought, was in need of urgent hospital treatment and before you know it, an ambulance (flat-bed truck) was on the scene. Little Ted was hoisted carefully onto the back by the amazing dexterity of the heroic fork lift, who would probably get a medal for all his efforts, "later" again thought Eric as he couldn't see anything that could be used for one.

With perfect timing, though unannounced, Cassandra appeared before him, smiling, with the aluminium pipe from the vacuum-cleaner clenched in her right hand.

All play suddenly suspended and Eric smiled in return and watched as his mother said "There you are. I've been looking for you everywhere you horrible child".

Confusion crossed his mind, as so many conflictions piled into one another. Where else would he be in a small, terraced 3-bedroom town house, no garden to play in and no back door to exit from? Horrible? Had Little Teds serious condition, now fatal, already been relayed for all to know? And the metal attachment of the hoover...how odd.

Still smiling Cassie advanced quickly, now hand and pipe raised, swung with fast and ferocious glee. Eric thought distantly that the "donk" he heard made a humourous sound as it resonated and glanced off his up turned head. His arms instinctively going up to protect his young fragile skull. Tears sprang immediately to his eyes as he retreated further back into the corner of his room and mind, like an injured animal fearful of its predator. He screamed out a second time, not hearing the first, imploring "What did I do Mummy, what have I done" pointlessly.

"You know what you've done, you nasty child" she sneered, still grinning with manic satisfaction as she swung the pipe a third and fourth time, each blow permeating more hurt than the last.

"I'm sorry Mummy, I'm sorry" came the screams of the terrified body of the child, though Eric had fled the scene after the first blow, not feeling the pain, but hearing the agony.

Exhausted by her possession, Cassandra knelt to the side of the child and cradled his heaving sobs in her loving arms. "There, there" she softly spoke "I didn't hurt you that much, I just didn't know where you were". She concluded, rocking the injured child.

Fear and survival retreating, the silence of the room cautiously crept in as the young boys heart started to slow its frenzied beating.

Offering a tissue, useless in size for the amount of damage done, Eric noticed his mother too was crying, though seemed to be oddly satisfied at the same time of her accomplishments.

ROOKS END '43

Bentley, the chauffeur, was already waiting on the platform, cap under arm, resplendent in his olive-green tweed uniform garnished with sparkling gold buttons, and infantry polished black boots. He had proudly served the family for some forty years, beginning at the same time "His Lordship" had purchased his first. Standing, waiting with quietly concealed excitement, he wondered how long it had been since he had seen young master Guy. Though only about 30 years stood in difference between them, he had watched him grow into a gentleman, narrowly survive the battle field of death and struggle to recapture his humanity that had been torn from him.

The last couple of years had been difficult for all, especially in his profession with fuel rationing now nationwide, though thankfully the aged Lord was still required for duties in London on a regular basis and spare allowances kept him, and the missus, topped up with the little extras.

Bentley heard the steam train whistle its impending arrival before it came around the bend to the open platform. Its brakes squealed mightily against the metal wheels as the pistons chuffed heavily for being forced to stop, hot dampness billowing the air. The whole train let out a sudden exhale of relief. With steam finishing its bellowing, the moustachioed station master stepped forward to assist the family alight from the first-class carriage.

The shock left him momentarily static. Though well attired, but not well kept, the three of them set foot onto the platform as if entering a forgotten land, grateful for its succour yet almost collapsing from the terror which they were leaving behind.

Wanting to race to them and gather them up safely in his arms and carry them forever under his protection, he slowly placed his drivers cap on his head and managed to wipe an ember from his eye.

Stepping forward, Bentley greeted the mentally lost family with a barely audible "Sr…ma'am" getting stuck between compassion and service.

"Thank you for coming to meet us. Our baggage should be getting delivered later". These were the only words passed or heard until they reached the family house of Rooks End at the top of the driveway after the ten-minute drive. The young girl disappearing behind her mother's garments was as quiet as a church mouse, as the door was opened for them to leave one entrance only to go into another.

Guy reached out and clasped Bentley's hand with unaccustomed gratitude, startling his nerves even more.

The simple sounding "Thank you" came forth, but it held with it a reserved silence as if whispering to God, the gratitude for all his blessings and hard lessons that had been delivered, whether recognised or not. All the answers that had been given in hushed tones, yet often fell on deaf ears, like the seeds of dandelion floating on the air, only to fall on rocky ground, unable to take root and blossom.

But this time his prayers had been answered.

The family were being made physically whole again, the trials of the previous weeks and months could be put behind them, like once before, and repairing would begin. For people in the security of open fields, where meadows still blossomed, lambs bleated want to their mothers and the birds sang their beautiful endless songs unaware of the buzzing of black fingers of death that tore through their sky, that made buildings fall and fires leap as tall as giants.

Bentley watched the family walk slowly to the greeting of the secure sanctuary, worried more for the lost youth of so many children, knowing that it could never be regained and fearful of what would become of all, as dark days lay ahead.

A WALK IN THE PARK (Part 1)

The black cab pulled up outside the unobscured old oak door that was tucked away in the corner of a small Bayswater building, wedged between the local tailor's cream frontage and an ancient looking cobbler, which displayed signage of thirty years before.

Fare paid, Cassandra took Erics hand through the door, into the smell of polish and floor soap. The dark brown wooden stairs angled upwards in sets of seven, broken with a small landing walkway, spiralling up to all four floors.

After passing the exit to a shared roof garden, clustered with pots and plants with an array of magnificent colours and hidden features hinted at by their tops peeking out from the back, they came to Gran and Grumpy's flat.

Knocking the door, the small head of Tippy appeared, peering out with well-coiffed white hair, understated lipstick and her soft, sincere and loving smile, an honest greeting to anyone who, especially, maybe, to gentlemen who might have frequented certain establishments in her younger days.

Her quietness was as elegant as a feather drifting on a lake of air, a breath could easily sail her away to heaven above.

Closing the door behind them, Tippy was already gone. Already returned to her small bedroom of broken dreams and loves many pillows.

The panelled walled corridor led to the kitchen at the end where Grandmother was cooking sausages. The smells mingled with the eau de cat and tipped with a hint of gas, from the entertaining cooker which Eric loved to light with a match and see how big a flame would leap out at his fingers, sometimes it was magnificent.

A cursory "Hi" and kiss to his Gran, Eric bounced off with his exuberant energy into the sitting room to find his Grandfather, probably sitting in his chair, and go through his routine of things needed to been seen and done.

Firstly, there would be the big hug and play with Grumpys wobbly bit under his chin, always requesting a flamboyant Donald Duck impersonation that would send ripples around the old man's face.

Secondly would be the examination of the felt lined tea caddy that had survived the trenches of the Somme and now housed a cut glass stemmed art nouveau bowl, conjuring images of their hedonistic socialite lifestyle, only to be sold years later by a heroin addict for a quick meaningless fix...but that's another story...

Next on the list would be a visit to wind up Pinocchio who

walked with a waddle and shook his oversized head, often falling over at each attempt. He lived in a basket of toys which lay in a small cupboard behind a hand painted, wooden fireguard. Residing with him was Sir Winston Churchill. A clay figure, of uncanny likeness, about the same height but not proportion. Arms clamped firmly to his side and hands cupped behind, had a small hole on the corner of his mouth which allowed a thin cigar replica to be placed and lit. After moments, small smoke rings would puff out which caused ecstatic happiness at such amazing ingenuity.

After the roll top desk had been stroked and puzzled over, a visit to the dining room to hear the clock being forced to chime early and see the delicate small, but detailed painting of a single sailboat out on lightly choppy waves.

As luck should be, sausages, peas and chips arrived as if served in the galley where Erics mind lingered. They had their usual coating of cat hairs, which was politely ignored and removed and eaten in no time whilst squirming around to look out of the window to the fascinating world below. Opposite in the small street was a restaurant that was always busy, day or night. Black tables and chairs, some with umbrellas, decked the path and a variety of people coming and going, seeming to get friendlier and louder through the evening.

"Seems like a lot of fun" Eric often considered.

Once lunch had been completed, a trip to the bedrooms would be needed. Grandpas, creams and browns, housed the gentlemen's quarters, smelling of shaving soap, leather and sandalwood with crisp hospital corners and newly starched collars.

Grans was smaller, dark and...smelly. "No bad smelly" thought Eric "a more sort of, familiar smelly." Her dressing table was draped with shawls and beads, the mirror and glass top reflecting Flapper girl days of sequins and loose morals despite that she preferred the company of ladies and questionable men.

A final visit was to be had with Tippy. Sitting on the edge of her bed, light conversation could be had, vague and distant as if memories would be too far away to put into words yet never forgotten and always treasured. Those little sparkling jewels dancing in her head and Eric thought sometimes, sometimes, if you looked hard enough, you could slip in amongst the dreams in her eyes and find yourself on the lone dancefloor, being twirled about the music and lights with muted sound of melody playing gently for none to hear.

Having being lost in his own fantasy world where he often went, where time was measured in adverts and cartoons ruled the roads, Eric noted that it would soon be time for tea and that meant a journey home. This was an adventure as well.

There would stand a combination of options to unfold themselves.

Depending on who was to take him home would decide which route to take, unfortunately however, this never led to the spectacular array of crocuses, resplendent in their cacophony of colours, planted years ago by the old pet cemetery, hidden in a corner of the park, that thrived year after year. Upon Grandfathers deathbed, his last wish would be to see these little flowers in all their glory, each one as special as the next, as new life waiting to be born.

One route would take them by Tube. A short walk through a wide street that had found itself protected from the devastation, passing grand trees and a busy road only to pass a Martial Arts shop with its windows blanked out so none could see in. "Very odd" quietly thought Eric, occasionally asking why they covered the windows, as he enjoyed the Kung Fu T.V series and didn't see anything wrong with it. "Its not a Martial Arts shop" was always the same reply.

"Very odd" he thought even more.

Just before the station, stood the tiny angular Flower Shop with its curved glass door and owned and run by a kindly spiv, who was a mixture of Flash Harry and Ratty from Wind in the Willows. Eric was always given a free button hole and not understood banter was had, especially when a notepad and lick pencil was produced and money furtively passed.

Then, down the depths to the platform, where you could feel history all around, and if luck was on his side, a casual stroke of the chocolate dispensing machine might yield a reward, to be enjoyed on the three-stop journey.

Once back into daylight a short walk to home, past the bakers and chemist with a contraption that, when one had figured out how to work it, would measure your weight, as well as a metal circular stand with an assortment of postcards. One postcard amused Eric a lot. A hairy creature, with thin arms and legs, eyes wide and crazed, fanged teeth smiling suggestively said "I FEEL SIXY". One day whilst passing with Tess and his mother, Eric asked what it meant "Sixy"?

"It's not Sixy, its sexy" said Cassandra.

"Oh" said Eric, "what's sexy"?

"Ask your sister" came the reply.

So, for the rest of that journey home Tess explained about 2 sexes, (male and female) and something to do with bees.

"Very odd" thought Eric, but sexy became his new favourite word.

Today though, they were walking and that meant through the park.

RETURN

The old black taxi pulled up in the late morning city air, to the broad pavement outside the theatre, just in time for rehearsals to commence of King Lear. The two lovers stepped out, fresh, happy and rejuvenated, ready to take on the world as a stage, falling over each other as if drunken clowns in love.

Robert had never new that emotions like this could be experienced, let alone shared, joyful in union, with no pain of separation, knowing of the exhilaration of coming together again would be mutual and acknowledged.

They had spent their time in a whirlwind of love. The sun shining on their every moment as the clouds tried to block out devotion, failing, yet glad of the outcome.

Once the proposal had been spoken, heaven seemed to pick them up on the wings of songbirds and migrate them to lands unexplored. Finding new beauties and jewels that could be hidden, but left, exposed for all to see and recognise, with winks of past loves and days less travelled.

As the pair silently joked in the midst of infatuation, Robert turned at the call of their names.

Cassandra was walking across the slabs towards them, feigning disinterest but with sarcastic gloryness of her own.

"Oh look what Tommys done" she said, brandishing her hand for Veronica and Robert to see. "He proposed, and wants me to marry him. Isn't that marvellous"?

"Oh…lovely darling" said Veronica, unsure of her wording and unsure for poor Robert.

Just a few weeks ago, she remembered how Robert had told her of his impending proposal and how he felt about her and how she had made him feel. In turn Veronica explained the course of true love never did run smooth and we know what we are but know not what may be, omitting that she thought Cassies life revolved around herself and affection was not always reciprocated.

But still, Robert relented in following his dreams and naïve desires, wishing to pursue not yet learnt lessons and damaged perspectives. In his literal pursuit of his conquest, he had been steered, as easy as a baby taking its first steps, by J and Ronald to witness Cassie and Tommy entwined in craving.

He was struck by how silent his hurt and anger screamed inside. The years of torture and abandonment by ones so close had prepared him well for this ordeal, yet nothing had equipped him for wrongdoings in this undiscovered country. Clutching at his heart, he now understood Macbeth's agony that drove to madness for all the inflictions made and staggered, wounded and bleeding, away from the vision that, even if eyes were plucked, would still burn to the bone.

He had fled straight to Veronica, who consoled him as she could, with gentleness and care, though full of life itself, not wanting to wait for the 'morrow nor care for what has already been. Innocent to start, plans that had already been made were quickly and easily altered and soon both were enjoying the Parisian life and all that the romance of the Seine could entwine. The centuries of a culture where passion is all.

Drama and pain are as essential to actors, as a stage and mask are imperative to the art, so when all are involved in life's rich tapestry...news travels fast.

Unsure how to respond to this interruption from Cassandra, as a life time had just flooded through under the bridge in the last two weeks, Robert graciously smiled and turned his back, pulling all the wind from the inflated gesture, and walked hand in hand into the theatre with Veronica, leaving his heart bursting with pain and Cassandra crest fallen but ready for vengeance.

As with all first day rehearsals, everyone was permitted to enter via the foyer, allowing reminders of how their patrons would cross the threshold from reality to distraction and enjoy a few hours where all were equal yet privy to a voyeuristic peek into an emotional tour. It was also used for all to see who had been cast in which roles, by way of publicity photos exhibited with characters names, an unusual but easy method.

This day, however, something different lay in wait. Word had circulated about an attractive acting couple, and an invitation for a lucrative modelling deal for a widely commercial magazine was ceremoniously pinned to the wall for all to see. Above it was a hastily hand painted banner "CONGRATS ROBERT AND CASSIE". A small smile, hidden from view, spread inside Cassandra.

THE ROOM

He stood, timeless still, his unseeing eyes only looking at memories past and forgotten loves with the sound of remembered children running about the house. His beloved Mother would surely ring the gong for tea soon, a task she took on herself as lady of the house and Father, in his study, would place his papers so, pick up his pipe and join the family in the day room to partake in this latest fashion. No doubt, his brother, scuffed knees from his latest high seas adventure, would regale all with his exploits, all whilst little sister fed her doll cooks sandwiches and cakes.

Staring intently out of the window at his memories, confusion crossed his brow, as worrying thoughts, deep set, disturbed his flow of flight.

For now, stood he, amongst the fields, wondering and lost, searching for something he could not find, even on such a beautiful day as this, cloudless and blue, the warmth bathing troubles away, the mists of misperception fell about him. Stumbling on, he had tried to ask his wounded friends, but they were as lost as he, each having their own paths of decisions to make.

He recalled a time... "A time"? he thought and tried to utter. When had there ever been "A" time? Everything was the same now, drifting like a leaf on a silver and golden brook, flowing against the rocks in one direction but being spun in circles, to come to rest against the soft bank, either to stay and rot or be pulled back into the eddies of the never-ending journey.

Was that his Father calling him, or just the sound of his horses' hooves clattering on the cobbled streets of a small French village. He liked to practice his vaulting skills on hedges down the lanes. Samson always ready to oblige, was a magnificent steed, strong and courageous, at all times ready for battle and a challenge, charging head on to meet threat and glory.

He... no, gone, lost, it was already getting dark. It seemed only just a few hours ago that Nanny had been getting him up from his mid-morning nap, yet already the sky was darkening and he would be alone again. He didn't like to be alone, he turned. Always alone. Especially when he remembered the pain. He felt he was becoming sad again. Why was he always left alone? He remembered saying goodbye to everyone when he left at the train station, the flags and waving, the cheers of happiness to be leaving, feeling a sense of duty and exhilaration, but he also recollected saying goodbye to them again in his prayers, but with a distant, intangible numbness that was lost to him.

The night settled in around him, wrapping him up in a cold, dusky embrace, the staleness of the air uncommon to his childhood bedroom. A slight chill brushed his bones as his thoughts went to the autumn afternoon and the lavender field that lay behind garden hedge at the end of path. How they collected the green stalks with purple fragrant heads only to take them home, back to the summerhouse and lay them out on newspaper to dry in the warmth of the wooden shed that held the croquet box, where sometimes now he could see his sister with Great Nieces and Nephews tea.

How long had he stood here thinking of his dreamless thoughts? No voice to spill from his lips, no visitors to pass the time. Just the light of his candle to keep him company as Great Uncle Crispin lay down again for his eternal sleep.

A FEW DAYS LATER

The rain had stopped, at last, its ceaseless torrent endured for days as if the angels themselves had wept and the wind had shaken the thin windows in their mountings.

He had been warned some twenty years ago, while walking through a Somerset town and confronted by an elderly man. From a distance he was noticed, small flat cap, glasses and moustache adorned his face, grey hair neatly cut and a well-dressed figure, hobbling gait with no stick was before him. A genuine simple smile was fixed under the facial hair and reminded him of a character they called Grandad at a church hostel where he had used to work. A balmy summers day hung around, slowing people in their pace, causing them to smile that little bit more and less likely to frown.

Despite the warmth of the day, this aged man had his coat jacket fully buttoned and tie and cuffs fastened well. No soon as paths were met, the aged gentleman spoke stopped in Eric's path and, in a kindly manner spoke "I'm sorry. I can't be your guardian angel anymore" then walked on leaving a dumbfounded silence.

And so brought about the beginning of the next chapter, just as he was now entering his final chapter.

Each step that was now taken was to be in territory unknown and unwanted. He felt as if he had been reborn, washed clean, yet as helpless as an infant child having no guidance to lead him and no options to offer him. Existence was passing full of loss and pain, though he seeked forgiveness and was filled with remorse and guilt, it was all the sustenance he could bear.

The days of confusion and pontification merged with seeking solace in letters written but forbidden to be sent, until the quietness descended upon him. Despair had been circling, like a white tipped shark sizing up its prey, ever watchful, feigning disinterest, though with each pass, looking for the gap to strike.

For decades he had been battling the demons that had been sewn into his soul which had led to a destructive and hedonistic lifestyle, trying to cover his insecurities and hidden memories with the overabundance of a sex, drugs and rock and roll lifestyle, topped off

with an alcoholic haze.

But all the tools of distraction were ages past and he had been left with the raw emptiness of nowhere to hide from the screaming that lay inside of the small boy being assaulted, behind the locked bathroom door, by the ravenous frenzied monster who he loved as his mother.

Now all was gone. All was silent. All had been lost. Suddenly, peaceful and still, collected and calm, clarity came to him as if the first gentle snowflakes fell from the sky. Everything became clear and transparent, everything was going to be alright after all, the solution was accepted with open arms and peace was at last in his being. Contentment spread about him as he planned his suicide.

PIRATES

The family had arrived a few days earlier after the two-hour drive (of smoke, vomit and cat mewling) which took them across the undulous green belt of the South Downs, with echoes of ginger beer and picnics, to their seaside destination. It was a yearly two-week affair, which saw the whole family, cat included, load into the old Rover P4 (lined with glossy oak and dark brown leather), crank started, to escape the confines of city life and arrive for the adventures that lay in wait amongst the gravel pathed woods, where pigeons made their wooing nests for all to hear on the quiet private estate.

Each grabbing their own bags or holdalls, ran fast through the small iron gate located in the middle of the front garden, between low aged hedges and onto the small winding stone path, down the little steps to the front door. The large house had been internally split in two, to allow separate accommodations for guest and owner, but still had ample space for all.

Rushing upstairs went the children, each desperate to claim a bed for themselves. From the bedroom window, looking out onto the front landscaped lawn, the sea could just be seen between the large trees that had enjoyed the view for years and the narrow pebble lined passage way. Arguing over the three beds, whilst performing acrobatics and smelling the fresh ozone, the two children noticed their mother walk past, with baby in arms, going to settle him down for a rest, at that, they noticed a picture had been moved since their last visit.

The pictures lined the corridor outside and in the children's bedroom, portraying bizarre alien beasts and birds with terrifying oddness but whimsical humour. Sometimes they watched you but they were always there, a legacy left from the owner's father who delighted in scaring children.

Once the routine of settling in had been completed the holiday commenced with a selection of stone throws walk to the shingled beach, lazy morning strolls to the shops to buy sweets and cycle rides exploring the area where none had been before, as well as one of the regular highlights, playing Pirates.

It was another glorious summer day. The clear, hot blue skies, the distant sound of waves folding on the beach, dragging small stones back in their wet grasp and the occasional bee, humming lazily to itself amongst the pungent buddleia bushes. The old rusty swing was waiting to be used as were the overhanging trees urging young feet to tread upon their grown branches like they used to.

The two children started pulling out all manner of furniture, from the back door of the garage that led into the back garden. There, among the few small cobwebs and spiders, were the two, dust covered, heavy rubber lilos, the white egg-shaped plastic seat with padded red cushion lining, that any young child could sit in and get rolled about with much hilarity and the two revered black sun chairs, decorated with golden flowers, that great grandparents had sat under.

The items were strategically positioned around the garden to act as a type of obstacle course. Rules were made, a bee suddenly ran away from, and directions of how each piece of equipment was to be used. The swing was holding its breath in anticipation. Whilst Mother and baby got comfortable on a sun lounger at the side of the arena, Father magically produced, with much delight from the crowd, a small brand-new paddling pool. It did not take long to blow up and fill with water, though an eternity of eagerness passed for some.

All was ready, nail polish and emery boards for Mother, an easy exit for Father and the two buccaneers who surveyed their efforts with exhausted exhilaration. Just before games could commence, it was suggested that the youngest of the three should enjoy a splash in the pool and was duly placed on the outside edge, so Mother could do her nails and not be disturbed in her worship to the sun.

Boarding of enemy galleons began. They swung on the old iron ropes and leapt through the air onto the rubber decks. Minding the hungry sharks that lay in the water below, splashing hungrily, they made their way around the ship, repelling borders and skewering them landlubbers.

Many laps were needed to kill all the invaders and throw them overboard to the sated sharks as the serene painted figurehead lay stretched and glistening under the yellow sun.

Father appeared, running towards them, they braced themselves for the incoming battle and were confused by the actions that followed. He swiped up their pale, blue lipped little brother, who was lifeless and still, after tilting like a seesaw face first into pool. Water poured out of his nose and mouth as he was pulled upside down by his ankles out of the pool. Calamity and activity erupted, shouts and running and the incredibly fortunate, though not needed, arrival of the property owner, who had been an ambulance driver in the Second World War. The quick and accidental action of being lifted by his ankles caused Eric to take a breath, thankfully, for him, the first of many.

(AUTHORS P.S: Pirates would always hold a special place in Erics heart. At the age of about 6 he would be given a fancy-dress costume, complete with eye patch, tricorn hat and paper parrot, for a party of one of Tess's friends. It would be such a treasure that it was worn for about a month, in bed and out, until the need arose that it had to be washed and subsequently, "accidentally", destroyed. This would not be the last time fancy dress or pirates would figure especially in his life. Apart from the game of the same name that occurred in P.E lessons in his last school (which Eric loved), Cassie took Eric to see a performance of Treasure Island, featuring Spike Milligan as the cheese fixated Ben Gunn, a regular fixture at London's Mermaid Theatre, so regular in fact, that Mr Milligan decided to ad lib his lines causing much confusion to the performance. As for fancy dress...many years later Eric was invited to another party where he would attend, wearing an almost perfect, Captain Scarlet costume. Walking back home at three in the morning he found himself having to walk through a notoriously dangerous part of town. Ray gun at the ready he was zapping shadows and Mysterons and being indestructible... well, almost, was ready for anything. With the end in sight of the area, relief was easing his tension, when out of the dark came a cyclist, slowly and erratically coming towards him. The gangly figure looked sallow and gaunt under the streetlights, the deep-set eyes of a scaghead staring toward him. Eric stopped shooting and got ready for the normal publicised attacks of the vicinity. Incredibly relieved, the cyclist peddled past and Eric berated himself for being so stupid and casually looked over his shoulder to see the rider turning his bike around and returning. Adrenaline kicked in, muscles built and breathing came focused as the man on the bike pulled up along-side.

"Are you Captain Scarlet"? asked the voice in an almost reverent tone.

"Yeah" after all, how else could he answer.

"Wow. Cool. Is that a real ray gun"?

"Yeah. I've been shooting Mysterons" Eric half lied.

"Wow. Awesome" said the young man and cycled off.

Eric couldn't believe this exchange had just occurred.

"Man" he thought to himself "That bloke must've been buzzing" and couldn't help thinking what the rider would say to his mates or how his brain would think back to "that" night in years to come.

UNLUCKY FOR SOME

Cassandra couldn't wait to tell Tommy the news about the magazine contract that had been offered. All afternoon, she had annoyed Robert with questions, interrupted rehearsals with flamboyant prospects and tired the cast with her missed cues and make-up checks. Veronica felt deep sympathy for Robert and his sensitive, yet unaware, nature but also understood how a too good of an opportunity this would be to miss and what it could lead too.

The theatre always fascinated Veronica. The different point of view that one has, backstage, auditorium, lobby, gantry, dressing rooms and the stage itself, each having their own character and smell. The symbiotic relationship twixt man and art, creating new worlds for all to explore, not knowing where it will take you even with a script. Yet today a great tragedy was unfolding in many ways, heartache was to be revealed and misery endured. She knew her days would be numbered.

The afternoon rolled on with everyone feeling more exhausted than ever. It had not been a good day backstage and front, thankfully, even the dedicated director manager elected to call it a day. Feet shuffled, boxes and chairs stacked, lights started to shut down by the Bakelite switches and a fresh breath of air breezed across the stage. It was then they realised that Cassandra had already left.

Though still early evening, she went straight to the club to meet up with Tommy and the boys, knowing it was their home from home, to share the fabulous news. The buses were still running frequently and it was only one change needed to be dropped off at the corner of the street. Staring out of the windows, dreaming of all the things to be, she was rudely interrupted by the bus conductor for fares, clicking his clippers with hat at a jaunty angle. Without even looking she lied "I'm so sorry, I left home in such a hurry. I have to get to the hospital. My mothers had an accident and I left home without any money". with tears in her eyes and a loving forgiving smile on her face.

"Well," the man replied scratching his forelock "I don't right know what to say"?

"I'll pay next time. I promise" she lied again.

"Alright then me dear," he said "just this once" feeling certain that he had just been hoodwinked.

And with that her stop came into view and she rose to alight the bus.

"Bye, thank you" she waved, stepping off the bus deciding which route she should walk to the club, as Cassie didn't want to have to explain herself or her actions again.

"Honestly" musing in her mind "people can be so tiresome".

Walking through the streets her mind conjured up all exaggerated possibilities that might unfold and all the attention that might result from such a potentially important photo shoot. She might get selected to be the face of Lux, be asked to open a new department store or spotted by an impresario or talent scout and offered a leading role in a movie, she felt the opportunities were endlessly exciting.

As her mind wandered, she barely noticed time pass while automatically taking the turns and crossing the roads needed to get to the club. Soon enough, the familiar corner of the street that cherished the venue came into sight and Cassandra's focus shifted, as did her momentum and her thoughts of how to tackle the issue of Tommy.

It was at that moment a plan revealed itself. A plan where she would avoid any uncomfortable questions, any recriminations, finger pointing or blame for what might unfold.

Her walk slowed as the idea rolled on and evolved and stopped her, literally, in her tracks. Thinking carefully, trying to weigh all the little nuggets as they made themselves known; she was surprised as to why the plot hadn't been exposed earlier. Slowly turning, Cassandra realised what had to be done, and started to walk home, away from the club and away from Tommy...for good.

ROOKS END (Part 2)

The weekend had been wonderful, as always, escaping across the roof top trying not to get caught, exploring the Victorian walled garden with its Mr McGregor water barrels, inhaling the heady fumes of lavender dust from over a hundred seasons of collection in the summer house and losing a kite (now stuck, waving for all to see) in the giant pine. There had also been a visit to Great Aunt Janes office, with her homemade jam cupboard conveniently secreted in the wall in the corridor outside. Years' worth of preserves lined the shelves, all with different coloured lids, all with different names, rarely two the same apart from the latest batches.

Jams and jellies for meats or toasts, for breakfast or afternoon tea, spicy or sweet all available to eat...if you were lucky.

There had also been the forbidden visit to the pavilion by the tennis court. Tess and Eric had convinced the adults of an escapade to the far end of the orchard, one of the furthest points from the house, though the ulterior notion was exploration of the crumbling wooden building on the edge of the sealed off, dilapidated and weed infested court. They had never managed to actually get inside before, but once succeeded, clambering carefully over brambles and avoiding nettles, mostly, they felt a sense of sadness, loss and disappointment.

The interior was certainly falling apart, beams had dropped, cobwebs hung about with little purpose, damp was bubbling the painted walls and a hole, big enough for a suitcase lay on the floor, also discarded and forgotten. The sadness though, lay not with them but in the air, the knowing of its numbered days and times before, long ago, never to be reclaimed. No adventure was to be had here, a journey of discovery maybe, but for here the adventures were over and the wait for the final blows suspended itself for all to feel.

Eric and Tess made their way back to the house, occasionally rubbing the hot stings which had been pointless accomplishments, deciding to split up and see what else could be found for entertainment.

Tess took the downstairs and headed straight to the voices congregated in the kitchen which had the large dining room and breakfast bar attached to it. If luck was on her side, a possible visit into the larder (the small room down some steps at the end of kitchen) and all the goodies that might be on show or offered.

Eric, on the other hand, took the small staircase upstairs, not forgetting to give a congenial nod to The Laughing Cavalier as he passed, in search for something interesting. No sooner had he reached the top, he heard a drawer sliding shut in the sewing room.

"Strange" he thought "I'm sure I heard all the grownups downstairs"? he concluded.

Going softly, so as not to disturb the monsters, he peeped round the corner of the door only to see his Mother in a most peculiar situation.

Standing, with her back to the door, in her arms she clutched a set of heavy tapestry, neatly folded, flowered curtains, and was attempting to force them down the waist of her skirt and under her red jumper.

"Hello Mum. What you doing"? Eric enquired.

Startled she turned, with an angry yet surprised look on her face said "They're mine, so I'm taking them home with me".

"Oh" said Eric "Why are you trying to hide them then"? feeling a bit confused and out of place.

Before an answer was issued, Father appeared in the doorway, shortly followed by Great Aunt Jane, people had been notably missed and curiosity raised, probably not helped by Tess mentioning to everyone that Eric had gone "Exploring" when questioned and had signalled upstairs. To all assembled that could mean another "Escape from Colditz" story being re-enacted, scrabbling across the roof to avoid the guards and so to jump into the large rhododendron bushes.

Instead, this time, they stumbled across and act of theft taking place and silence fell instead of the foolhardy young boy.

This was a stunned, awkward silence which Father broke, understanding, as all did, what was occurring.

"Cassandras been under a lot of pressure. She hasn't been well for a while". the words came out staggered as he spoke.

"Well my dear," replied Aunt Jane "you only needed to ask".

The air felt heavy with embarrassment and Cassandra looked more childlike than ever. No apology came forth, but things were tidied away and people led to cups of tea, no one quite knowing how to end this episode that had not been encountered before. The polite conversation steered itself towards the better notion of time to go home and bags were conciliatory packed and loaded into the car.

Great Aunt Jane neatly placed the curtains on top of the cases in the boot and gave a seldom show of affection to Cassie as another fare well gift. The car, with all occupants present pulled away, still inwardly reeling from another episode of Mother.

Cassandra looked out of the windows at the countryside hedges going by wondering what she was going to do with two sets of curtains.

A WALK IN THE PARK (Part 2)

The black iron railings had stood guard through many years and ran the length of the northern part of the park, from Marble Arch (where an incident would take place involving a store Manager, a selection of sweets and an embarrassed Eric…with the "innocent" culprit, Mother) down to Bayswater. If patrolled on Sundays, with the gentle hum of traffic behind you going nowhere in a hurry, one could expect to see a mile of artists, from beatniks to squares, and each exhibiting and expecting to sell, their array of pieces, from pin art to oils, abstract to pointillism, the abundance of colour and shape was yours to peruse.

But today was not Sunday, today was another sunny day of youth, full of excitement of the prospect of a walk in the park and all that would be seen on the journey.

Despite the need for the wooden walking stick, Grumpy enjoyed the strolls with his grandson through the historic gardens, bringing back memories of his daughters' childhood and a slower, genteel way of living and imaginings of the royal hunts from hundreds of years gone. The large trees, with arms outstretched, were spread throughout the park, where children ran around them, lovers lay under them, but all enjoyed them as they brought a hidden tranquillity and calm.

As they walked in, Eric was already eager to run around the understated, majestic Italian Gardens, resplendent with four formal, rectangular stone ponds centred with umbrella fountains, each separated by wide walkways for the ladies and gentlemen to promenade and the low balcony with the stretching view of the Serpentine lake below. This was not the highlight however, for surrounding on all sides, were the tall willow trees. Branches and leaves hanging to the ground calling out to children to hide under their green protective skirts so as to frighten their guardians by disappearing when backs were turned.

This was a somewhat regular occurrence for Eric, for some years earlier a Nanny had been hired, much to his dislike, and had taken the child for a constitutional. On the walk back home, Eric had lagged behind and ducked into an open gate of somebody's front garden and hid behind the low wall. Much internal sniggering ensued as Nanny couldn't find him anywhere and went home distraught at losing her ward. Not realising this severity, Eric decided to present himself, but was taken aback to find no one to reveal himself to.

With slight disappointment, the owner of the house presented themselves and questioned the young child on his circumstances. Once the story had been explained, the kindly gentleman decided to walk Eric back home himself and inform all of the hilarity that ran through the boys' veins. Eric was surprised, when arriving home, that he found a hysterical mother, a father on the telephone to the police and a weeping Nanny, who he didn't like anyway.

After burning off some energy, running rings around his grandfather, ponds and trees, it was elected that they would go via a visit to Peter Pan rather than the Round Pond (where Eric had slipped in many a time…sometimes accidentally) and the Band Stand (where great tragedy would one day unfold). This was also the shorter route and Grumpys leg was already beginning to hurt, returning with it visions he would rather lay as buried as "they" did, another lifetime away in green, bird song filled fields now unrecognisable to the black, smoke holes that they once occupied.

Peter stood, as always, atop of a hill of bronze, with faeries, rabbits and all types of creatures poking out, burrowing in or enjoying the view of humans going by in their odd ways of living. His horn, which Eric could not discern whether it had already been blown or not, was still held in his hand, though someday it would start to disappear, reflecting the loss of innocence and beauty in our world.

Many passes around the statue were taken. Hand trailing over the smooth and lumpy, warm metal surface, holding protruding ears and smiling to the hidden mouse. How many other eyes and hands had feasted on the work, how many seasons had gone and when would it be seen again echoed in his heart.

Moving on from eternity with a skip and a jump, he caught up with his grandfather and held his wrinkly firm, soft hand, as he thought of nothing but warmth and of each step he took. Questions asked, answers given, they walked in silence, one looking at life, the other looking not to fall over.

Before time had to fly, the mews arch came into view, signalling that the end of their journey was soon. Eric had enjoyed his walk, as always but was curious on how his grandad was going to get home, having only betting slips in his pocket. He knew if grandmother was to do the return journey, then father would oblige a lift rather than take the tube, but for some reason it wasn't the same for Grumpy. He had often heard funny talks between his parents but could never fully understand them. "Adults"!? thought Eric.

Skipping had resumed as the two neared home. Thoughts of milk and possibly a doughnut or marmite sandwich was spurring him on, when Grumpy interrupted his train of food with "I'm going to have to ask your father to lend me a couple of bob" he said.

"Oh, he won't do that" said Eric somewhat emphatically "he said he would never lend you money if you were the last man on earth". he concluded.

Eric had never seen his Grumpy angry, and was quite intrigued in the sudden change of mood. Unfortunately, they arrived home, greeted all and sat down to cartoons, milk and Jaffa Cakes. "Nevermind" he thought.

ROBERT

Robert lay on his bed, head propped by three pillows, asleep and unaware, even of his dreams that visited him with tenderness care. Eyes flickering gently as he walked back up the dirt track to visit his family who all had long passed, yet greeted him with waves and smiles which had not existed in life. It felt good to be home and to see them all, even his brother, who had spent their childhood in a jealous rage, beating and raping his younger sibling with vengeance and hatred running through his veins.

His father was there too, standing by his seated beloved mother, who sat for pleasure and not for need, no longer tied to her wheelchair. Even his father radiated a loving warmth, giving Robert the urge to run to them all and scoop them up in his arms yet, at the same time, scared that if he touched them, they would vanish in the mist.

He felt at last a peace in his soul, balanced out and complete, no longer tired or confused, no need to worry about the past or regrets, no need for anything.

A hand reached out and gently brushed the fine hair off his brow and stroked the top of his head, it felt good and loving and opening his eyes he saw familiar faces.

Their three children, all with children of their own, sat around, still dearly loved, though never fully understood. He knew he had failed them all, but had tried in his own way, trapped in his own prison, not seeing where the doors or windows lay nor how to escape its constraints.

For once they were all here together and that itself was gladdening, the exquisiteness spread through him and made Robert smile. He wanted to tell them all about his gladness and joke and make them feel how good he felt, but speech had departed, unable to make those connections, so instead he pulled funny faces and gesticulated exaggerated hand movements which produced the desired effect. Chatting and laughter entered the ward. The other elderly gentlemen being infected by the life rather than the dying joined in with the chuckles of mirth and then needed the toilet.

A nurse came in to check on the unusual activity, and aid the desperate, and left, eventually, when satisfied with the circumstances.

Now that Robert was awake, conversation sprang up between the divided, brought back together, soon to be divided again family filling in for their father where necessary, unsure of how much precious time there was left.

This had not been the first time of gathering around a death bed, several false alarms lay in the past, each harrowing in their own way. The alcoholic induced coma, the lung cancer, so many hospital visits to both parents, each taking it in turns as their ages grew. Now though would be the last. No more pacemakers, no more accidental falls or missed medications, now the book was being closed but never finished as chapters were still to be finalised, questions not yet realised answered and secrets unearthed.

Time had ceased to be important, as too their differences, suspended for a short while, some uncertain and more confused than ever in what they were meant to be feeling or what they had done in their lives and their own frailty.

Slumber had taken the once proud man into its domain again, giving respite to a troubled soul whose dementia had already rid him of the complexities and insecurities of the vast ocean of life. He had been a wounded prince, washed-up on the shores of a foreign land, kingdom lost, never healed no matter how he searched in all the wrong places, for the elusive cure that hung around his neck.

His lady, an Egyptian slave in another life, had already passed suddenly, without warning or reason years gone but the love and turmoil still twisted in his mind like a peaceful, white dove wrestling with a snake.

He awoke again, Eric still by his side, winked and patted his hand with an almost toothless smile then returned to his dreams.

Eric stood, for unknown reasons he had decided to leave, there didn't seem to be any need to stay, Tess and Dicky stood guard and the last rites had been administered, so that was protection enough he thought. He kissed and hugged his older brother and sister and told them he loved them. He bent over his dying father and kissed his temple and told him he loved him too. Standing upright he instinctively said "See you later Dad" paused, knowing that he would not, turned and left feeling empty and lost.

Silence fell again on the ward, Tess and Dicky talked gently to one another as Robert, only a short while later entered his deepest sleep, troubled no more by pain or sorrow as the traffic carried on outside.

TESS

Tess sat up to the square, wooden kitchen table waiting for the large sheet of taped down paper to dry, preparing it for a new masterpiece that would hopefully materialise. She checked over the table making sure she hadn't forgotten anything before painting started.

"Brushes, paints, obviously..." she pondered "water, gin, palette, cat". "Get down puss" she said waving her hand and Celia taking no notice whatsoever. "Wine," crossed her mind "can't do without wine". The last word came out as she stood and walked to her large canvas bag and produced two bottles of wine, Red and White, decisions, decisions. Returning to her table, Celia had got more contented, but there was still room enough for a glass and two bottles amongst the utensils of her trade. Seating herself once again, Tess poured a glass of gin and a glass of white, saving the red for later and stared at the blank space again, hoping for inspiration to call, or perhaps another sip was needed.

Taking a hefty swig of the juniper flavoured alcohol, her eye was caught by the shade of red on a metal pencil tin and reminded her of the small blue and red cardboard handbag that once was a prized possession. Always on her arm, it had accompanied Tess through times of need. Whether to be used to slap away a gentleman's unwanted advances in a cartoon cinema (where she sat with her Mother and little brother) or to carry a butter knife, used for flower bed digging, which often disappeared and the blame was centred on Eric (unbeknownst, though would be resolved decades later). The little bag would also be a trusted companion in which she could hide in when being sexually abused by the black clad family doctor.

Another sip. Still no inspiration. Another sip.

The painful memories were never far away. Remembering being torn away from her friends of years and the sudden death of her closest, the two sisters who she often played with when younger and the tragic housefire that followed, the sexual discomfort she felt from her fathers' touches, but her earliest and most confusing was the almost murder of her brother.

He had been born at home, on a quiet winter's afternoon, snow falling softly in the quiet hush of the city, with the cleaning lady helping delivery as the snow hindered midwife battled on bicycle.

Erics cot had been placed in Tess's bedroom, by the window, so not as to take up valuable playing space, but Tess didn't mind, having a baby brother was fun in itself, she liked to play mother. As the two grew, Tess would always be the older one and Eric would have to be told what to do, marry her friends, be the baby, carry the bags, whatever game they were playing Eric would have to obey her friends as well. Secretly he didn't mind, but sometimes Tess's friends said as they were married, he had to kiss them. Yuck.

Months had passed from the snows and early spring had sprung, a gentle warmth in the air was trying to battle the cold and Mother had put him down for a rest in the crib. Tess was downstairs sorting through her handbag, organising her toy makeup, like ladies do, tutting at nothing in particular, like ladies do, when she thought she would go and fuss at baby Eric, like ladies do.

Once up the stairs, she noticed Mother was not resting on her bed, like she often did, and turned into her bedroom to check on the cot.

Cassandra was leaning over the crib in still silence as Tess drew up alongside. It was at that moment she saw the pillow being pressed over the baby's head and a soft muffling coming from underneath. Tess touched her mother's arm, which caused Cassie to leap backwards saying "He's fine, we were just playing" with a look of distance and craze in her eyes.

Tess reached out and took yet another sip of her gin glass only to find it empty, so swapped it for the wine. Still no inspiration.

TOMMY

Tommy had been working hard, harder than usual. He now had a fiancé to keep and a wedding to fund as Cassies parents had lost a lot in the Great Slump and had never fully recovered from the heavy burden that was felt the world over. The club had been doing better than expected, good turnouts most nights where people were hungry for colour and change and that was what they were offering. It was a happening scene, with many musicians wanting to explore new avenues and experience the sounds coming out of America. The likes of Miles Davis, John Coltrane, Monk and Mingus were some of his personal favourites, Miles Davis being the only trumpet player amongst them. But he figured if he worked hard, long enough, something would give, maybe one day a tour in the U.S would come out of it despite what Ron and J said. Tommy knew he could make it, he knew it wasn't far away, the boys just liked to drag him, probably jealousy he thought.

He was surprised not to see Cas in the crowd tonight as she said she would be there, perhaps their rehearsals had run over and she went home tired crossed his mind. "I'll check in at the cloak room and see if she's rung when I'm done" he thought, whilst sweating under the lights, almost missing the beat.

It had been another good turn out tonight, some fresh faces in the audience, no trouble and plenty of good feedback. It was always satisfying to see tapping hands on the table and nodding heads, it helped really get into their rhythm.

He finished his set and wiped his forehead with a wet hanky from his trouser pocket and stepped off the small raised stage with his horn, smiling and a small salute wave headed to the bar. A scotch on the rocks sat waiting for him but didn't hang around long. It was joined by its brother who also exited rather quickly, the third would have to be paid for. Gus, the barman, kindly offered a smoke and Tommy accepted, striking a match off the counter for light he took a long puff and exhaled. Third whisky in hand, smoke in other, he strolled though the seated bodies, heading to the cloakroom where Mandy was on duty tonight. Mandy didn't like cloakroom duties, feeling it was always a cruel joke of the establishments.

Tommy approached with a smoky wave of acknowledgement and enquired whether Cassie had rung and left a message.

Mandy, busily, in the quietest period of the night, was doing (trying to do) a crossword. "Hi Thomas," came the husky voice "No. No message. 7 letters: Ball on the Door"?

Tommy stared incredulously. "Mandy, come on" he said "What do you like doing best"?

"Knocking people owt…. oh, bouncer".

They both laughed and a couple came round the corner to collect the lady's coat. Mandy stood up, his 6ft 6 frame could barely fit in the small cubicle, but it was policy for all staff to rotate job positions, it just seemed unfair that he was never allowed behind the bar or waiting on tables. He liked waiting on tables, though was a bit clumsy.

Tommy returned into the club and saw Ronald and J now propping each other up, where they had come from goodness only knows, but they were here now, so they might know something, they usually did.

A brief chat later and none the wiser, Tommy felt uncomfortable of the no news situation, but figured that no news was good news, and he was sure that something would appear before the end of night.

The end of night came and still no news. Nothing. He couldn't understand it. He said goodnight to Ronald and J, who could hardly stand now, waved again to Gus, and told Mandy he should wear a pinny if working. Mandy said something in return, loudly, but Tommy and the last customers were laughing too loudly to hear the reply as they left through the door.

He hopped into his black Ford Anglia and decided to call round to Cassies house. He knew it was late, but he wanted to make sure his fiancé was okay.

It wasn't a long drive and as he pulled up to Hyde Park Square he saw the lights were still on. Relieved and surprised, he bounced up the small steps and rung the bell for her parents flat. It was promptly answered by Cassies mother.

"Good evening Mrs Pope" desperately trying to sound very sober "I'm very sorry to disturb you so late, but could I speak to Cassie please"? he softly said.

"I'm sorry Thomas" recognising him instantly "Cassandra doesn't want to see you"

"Oh" he replied with confusion "Well, tell her I'll see her tomorrow then".

"No Thomas, you don't understand. She doesn't want to see you... again...ever". Came the firm reply.

And with that the voice was gone. Tommy tried buzzing again, and again and no one answered. He stood in the street and shouted up, the lights in the flat went out. He shouted a few more times and remembered some lines to a poem "Tell them I came, and no one answered..."

All was still in the night, but his beating heart. He didn't understand anything of what had just happened, none of it made sense. He just wanted answers, something. Reeling he climbed back into his car and headed back to the club. Tomorrow, he thought, tomorrow.

AFTERMATH

The more he planned his suicide and nearer the time came, the calmer he was. Hitching to the Dorset sea town seemed an easy path to take, no need for stops for food and water was somewhat liberating as was taking his future in his own hands, albeit a destructive one. He had always had a fear of open water, especially concerning sharks, even in a swimming pool, when younger, the irrational thinking made him swim faster, often leading him to win races with his secret intact. It wouldn't be until years later the fact would emerge that his Great Grandfather had died mid-Atlantic, torpedoed then all people lost at sea by the hungry denizens of the waters.

He decided that there was no point waiting another day, why put off the inevitable, he would wait until movement had rested for the afternoon break and then leave quietly and unnoticed, no need for drama to spoil what was looking like a lovely day outside.

A final check around the room before he left, making sure it was tidy, and there was a knock on the door. Startled as to why anyone should be knocking, he answered and pulled the thin wooden fire door open. There stood his sister. His sister. He could not take in the sudden appearance of his own sibling, especially on his imminent departure. Since he had left their family home, some thirty years previous, his sister had only visited him three times, for a wedding, a christening and a funeral, he had visited her many but not the other way round. And now! Now!

All that came out of his mouth, sounding alien and disjointed having not spoken to anyone for a couple of days "What are you doing here"? was all he could muster.

"I was worried about you" she replied. As simple as that. His world collapsed. Someone was showing him compassion and concern at the pivotal point of his destruction. He tried to talk but his legs felt weak and the part of him left that had been keeping him under control departed. He had previously been wrong before when thinking that he had lost everything, now even his very being fled screaming. That one simple gesture of care and compassion finished him completely. His mind crumpled as he managed to sit on the sofa and he wept. He had never wept like this in his life. He could not stop, he could not talk, he could not see or hear. Just blackness and the outpouring of the sea of sorrow. No longer was he able to carry a load.

A hand rested on his shoulder, firm, authoritative. He heard his voice being called but could not register, still possessed by the escaping monster of his past, draining him until exhaustion.

He heard his name again, asking him to talk, but he could not, how could he. They asked him to look up yet he could not open his eyes, he could only weep uncontrollably.

Another voice, his sister "They're paramedics come to help you".

Confusion entered his mind. Uncomprehending confusion. "I was leaving. Paramedics here"? he blundered in thought. "who, how could…,… know…".

It was then senses started returning. Darkness lay outside. He was no longer in the room he had started to call his, but on the ground floor, sitting on a hard chair. Coldness was about as night set in. Hours had disappeared.

It was now that shock overtook his malaise, trembles shook his body and his teeth started chattering. Water offered and a sip taken. He heard a voice. "I think he's going to be okay now. Can anyone keep an eye on him"? was questioned.

"He can't stay here" a voice said.

"I'll take him home with me" his sister declared as a reply, "he can stay with me for a while. Until he feels better".

The crying seemed to be going away, drifting off downstream leaving behind the aftershock and solitude.

"Feel better"? went through his mind, not fully comprehending words or meaning.

A taxi was called for whilst the paramedics organised their farewells and thanks given and the vessel stared blankly in his seat.

He was led out into the night to the waiting car, buckled in and stared out to the passing void. Time nor distance had no meaning. He was suspended to the world where only the clock expressed any movement. Nothing made sense, yet all had been laid bare. Death would have to wait another day.

CHRISTMAS AT ROOKS END (Part 1)

Rooks End, covered in a pristine covering of snow, was waiting, as always, at the end of its familiar drive, waiting to be
filled and give its appreciative embrace to any soul that might
cross its threshold. Its fire was lit in the second sitting room,
with its water clock, Dansette sideboard and television which
was only tuned to BBC 1 or 2. The cupboards were full with a
plethora of festive treats, a freshly baked ham lay in the larder, a newly plucked turkey hung by the back door and Great
Aunt Jane (and Ruby) were putting the finishing touches to the
Christmas Chocolate Log.

The Christmas tree stood subtly decorated in the first sitting
room, up on the small stage next to the dressing up chest
(which had been used by a hundred years of children at least)
looking out of the window expectantly. The air was heavy with
anticipation and suppressed excitement.

The car pulled up and out poured the family. As always, the
children made it through the door first, shouting hellos and
heading for the stairs only to be stopped in their tracks when
replied by the two voices in the kitchen. As if a switch flicking
inside their attuned heads, each slowed and turned and wan-

dered casually to say their greetings.

Calls came from outside for a hand with luggage as Robert was having to make a hasty dash to the train station to pick up Grandparents and Tippy so as not to leave them waiting.

Cassie looked at her husband curiously.

"They don't get in until half past" she pointed out quietly."Oh, don't they" came the non-reply "well, I might nip to the pub for a quick one while I wait then" he said climbing back into the car with an air kiss goodbye.

She felt another one of her headaches coming on.

The children knew the drill and had taken all the unloaded luggage to their rooms, squabbled who was going to sleep where, who slept where last time, whose turn was it to sleep where this and next time and "Well, if you don't like it, you can always sleep upstairs on your own". Both parents' bags had also been deposited and a little bit of sorrow shed that no visit to Rubys hideyhole would be included. Once done, all congregated in the dining room, that was one half of the semi open-planned kitchen (the dining room being separated by a breakfast bar) to await the arrival of the Great Aunt Janes brother and wife (and Tippy) so festivities, and tea, could commence.

An hour or so passed until they heard the car on gravel and snow and Dicky, Tess and Eric dashed out, smiling and waving, the cold making no difference to their warm hearts, to see the newly arrived and offer assistance, only to see unimpressed faces staring back, except for Tippy with her gentle little wave just reaching above the car door.

The car pulled to a gravelly halt and doors were grabbed and chatter commenced from the excited children, falling on tired and weary ears. Behind the activity, Cassandra and Aunt Jane appeared, waiting to greet the thirsty travellers and to sympathise on the hold-up that must have occurred.

A hefty waft of alcohol and a rosy faced, unhappy grandfather came into view, followed by grandmother and ever smiling

Tippy.

Great Aunt Jane spoke first "I'm sorry you were delayed; it must have been awful for you".

"The train was on time. Robert had an unfinished drink at the bar" came the curt reply followed by stony silence.

"Hello everyone," broke in Tippy softly "lovely to see you all".

"Well," said Robert "I only had a couple".

And with that, the episode was closed. Everyone knew the well performed dance that would be performed by all and were either too tired or relieved not to play it out again. Out came the suitcases, handed subsequently to the carriers who stared at them curiously, only just starting to realise where they were to go. Dawning realisation that they, after all, were sleeping in the attic, opposite old Uncle Crispins. It was Christmas.

KINDERGARTEN

Both Tess and Dicky had attended Market Lodge Kindergarten and it seemed obvious that Eric should follow in their footsteps. Eric, on the other hand, had a different perspective. Eric was quite happy staying at home, plugged into the radio or television, whilst sitting on his most comfortable seat (his potty, though not needed) or playing with Teddy, or Ted…or Speedy or even Wolfie the Hamster, life was pretty good, why change it?

Being the youngest of the three, he had been spectator on the unfolding life of schooling and really didn't understand what all the excitement was about. After all, Bleep and Booster taught him a lot as did The Pogles, he didn't trust Andy Pandy, weird girl, but did enjoy Open University (and the funny clothes and hair) and listening to the variety of music that came out of the warm, fish smelling speaker of the fitted radio.

"What more did he need" he thought deeply to himself whilst

picking his nose. Butty, the house cleaner, had taught him how to clean and he often helped with his little red bucket and cloth. Snacks were delivered daily at lunch and tea time, and if he was feeling sleepy, or not, Mum would always give him one of her special pills, which always seemed to give him really vivid dreams. Yup, why bother with school or kindergarten.

Unfortunately, the inevitable day came and explanations given.

To start it was going to be just the morning, just to see how things go and "For you to get to know everyone" his mother said.

Hand in hand they walked down streets and lanes, waved good morning to John the Milkman, passing tall houses, small gardens and Timmy, the squirrel monkey in his cage, arrived at the school which was tucked away at the end of a quiet mews, unassuming yet cosy and humming with activity.

Being left with a stranger, wearing a tight polo neck top, nice smelling, long, centre parted hair and attractive face Eric was settled down at a table surrounded with other prisoners who seemed happy in their play.

Words were said and the children looked and responded, obviously used to such instructions and knowing where to find pencils and paper. Sitting at the small square table, on the miniature wooden chair, Eric was given a large piece of paper and handed crayons, "...of all things" he thought and asked to draw something. Eric thought long and hard "...something..." he contemplated "...what is something..." he continued to ponder to himself. Time continued in this way as he looked around him seeing many hands at work, all creating feverishly their imaginations, sharpening their tools or sucking their thumbs looking blank and distant.

Not achieving the task, though quite happily watching and dreaming, it was suggested that maybe a jigsaw puzzle might be more fun instead. "Hmm," thought Eric "I'm good at jigsaws". He was, in fact, good at drawing and had demonstrated a number of times on his bedroom wall.

The boy sitting next to him was also offered a jigsaw, "Obviously a kindred spirit" Eric would have thought if he knew the words, though possibly being a little younger and not very nice. The two children settled into organising their pieces when Eric noticed that his jigsaw had smaller, and more, pieces than his neighbours, who's also had redder colour in the picture.

All started well, until the other child leant over and took one of Erics pieces and tried to insert it into his picture, where it certainly wouldn't fit. Eric reached over, recognising the mistake immediately, and retrieved the error and was faced with a wall of wails and pushes. The angry child's face got very wet, very quickly, tears were streaming, nose was running and the noise and pushing wasn't much fun either.

Another grab was made at Erics jigsaw puzzle and it was at this time that a change of action was required. Making a small fist, Eric passed it, in a wide-angle swipe, in the direction of the noise emitter. The result was spontaneous. The room was suddenly silent, (he had not noticed much noise before, apart for the annoying child) except a couple of adult gasps and he was lifted out of his chair and moved to the grown-up chairs.

Unhappy with life, Eric too burst into tears and attempts of consolation were made, but to no avail. Tried as they might nothing could placate this unhappy child, until someone mentioned Cherry Cake. A small glass of milk and a slice of cherry cake appeared and looked at. He had never tried cherry cake, but it looked inviting. Sitting on his strangers lap the world became right again and before he knew it, his mother appeared to take him home. "What a fun day that was" he thought to himself again. Funnily enough, he never went back there again.

BIRDSONG

Ronald and J sat at the front of the church with a seat beside them, reserved for Tommy, who was running late. Most of the regulars were there, as were the staff of the club. Cassandra, sitting on the other side of the aisle was looking very glamorous wearing a large corsage and standing out from all around.

They had known Tommy ever since they were kids, growing up on neighbouring streets yet moving in different circles but being united through their love of music. Many were envious or suspicious of their relationship, but only they knew how deep their friendship was.

Ron's mind drifted back to playing amongst the bombed out derelict streets, exploring the ruins and finding damaged treasures they would prize or share and one time making a grisly discovery of an undiscovered skeleton in a buried entrance to a cellar.

Life had sped them through the years of changes, the biggest in the last five years with the end of rationing and the Suez Crisis, where once again fuel disappeared for some, opening up the black market once again, though this time more organised.

It was strange that Tommy should be late, he never usually was, but being such a special occasion, he wasn't driving himself.

J turned round and caught the eye of a fresh, young gentleman who he didn't recognise, and connected on some level "Maybe later" thought Jay in silent conversation. He remembered how he once came on to Tommy, mistaking his friendliness as solicitation, but was gently let down with such kindness and understanding that he knew he would always have a true friend to rely on.

As if in some mutual psychic understanding, Ronald put his hand on J's leg and gave a gentle squeeze, as if signalling it was meant to be the brides prerogative to be late.

Lateness was never Tommy's thing. He didn't miss a beat, a payment or a meeting, only once had he been late and that was in their teen years.

All three of them were working at a local pottery factory, it was long and hard work but it was good, regular pay and Tommy was saving up to buy a trumpet rather than renting one all the time. It was early starts and late finishes, the foreman was a fair but strict man, a stickler for timekeeping.

One morning, Tommy didn't show, causing the other workers to get the short end of the stick and abrupt temper meted out to all. Eventually a drunken Tom showed up just before lunch with raw knuckles and bruised jaw. The swearing match between foreman and worker was a spectator sport of its own, fascinating everyone around, even passers-by peeped through the open windows. People laughed, cheered and gasped at the tirade, neither side backing down or showing any signs of contesting the fight.

At last, the management had to intervene the contest. Tommy was led away to his corner, the staff canteen, by Ronald and Jay, whereas the opposing team retired to the manager's office. Words were still being bandied about, but after some 10 minutes peace descended and an adjudicated meeting attended.

There was considerably more silence, then apologies heard when the truth was revealed. Tommy's mum had passed away in the early hours and both he and his father had drunk themselves into a stupor and come to blows in their joined grief. Hands were shaken and time off was given, with pats on backs and tears in eyes, life went back on course.

A gentle breeze wafted through the church and the sound of a car pulling up, at last, outside made the organist spring into action, finishing his non-descript tune for something more suitable. Ron turned to Jay and smiled, gently holding his hand by his side as Tommy's coffin came into sight.

LOST IN THE SUPERMARKET

Window shopping was one of Cassandras pastimes, a handy diversion and means for of the chore of childcare but at the same time an opportunity to get noticed or gain attention, be it department store, shoe shop or museum.

This day would be an extra special trip, to Harrods, rather than Fortnums (where she once worked for a short while in her acting days), a chance to see and be seen, the food hall and possibly a look around the music department or pet shop, quite enough for an afternoon's entertainment.

Making sure that Eric was clean and well presented, she applied her make-up with care and sprayed a little hairspray in place. Checking her purse, she noticed that she had a couple of shillings more than she thought but didn't think that it mattered, as there was little intention at buying anything.

The thirty-minute walk took them past the lower part of Gloucester Road with its tube station (where, one day, a Dalek would be spotted, trundling around, jokingly terrorising people), Lyons Restaurant (visited at times when there was the need of a free meal, where a matchbox and dead fly would come in handy) and the butchers (where tick was often given yet frequently forgotten to be paid). Then up the Cromwell Road and past the Natural History Museum with its grand flight of stairs, past the unassuming Victoria and Albert and up into Knightsbridge.

Harrods was spotted a long way off, its flags fluttering high on the imposing building giving it an air of expectation. On approaching, Eric gave his slight customary bow which he enjoyed doing and received one back with a subtle tip of the hat from the green and gold uniform clad doorman. His white gloved hands pulled open the large door with ease for the lady and child, who entered into an afternoon of otherworldliness.

The first and last visit was to be the coolness and tiles of the Food Hall. Epic displays of foods from around the world surrounded the drinks bar which served exotic coffees or freshly squeezed orange juice. A tower of shrimp and sea food, a mountain of cheeses all shapes and sizes and a wall of hanging meats, coloured and cured to satisfy any palate. It was a dizzying sight to a child who lived on sausage and chips and marmite sandwiches (not forgetting the doughnuts).

Cassandra led him through the sights by hand, towards the lifts to take them upstairs. It was at this point that Eric realised that he had never got lost in Harrods. Many other smaller departments store he had been "mislaid" and had often had to hand himself into the Lost Property section, which his mother had always explained to him how to find it. It had become a frequent occurrence that Cassie had resorted to tying a helium filled balloon to his belt, so as to track him more closely when wandering struck. It would eventually dawn on Eric, when he had children of his own, how odd these events were and perhaps it was never that he wandered off, more the other way round.

The lifts in Harrods were a treat in themselves. Hosted by an either an aged, well-informed gentleman who would professionally give details of the floors and their history, or a younger, uniformed man (complete with cap) very precise in his wordings.

The doors slid open revealing the young man in his empty domain with hand on well-polished handle beaming a welcoming smile.

Before his request of "Which floor Ma'am" could be uttered, his face changed to a startled gasp. Cassandra was falling towards him; child being pulled along into his nice routine of his day. Eric was watching this in slow motion, hearing the howls of exclamations from shoppers behind and the thud as his mother's head hit the wall of the wooden interior whilst being manhandle by the poor surprised youth. The emergency bell was rung. The floor manager came running. Room was "made way". "Give us some air, please" came the calls. All the while Eric stood and watched, "it's a bit like Tom and Jerry" he thought.

Cassandra, dazed and confused was helped to her feet and flinched in pain of her ankle. With great concern, the Floor Manager berated the lift operator for not levelling out the base of the elevator and went to call for an ambulance. Before he achieved his departure, Cassie implored him not to go to such trouble, she was certain that she would be fine soon and it was nobody's fault, but her own and didn't want to make a fuss.

Somewhat relieved, he insisted that Cassandra and her son should rest for a bit, just to make sure, and have a drink of their choice in the Food Hall, with compliments. Leading the way, he instructed all staff to assist this young lady and give her anything she desired. Hobbling to the barstools, two tall glasses of freshly sieved orange juice was produced and the Section Manageress took over care.

Enquiring "Is there anything that I may get you Ma'am" the reply came instantly.

"I'd love some smoked salmon and maybe some prawns and maybe some of those..." pointing to the dessert section "choc ice polar bears, please". Slightly taken aback the order was completed, as directed by both parties and duly delivered, wrapped and bagged. Climbing down from the stool the pain shot through Cassies ankle again and she rubbed her sore head, flinching in pain.

The Manager came over again, quietly watching from the sidelines and insisted that a taxi be called for to take them home, all expenses paid for. Helped to the front exit, a cab was hailed and instructed and delivered the mother and son home. Cassie thought "Bother, I broke a nail. Next time I won't trip so hard".

BACK AGAIN

His father had died in a car crash, when he, Robert, was seeking a company to join and start his professional acting career in England. A well liked, confident and charismatic local sportsman, he had admirable reflexes and had avoided many accidents growing up and living in the South African countryside. Unfortunately, those abilities were also his undoing. Travelling in a car one evening with a group of friends, they were confronted with imminent destruction and swerved to miss the onslaught. The car veered off the road and started a high speed roll down an incline to rocks below. The quick-thinking man flung open his door and launched himself out to safety, only to be struck by another passing vehicle, ending his life immediately, whilst all the remaining passengers and driver came to a safe and abrupt halt before plunging into a ravine.

Robert had been obviously traumatised by the news, and the journey back to his home land and subsequent funeral and return had difficulties of their own. His brother was still arrogant and cruel, despite the sorrow, and taking lead of the household even furthered his malice, though his mother tried to alleviate the open pains they all felt.

There was no closure for Robert. He could find no place to reflect on his relationship with his demised parent, too much noise littered his head, even in the stillness of the night with the crickets chirping their gentle lullabies. Anger and resentment, confusion and rejection all tumbled around each other fuelling his solitude, with questions unknown and answers not given he felt lost in the place he knew so well, so had to flee back to his goals and aspirations.

It was upon his return, that he found a new member had joined the cast. An attractive young lady, always giving him a smile, touching his arm (three Mississippi) and showing interest in what he had to say with no judgement, no conflict and no denigration.

Their friendship grew more obvious, on stage and off, as he felt the electricity spark between them and course through his being. For the first time, for a long time, he felt alive again, washed clean with something new to cherish, something good and pure.

They had been standing in the wings, waiting for their cues, he slightly behind her as she faced stage front. She leant back, the smallest amount, the warmth of her body climbed his chest and filled his senses as her shoulder touched his chest. He leaned his head gently forward to take in the fragrance of her hair, only to see her face turn slightly to meet his and their lips touched.

This small act, this small token gesture, insignificant in the history of the expanding cosmos where worlds collide and stars are born was all that existed for that fleeting moment. No thing had gone before this moment and no thing would exist again. Somewhere all those treasures live on and grow the exquisite flowers of romance.

He had never felt wanted before, apart from his adoring mother and now he knew what he had been missing.

A call came out, for all to hear, loud and clear, waking the

THERE FOR THE GRACE OF GOD GO I

new lovers from their slumber. Cassandra had missed her cue. Gently flummoxed and clearing their throats, Cassie came on stage still under the spell, unsure of what just happened. She too had been a participant of a too short-lived touch of something wonderful, something she had sought through the years and never found and here it was, in a small unimportant theatre, surrounded by small unimportant people.

But all of those events had been and gone. Robert's love had been lost, then found in another, another type of love and now Cassie wanted him back. Tommy was gone for good, she said, it had been foolish of her, she only wanted him, she said.

"Our modelling job is still on" Cassie said to Robert, admittedly, and "we will be working together for a couple of days" she continued softly, getting closer. "I have missed you" she sighed.

With that the fish was hooked, though the reeling in would be more arduous.

CHRISTMAS AT ROOKS END (Part 2)

Morning came around quickly despite the three children having to spend the night crammed into the small, spartan two-bedroom attic room and Eric complaining about the army surplus camp bed. There had been the suggestion that they could sleep in the more spacious room across the way, but all had emphatically declined.

Breakfast was always a plain affair at Rooks End, toast and tea were all that was provided, but enlivened with the ancient flip toaster which, when the side was lowered, allowed the uncooked side to be rotated, as if by the magic of physics. A lot of toast was made on those mornings.

Time was wasted around the house in awaiting the feast of luncheon, playing in the garden, though not being allowed to set foot on the pristine snow of the croquet lawn, hunting around the house, though being forbidden to play hide and seek, so, much time was spent staring out of the windows and dreaming of childhood things and what had gone before.

The gong went for lunch, resonating its call throughout the old house and all and sundry beckoned to its call. Grandparents had already been strategically placed around the large, curved oak table with matching high-backed chairs, interspersed with the remaining family attempting, but failing, to go boy girl... Once the unannounced game of non-musical chairs had been agreed upon, carving commenced. Robert stood proud and brandishing the sharpening knife decided another drop, or two, of whiskey was needed before plunging in. With ceremonies taking an unexpected halt, expressions were made of hunger and "food getting cold" amongst other whispered mutterings.

The anti-climax was soon over, as the meats, ham: hot, turkey: not so, was passed around for all to place their own helpings of assorted vegetables and potatoes on the antique china and silverware. Eating still had to wait until all plates were filled, bottoms seated and grace said, but once completed the chattering of utensils and appreciative talk commenced, along with the pop of a champagne cork and a "Mind where you're aiming that Robert".

Ruby was still beavering in the background around the kitchen, tidying and cleaning away and getting the mince pies warmed, cream whipped, brandy buttered and inserting charms and coins into the festive pudding.

Once completed, Ruby came to the table to start clearing away, only to be shooed away by Great Aunt Jane in mock surprise to see that she was still there and insisting that she was to take some food for herself. Disappearing, the children were put to good use, collecting the empty plates and finished with bowls of excess food, making way for the grand finale as Robert was already in the far end of the kitchen sampling and heating the brandy, ready to be poured on top of the pudding for some lucky person to set light to.

Ceremoniously carried to the table, it was elected that Eric, of all people, should be allowed the privilege of lighting, much to the annoyance of Dicky and judging on his track record of when it came to fires. Match in hand and smile in his eyes, the flame was struck and reached out to be greeted by an enormous WHOOF! The fire jumped for joy as chairs pushed away in unison from the table and the youngest person in the room chuckled with mischievous pleasure.

The flames died soon enough, leaving a slight smell of singed fringe in the hair but no harm done, just a few tuts from the older members present, while Cassandra seemed unbothered by the whole affair, perhaps it was her pills.

Great Aunt Jane took control again and dished out portions, regardless of like or dislike, of the sticky fruit substance to all, with no objections, due to the hidden, exciting possibilities that lay inside. Normally, a single silver sixpence would be placed for the lucky finder, but this year was the inclusion of silver charms: a wishbone for a wish, horseshoe for luck, a button for a bachelor, a thimble for a spinster and a bell for a bride-to-be.

Again, all bowls served and toppings selected, eating began. Disliking the food most, but eager for the prize, Eric found the silver coin to his triumphant delight. Yelping out his happiness, congratulations were made, apart from Dicky, and polite conversation resumed followed by an explosion of coughing from Grumpy. Red faced and spluttering he produced a small, shiny horseshoe from his mouth that had been unwittingly swallowed, much to the amusement of Eric, who felt he'd just won a hat-trick, and to Robert who thought "Serves you right".

FIRST DAYS

Eric never really liked school. From the early days, where he would cling to railings and scream to be allowed home or at dinner times, where unwanted food would either be thrown, secretly, under the tables or stuffed into his shorts pockets and disposed of later (normally, rhubarb crumble and custard). Unfortunately, these tactics didn't always work and resulted in being stood over by an ever-watchful teacher, forced to clear one's plate, often resulting in a torrent of tears and excessive nose juices mixing with the forkfuls going into the mouth, either to be swallowed, spat out or recycled out through the nostrils, always pretty amazing when all three happened at the same time. Sometimes, a distant part of Eric would marvel at this process..." wow, a whole pea".

Apart from dinner break, Eric enjoyed the walks, often in crocodile style, around the busy streets, and didn't mind walking next to James as he had very soft hands or Andrew, as he was quite chatty and friendly. One lovely, crisp Autumn day that would change. Hand in hand with Andrew, who also tended to be...individual, he pulled away from Erics, not breaking his grip and started kicking a huge pile of raked up leaves, which he promptly, rather flamboyantly, fell into.

The whole line came to an abrupt halt as the teacher, ever watchful, came to assist. As Andrew lay, somewhat dazed, the smell hit everyone's nose with a resounding "Eurgh"! Even the teacher faulted in her tracks. Andrew rose out of the leaves, only to exhibit an impressive coating of dog mess, legs, hands, arm, shorts and particularly well inground in his shoes. Needless to say, the walk back to school wasn't pleasant, for anyone.

Another issue that Eric didn't respond well to, was toilet time. Regardless of the need, pupils would have to queue, and perform on demand, all while a male teacher watched proceedings, twice a school day, and that, in itself, created its own future issues.

Following in family tradition, Eric was sent on to Prep. Skool, which he detested even more.

The work was easier enough, daydreaming was easier and the teachers were a mixed bunch, ranging from borderline psychotic to character filled personas. There was the monotone chemistry teacher who often crossed his arms in an exaggerated fashion; a tall, thin, dark haired pleasant lady in charge of Art, always encouraging pupils to find their voice; the round, Italian, very patient French lecturer; the diminutive, green tweed, skirt suit wearing Scottish Maths teacher, her red hair tied severely back giving a no-nonsense air, yet incredibly good at her skill. Then there were the three English teachers. The Good, though often exasperated; The Bad, chain-smoking sadist; The Ugly, explosive, violent and terrifying.

But to Eric, life was a playground, unable to take much seriously, so it understandably came as a bit of a shock when he was informed that he was being sent into boarding. His brother had done it, his father had done it, in fact it was regarded as a norm to all male children for many generations (though unbeknownst, Robert rejected the idea, but Cassandra was the instigator).

Originally, he had started as, what was colloquially known as, a Daybug, taking the 50-minute journey to school on a daily basis, predominantly on his own, consisting of a 7-minute walk to a tube, then a change to a main line and another 7-minute walk the other end through a housing estate, where the arriving and departing school kids were often shot at with air rifles and catapults.

The constant expenditure must have been a calculating factor, so weekly-boarding came into effect. This however, led to more problems than resolved. The first night at the boarding house was traumatic for most. In a dormitory of about 15 rejected nine-year-olds, the crying was constant, gently dying away, as one by one, fell asleep, only to awaken the following morning to years of traumatising unhappiness.

And it certainly didn't increase Erics like of school. Often, when being returned he would either try and cause the car to crash, (if being taken back in the family vehicle) either by unlocking the clip that held the driver's seat in place and suddenly pushing Robert forward from behind or lunging for the steering wheel at some inopportune moment. After a while he was returned by train, a safer option, but as the train was pulling away from the platform, would fling open the door and throw himself out. "Quite impressive" he would think to himself. This option would never be the more comfortable option. Nothing to do with the landing, but the kicking he would receive from an angry father as he was booted down the platform.

It was this that caused him to be entered into full-time boarding.

THE CENTRE

The shop was meant to be a new start, signalling a new direction for the family and business alike.

Dicky was coming to the end of his education, which would free up some monies, and had won a scholarship for some travel or something or other, Robert did not understand the complexities and found it difficult to talk to his now estranged son. They had always had communication problems, Robert being resentful and quick to temper with Dickies frustrated anger, which grew when Tess was born, but went to a new level on the arrival of his little brother. Sometimes they came to blows, which only served to divide them more and reminded him of his own childhood.

They had managed to secure a rented property nearby in a backstreet of Kennington, that would suit their purposes, and had set up the company with an old advertising executive that he used to work with, each fronting equal equity, though Robert would do the sales side and Larry would be predominately in charge of production. Accountant and a secretary (of a more mature age to avoid…" distractions") hired, the shop was fitted out with black and white cuboid displays, with clear glass panels to present their unique and prestigious replica metalware, and chesterfield sofas for wealthy clients to relax on and be served coffee.

Cassandra seldom assisted in the business, turning up occasionally to check no shenanigans were about or to happily (and outrageously) flirt with an American businessman (or two) who might need to be cajoled into an extra expenditure. Besides, she often had her own diary to keep: hairdressers, beautician, people to see, pills to take and plenty of rest booked in. The "hairdressers" seemed an important part of the agenda, more so now to when the children were younger, as to having to take them with her tended to cramp ones glampuss style. Eric recalled, on one such occasion, happily playing with a small wooden giraffe whilst his mother went into the back of the hairdresser's salon. Time passed and then did some more. He elected that giraffe had enough playing with and asked the nice-looking receptionist "Do you know whether my mummy is going to be much longer"? The kindly looking young lady said she would check and disappeared (not literally, you understand). A few minutes later she returned with the proprietor and head stylist. He knelt down in front of Eric and said "Your Mummy's not here at the moment, she'll be back later" and left. So, he sat…and waited, and after what seemed like a very long time, did come back, through the door they had entered from when they first arrived. "Very odd" thought Eric.

He, on the other hand, enjoyed helping behind the scenes in the shop. Whether it be gift wrapping sales, sniffing the ink of the photocopier, or pulling a wall cabinet over his head, by mistake.

It was on one of these days, the first of many, that confirmed that his parents perhaps weren't being totally faithful to one another.

The first time he remembered the penny dropping, it took a long time, was at home. He was engrossed, as always, playing with his truck and, as always, someone/s were getting seriously run over on the upstairs landing. Mum was out...who knows? Dad was downstairs with a very attractive Australian blonde (a cousin, apparently) with a tight blue polo neck on. "She has a lovely smile" Eric said to Action Person who was naked and getting tied to a Cindy (who was also naked) (by the way, the names have been changed to protect identities). The game was going well, but a glass of milk was needed, so down Eric went to garner his chances. As he came down the stairs, he noticed an intriguing sight. According to his father, the cousin was just showing him her new bra. "It looked pretty enough" thought Eric. "There wasn't very much of it" he told his Mother later.

But, at the back of the shop, and many years later, his Father was on the phone, with his back to the door, when Eric arrived for duties and overheard a "Yes, of course I love you" and a "Don't worry, I'll see you later". Assuming that it must be Cassandra on the other end of the line, no thought was given and Eric went through to the back to make a Coffeemate special.

No more than 5 minutes of his arrival, his Mother walked through the door. "Well," mused Eric "I guess that proves that then".

DEAR DIARY

Dear Diary,

I died and drifted in limbo and pain, free of the being that had laid hidden in plain sight, seeking out answers yet hearing none be-

cause I still wasn't listening. I earnestly prayed for forgiveness, sincerely sorry for all my wrongdoings, sorry for the path I had tread, sorry for blaming others, I accepted my life and all my mistakes as mine and mine alone. I no longer heard my inner child cry in pain, all my pasts came to me, just as Scrooge had been visited by his ghosts.

Yet still I prayed.

It was all I had left, all I could do, I offered myself into his arms, not deeming myself worthy or wanting acceptance, just mercy.

I tried to run and die a second time, more determined, but was found and stopped by the person who had faced his own demons, though had not defeated them all.

That night I went to the unfamiliar bed, with its unfamiliar smells and unfamiliar sounds and slept. I slept the deepest and most restful sleep. I had not felt this way for many years. And as I slept, the heavens cracked above my head. An almighty boom was heard and the snow fell hard, out of season, not stopping until the morning.

People awoke in the town with astonishment. Roads blocked by the snow quickly melting to flood water, impassable to traffic, only this small town had been affected.

I arose rested and peaceful, I felt afresh and ready, though walked around just as amazed at the spectacle as others.

I felt that, as all things were changed, I should change too. I know I said I had prayed, but I seldom visited church, but being Sunday... I asked a passing stranger what time it was and I realised that services would soon be over. The stranger looked at me and said "Goodness, I'm sorry, I didn't change my watch".

Glad, I attended a local service where the sermon was about my wrongdoings and the pain of sufferers, I couldn't stop the tears or believe what I was hearing. A lady gave me a sympathetic look. As I left I vowed to listen more carefully and sat in the churchyard patchy white and green. I sat and listened in peace and silence. I have not felt like this in over 40 years. I could have been sitting *at my birth home watching the raindrops roll down the window. It was then I heard the voice, soft and clear. Startled at first, I let it direct me, I followed its course, curious to see what would happen and where I was to go.*

I eventually came to a bench, a normal, wooden roadside bench. The voice told me to wait. Three times I asked or questioned, each time the same answer "Wait".

So, I sat and waited, wondering what I would see. I looked around at the normal street, the snow almost gone and traffic resuming it day. Trees and buildings around, fire station, a red bricked bungalow with a large car park, I considered some type of social hall. I sat and waited and watched. A car eventually pulled into the little car park opposite, a person got out and went into the red building. A few minutes passed and then another car, then another. Soon, a considerable number of cars were arriving and people entering this small building. I stood up, intrigued and crossed the road to enquire what event was taking place. To my amazement it was a Catholic Church and I was invited to attend, despite my denomination.

Incredibly, this service too pinpointed my errors.

I do not forget this time in my life. I was offered a new beginning and intend to take it and make a difference. I am truly free at last and do not intend to go back on my destructive path which was being used to hide my hurt.

MRS JARROW

The_old Dorset hamstone cottage had been nestled in the middle of the quiet, rural village for over 400 years, at least 200 of which had been in ownership of the same family. Its tall walled garden at the front and side had small, gnarled fruit trees, pruned by generations and a magnificent horseradish, so deep in flavour, it was strong enough to "scare the devil 'imself". The wisteria was "roight 'eavy 'n bloom" and bees were bumlin', "twas garn b proper roight 'arvest dis un" said young Tim (who was probably about 95) admiring the distant apple trees and Old Mary chuckled behind him with her toothless grin.

Old Mary lived on the edge of the village, in an old brick and wooden shed, no water or electric, just tilly lamps for light, a small open fire for heat and cooking. There were daily visits to the spring with her buckets, where, if your paths crossed, she would entrance you with her tales as you stood there, spellbound, not knowing what she was saying, but loving her honest company. She always wore her heavy woollen pointed hat and thick tweed overcoat with bare legs and wellies, how long she had lived, no one knew, she had always been here, with her boyfriend and talked with the broadest accent that even some of the old folk didn't understand. Old Mary knew all the herbal cures of the land and grew fist sized strawberries with the taste of beauty and purity, so much so, that you would have to stop whilst eating and marvel at life.

Mrs Jarrow sat on her padded window seat looking out through the lead lined panes at Young Tim and Old Mary conversing, looking up into her apple orchard, while the small round oak table in front of her stood on the cool flagstone floor, and gladly held her cup and saucer and, as yet, un-cut seed cake. She sighed as she turned away and looked around the room with its large inglenook dominating the space and remembering her childhood stories and the flames that used to dance about. She would be sad to go. But the house was too big for her on her own and there was none to leave it too.

The house creaked in agreement, as the old footsteps walked the floors going nowhere, but retracing their well-trodden routes.

The 3 bedrooms and attic were crammed with the past occupants' clothes and trinkets, hundreds of years' worth of dresses and tabards, hats and fascinators, jerkins and jodhpurs, all stacked as high as the ceiling, as well as the sawn-off Elizabethan four poster, cut down to size to fit. And if the rooms were not filled satisfactorily, then the barns had their treasures also. The cider press, not used for 25 years, still hadn't been repaired since the day it was made stood wanting and covered in dust. The dipsomaniacs delight, the pile where bottles of all shapes, sizes and uses, lay discarded and had been covered over years of leaf fall and fire ash.

There was one bottle though, a special bottle, that lay hidden, even from Mrs Jarrow, a Witches bottle. A few feet from where she now sat, were her stairs for taking her to bed, behind a small wood panelled door. Under the stairs, boarded in some 300 years past, someone lay a glass bottle. The size of a flattened 1-pint milk bottle, though mottled, a rich black, blue and green, as if oil had been kept in it yet permeated the glass itself.

And inside, inside clippings of hair and nails lay and a scrap of paper, now too faded to read, but would have revealed the true purpose of this hidden, cloth covered container. Used to protect or curse, none would know, but one day soon, it would become discovered.

RIFF-RAFF

The photoshoot contract had gone well and had immediately garnered possible fruits, in the guise of auditions and modelling contracts, more so for Robert than Cassandra.

They were driving back, in Roberts recently purchased banger, from the final day when Cassie suggested dropping in on the club to see the boys and let them know how it went and how wonderful it all was. Robert was a bit unsure and was tired, but after some persuasion relented, "As long as we don't stay too long" he suggested.

They pulled up outside the club, easily parking and went down the stairs, ignoring the hat check, and went straight to a table. No sign of the boys as Cassie scanned around, but she was certain they would be here soon, instead she signalled for service, keen for a bit of attention.

"So," a familiar voice said behind them "you're here. Bit late aren't you"? They turned in unison to see Tommy standing, with arms crossed, horn in hand.

"Oh, Tommy darling, how lovely to see you" cooed Cassie with ease.

"See you brought your fellow with you. Hard luck chap, lookout" came the reply.

"Yes, erm, Cas told me you broke it off" Robert replied.

Tommy laughed, throwing his head back "That's what she told you, ay? Other way round dear boy."

Cassies face faltered when her eyes met Roberts. She didn't understand why he looked so shocked and unsure where to put himself. He stood, knees weakened and walked away out of the club and passed his car and walked again into the night.

Back inside, Tommy sat down with Cassandra, who was feeling uneasy and cornered.

"You've been a bit of a minx Cassie, haven't you"? Tommy said, signalling for his usual. "How about we start again Cassie, you know I love you".

Cassie was stuck. On one hand, Robert financially secure, handsome and then there was the modelling and acting to think of. On the other, Tommy, was here and Robert had left, how else was she going to get home.

Robert was tired. Tired of it all. Tired of trying to keep it all together. He missed home. Missed his family, even his brother, perhaps not, but he missed what his brother could have been. He missed his father too and the unresolved issues. He felt played, he felt used. Used and abused by so many people for their own benefit. Dumfounded, Robert walked. The years of upset grew with each footstep he took. It started to rain again. "English bloody weather" he thought to himself. He started to feel hemmed in with all the tall buildings reaching over him, crowding around and suffocating and the raindrops themselves were too heavy to bare, adding insult to injury, smothering him with their dampness. Robert needed open space, the all-encompassing veldt, wide open, glorious skies where you could breathe and fill your lungs, gallop for miles with simple life in your heart.

His hand reached and touched Inkosi, his trusted childhood steed. He reached up and stroked his mane, pulling their heads close together and whispered soothing clicks into its ear. Robert told Inkosi, not to worry, everything was fine, its just a distant storm, they'd be home soon. He swung up with ease onto the horses back, and steered it away from the dark foreboding clouds and galloped off in whatever direction they were heading. He called out and waved to a group of locals and servants working along a fence fixing the road and putting up new posts. The lights flashed as the storm clouds neared, but he was happy to be riding again, happy and free, though his head hurt and part of him felt cold.

The horn blare surprised him as he got up off the wet road and stumbled onto the pavement. Warmth trickled down his face with cold wetness and he staggered on, confused at his surroundings and trying to reach again for Inkosi who had bolted. A man leant in to face him, to close and scared Robert swung wildly at the figure, screaming at the nightmare and calling for the buildings to stop laughing at him. The swirl spun around him like a nauseating wave, flipping him inside and out, desperate to unsteady his connection, scratching at his eyes and dancing the black belief.

It went on forever. He was there and nowhere. With time and without. He felt nothing yet everything. Hot, cold. Heard, silence.

The light made him shake. His eyes flickered open and he was awake. Tired, confused, but awake, lying in a hospital bed with Cassandra by his side.

CHRISTMAS AT ROOKS END (Part 3)

Plates had been cleared away, the Queens Speech watched with reverence (including Grampa and Eric standing for the National Anthem), after lunch games played amongst the whisky fumes and Afternoon Tea consumed with Great Aunt Janes Chocolate Log.

All the grown-ups retired to their rooms, for a brief siesta and to reboot themselves ready for the evening's drinks party, leaving the three children alone. It was the only time this ever occurred and they were always lost at what to do. Knowing their strict guidelines, as dictated by Aunt Jane, they sat virtually motionless watching television, not daring to move in case something got damaged, it seemed different with all adults absent.

Time thankfully passed quickly and before long started to hear water going through the old pipes of the house, and doors opening and closing upstairs. This only made Eric get more fidgety and got told to sit down and behave by Dicky who was seriously and intently interested in motor racing. Things got the better of Eric however, when he heard movement in the kitchen, he slowly moved backwards away from the television engrossed Dicky and when he was out of view materialised smiling in front of a startled Ruby, who was preparing cocktail snacks for the imminent guests.

He was closely followed by Tess, enquiring if they could "help or taste anything"? Ruby directed them to some sandwiches she had already prepared, that needed crusts cutting off. "Hmm, crusts" thought Tess, she loved bread and she hadn't eaten much lunch, having been told once that she should always leave some food on her plate for Mrs Manners, it was polite. This would be the start of her life long struggle with bulimia.

As they were busy trimming, and nibbling, Robert came down to prepare the drinks and get a head start on everyone else as Cassie was still having a lie down after taking one of her pills.

Dicky appeared and automatically was given the task of carrying the bottles and lay out nuts as the first of the invited guests knocked at the door. They walked in, before the door had been answered and Eric was surprised to see them being escorted by Aunt Jane, not realising that she had actually gone to pick them up in her car.

Soon enough more familiar faces started to turn up and as Eric had been given the duty of Doorman, kept getting patted on the head with comments like "Oh you must be Derek" and "Haven't you grown". It was cold in the corridor by the front door and the party sounded like it was warming up, no other cars could be seen coming up the drive, so Eric decided he needed a drink as well...

Entering into the first sitting room the fumes hit. The heady mix of smoke and laughter, gin and music, port and lemon. Weaving around the head patting and perfume he searched for the drinks table to see what he could find. A bowl of salted peanuts and cheese balls looked at him, all alone, so Eric thought he'd take it for a walk into the kitchen for a quiet chat instead, just like he'd seen his parents do with the occasional guest at other parties.

Ruby was just finishing off tidying and getting ready to retire when Eric arrived with Tess, unknowingly behind.

"Look what Miss Jane bought a while back" she said, bringing out a blue metal tube fixed to a stand. "It's called a Sodastream". She explained its use and how it worked and made him and Tess a fizzy orange, which tasted disgusting but drank it anyway and asked for another. Ruby obliged and chivvied them away.

The Spirit of Christmas was definitely present and Poor Pussy was being suggested. Eric found this game hilarious but didn't really understand it. One person was chosen to be "The Cat". They would, on hands and knees, have to circulate and behave like a cat, rubbing themselves against other people's leg and get stroked on the head with the person saying "Poor Pussy". For some reason, which Eric could not understand, some adults found it more humourous than he, especially when people over acted. It was normally about this time when he would be sent to bed.

"Eric," called his mother "time for bed".

FULL-TIME

Being a full-time boarder had its perks, few admittedly, but some. There was being allowed up the main staircase, usually only permitted to Teachers and Prefects, no specific bed time on weekends, but the best was less competition with the television and cooks treats.

Most weekly bugs went home on Friday after school, so when the full-timers got back to the boarding house, the lucky first few would dash downstairs to see Cook, who, hopefully, had just finished baking some biscuits or scones. Piping hot from the oven she would allow a few to "disappear", they would be scurried away to a hiding place, behind hanging coats or part closed doors, sniggering and scoffing and "ho..., ho..., hop". Crumbs dispersed, a dash back up the concrete stairs so as not to be missed by a prowling teacher, meeting hopeful late-comers descending and hearing "Aw" in the background. This was counterbalanced, very unfairly, with a Saturday morning of triple Latin with an equally ancient Mr Oarman, who often fell asleep during class and would berate any pupil disturbing his slumber or failing to notify him of end of class.

Eric felt himself lucky among some other full timers. Others were sad all the time, not matter whether in play or work, a handful only seeing one or both of their parents maybe only twice a year, if they were fortunate. Children of international models, politicians, celebrities or the affluent, they all shared the same pain and tears, no matter where they came from. Unfortunately, in their future, they might put their own children through the process, forgetting how they were damaged only to pass it on from generation to generation.

Being a target for bullies didn't help with a healthy welfare. No matter which school attended, someone was looking for a way of spreading their problems, looking for an outlet. As he grew older, the imagination of the torturer grew as well. Starting with plain old kicking, punching, tweaking, headlocks (all favourites of teachers as well, not forgetting blackboard wiper and chalk throwing), things would progress to strangulation, filling a bath with water (by way of a milk bottle filled at a river, a 5-minute run away), whipping, but the most uncomfortable was hanging. No noose was needed, just a coat hanger. The unsuspecting victim would have a coat hanger placed inside their coat, which would then be fastened up and the victim would be hung up on a nearby coat hook. Seemingly humourous, rules applied. Left dangling, passers-by were expected to irritate the child further in any manner they felt fit, you decide, but on no account was help to be administered, unless you wanted the same treatment. Tears and pain came quickly for many, sometimes being left there for a long half hour.

After a prolonged period of unhappiness, Eric decided to make a change and runaway back home.

He thought carefully how to do it, having little access to money and a long walk that he could get busted on, he then remembered that one of his teachers, a friendly History teacher, lived an easy walking distance from home, with many well-known routes. The end of the school day, midweek, loomed and he spotted Mr Cuthbert at his usual desk, marking some books and finishing his cup of tea. Eric knocked at the door.

"Afternoon, Mr Cuthbert" said Eric "Mum asked me to ask you if you're going straight home tonight" he lied, with his heart beating fast.

Mr Cuthbert looked up, over his half-rimmed glasses and spoke "Oh, hello Eric" he said in his usual quiet and unfaltering manner "Yes, yes I am, but aren't you meant to be going back to the boarding house this evening"? he enquired.

"No" came the instant reply "I've got a hospital appointment first thing in the morning. It's my ears again. Dad was meant to come and get me but rang to say he was held up in a meeting".

"I thought you said your mother rang" came the response.

"No, Dad rang and so I had to ring Mum and Mum asked me to ask you" wow, he was proud of how well he lied.

"Well, actually" Mr Cuthbert said tidying up the books "I was just about to leave, so you've timed it well. Come on".

Eric couldn't believe his luck, unfortunately the opposite would be the case the following morning when Mr Cuthbert was called in to see the Headmaster.

OOPS !

This was to be Erics first funeral, though he didn't know it yet and at the age of 9 his grandfather was dying of Lung Cancer. Spring had sprung and almost gone and his mother said they were going on a visit to his Grumpy at hospital, where he had been for a couple of weeks, ever since they had taken him for a drive around the top corner, of where Kensington Gardens meets Hyde Park, to see the beautiful, breath-taking crocuses.

They arrived at the hospital and were led into a quiet room where two strange, elderly ladies sat, weeping, talking to a very frail, small looking man, who didn't move or seem to register anyone. The ladies reminded him of a time when he had been ill some years ago. He was always ill with something or other, often bronchitis, sometimes worse.

He had been in bed and the doctor in black had visited him and sat by his bedside. Eric liked the smell of the large black square case the doctor opened, something reassuring and friendly about it. He turned and looked back at himself, he was standing at his bedroom window and saw his parents, sister and doctor gathered around his bed as he lay there, though they were all in Victorian clothing. It reminded him of the time he saw the White Horse come through his bedroom wall and the skeleton trying to open his eyes.

His mother looked the same way now, at this wasted figure, as she had at her son then and Eric wondered who he was. He sat down on the floor and pulled out his little scribble pad and pencil and started drawing some monsters, he liked drawing monsters. The teacher didn't. She even talked to his father because she was concerned about his painting and drawing sometimes, thought something bad was happening at home.

Eric sat, using the chair as a rest, and went into his dream world until it was interrupted with "Don't you want to come and say hello" his mother asked. Eric frowned" No" came the direct reply, "Why would he want to talk to a stranger" he thought.

They were there for a while, not as long as they would be when his Grandmother was in hospital though. That time would trouble Eric for years. His Grandmother and Mum never saw eye to eye, though eventually they would be peas in a pod and when she came to stay, circumstances would cause her to die of pneumonia.

But that was a long time off, and for now it was time to leave and Eric wanted to see his Grumpy. Instead, they left the hospital entirely, his mother in tears and Eric asking "Aren't we going to see Grandad"? and "Who was that you were talking to"? "That was your grandpa" came the answer. The funeral was two weeks later and Eric was still convinced his Mother was wrong.

The ceremony was a very black affair. The church was filled with very well-to-do people who Eric didn't know and would never see again. Cassandra dabbed her face all the way through the service, but would scorn Eric for it years later at his Grans funeral. But today he was interested, looking around at the different hats and outfits, all the cars outside and where all these people had come from.

The service ended and invitations were issued to meet back at the flat for drinks whilst Tess and Eric were led away to a waiting limousine. The driver was asked to take them on and return as soon as for the rest of the party. The long vehicle pulled away with Tess and Eric looking out of the back window at the shrinking scene and couldn't believe their luck. A whole stretch limousine just for themselves. Wow! They rolled around on every possible surface going, much to the amusement of the chauffeur, "Carry on kids, it'll be your turn one day. Make the most of it"

CAS

Despite her sudden outbursts of violence, lies, inability with confrontation, jealousy, secrets, emotional breakdowns and general madness, Cassie was a loving Mother. Desperate for attention and affection, flirtation was a handy, well used tool as well as her acting background, giving her the ability to lie convincingly (a trait that Eric would adopt and excel at, bringing him a lack of satisfaction of his own).

There would be occasions of bills or shop credit that would need to be paid, often leading to hiding behind the sofa when the milkman came calling or sending her 5-year-old son into a shop, where credit was already exceeded, to purchase some goods, to spin a yarn and look innocent. It often worked and Eric learnt the skill quickly to make his life easier.

Tess would often take on responsibilities during one of Cassies "moments" (Dicky being away as usual) having to tend house, cook and call the Doctor. On one such occasion, Robert was out playing cricket, a regular event, as well as golf or polo, any sport activity except on Saturdays when an afternoon of fixtures was displayed on the box, and Cassie was distraught.

Tess rang the doctors, as per instructions, and relayed how bad her mother was, as per instructions, and emphasized the lack of paternal aide, as per...The family physician appeared within the hour and checked on her patient, lying dramatically in bed, too ill to raise her head and wipe her own brow (though, oddly, thought Tess, fine not 10 minutes before, reading her book) and was furious that Tess had not contacted her father, and should do so immediately "Do you not realise how ill your mother is" she said.

A faint murmur emitted from Cassandras lips, and both Tess and GP turned, the destination was given weakly again. "Go on then girl, ring your father". Was barked. To a young 9-year-old, already confused and injured, she tried her best, with the doctor leaving and mother shouting demeaning comments, she sat on the downstairs sofa and waited for the rest of her family to return and ease some of the pressure from her small shoulders.

Apart from her usual illnesses, Cassandra had experienced two miscarriages, potentially harming to any psyche, one requiring a fortnight stay in hospital and an erratic couple of years to follow that would entail disappearances from the family home in the middle of the night, only to return days later, hair dramatically shortened or coloured and dressed in unrecognisible clothing. It was always a stressful time for the family, constantly walking on eggshells, which came to a head (at least one of many) when a month's hospitalisation occurred, with no visits allowed or contact made (it would later be speculated on, though never talked about, that sectioning had taken place).

For a while after Cassie felt better, new medication was prescribed (and shared with Eric) and she started applying herself in new directions, for the first time in years, life seemed on the up. The new fall was around the corner.

The Centre had been doing well, attracting international buyers, especially from America and Japan and a sales meeting was taking place in Scotland, organized and presented by Robert. She felt very proud of what he had achieved in such a short time and with so little, and was already reaping the legal rewards from all his hard work and long hours. It was a ten-day event, but she felt prepared enough to handle the shop and children, especially as well behaved they now were. The time went quickly, with no hiccups and Robert returned with an abundance of positive feedback, potential contracts and possible investors and contacts. He rang Harry, his business partner with the good news and received devastating news in return. Robert put down the telephone gently back on the cradle. He was no longer a part of the business, Harry had bought him out for £1, "...a legal loophole" he said, "Sorry to tell you" he said. Roberts face drained white as he faced Cassandra to tell her the news. "What would he do now" he thought, terrified.

MR LUTON

It was late evening and Eric was enjoying the evening. He had been disturbed from his slumber by the flashing lights outside his bedroom window, not for the last time, and, bleary eyes being rubbed while pulling up his striped cotton pyjamas, stumbled to the window (yes, the same window) and peered outside behind his curtains.

Much to his young delight, it was a most impressive scene. A large red fire engine, illuminated by its own and street lights, was trying and failing to manoeuvre around the tight corner into his cobbled road, with fireman shouting orders, dashing this way and that.

The last time he had seen an active group of firemen was when he had got his head stuck in the local public gardens railings. It was another lovely summer day, so himself and Cassie had gone for a walk to the park and, at the front entrance, spied the Balloon Man selling his wares next to the Flower Lady. The black balloon looked particularly interesting and attempted to persuade his mother to purchase one. Today, however, was not his day, he was going to have to find another way to amuse himself.

Walking along the low brick wall, with arched railings above, Cassie suggested (though I don't think literally) that Eric should stick his head through the railings. Eric couldn't believe his luck. He had always wanted to try but always got told "Don't be so stupid". So, with invitation opened (and checked, just to make sure), obliged.

It wasn't as much fun as it looked. Easy going in, not so much coming out, actually, not at all coming out. Stuck. A few kindly passers-by tried to assist and offer helpful suggestions, but all Eric heard was "why would you do something like it" and, yes, even "Stupid boy".

He tried telling them it wasn't his fault but no one listened, not even the kind fire chief who brought a hacksaw and laughed saying "Which do you want me to cut? The railings or his ears". Hmm, very amusing.   Eric called downstairs to his mother from his bedroom and was soon joined by she and Tess. Cassandra explained that a television had been left on by one of their neighbours, in a drunken stupor, and, being old and faulty had set light to the sitting room. Eric pushed up the window for a better view and was disappointed that he could not see any flames dancing about, though plenty of smoke was puffing away, which alarmed the firefighters more as their hoses would not yet reach from their stuck engine.

Eric enquired about the safety of Mr and Mrs Luton, a funny couple he thought. Mr Luton, a large, rotund, red-faced man, always wearing a caracul hat (no matter what the weather) could often be seen pedalling his penny farthing, with great gusto, looking the worse for wear and on Sundays would return, from somewhere, with a car full of children in his convertible Rolls Royce Phantom.

Apparently, no harm had befallen to any party, much to the disappointment of Eric, not that he wanted anyone hurt, it just would have sounded more...entertaining. Unfortunately, the first love of his life, a young girl down the end of their street (who, with her sister, would attend a series of "secret" midnight feasts with himself and Tess) would one day soon sadly die in a house fire, leaving a large gap in his life and his first introduction with real loss.

But for now, the smoke carried on billowing as did the excitement of Eric and the fireman, as the truck kept going backwards and forwards, slowly edging its way around the corner. Eric hadn't seen this much commotion since a time near the Tower of London, except for the Dalek (and the man who threw a case of money in the air), when, walking with his Dad, stopped to witness a crowd enjoying the stunts of an escapologist.

He had managed to escape from handcuffs and had done a spectacular dive from a ladder into a paddling pool (some years later, re-enacted by Eric, knocking his front teeth out). Now was his Grand Finale. Straitjacketed, chained and tied to a rope, was hoisted, upside down to wriggle like a worm on a hook. Not satisfied with this foot of expertise, fire was added to the rope and the countdown was set. Lots of "OOHs" and "He'll never do it" was heard...and, they were right.

Shouts started coming from the upside-down man "I can't undo the lock, Steve, I can't undo the lock"! People were running everywhere.

"Now, this is getting interesting" thought Eric, hopping up and down, trying to make sure he didn't miss anything, yet at the same time getting pulled in with the excitement. The burning rope was lowered in time, the flames dowsed and The Great Escapo freed, it was all a bit of a disappointment thought Eric.

RETURN

Robert returned to London after six weeks convalescing back in South Africa, trying to come to terms with his life and experiences after his breakdown and shock treatment and was greeted with welcome arms back into The Company. He wished he could have said the same about home. His brother was as cruel and brash as always, fervently machoistic, domineering with unflinching superiority and a general buffoon. His mother on the other hand was as lovely as she was good. Patience, understanding, sympathy and beauty fell easily off her shoulders, he could understand why his father had married her. The farm was in good order, though the stables had been torn down and replaced with a large open garage, his Dads old motorbike covered with a dusty tarp at the back, and new trees had been planted where some of the older ones had been chopped. His mind was taken back when out working with Timo and Julian, a couple of land servants with a group of others, out at a part of forest that needed some scrub and timber clearing. When chopping and felling, you had to have your wits about you and always call out warning to avoid harm. A young inexperienced local was taking a break, eating from a cloth bundle his mother had prepared for him of dried mealie pap, while sitting on the root end of a downed tree. A call went out and he turned to see a tree falling in his direction, but would clearly miss, so returned to eating, not realising his predicament. The two trees, fallen and falling, made contact with each other and projectiled him into the air with devastating circumstances, falling himself, hard and broken, the vision staying with Robert for a lifetime.

He had stayed at the farm for most of his time, revisiting favoured landmarks and hideaways, but found nothing except for the knowing that these places were used as escapes and not attached to happy memories. On one hand he loved his home and country that bore him into life, the vast open spaces where early man would possibly have marvelled at the beauty and abundance on offer, yet if offered him no solace, no escape and no promises for the future, he had to find his own path. So, with weight in heart, he decided to leave and resume as soon as able, as not to miss the early worm.

The Company were in full swing of a run, but rehearsals were also taking place for a matinee production of Maria Marten (Murder in the Red Barn and the lead had not yet been allocated, so a possible opening for Robert), a melodrama, an unusual choice for this group but a crowd pleaser nonetheless. Robert walked quietly to the wings of the evenings show, receiving hugs, kisses and pats on the back by passing cast and crew, and saw Cassie on stage. She turned, on cue and unflinching, contact was made and she smiled at him, whether it fitted the moment or not, neither cared, but the connection was remade.

The performance ended and bows given and Cassie fell straight into Roberts arms.

"Oh Darling" she said, resting her head against his chest "I've been so worried about you. Have you missed me"?

Robert kissed the top of her head "Of course I've missed you darling, you're all I've thought about".

"Oh, my Darling, do you forgive me? I do love you so". She continued.

"There's nothing to forgive" he said feeling slightly confused, like he had forgotten something inside, possibly important, though couldn't be otherwise he would remember "I love you too".

They embraced and kissed and received more slaps on backs.

Make-up and costumes needed removing and congratulations and suggestions given, so Robert waited by the Stagedoor for the ensemble to depart, thinking "This time, this time. This time I'll make it right".

He turned to hear the voices coming closer, the first wave, normally the ones who hadn't been on stage last or the ones hurrying off, furthest to go, or the ones, like Cassie, rushing to see her beau.

He stood upright as she came into view and noticed she seemed hesitant or not so confident. She took his arm, as she had so many times before and exited under the old light, it still watching yet not being able to tell. Robert went to lead the way to the little passageway out to the front and Cassie pulled at his arm.

"Let's go a different way tonight" she said softly "I haven't seen you for so long, I do want to catch up". She said "There's a new café round the corner that will be open. We could go there".

Robert faltered slightly, but smiled and kissed her once more and they turned and walked into the darkness of the night, leaving Tommy out front, waiting in his car.

EASTER AT ROOKS END

Tess and Eric (Dicky being otherwise engaged) were excited as always to be visiting Rooks End, especially now that it was Easter and the promise of an Egg Hunt around the gardens. Pulling into the drive way, they looked out of the car windows searching the hedgerows and bushes to see if any eggs had already been concealed. Alas, none.

Pulling to the usual handbrake stop, Tess and Eric dashed off with permission to their first port of call. Running through the house, shouting hellos, they headed upstairs to their favourite corridor and bumped into Great Aunt Jane coming down.

"Ooh, mind where you're going children. Where are you off to in such a hurry" she said, knowing full well.

Thwarted, disappointed and not wanting to offend, in unison

said "We were looking for you Aunt Jane"

"Well, come along downstairs and we'll see if we can find anything in the kitchen". That worked.

In a full about turn, the little feet pounded down the stairs and hurried through the door and sat in their trained positions, at the breakfast bar, like good puppies they were, awaiting treats.

Moments passed slowly, dishearteningly and droolingly as they heard Great Aunt Jane saying hellos to Cassandra and Robert, how was the drive, how was Dicky, how was work, blah, blah, blah. They looked at each other and decided action was called for, so slid of their seats and sidled into the corridor to chance their luck.

"Oh, sorry children" said Aunt Jane smiling "I forgot all about you, lets go and get you a biscuit each".

A biscuit! They had hoped for more, but supposed a homemade biscuit might mean two…or three. Tess couldn't help but lick her lips.

"Don't worry about biscuits Jane" interjected Cassandra "They won't eat their supper if they fill up on biscuits".

"So"? thought the two, now desperate tummies.

Being steered away from the house (and away from their prizes) and led back to the car, they were handed their bags and told to take them in.

Begrudgingly doing as they were told, received an update.

"You're sleeping upstairs" stopped them in their tracks. That meant the attic. They turned, enquiringly silent. "Tristan and Blanche are staying tonight as well" ended the sentence.

"Yuck, not nasty…" (freckled, permanently runny-nosed, spoilt little brat) "…Tristan and smelly…" (oh, so smelly, whiny…) "Blanche" retorted Tess.

"Now Darling" replied Cassie "They're not that bad"?

Tess turned and signalled to Eric to move "You don't have to play with them" she thought, whilst Eric pondered "I might get on the roof again".

The evening was a bit of a sleepy blur, that consisted of lots of food, people coming and going, lots of grown-up talk, a snotty Tristan and a not smelly Blanche who had ringlets and a white puffy dress, she seemed "quite nice" thought Eric. "No" said Tess later "Still yuck"!

Morning came soon enough, after the usual ghost stories, the night before, of Great Uncle Crispin that kept them awake, each taking guard, in case he came into their room with his candle and ate them alive. As per house rules, they had to wait in their rooms until the gong had struck three and then the stampede could commence.

A full breakfast was laid out this morning. Bacon, eggs, sausages, tomatoes ("yuck" again from Tess), Tea and, as it was Easter, Coffee (with a secret six sugars) was allowed for Eric, a special treat (he actually drank three unbeknownst to the adults, but much sniggering and icky snorting from Tristan).

Filled and content after fast breaking, children were directed to amuse themselves for a couple of hours before luncheon, which would be a light affair of salads and cold meats, which were always fantastically cooked by Great Aunt Jane (Ruby).

Orders given, the parents stayed talking, tidying up and drinking "Bit early isn't it Robert"? "No, no, not early" came the reply.

The four children ran outside to the front garden, another lovely day at Rooks End, the magic and warmth never stopped. They all had the same idea. "Let's see if we can find any eggs yet" they agreed upon. Dashing around the beds and trees, not going too far afield, a blank was drawn very quickly, knowing full well that they would have to wait until well after lunch.

"I know" said Tristan "let's go to your bedroom" he suggested.

"Why"? enquired Blanche.

"They've got the window onto the roof".

Erics heart momentarily stopped, changed gear, then went full speed ahead.

"You know about the roof" he swallowed lightly looking at Tristan.

"Yeah, c'mon" he said dashing off.

The eight legs hurried into the house and as quiet as a spider dashed up the stairs only to slow on the wooden flight up to the attic room where the window was beckoning.

"Ooh" said Eric, doing his little jump up and down "Can I go first"?

"No, said snot face "It was my idea, I'm going first". Pushing his way forward.

"Well, I don't want to go out" interjected Blanche as Tristan opened the window and started clambering out. Still doing his hopping, Eric turned to ask Tess if she wanted to go before him and that he might have to have a wee out there, all this hopping. But Tess was nowhere to be seen. "Odd" he thought and went to the bedroom door to peer round to see if she was on the small landing. Instead, he saw his mother coming up the stairs. Mouth open, Eric stood there, defeated again. "No Egg hunt for you, young man" came the sentence as she walked past to collar Tristan, alerted by his sister, desperately trying to scramble back in through the window.

Tristan was sent home and Eric had to sit still for the rest of the day, even while Smelly Blanche and Tess hunted for the not very well-hidden eggs. "Hmph" he thought "I can see them from here".

His sister had collected the most, "because of her betrayal" thought the gloomy Eric, head resting on one hand, feet swinging on the garden bench. She came over and sat by him and smiled.

"Ten tonne Tessie, more like" he grumbled, possibly aiding the start to her anorexia.

HENRY

Henry sat on the back of the sofa, his favourite sitting position, which annoyed everyone immensely. It wasn't that it was a small sofa, far from it, at a squeeze, it could accommodate four adults, it was the fact that he would sit in the middle and on top of the cushion, making it very awkward for anyone else who knew him.

Henry was an aggressive, short-tempered toy poodle and he hated everyone.

The problem was thought to be that he had been nurtured by a matronly cat, who taught him the ropes, as best as she could, and made sure that everyone knew where they stood. Unfortunately, Henry didn't have a clue what she was talking about, so made it his mission to alienate one and all.

Hence the problem with the sofa. Even sitting at either end could be seen as an invasion of his territory, with low high-pitched snarling coming from those sharp little teeth.

One day, Eric had been invited to a party. Not a friend's party, Eric didn't really have any friends. Tess did, Dicky did, but not Eric. He had made friends a couple of times, but they had not met with his mother's satisfaction, so had been readily dismissed with "Nasty child"! (them, not him…I think).

Dickies friends were the favourite, Tess's were just girls (barely tolerated), and Dicky, his mates and Tess used to go to Saturday Morning Cinema, by bus, on a regular basis, which sounded so mysterious and fun, "and no adults" he thought. Eric was very envious. Sure, his favourite cartoon, "The Impossibles" was on T.V on Saturday mornings and he would be reluctant to miss it,, but the sound of the cinema…well, excitement overload.

Every week he tried to go and every week rejected.

"I don't want HIM to come" said his brother to his mother.

"He'll get in the way. He's so annoying".

Eric wasn't quite sure what made him so annoying, his brother never had liked him, even when rough'n'tumbling Dicky would get short tempered, but he was determined to keep trying. "Wear them down," said the quiet voice.

Eventually, it worked. The group pilled on the bus, pennies rattling in pockets, with Dicky, Richard and Graham taking the upstairs and Tess and Suzy, with Eric in tow, downstairs...he wasn't a "big boy". As usual Eric spent his time looking out of the window, watching the busy world go by, all the different vehicles, buildings, trees and people you see in one of the planets largest cities, centuries old with highlights of the modern touch. He especially liked to see the old alley ways or unusual feature, tucked between, or on, unassuming buildings, but offering a glimpse of life gone by, as the pedestrians walked past, oblivious, of their ancestors.

Tess and Suzy rang the bell for the bus to stop and they all bundled off into the crowd of expectant, noisy children all waiting for the doors to open. Eric had never seen so many bodies in one place before and was quite excited already. A stern looking man came out of the cinema at the top of the steps and before he could finish his first sentence was stormed by the throng of pushing and shoving and shouts of joy. Tickets paid, the pushing and shoving continued to their seats. They had lost sight of Dicky and Co., no doubt somewhere amongst the full cinema of noise and activity, so many excited and ill-behaved screams and shouts. A momentary hush descended, as did the lights, but resumed to fever pitch as the organist arose, playing his wurly music, from out of the stage and a hail of popcorn and sweets hurled through the air, directed at the poor unsuspecting man. He tried to turn and shout condemnation, but was drowned out by the ridicule and confectionary, so retreated below, never to return again. Years later, Eric would often lie on his bed, late at night and listen to "The Organist Entertains", often feeling remorse but enjoying where the sounds would take him. After the man descended, they were treated to an array of serial films, Flash Gordon and Champion, the Wonder Horse, a couple of cartoons, a news reel and a main feature about some children finding a Dragon egg and hatching it. Never once did the volume and food throwing abate, but Eric was focused on what unfolded before his eyes, escaping into his own world of safety and daydreaming and wondering what it would be like to have friends.

The party, as always needed a present, so magically, one appeared that needed to be wrapped. Cassandra and her youngest son sat on the unmade double bed, scissors, tape and paper at the ready but no gift in sight.

"It must be under the blanket," said Cassandra.

Eric slid his small hand under the bulging blanket, eager to see what had been bought, only to find a warm lump of fur that proceeded to clamp its sharp teeth onto the inquisitive hand.

By the time the hand had been cleaned and dressed, tears wiped and present wrapped, dog admonished, the party would already have been in full swing, but Cassandra was adamant that he should still go. A miserable walk followed, still with the occasional sniff in tow, they arrived and coats were taken, with sympathies poured onto his mother for her terrifying ordeal, as Eric was given a glass of squash and told to go and join the others.

MONTE CARLO OR BUST

The day didn't come round soon enough. Tess had left home about a year before and Dicky had had the sense never to have returned, apart from a brief spell after returning from his tour of South Africa and his attempted foray into joining the forces in order to win the hand of a lady. Since Tess's departure, the onus fell more on Erics shoulders to be more persistently reliable (not that Tess had performed many duties or chores herself) without fiscal recompense (food and lodgings were considered payment enough), forcing him in the end, to seek out a full-time job as an apprentice in a local builder's firm.

The work wasn't the problem. He enjoyed the outdoor life and found manual labour instantly satisfying and enjoyed the challenge of learning. No, the problem lay with his parents, as with any teenager.

His father had become dourer and easily tempered, working longer, unfruitful hours with little reward with a wife who, with possible good intentions, hampered progress or was a drain on valuable resources. And that was his main drive to leave. He realised that he no longer needed to put up with the, what he considered at the time, erratic and crazy behaviour of his Mother, and nor did he want to.

The deciding factor came a few months before. He had already declared his intentions of departure, having seen his Mother attempt to throw stones at horses in a field, or find her hiding one day, preparing to run away, with a fanciful idea of making some money to send back to the family. One morning, sitting at the breakfast table, innocently eating his bowl of cornflakes, his mother strode in, that look in her eyes that he hadn't seen for years, but not forgotten.

"How dare you read such disgusting filth" she shouted at him, picking up the box of cereal and striking him over the head with it, cornflakes exploding everywhere. Confused, a switch flicked inside.

"I don't have to put up with this anymore" the small voice said inside and he immediately stood up and pushed Cassandra.

She stumbled back, shock in her eyes, incredulous at the response. At the same time, Robert arose and punched Eric full in the face.

"Don't ever do that to your mother again" was shouted.

Mother fled sobbing to go and have a lie down.

" How could anyone be so horrible to me" Eric heard as she went.

He no longer cared, enough was enough, though was still confused at what she had been going on about. It was then that he spied a book he had been reading, a standard yet very popular, semi-fictitious, risible, American crime novel about the New York Police Department and had passed it on to his father. Pages had been torn out, a mild yet humourous sex scene and another concerning a donkey.

Erics face throbbed, but he really didn't care. The years of abuse had piled up and he wasn't going to take it anymore, though not realising that nature abhors a vacuum, the void left by his mother was going to be filled by years of damaging hedonistic behaviour.

And so, his determination to flee the nest manifested.

His bags were packed into the car.

Robert was going to drive up, with Cassie, not wanting to be left behind (more likely wanting to keep an untrusting eye on Robert) to lead the way and carry the luggage, as Eric rode his motorbike on the longest journey he had yet to make.

Familiar lanes and roads soon disappeared with the arrival of the rain, and as the roads became busier and wider, Robert's speed increased also.

Eric, though a competent rider, had no experience or desire, to ride at such excessive speeds as his father (often above 80 miles per hour) in the rain, especially as he only had two wheels compared to the dry, warm comfort of four, in addition to not knowing which directions to be taking, relying of his fathers' bluster of "you'll be alright, just follow me".

Eric wasn't "alright". Far from it. The rain had been insistent and wintry cold and traffic as steady as his Dads foot on the pedal. A window ("if only he had one" he thought) arose. Stonehenge came into view, marking a rough half way point of his sodden journey and his parents' car slowed to allow Cassandra a view of one of her favourite landmarks. Old churches, brass rubbing, ley lines, dramatic skies, they all featured heavily on her list. Eric flashed his lights at his family and signalled to pull over, indicator flashing and arm gesticulating, all to no avail. The rain was as hard as ever, as was his resolve. Eric opened his accelerator and pulled up alongside the f'"*|^£$g … sightseers, shaking his fist with a tirade of expletives.

Fortunately, and coincidently, a small roadside café loomed and was manoeuvred onto, with Eric still doing his Captain Haddock impersonation as he got off his bike, striding towards his bemused looking parents.

It took about an hour's rest to go from drenched to damp

(a wonderful difference) and calm down. Thankfully the rain eased to a fine drizzle and they resumed their uneventful journey.

Eventually, the first address of <u>his</u> new life was reached. A picturesque two-bedroom house nestled quietly (for now) in a pleasant back road of student town.

HOPE HOUSE

Weeks of worry and searching had proved fruitless. Work for a man in his late 40s, with plenty of valid experience in sales and marketing, though no formal qualifications, was far and few between, especially when coupled with pride.

The weeks turned into desperate months, causing a shoe string existence and pulling Eric from public school life (much to his elation). It happily, or unhappily, coincided with a call from the college, asking his parents to attend a meeting due to some undesirable behaviour. The conference was held with both parents, Eric and House Master, who laid out the seriousness of events which had involved streaking after lights out and Eric being witnessed on the House lawn by the Headmasters wife. The story omitted the circumstances of clothes being tied together to form an escape rope, thrown out of the window and the victim being towel whipped while trying to retrieve them. House "pranks" were common. Ranging from Apple Pie beds, where the top sheet is removed and the bottom sheet folded in half to represent a fully made bed, to wet flour in pyjamas, not fun to be made to sleep in. All the while the Housemaster was extolling healthy virtues and unwanted miscreants, Erics mind wandered to an event a couple of weeks earlier and how three fellow pupils had raided the secure arsenal, housed behind the Captains lodgings, and borrowed some rifles, ammunition, smoke grenades and flash bangs. They proceeded to terrorise the local village in the middle of the night and caused much commotion (and hilarity to the admiring, innocent understudies) until eventually being caught, absconded, then caught again by the local constabulary. Only one was expelled, the other two told off (with no parents having to attend "a stupid meeting" thought Eric) as their parents were too wealthy to attend.

Meeting over and "drivel" talked, Erics parents took him for a drive and "a word". The word was:

"Eric, if you don't behave, they'll kick you out of College. Then, when we move, you'll have to live with us in the countryside. And you don't want that, do you"? was delivered intermittently by both parents.

"What"? said Eric "We're moving"?

"Yes" Cassie said.

"We're buying a small place in the country, a few cows, chickens…" said Robert.

"Oh Great" came the unexpected, enthusiastic reply "when are we moving".

"Don't you want to stay at College" his mother nervously asked looking at Robert.

"What"? came a shocked exclamation "No, thank you…" emphatically came "farming sounds great". He said sitting back in his seat smiling, free at last.

Things began to move very quickly from his point. For Eric it was to be a new lease of life, opening up a whole world of possibilities, but for Tess, it would be leaving all her beloved friends behind to an existence she did not want or care for.

The contract completion was being held up by the sale of their house in London and Great Aunt Janes family solicitors, who were helping in part, with Cassandras "one day" inheritance, raising some funds now, sooner than later.

The new school term was looming and it was decided to send

Tess and Eric ahead, in order to get settled in with their new education and get to know the pupils and the area.

They were introduced to the large Hope family, a friendly 5 boy family who sometimes took in waifs and strays and directed them on a new course of life, with them popping in, out of the blue, years after being given a chance in life to succeed. It was a strange period for both Tess and Eric, happiness and communal efforts not marred with suffocating seclusion was a refreshing change, as was the ability to cycle around tall hedged lanes, smelling wild garlic and cow muck instead of car fumes, and nothing more dangerous than a slow-moving tractor chugging along with a wurzel at the wheel or a wellie-wanging competition.

MY FUNNY VALENTINE

Tommy was devastated. He sat in the quiet of the club, last man out, with a bottle of scotch in front of him, half drunk and an ashtray fit to burst. Cassie had stood him up again, he couldn't believe what a putz he had been. She flitted between men, depending on what they offered, tiring of commitment, seeking the thrill of the chase and the attention it brought. A month ago, he had gone to meet her outside the theatre, only to wait forever and find she had walked off with that Robert. It stung. He took another swallow, that stung too.

She'd come back, mind. Came running back like she always did. "Oh Tommy, I missed you" she said, "how could I be so foolish" she said. Again, another hefty glug.

He leant back in his chair and wiped the hair out of his face and reached for a packet. He pulled out a stick and put it in his mouth and struck a match. The end fizzed as he drew in a smoky breath and exhaled, blowing out the match at the same time.

She only stayed a couple of days before disappearing again, only to reappear at that same weekend. "Why was he such a mug" he thought, tipping the bottle to refill his glass. He took another drag of the cigarette and blew out its blue smoke hanging low over the table.

Ron and Jay had told him things would end up bad. He just hadn't wanted to believe them, he had faith in the old girl. "What a mug"! another slug easily gulped down his throat.

And now this evening. Well, this evening was a beaut. One of The Girls was in, gossiping away like they do, and word gets out. Only it's a word that's not his. Pregnant they say. Cassies only gone and got herself pregnant with Robbo's baby. Two hefty swigs from the glass followed by an "ahh" and another puff. Glass empty, Tommy reached for the bottle for a refill only to find another bottle was called for. He stood and wobbled slightly and staggered for the bar, more difficult than he thought. Rather than going round, he leant over and just managed to fumble a bottle off the shelf and told a chair to get out of his way as it threw itself into his path on the journey back to his table. He fell into his seat and reached for his smoke only to find it had disappeared, so lit another. He unscrewed the lid of the fresh bottle and chucked it across the room "won't be needing that" he said. The liquid sploshed over his glass wetting part of the table.

With glass now well topped up, Tommy drank heavily and refilled again. "I can't believe my Cassies gone and got herself pregnant" he said to the bottle that stood there ignoring him. "Why would she do that to me" he said again, but no response came. Another puff of the cigarette was followed by a hum of F, Dm7, Fm, G7 which made him laugh. F, Bm7-5, E7, Am, C7 which made him cry. The cigarette was almost out, it had had too much whisky, but it tasted okay. That reminded him, more whisty. "What was he going to do now"? he thought as he drank, "Cassie was my life" another slurp, "I wanted to marry her not him" refill again.

Silence fell like a heavy brick as he already knew what he was going to do. His Uncles World War 2 revolver sat also on the table. It was what it was for after all, thought Tommy, his hand reaching out to feel the cold metal. He picked up the gun in one hand and glass in the other, wet cigarette in mouth. For a moment he contemplated what a mess he must look. He put down his glass and gun, lit a fresh smoke, tidied his hair, shirt and tie. Put on his jacket, kissed his trumpet and had another large swallow of scotch. Another puff and gave out a laugh as he pulled the trigger goodbye.

TOM THE MILKMAN

The stables doors often had the top left open in the quiet cobbled mews, allowing the noises and smells of the city to come and go as they pleased, but bringing the scent of the ivy (growing up the front of the house) in along with what plants were blooming in the small flower boxes.

When Cassandra and Robert were first married, they rented a quarter of an unimportant mews house, a glorified, but run-down bedsit, the Belfast sink with dripping tap and haphazard gas cooker sat in a partitioned off corner by the window and the rest of the room had a small, Formica covered table (with two straight back wooden chairs), a china wash basin and jug and a small double bed. Each time one of the other tenants moved out, they were able to expand their living quarters with agreement of old Mr Coxton, the owner and landlord, a kindly chap, though tired of life. Eventually, as time passed on, the longterm tenants and proprietor became good friends and the house was sold to them on condition of him being allowed to stay in his humble abode until his time came to fly to pasture new.

Life grew quickly for the newly-weds. 9 months after their happy day their first son was born, two years later their daughter and another two years would pass until their final, though not last child.

Life, in the unassuming part of the city, was like living in a miniature town of its own. Everything you needed was within easy walking distance, shops, transport, doctors, carpenters, park, casino and brothel. In fact, the last two were actually opposite the front door of the small residence and someone had very kindly daubed, in big white letters, BROTHEL, on the side of the building, just to make sure you didn't miss it. By the time Eric was three it had been painted over, looking a bigger eye sore than ever, and a trailing plant was attempting, and failing to hide it. Clampdown came on criminal activities after a celebrity was found dead, in the back of a car, down a quiet alley way, too close to common folk, moving away from the East End where trouble and strife were more noticeable.

The Rag'n'Bone man was a regular visitor to their area. Hearing the shouting from a distance there would be a dash around the house to find either a sugar cube, mint, or apple to feed the cart horse as it came clopping along, pulling its cart, but appreciative of stopping to put its head over the stable door and snuffle at the offering from young hands.

There was also Tom the Milkman. A thin, tall, kindly man, ex-services, always well dressed in his uniform and blue and white striped apron, leather satchel at side, mimicking the angle of his cap, which was supported by his round spectacles.

He would lead his horse for a few years more, until it was sadly replaced by an electric three-wheeler milk float, full of rattling crates, loaded with the day's deliveries and empties of the 1960s housewife. The wooden slatted flooring, studded with brass tacks, the hum of the motor sang to the rubber tyres, who tirelessly carried the load and the solid bakerlite steering wheel all struck an encompassing picture to Erics eyes.

The children of the street would often dance around the delivery vehicle, sometimes being given short rides and sometimes allowed to help steer. It was one such day that this would end. The big round pedal on the floor was a stop/start affair. No acceleration or braking, it was either going or not and Eric had been watching carefully for some time, growing in confidence and ability. After considerable nagging, Tom relented and let Eric take control of the whole cart. All went smoothly enough to start, sitting next to Tom, being allowed to press the pedal and steer, chasing Dick Dastardly and Mutley, catching the pigeon, "look out Cavey", Zoiks!

There wasn't too much damage to the car.

SUMMER AT ROOKS END

Pulling into Rooks End already felt different, change had occurred and not fully understood or explained, but to Tess and Eric part of the heart had disappeared. The car pulled up with its usual crunch on the gravel and everyone got out of the vehicle and stretched away the journey and inhaled another beautiful day. It was always sunny at Rooks End.

The heavy-hearted children carried the bags into the house, calling out hellos to Aunt Jane and made their way past The Cavalier, nod, past the wooden cabinet of curios and dolls house accessories and put their bags in the large middle bedroom. The big windows and curtains giving a cruel reminder. Before heading back down to the kitchen, they looked at each other in mutual agreement and headed toward the narrow twisty corridor which led down to the back of the house and the magic chamber of Ruby's. Walking along to the rickety stairs, their hands trailed the walls and they stopped at the end to look out of the tiny window that peered out onto the orchard.

Tess asked "Are you coming"?

"No, what's the point" replied the gloomy Eric, sighing.

Tess went to the door and turned the knob, which didn't open the door, it was locked, so came back up.

"It's locked" she said.

"Hmm" said Eric, turning and heading back into the main house, "perhaps there might be a biscuit somewhere" he thought to himself as if in a dream.

The house felt emptier, as they entered the kitchen, where drinks, soft and not so, were being consumed and a plate of, not home cooked, biscuits sat waiting.

"Now children" directed Great Aunt Jane "I've got a surprise coming this afternoon".

Interests perked, Tess and Eric were brought out of their malaise.

"Ooh" said Tess "what is it"?

"Well, if I told you, it wouldn't be a surprise any longer, would it dear".

Eric stood listening, mind tumbling, a surprise, hmmm.

The afternoon rolled on into early evening and nothing transpired, despite all the pestering.

"You'll just have to wait until tomorrow, won't you dear" Great Aunt Jane said to the now tired children. Disappointed, they dragged themselves to bed, only to be reminded by the open curtains, that there would be no morning ceremony of curtains being thrown open by Ruby, to awake them with the words "Lovely morning, breakfasts waiting" now that she had left after all these years and they never got to say goodbye. It just wouldn't be the same.

Morning came and greeted everyone with a fresh "Hidey Ho"! the children stretching awake in the large open room with the Victoriana sink in the corner. After a cursory splash, they trotted downstairs to be greeted by the three adults, smiling, the smell of bacon and a glint of sun on metal through the large bay window. Saying their mornings and ignoring food, they stepped toward the glass to get a better glimpse. Outside, parked next to the car, gleaming silver and chrome, was a homemade go-kart, complete with crash helmet.

Great Aunt Jane explained that her next-door neighbour had built a couple and knowing she was to have visitors, suggested she could borrow it to have some fun with. Eric thought "Fun" would definitely be a good word to use.

Breakfast was very quickly consumed and with eagerness and enthusiasm proving good incentives, beds were made and rooms were tidied (though teeth weren't brushed).

By the time Tess and Eric appeared outside, they had already heard and smelt the engine being primed and warmed up by Robert, who was a little disappointed that he would not fit, but was already making up for it with a glass of whisky in hand.

Tess, being eldest, was to go first, with a few steady laps around the circular gravel drive outside the front, while being watched by father and son. Around and round she went, slow and steady, with Eric watching, contemplating the toilet. Robert and Dicky had been to Brands Hatch and Silverstone on numerous occasions (once taking Eric) and had also been to see the James Garner movie Grand Prix, which had, according to Eric "...some very exciting bits, but I don't understand why it's called Grand Pricks".

Tess pulled up smiling and got out of the Kart, engine still running and removed and passed the helmet to Eric. Sitting in the Kart, Robert explained the controls and directions to the ever-impatient child, who was already envisioning the starting grid, at pole position, awaiting the chequered flag to fall.

As soon as he heard the word "Okay"? he was gone. Tearing around the corner, foot almost pressed flat on the accelerator, gravel flying, he saw his opening. Rather than going around the roundabout, like he was supposed to, the straight part of the drive looked more preferable. Off he shot, in the lead, he'll be bound to get the cup, no overtakers. It was at this point, realisation that the track ended and the road was about to start to hit home. "Brakes" he thought "What did Dad say about brakes"?

Too late to worry and hearing plenty of shouting behind him, he decided to turn into the long grass and head towards the pavilion. Not being able to remember where the brakes were, he lifted his foot (still happily pressed) off the accelerator and glided to a bumpy halt. "Gosh, that was fun after all" he thought.

...AND AWAY

The years of self-medicating had at last caught up with her. Depending which decade, there had been prescribed anti-depressants, tranquilisers, statins, beta-blockers, pain killers, antibiotics, pills for the heart, liver, kidneys, colon and a profusion of ointments and powders, the list was as long as the varying ailments. As her years on the planet progressed, so did the number of illnesses she suffered and with, each came a different treatment, with surplus medications being squirreled away to some hidey-hole, the same treatment met out to unwanted bills or communications.

On visits, one could turn over a sofa cushion and find a final notice or a spare tablet, years out of date, yet kept for special occasions, depending when or where you were in the house at the time.

Despite what was occurring in her life at any time, you could always be sure to find a healthy selection of ProPlus in the cupboards and even towards the end, a venture into energy drinks.

At one time, when moving to their poor choice of bungalow, the garage-cum-scrapheap had to be sorted and cleared. Years of official letters (denied at the time), Christmas presents (not sent or given), canned food (thought to have been disposed of from their last move) and vast collections of expensive cosmetics (some trialled, others untouched) were all found, carefully hidden and forgotten.

But now, she lay in the hospital bed, one mix of pills too many had taken its toll on her liver, though the blame was being squarely directed to the G.P for misdiagnosis and incorrect remedy.

The three children, now, most grandparents themselves, stood around as their father sat holding Cassandra's hand, convinced that all she needed was a good holiday to get over this current malaise.

The nurse came in to check on the situation, since the intravenous had already been removed, it was only a matter of time. For once, for Eric, this time felt different. His parents had been taking it in turns over the last few years in hospital visits, each possibly more serious than the last, though each time coming back, weaker than the last, like a sculpture being chipped away at by its creator, or going down the stairs, each step progressively worse, never being able to attain its previous height again.

There had been plenty of hospital visits for his mother in his youth, broken leg, thyroid operation, car crash, bumper car crash, the miscarriages and possible sectioning, but mortality wasn't visited until his father's drinking overtook his ability to work it off and an induced coma was called for. Last rites were administered, with the family present, though Eric felt this was presumptive but was rebuked for this train of thought.

He left the hospital, well into the night and started his long journey home. In the emptiness of the roads, he lit a small pre-rolled smoke and put the radio on. Time and road passed and he threw the spent roach out of the window, thinking about death and lines being etched in the sand being drawn by the pulsing sounds coming from the speakers. Sudden ethereal awareness punctured his thoughts. He had travelled some miles, and over twenty minutes had elapsed in a semi-hypnotic state, yet the radio was still playing the same track. Unheard of in '91 and disconcerting, almost panic set in. Thankfully, before sanity was lost, if it had ever existed, John Peels reassuring voice informed Eric "Well listeners, that was The Orb, and the longest track I've ever played on the radio...". Normality resumed and his father didn't die that time.

Their mother was lapsing in and out of sleep, waking to tell her spectators of visits from long gone friends and how she felt a lot better about dying now, knowing that they were waiting for her.

Robert was somewhat alarmed, saying "You're not dying darling, you just need a good holiday" looking at his children for confirmation.

Dicky was the first to depart, taking the father home, who was in need of a drink and cigarette, knowing that left to his own devices, would head for the nearest ward toilet and light up accordingly, causing alarms to wail and nurses and orderlies frantically dashing around, trying to locate the outbreak (as he had done so before, unfortunately, not once). Dicky left instructions to be notified, no matter what the time, of imminence and pushed Robert quickly out of the ward in his wheelchair before temptation got too much.

Tess, in tears and distraught (and still slightly drunk from breakfast), chatted briefly with Eric when Cassandra came too again.

"Oh bother" she said "I'm still here". Which made Eric burst out a laugh. He recalled two of his mother's favourite comedy quotes and ongoing joke that he had shared when younger. "Funny he never married" by Marty Feldman and "I'm getting better", a great piece in The Holy Grail (I'll let you discover them).

She explained that she visited them all again and she must hurry up, and in mid-sentence saw Tess crying. Her hand reached out and comforted her daughter, reassuring her and thanking her for all her years of support, but for Eric, there was no apology for the untold abuse and violence and she died in the early hours of the morning, no family by her side. Different reasons were for the lack of tears shed by Eric, not malice or resentment, but those attributes did disappear from his being once his mother had died.

YORICK

Robert had returned from working in Cambridge after a number of weeks, on a short-lived production, and as usual, fallen easily back into city life and The Company.

Cassie and friends had written plenty of times, keeping him up to speed with the latest gossip and found that, at times, stories differed. It was great to see everyone again, a pleasure to feel recognised and accepted, though was starting to tire of possible unwanted attention.

Perhaps too much water had gone under the bridge, too many comings and goings or too many variations of the truth being spun, he felt that maybe, maybe, it was time to cool things off and perhaps, change direction. He had certainly found a sense of freedom since being away, had found it quite liberating and realising a new self-confidence.

Despite his lack of trying and his disinterest, Cassandra pestered him more and more for recognition and attention, holding onto his arm at any given moment and making sure an available seat was always by her side.

On a couple of occasions, he relented, but each time, sooner or later, found her back in Tommy's arms, which no longer left him feeling a fool.

One evening, he spurned her advances totally and for the first time, witnessed the venom rise from pits unseen. Vitreous and as black as pitch, spat from the depths and flung in all directions, unleashing fury untold from hidden nadirs. Shocked and unable or un-wanting to tackle such a creature, left to protect each other from harm or further onslaught, only to be greeted the following morning by beauty and serenity as if the demon had been chained and forgotten.

A short time later, at his small flat, life would change for good (or bad). Cassandra knocked at his door one evening and immediately informed Robert that she was expectant and the child would be his. Feeling incredulous, he took the news lightly and inferred possible other candidates or scenarios and reflected the allusions that were being directed towards him as fanciful and untrue, quoting "to thine ownself be true". The demon was released again, but Robert let the harpy fly its course and when exhausted, calmy suggested that "Perhaps we shouldn't see each other anymore"? and escorted her out.

Two nights of silence came, yet on the third, returning from his new part-time job, he found Cassandra and her Mother waiting for him outside his rooms, waiting to be invited in and waiting for justice.

"Well Robert, what do you intend to do now you've got our daughter...pregnant"? the word being forced out with discomfort.

"If I knew it was mine, I suppose we would have to get married" he said out loud, half thinking to himself, half not realising that these were the words waiting to be heard.

"Well, good then" carried on Cassandra's mother "I'm glad to hear that you're going to do what is right".

"Now I never..." Robert replied, getting cut off as both ladies turned and walked away down the stairs.

For the next few evenings, each time he returned to his flat, he found Cassandra with her Mother, waiting for him to return, her mother doing the talking and Cassie silently being submissive, slowly eroding his resolve and convincing him to "Do what is right" and for him to accept "What he has done".

Eventually it worked. News was heralded to one and all, the bells rang out in the land for each soul to hear of the forthcoming ceremony. Happiness was to be shared from John'O Groats to RooksEnd for the ecstatic couple.

It was to be a brief engagement, a mere 2 months, as the young couple were eager to be betrothed and life was but a fleeting blink in the eye of the universe (and no parents would want their bride "showing" under the white of the gown).

They were married at the beginning of the new year, symbolising new starts and new beginnings, their son would be born in October.

DICKY DOES

Going through the motions and jumping the hurdles was important for Dicky. Life was no joke, as he had experienced through the violence of his father growing up, and in order to succeed he needed to take things seriously and professionally to ascend the ladder. Unbeknownst to him, the ladder didn't really exist and if it did, there were plenty of rungs missing to stop people climbing too high, after all, those at the top didn't want to be toppled from their comfortable position. So, the endless game of cat and mouse continued, with bored "executive" onlookers chasing their own dreams, seeking out distractions or power whilst the minions strode to what they believed in.

Dicky had always been a serious and studious child. Tess tried to focus on being a girl, though looking at life from two steps away, unable to run but skip, not really having a reliable role model to copy. As for Eric, he was the joker in the pack.

As the children grew, Robert would issue ideas:

"Why don't you three form a band".

Admittedly, Dicky had learnt guitar and flute, Tess guitar and piano and Eric...well, he tried piano, but found the drums more to his taste though the noise did interrupt his mother's "rests".

Then there were suggestions like:

"I think you'll make a fine writer one day" to Dicky (despite no encouragement or direction, 50 years later did).

To Tess "I'm surprised you never became a Tennis Player" which astounded all as she had ever, barely, lifted a racquet in her life.

And to Eric "I thought you'd become a Racing Driver" confused everyone. Instead, Dicky had turned to the Music Industry, diligently working in many areas, sound libraries, mixing and editing, publications and most recently, management.

It was this last foray that laid the path for Eric to springboard away from home (becoming a roadie and engineer for one of his bands) and into a place he could call his own, not in a way he expected, but might have seemed obvious to an outside spectator.

Eric was settling in to his new life, in the compact yet attractive two-bedroom house. The floor was comfortable enough, as the small bedroom only had room for a single, and that was mostly occupied by Tess (though, when spending time away, allowed Eric the comfort of a mattress), the larger room was being rented by John, a friend of both the owner and old school chums of Dicky's. Tess had kindly persuaded in her boss of a local Bar/Restaurant/Bistro to give her brother a go and they worked well together, with a free hand all aspects of the Bistro, including the music. This delighted Eric considerably. Mix tape after mix tape was provided, even if the record had stuck and the bistro was packed every lunch time, from opening to close, with a vibrant mix of office staff and public, enjoying the sounds and food offered fresh each day.

It was here that a regular group, all of similar age, attracted his attention one day. Bringing a plate up to the bar, Eric was verbally pulled to the side and shown a slug in their salad. Immediately and automatically, Eric unfortunately, burst out laughing but quickly extinguished it, it had reminded him of his mother's antics when young, but quickly and honestly apologised and rectified the situation with recompense for the whole party. They were a pleasant group and would one day become his brothers he never had and loves of his youth, but for now, they were looking for a drummer for their newly formed band.

And so, his life was filled. 9 to 3 was spent cooking, baking, slug bashing and serving and evenings was juggled around either band rehearsals or being taken off to set up for gigs, and such like.

It is the "such like" that started to take a hold of Eric, for a number of years. Distorting and warping reality, almost ending it on a few occasions, but almost certainly always being a learning curve.

FIRST DAYS

Life had changed dramatically for Eric. His past had been shaken off and puberty had attacked his body with gusto, empowering him with super strength and invulnerability, at the same time as taking him from inner-city habitation and the confines of male dominated public school, to open fields and pastures new of the rural countryside and mixed comprehensive education.

The picturesque village of their new home fed his senses every day, so many new things to take in fuelled his natural curiosity as did the local pub that lay 100 metres from their front door.

The quaint pub, far older than its name implied, was fitted perfectly with dart board, bar billiards and both types of skittles, along with both types of farmers, either the cap wearing gentry or down to earth, who would be more accepting of a shove 'aypny challenge and pint of dry cider, though admittedly you rarely saw the cap wearers in the bar. It was most frequented by the people that Eric learnt to admire the most, the hard workers and day to day poachers, who would teach him how to fork hay and make ricks, lay hedges, milk cows, wring chicken's necks, shovel shit (properly, it is a skill) and most importantly, how to drink (especially at lunchtimes).

The house stood emptied of Mrs Harris's life, but now was a strewn with tea-chests and boxes, all waiting to be emptied and contents fitted into their new places. Dicky was in attendance for once, with an ulterior motive though, having rescued a dog from being drowned, had brought him to the farm with the intention of giving it a new life, though not governed by him.

The two, family cats, that had been caged and driven down carefully, were suitably disorientated and were let go in the upstairs area so as not to be able to flee as activity progressed with the unpacking.

Cassandra, having her afternoon lie down suddenly stirred, concerned about the two moggies and needing to check on their welfare. Searching around the bedrooms she found no sign and called her sons to the rescue.

Dicky took the bedrooms, rechecking under beds and in wardrobes (just in case), whilst Eric went up the creaky and rotting stairs to the attic, where at night, what sounded like a body being dragged across the floor would be heard, but fancifully dismissed as rats.

Carefully walking across the beams of the floorless floor, in the dark and misty gloom he thought he saw a movement in the far corner. Instinctively, Eric stepped in that direction, only to suddenly plummet through plasterboard, his feet and legs appearing right before an astonished Dicky. With inherited reflexes, he had caught a cross beam on the way down and stopped his descent, abruptly and almost fatally. His brother, laughing out of surprise, called.

"It's okay, you can let go. I've got you".

Sensing that all was not well, Eric replied "Yeah, don't think that's a good idea. I think you better come and pull me up" as he stared down at a long protruding nail that had skimmed his chest and wanting an excuse to plunge deeper.

It would be later that day that the Witches Bottle was found and removed from its decades or centuries long resting place, from that night on, noises would be heard and things would be seen until, some weeks later, the house would be blessed and peace would descend until they were to move again (but, that's for another time).

For now, everyone was getting used to their roles and finding their feet in village or school life. The shire people being friendly and welcoming, especially as the newcomers were adopting their ways and not trying to insist on the tried and tested communal life, unlike some who move to the country and complain of cockerels or the church clock striking at 5 in the morning to call out the workers, or buy a house near a runway and grumble and protest about planes. No, here the status quo would be kept and humbly added to, grateful for the new life and new loves.

THOMAS AND TUPPENCE

The small farmhouse stood in the middle of thirty acres, the highest field giving a glorious view down the southern valley while sitting under the perfect tree, its arms symmetrically proportioned and roots forming a lover's seat, admired by each person who saw it and even the cows, who like to use the base of the tree as a rubbing post.

Needing more acreage for the increasing herd, the decision had been made to move again, more rural than before, no village life here or pavements here, just a dirt track to walk on for ten minutes to reach any sign of tarmac and then a ten-minute drive to the local post office-cum-community store, nothing like keeping away temptations and focus more on mere existence.

The dilapidated milking shed, attached to the back of the house, had touch and go electrics, you touched a switch, then didn't dare go anywhere near it, particularly as a small stream ran by your feet, through the centre of the barn and whether you were wearing wellingtons or not, the idea of checking a shock near a cow* wasn't the idea of Friday night entertainment.

*electric fences are more effective on cows for one main reason. Cows have four legs rather than two. If you're still not sure what I mean, next time you're near an electric fence for cattle, touch it. "Ooh, hmm, not bad" you'll say. Now try it while on your hands and knees...yeah, big difference.

A lot of work was needed doing to improve the place. The rats had had time enough to overrun the hay barn, holes in the walls could easily be used as climbing footholds, and the range, in the tiny kitchen was hazardous enough to poison the residents within a week of being there, with the coke fumes permeating the whole house.

Ramshackle repairs were done, though more were needed and as Robert was no DIYer, had to rely on outside help, a bigger drain on resources on top of the high phone bills created by Cassandra trying to keep up with the latest with her ageing friends. Being now in their 50s, it wasn't the best time to be accelerating, especially with Cassandras back.

In her teens, Cassie had been a promising ballerina, performing for the future Queens Mother, and receiving accolades and recognition, widely regarding her as another Fonteyn until tragedy struck. During one tragic rehearsal, a trapdoor on stage had not been properly secured, causing her to fall and fracture her leg, hip and damage he lower back. Recovery was hampered by sitting in a curled position on a sofa, rather than legs straight, as her parents each vied for her attention, an only child getting all the things she wanted at the cost of her parents' marriage was a good starting point for decay and only fuelled he distaste for her mother.

On occasion, Cassies mother would come to stay, insisting on being driven and bringing her two feline friends Thomas and Tuppence, both of which had never set foot outside her London flat and lived mostly under her bed when staying, obviously terrified. A small bedroom by the downstairs bathroom was created, solely for her use, as the stairs to the bedrooms were steep and only had a rope rail to hang on to.

The routine of the farm rarely changed, nor can it, when the ladies need milking and feeding twice daily, morning and evening tide.

The girls were, mostly, a friendly bunch. Well looked after, loving eyes, good coats, pleasant manner and each as individual as they come. A large proportion of the herd were home bred, raised from cow to calf to cow, Annabel and Seven being the original two, had sired many a calf, thankfully mainly cows and Seven liked to sing to them all. At nights, after milking and being settled in their barn, fresh straw laid down for their beds and fresh hay put out for when wanted, the cows would settle, chewing their cud, snorting softly and getting ready for a night's rest, Seven would start her song. She would be the only one to make the rhythmic melody, soporific for any listener, possibly telling tales of days gone by or just reassuring the ear, that they were in good hands.

During one afternoon, between the milks, Robert was attending the land when a desperate Cassie appeared waving her arms for attention. He drove the tractor to her.

"What now" he muttered "Can't I get any work done".

Pulling up alongside her, Cassie was shouting.

"Wait until I turn the tractor off" he shouted short temperedly.

"Its Mum" she shouted "she's fallen down the stairs" in a fluster.

Robert jumped out of the cab and rushed into the house to find Cassies Mother lying at the foot of the stairs, unconscious.

"Have you called the ambulance"? he urgently asked.

"No, not yet, do you think I should"? replied his wife.

He looked at her incredulously "Straight away".

Despite their location the ambulance arrived within 30 minutes and rushed the old lady to hospital, where, after x-rays, a broken leg and hip was diagnosed, only to die a short time later from "unforeseen complications" and pneumonia.

Questions lay unanswered and officially unasked. How did she fall, but most importantly, why was she upstairs, yet at all, on her own as stated by her daughter?

"I was in the kitchen and I heard a crash and found her lying there".

Whatever the reasons, the truth will never be known. But Thomas and Tuppence became farm cats, preferring to live in the barn, roaming the land and excelling a reducing the rat population. Its never too late.

ROOFTOPS

The dreamy spires were a magnificent sight, much of the architecture reminded Eric of parts of his hometown and he was getting familiarised with the alleys and secluded courtyards dotted around the city.

Most of the pubs had individual characteristics of their own, each lending themselves to different styles, but predominantly catering for the student market. One pub in particular didn't favour the establishment, instead offering a safe (not really the appropriate word, considering) haven, where punks would accumulate, thanks to an excellent juke box, ability of underage drinking, the turning of the proverbial blind eye and being allowed to "smoke" in the back room. It would see its fair share of "busts", since "Operation Julie" had only recently taken place and it would only be a matter of time until it died, but being a student town of the elite, there was little impact on the other venues where the wealthy still floated the laws.

Many young "gentlemen" to be, maybe from Harrow, Eton or Winchester, who already, prior to Uni. life, had jobs and careers lined up for them, would be dallying with substances and nuances, buying, using and selling as common knowledge. This is what made people dislike them more, whereas, at the time, the lesser folk would be targeted as easier to prosecute.

The mix of lesser people was immense. From Skins to Bikers, Soul Boys to Rasta, Townie to Punk, they were all there and more. And into this cauldron, Eric found himself fully immersed, a whole new chapter and set of experiences to be sampled and sample he would, but that was still to come. For now, work was unfolding its opportunities, and during a break from prep., coffee was to be had with the boss on the rooftop overlooking the High Street.

The roof was large and flat, easily able to hold a kick around, though probably ill advised. Looking down over the pedestrians, going about their daily routines was a comforting and enjoyable sight, them being mostly unaware of being watched and talked about, at the same time seeing how they behaved when not realising scrutiny.

Erics mind took him back to his childhood bed and the skylight that lay above his bed, fitted with misted security glass. He would often stare up it at night, seeing shadows of movement, scared of vampires or werewolves' visits, until one day a pigeon would die, spreadeagled on the glass and over the months of decay, leave its forever imprint. But still he saw the shadows flicker, often calling his mother in fear, only to be told not to be silly and given another pill to help him sleep. But one night the shadows were different and had sounds as well. The big black figure, hunched over the glass, made the young boy scream in terror. Turmoil ensued and police were called. The next-door neighbours had been burgled and they were next on the list.

Eric entertained his manager of the stories of various rooftop exploits, not knowing that they weren't yet over, and told of how, when at school, his most dangerous stunt, to date, was performed.

In the main class area, an old courtyard, with a tithe barn that was used for gym, services and movie night, was the large red slate roof that covered the semi-circular building. No one had ever achieved a whole circuit of the roof and not been caught, so to Eric and one other, the challenge was open to be had. Speed was of the essence. Spotters were sent to strategic locations, ready to shout the ridiculous "Cave" (K.V), giving the game away instantly, rather than a subtle bird call. With the help of a boost or two, Eric and comrade found themselves scampering quickly along the ridge, occasionally slipping, almost falling, with much hilarity and goal coming quickly in sight, only to be halted by a loud, severe, masterly shout from below.

Busted.

The lookouts, had failed, but were now joyful spectators, cheering the fact that people had been caught. Standing upright, instead of scurrying position, the two assailants could no longer escape Colditz and were bound to be shot by the guards. Fortunately, there was only one route down from the position they were in, they would have to complete their journey, making the mission a success…of sorts.

RETURN TO ROOKS END

It had been a long and hard 9 months, but the news came through, Great Aunt Jane had died. Tess, the only family member, had visited her a couple of times in hospital, brushed her hair and reminisced about days past, the last to have seen her in almost 10 years.

As Eric was living, with family, near Robert and Cassandra and she had just come out of hospital, following one of her "episodes", it was decided that Eric should accompany his father to the funeral, helping with the arduous drive, despite having a new born at home. Assurances were made of only a one-night stay at RooksEnd and they would be home before they new it, hopefully comforting words to a convalescing wife looking after four children.

The drive was demanding, in more ways than one. The most challenging part was the excessive speeds and erratic driving of his father, who rarely dipped below 100, unable to see the near misses and getting side tracked by his cigarettes. The hours rolled by and as dark started to set in they arrived at the familiar entrance to RooksEnd. They drove past the almost disintegrated pavilion and tennis court and noticed how the apple orchard had all but been chopped down. Only two lights were seen in the house, the kitchen and porch, lighting their way to one of the last times they would arrive at this house. The car pulled up, though no characteristic gravel crunch was heard, and the two men got out and stretched their muscles looking up at the building, each in their own memories, each in their own thoughts.

The front door opened and were greeted by Meredith, the latest housekeeper who had cared for Aunt Jane the last year or so, her lack of warmth disappointed Eric, not for himself, but for his Great Aunt. The house felt empty, even the echoes of the past had left, he was surprised that the walls themselves had forgotten who he was now that Jane had gone. It was a that moment he realised, it had been Great Aunt Jane herself who had kept the place alive, every room and everything had a piece of Great Aunt Jane in it, and now she was gone. The house, regardless of familiar furniture, was empty.

The morning of the funeral came quick enough, after an uncomfortable night's sleep and it felt peculiar making coffee and toast for his father in a kitchen where Eric had only been allowed to be bystander. But now, breakfast had, they changed into their mourning attire with Eric unfortunately tearing his trousers and having to wear his black jeans instead.

It was a short drive to the church, which was packed with the influential and affluent well-wishers that had been associated with the family, one way or another over the many years, but no recognisable faces were see. The service progressed, formal and to the point until the eulogy. To both his and his fathers surprise, Dicky took the dais and delivered an unsentimental speech about his aunt and the work she had done during the war and its after effects on global commerce and business.

Back at RooksEnd the after service do was held and Eric seemed it right to offer his help with the serving of drinks and canapes to guests. Circulating around, cold shouldered by Dicky, but trying to be friendly to all, despite having just buried his great aunt and memories, received a rebuke for his attire "Hmm, bad breeding stock no doubt" came the gruff, pompous voice from a man he'd never seen, but certainly directed fully at him. He smiled and passed on, looking forward to be going home once Robert had had his fill.

Unfortunately, time dragged on and Eric pulled his father to the side and informed him of the time and how they ought to be going soon. "Oh, we can't go this evening, I've already arranged to stay another night" said Robert filling his glass, "it'd be rude to go now, besides I want to talk to...Ahh...hello Andrew, good to see you...". It was probably the most fun Robert had had in ages.

Eric was speechless, he tried to intervene again but got cut off again by his father's drunkenness. He left the soiree, nauseated and angry and called his wife to break the bad news. Upset but understanding was all she could be. He sent his love to the children, one already tucked up in bed and wished them all a goodnight. He always missed his children and didn't want to be the same parent as his. He went to bed, listening to the people forget why they were here, to mark the leaving of a Great Aunt Jane who he never told he loved her and if he had? She probably would have said "Nonsense, silly boy" x

BEGINNINGS

Having left London for the rural idyll of self-sufficiency, Cassandra sat in her new kitchen, now all unpacked, and picked up her guidebook, from The Ministry of Agriculture, on how to farm.

They already had been visited by some of the very friendly and accommodating locals, welcoming them to the village and letting them know of do's and don'ts, why's and how's, when's and where to's and buggers an' rascals.

There was the Major who lived on top of the hill, the Captain who lived by the church, the new lady (who didn't mix much with village life) lived by the pub (and had pigs), the geese "mind" up the road ("best take a stick, when going to Post Office"), the ghost up the lane and "mind youself with that young Billy Hunter".

There was a lot to take in, Robert had already thrown himself in head first, organising chickens, buying a cow and the basic equipment needed for milking, sorting out an old red Massey Furguson and working out a timetable for the year ahead, pruning, feeding, planting and harvesting, of both veg and grass alike. It was going to be hard. With no machinery, except for the tractor, everything was going to have to be done by hand, from cutting and stacking the hay, to the milking of the cow (soon to be plural), it was going to be an arduous task and a steep learning curve, but "as long as everyone (meaning Eric, Tess, Cassie and himself) got stuck in" thought Robert, "it should be easy enough". Unfortunately, only half the task force was up to the job.

Cassie sat at her kitchen table with her cup of tea leafing through her book and chuckled when the Min. of Ag. mentioned that "Jersey Cows were right little sods".

She suddenly realised that the Aga hadn't been attended to and had once again gone out, meaning one of several situations were to occur.

1) She could attend to it straight away, probably get dirty or worse still, chip a nail.
2) Leave it and act surprised later either confessing that she forgot or didn't know how to do it, or tried and it didn't work
3) Call Robert to do it for her.

Cassie contemplated what food they had in the kitchen cupboard and wondered which she would prefer: a hot or cold supper. Looking at the clock she realised that if the range got lit straight away it probably wouldn't be hot enough anyway to get an evening meal ready, so stood up, pushed in her chair and went off to be busy lying down with a headache, so, option 4.

Meanwhile, outside, Robert was giving Eric a lesson in the importance of cleanliness. Having thoroughly cleaned all the milking equipment, churn, bucket, sieve and muslin with sterilising fluid, it was onto the importance of milking parlour hygiene. Robert handed Eric a shovel. Looking at him, his Dad explained "That's a shovel son, that, over there is a wheelbarrow", signalling behind his son "you need to shovel that" pointing to a fresh pile of cow dung "into that" pointing to the wheelbarrow.

For a 13-year-old boy, having never done physical labour and, essentially, only used to city life and the over protectiveness of boarding school, there was only one reaction.

"What, me? Urgh. Why"?

"Someone has to do it. We'll make a big pile over there" his Dad said pointing behind a wall "and when needed, spread it over the fields as a natural fertiliser".

"Oh," came the reply "do I have to"?

"Yup" was the emphatic response with a big smile.

That was the first of many wheelbarrows. And after barrowing away the manure, the clean up (spraying down the yard) would follow (Erics favourite bit), leaving a wet but pristine canvas for the dears to mess on again.

Over the years, as the herd grew, the wheeling would be suc-ceeded by a manual scraper, a large curved rubber type broom, and then a tractor with a drag scraper attached to the back. This wouldn't be until the next move and the muck would be scraped into a slurry pit, a large swimming pool sized hole in the ground, about 8 foot deep, at the back of the cow shed where all waste was collected.

Unfortunately, the sluice ramp wasn't steep enough for clear drainage and would often need to be manually cleared with an old two-pronged hay fork, sometimes a risky job. It was on one such occasion Eric found to his cost.

Standing on the bank, to the side of one of the ramps, Eric had climbed out of the cab and was attempting to shift a large heap of muck and straw that was refusing to slide down the slip, despite the plentiful rain that might have helped.

Nothing was shifting. Taking the calculated decision, he stepped onto the top of the ramp to try and push the pile from above. With the first effort, it worked, dramatically.

The ground underneath him slid instantly into the waiting pit taking him with it. He was instantly "dipped in shit" up to his eyes. It filled his ears, mouth and nose as he, fortunately, managed to heavily scrabble a foothold and save himself from being fully submerged and drown in the stuff.

Clambering out, like something from an old Tarzan movie, escaping from quicksand, he made it to the bank, spitting and blowing out of his nostrils. Squelching his way back up to the farmhouse, the cows gave him a wide berth, a look of surprise in their eyes as he sloshed and sploshed his way across the yard.

Cassie saw him coming and rushed to the door, stopping in her tracks.

"What on earth happened"? she called.

Eric raised his arms and shrugged his shoulders, still spitting out large chunks and trying to clear his breathing. "I fell into the pit" was all he wanted to say, not wanting to swallow any more.

"Well strip off here and go and have a shower".

Eric stopped and kicked off his boots and pulled of his overalls, amazed to find how much had made its way through the layers. Once down to his underwear he was allowed inside and made his way to the bathroom. It took a while to get fully clean but it would take weeks for the smell to go.

BATH TIME

The bath was run. It seemed like a good idea to have a bath before going to bed, "Try and get a bit sober before going to sleep" was the logical thought processed by Erics once again alcohol induced brain.

It had been a lonng day. Sitting on the toilet next to the bath, ears and head still ringing from the gig, he wondered whether the last drinking session had been that a good idea. Last night was still very present when the morning started, but being followed by a coach, ferry, then another coach journey, all with proportion of drink, well, he did feel drunk. "Ha" came from somewhere.

"Wow, it had been loud. I think the loudest yet" he half said to the bath. The bath wouldn't have understood what had been said, since only some of the words came out, more of "Wow, loud, think, yet", perhaps to some, a deep philosophical problem trying to be posed by someone who could barely crawl.

The room was certainly spinny, so the bath really was going to be a good idea, the next serious decision forming in his head was "Am I meant to get undressed"? it seemed like the right thing to do, but it felt odd at the same time. Eric couldn't actually remember the last time he had taken his clothes off, it had been a while, he knew that. He tried thinking, very hard, perhaps if he "Hum"ed or even "Err"ed while tapping his chin it would look like he was thinking and, who knows, might help. It didn't. he just forgot what he was thinking about and got side tracked by the three double gins and fizzy orange he had recently consumed at the little night café round the corner from the 4star hotel, where the two coach loads of Motorhead fans were staying.

Licking his lips, needing fluid, he scooped up a handful of bathwater, with bubbles, and had a drink.

"Ooh" face wrinkled "Too warm".

And bumped his way to the waiting courtesy fridge, door open and waiting and already plundered, to see if anything left was worth consuming.

"Ah, peanuts" he said as he spied a can of salted nuts not yet open.

"They're mine" came a distinct yet muffled voice from a pile of upturned furniture. It was his travelling companion and second drummer of the band, who had also come to Brussels for the weekend, but was now crashed out in his own fort, a result of raids committed earlier but at least thirty metal fans on all rooms.

Eric popped open the can with a swift hit of "eau de penut" and a shout of "Bastard" and decided his bath was more important. He didn't understand why he felt so drunk, after all he had eaten before they all went out to the red-light district, apparently where the best bars were to be had, but he couldn't for the life of him remember how they got back to the hotel.

Back at the tub he turned the taps off, he guessed it looked full enough, so automatically stripped off, wondering whether he should put his DMs back on or not and climbed in regardless. He sunk down under the bubbles and had another slurp.

His mind started to wander as soon as the warmth spread into him, soothing and relaxing.

More recent flashes of the past, namely Tess's birthday, flew by, "Boy, he had been drunk" he thought, he'd gotten in the bath with his pyjamas on at that party (long story), "Man, the water was dirty" he mused.

"Then" he said, talking to himself "school... Being made to fill the bath with a milk bottle" he continued, remembering have to run to and from the river to the boarding house with bottle after bottle to fill the bath as punishment meted out by prefects and masters alike. They were all sadistic. One master came to mind at the top of the list. This English teacher doubled up with P.T (Physical Torture, not Training). At boarding, the afternoons were put aside for all sports (except for Fridays which were reserved for C.O.R.P.S training and punishing) and a usual 3-to-6-mile run was required to start the session if one came under the jurisdiction of this Mr Walsh. The run itself was easy enough for Eric, who always enjoyed long distance jogs, finding a natural rhythm of music in his head, but more often, couldn't take sports seriously so got sent on laps around the pitch instead of following rules.

On one such day, Mr Walsh was particularly smiley, disconcerting in itself, and a 9-mile run was set, the maximum the route allowed, along the river to a lock and back, so flat all the way. It started well enough, the keen and determined at front, dashing off with eagerness, already wasting their energy in wanting to climb the ladder of success, whilst Eric put on his internal hum and drifted away on the beauty of the scenery with Elvis for company.

A few miles of gentle jogging brought you to a small woodland with little twists and turns, jumping logs and sploshing in undrained puddles. Rounding a bend, he heard calls from behind and looked and saw a halted group who had decided they had had enough and were going to wait there for the leaders to return, then follow back.

Eric halted to try and encourage continuation, but by the time the conversation had been had, the pack was probably a mile away, with no chance of catch up, so he resolved to stay and wait. An unfortunate move.

As the pack returned from their turning point, the remainers tagged on behind and looked suitably exhausted at the finish line. One by one, names were called out of all who didn't complete the full run and beaten, severely, with The Plimsol, kept for such occasions, by being hoisted over the boathouse workbench, wrists held and pulled by two pupils to ensure the feet left the ground. Sadly, for Mr Walsh, the days of such punishment was limited. Not because of reprimand, but when adjusting the tension of his motorbike chain, with the "help" of a favourite pupil, mistimed instructions caused the amputation of the fingers on his right hand, above the main joints. "It's a funny world" Eric pondered.

The bath was very relaxing. Even the reminder of his Mother trying to strangle and drown him in their bathroom, with Tess banging on the door after hearing the terrified screaming and the beating didn't phase him. Instead, he slipped into peaceful unconsciousness, comforted by the bubbles and warm water... and an incredible amount of booze.

Something didn't feel right?

Cold.

Cold and wet.

Cold, wet and a funny smell.

Hard...

"Oh, I'm still in the bath" flashed through Erics brain as he stood up. "Odd"?

There was no water left in the bath to speak of. Just a couple of inches of reddish-brown liquid and dried spaghetti stuck to the sides with plenty clogging up the plug hole.

Still in an alcohol stupor and limited brain function, Eric quickly surmised that he must've fallen asleep, his Bolognese from the start of the evening came to pay a visit, somehow, he kicked the plug and water drained. "Ta Dah" he thought brilliantly.

Climbing out of the bath he realised he looked very red and greasy, so attempted to dry himself off with a very soft and luxurious towel and climbed into bed, gone in seconds.

Morning came too soon. Breakfast missed, room in total disarray and waking up in a slimy orange bed was an experience too much for the brain to fully comprehend. Baz was already up and smoking and suggested they depart to the waiting coach, quickly. Quickly wasn't available at this time, so Steady had to do. Carefully making their way down the stairs, the lifts were somehow broken, they made their way into the foyer, where management and staff were trying to cope with 60 leather and denim types trying to avoid payment of consumption and destruction. Keeping eyes to the ground, it was too bright anyway, Eric and Baz slipped out to the waiting coach, not looking forward to the ferry back or the comments concerning the smell.

MAURICE AND THERESA (and all)

Morris and Theresa lived at the far end of the cobbled Cul-de-Sac, the narrow door tucked neatly between two others, almost unseen, but when opened, certainly noticed by the smell of cat and air freshener.

Both Italians, even to younger eyes, how they became a couple was a guess in itself. Theresa, dark hair always in a tight, compact beehive, pencil skirt and polo neck, was an attractive older lady with a beautifully friendly smile, relaxed and at ease with herself and nothing being too much trouble for her, even Morris (and boy did he challenge her).

He was sharply dressed. As sharp as a stiletto blade. As sharp as his tie was thin. His light grey suits with very subtle black trim were always tailor made and came with matching trilby, pulled down at the front, but not so low as to hide his pencil moustache, but enough for the need to walk with head slightly tilted back. An amiable gentleman in his twilight years, but would not look out of place in a dodgy, backstreet market or with switchblade in hand. Neither would he be seen dead in, for his main occupation was cat collecting, a passion shared with Cassandra.

Everyday had its routine. After his breakfast and morning coffee he would take a walk to the nearest newsagents to buy the mornings paper. Only located a few hundred yards away, as the crow flew, it might take him an hour or so to complete his task, yet somehow managed to return most days with a cat under his arm.

"Maurice"! Theresa would exclaim "Watta you got"? "Ah, *another* CAT"! she would shout exasperated "Where you find it this time"? would be asked but definitely not wanting an answer.

No sooner had one cat been turfed out, another one or two would arrive. And so, the game continued. Occasionally, Cassandra would receive a knock at the door. Either Maurice trying to hide a new discovery "Cassandra, my love" would be the opening line "I found this poor creature abandoned, would you look after it for me, while I buy some food for it, please"? (Once, she agreed and got stuck with the animal for several days) or it would be Theresa in tears, wanting to go back to Italy and get away from the ever-growing pride.

The quiet little backwater of the hustle and bustle of city life, lay nestled amongst the tall surrounding buildings with hundred-year-old cobbles still in place. It was home to many a character. The aforementioned Mr and Mrs Luton, she small and stout of stature, possibly of Cossack descent; Wol and Phil the carpenters, who owned the corner property, with its double floor doors that could fold open like a giant dolls house to expose the full workings on its insides, workbenches, sawdust and a plethora of timbers. Many a time as Eric grew, he would wander in and be allowed to watch them work, sitting on a saw horse, legs swinging, twirling the ringlets of freshly shaved wood. Offcuts scattered the floor, swept into piles, or fallen from shelves and would often be given to him to take home where he would imagine himself hard at work nailing and chiselling, or fashioned into some nondescript item for Erics imagination to fill in the gaps.

The small community had its benefits. Dickies closest childhood friends lived around the corner, as did Tess's in the flats of the neighbouring square and her Godmother living next door.

She was an elderly lady, who had also driven an ambulance in the Second World War, losing her fiancé in battle, at a tender age, never married, but had the company of her two short-legged, black and hairy Griffon dogs, Topsy and Turvy. In the early evenings she would sit in her chair and listen to the wireless, a favourite being Radio 4's The Archers and Topsy and Turvy would howl along to the music, not stopping until a small treat arrived in their mouths to quieten them.

There were many characters and buildings that stood out to a young boy's eyes. The ivy-covered corner builder next to the tall double doors of the beloved carpenters, the sloping road that ran the power station and flats, the cobbles and manhole covers that Eric practiced his brass rubbing skills on, the external metal spiral staircase in a front garden, the squirrel monkey kept in a large cage, the noise of the tube trains rattling on their tracks and the embankment full of daffodils in spring that could only be reached climbing the wall.

The old Russian Orthodox church lay nearby, opposite the small private garden, and Eric would pedal his little, chunky, red bike to be able to watch, from a distance, the austere and sombre, yet incredibly attired priests arrive for ceremonies.

The stream of clergy and patrons fascinated the small eyes, wanting to know where they kept themselves, what they ate and how they prayed. A tall and dark-long-haired clergy man acknowledged the young onlooker, making him feel exceptionally privileged, yet witnessed an exchange of words with a elder, who seemed to be rebuking his juniors behaviour.

The square (triangle), of which they lived off, was a mix of creeds, and Eric would enjoy the smells as he cycled around, sampling some more interestingly than others, yet all creating a homely feel to his little microcosm. Whether it was the biker's fires and 'erb in the recess of knocked down buildings rubble, or the fragrant earth of the Norwegians abode, or the tang of spice from the newly arrived Indian family, whose patriarch would sit daily on their step, reading the Financial Times in his lopsided turban.

MUSIC

Eric sat in front of his laptop, slightly amazed at what he had found out but still uncertainty lived, to hover about like some curious bee looking for a plant to settle on, yet none fulfilling the brief.

For years his mother had spun yarns about her brushes with the famous and her exploits, many not being uttered to the family directly, but to outsiders who admired her achievements and varied life.

When very young, skipping around the streets or pulling along his metal truck, just big enough to hold a loaf of bread, Cassandra would point out, with great affection in her voice hinting at a more than casual acquaintance, the house where John and

Cynthia lived, or how Lady Madonna was written about her, or the nearby church where Eleanor Rigby had worked and died. As thanks to her, when leaving the area, Cynthia and John gave Cassie a beautiful blue and gold tea set, which stayed boxed and hidden in the kitchen cupboard for years, all confirmed, dismissively, by Robert, but never knowingly witnessed by Eric, which, over the years, grew in suspicious speculation of authenticity.

Being brought up with parents who had been actors and living in the nation's capital, it seemed natural to rub shoulders with the rich and famous (sometimes infamous depending where you were) and very soon became humdrum and meaningless for the youngest of the family (whose early years consisted of being plugged into either the radio, t.v or record player, with a possible crushed pill to keep him quiet) who saw them all as just people who sometimes behaved in odd ways.

The flamboyant Glam Rock star (looking just as he did on stage, leaving him instantly recognisable) sat across the busy and now fashionable Italian restaurant with its sunken garden styled seating, with large palm fronds and gold tinted mirrors around on the split levels, as the large circulating fans in the ceiling cooled the already "chilled" clientele. For the first (and only time) in his life, Eric was in awe. He was sure he was gaping at the smiling face (who gave a friendly little wave from across the tables), as he recounted all the times he had stood on the table at school doing his extravagant and flamboyant impression, imagining roaring crowds as he pranced, waving his arms in the air singing, strutting and stamping, tossing his head around with gay abandon and living the moment of exuberant passion. The other kids just thinking he was odd, but Eric was sure they were just jealous. It never dampened his enthusiasm though. If anything, it urged him on to be more and more outrageous as possible (and reckless), glad to have found a niche he could call his own.

Too shy to go and ask for an autograph, Eric turned to his

father.

"Dad..., Dad" he said trying to get his attention but unable to take his eyes off his namesake, he understood what it was like to be him. "Dad, would you go and get me his autograph please"?

"What, Who"? replied Robert, unaware of the world that his son had just been in.

"Gary Glitters, he's sitting over there". Eric signalled with a movement of his head, still SO much in awe.

"What"? came the reply "That creep. No, I don't think so. Ask the waiter".

Double whammy. Creep? Ask a waiter?

"Dad..., Dad" Eric persisted, not bothering with the creep bit, after all Dad said that about The Goodies "Dad"!

"What"?

"Dad, can you ask the waiter for me"?

"Oh, all right" he said.

Signalling "Gaston" an Italian waiter came over discreetly and words and head movements and smiles were exchanged with the waiter moving off on his mission. Eric watched as the waiter approached the table of his task and brief were had, another big smile and wave, a scribble, third wave and the waiter returned with a card saying "All my love Gary Glitter".

"WOW" thought Eric "bit heavy on the love bit" thought his mature voice inside (one that would often pop up), but never the less "WOW".

He could not look in that direction for the rest of the evening.

Eric collected many autographs over the years, some easier collected than others. By way of an example was John Cooper Clarke, a Manchester punk poet whose first album made quite an impression on Eric, was giving a lecture at the Oxford

Union, a discussion hall predominantly for students, but a place he would often go, blagging his way in, like so many others places. After the lecture he dug deep in his trench coat pocket, only to find a condom packet (and a newspaper fold of "seeds") for Mr CC to sign, which got a seal of approval and an amused comment. Amazingly, their paths would cross again about three years later.

Dickie was working hard and seriously for a London based music magazine (most of Dickies work had to be taken seriously), and was organising a celebratory birthday bash ("No, it's an event"), hosting an array of bands at a well-known Victoria club. Being a roadie for one of the performing bands, Eric was roped in to help with the whole event, much to his delight. Eric enjoyed the work, but the bigger the "event", then bigger the after party, which he was seldom invited to, but it did mean that more people would be milling around backstage and more people meant a wider variety of drugs available… and that could only be a good thing.

Setting up was pretty straight forward. The first job was to hoist the giant backdrop for the stage, a giant Happy 100th Issue banner needed attaching to a large pipe running the length of the stage. Normally a boon would be lowered, banner attached, then hoisted in position, but new regulations meant that a non-electrical engineer was not allowed, by union law, to operate the equipment, so a ladder and Eric was called for.

Eric strolled onto the stage, slightly worse for wear, to be greeted by an enthusiastic Dickie.

"Right E, I need you to take this corner" (signalling to the immense banner) "and rope and climb up the ladder" (easily 30 ft tall) "and tie it to that pipe up there" (pointing) "it'll been fine".

Eric wasn't quite sure what was meant by the last bit, but not being of sound mind, Eric agreed, as usual, trusting his brother.

Hands full and climbing up the ladder, the very long ladder, he decided that, yup, he didn't like heights. Especially on wobbly ladders. With his hands full. He nervously reached the top, which was good and bad. One: he couldn't decide whether it was his knees or ladder shaking and Two: he could hold on to the pipe. Now this too was good and bad. One: the pipe was definitely robust, but Two: it was very hot. Obviously, a hot water pipe.

Carefully tying the corner of the banner onto the pipe he started to make his way back down, until…

"Don't bother coming down" came the unwanted command.

"Grab the next loop, hold on to the pipe and I'll jig the ladder along"

"What"? shouted Eric in disbelief.

"I Said" Dickie called back.

"I heard what you said, I just didn't believe you" shouted Eric again, feeling that he had only just started his life.

"It'll be quicker this way" called back the ever mature and knowing older brother.

And so, the exploit began. Once Eric had managed to burn his arms by clutching to life too hard (as he was only wearing his Motorhead TShirt) and almost soil himself on at least three occasions when the ladder almost disappeared, it wasn't so bad, and after all Dickie was right, it was quicker.

By the time Eric was allowed to come down there was only a short time left until the opening. Time enough for a few beers though. The first two that were gone in seconds, as they were only cold half lagers (with brandy chasers, especially good when taken with Whiz (Speed/Amphetamine Sulphate)) just to bring him back to normality, the third being Guinness, to level him out (and apparently, to protect him from BeriBeri). Black glass in hand he wandered over to the pinball machines, now with a slight fuzz starting to soften his edge, to eek out any other lingering stress he had suffered.

Coins in, lights and noise commenced, the now familiar ping ping of the machine, instantly recollecting memories of his first attempt playing at an amusement arcade and failing, unknowing about flick buttons and bumps, only to be embarrassingly tutored by a well-meaning older lad. He also recalled getting banned from his local, until repairs had been paid for and apology made.

Eric noticed he had been joined by a competitor, on the identical machine next to him, and they spent the next ten minutes or so in a head-to-head, enjoying the simple diversion. Glass emptied, Eric decided on one more shot before retiring backstage for duties and offered his now partner a drink.

"Can I get you one"?

"Nah, it's alright, thanks" said the tall hatted man in a gravelly but smooth voice.

Eric paused and momentarily realised that he recognised this bloke from somewhere. Not surprising though, he covered a lot of ground and when gigging he tended to bump into fellow roadies and engineers etc. all the time.

"I know you from somewhere, don't I"? he innocently enquired, still not managing to find this person in his stored data banks.

The man grunted and left. Totally perplexed at this reaction and standing like a confused lemon (trying to figure what he'd done wrong), he heard the doors open and people came flooding in.

"Wow" someone excitedly said to their friend "That was Lemmy, did you see him"?

Now just a lemon.

Unfortunately, Erics stay at the foyer bar lasted a bit longer than intended, mainly wasting time, chatting-up possible conquests.

Realising that time had passed, he headed towards the sound-proof doors of the main auditorium and pushed one open. He was instantly transported to a totally different world. The heavy tribal, rhythmic thud of tight drums chocked and pounded out a fierce energy. The skins (Skinheads) were stamping hard to the beat and a flame thrower, only clothed in a loin cloth and dreads, was spitting out flames above the masse of bodies. The earthy, chemical smell of fumes filled the air as did the palpable feeling of threat and danger. He was glad that Todd (a skinhead friend, filled with dubious exploits… we'll come to him later) was not here, because as he made his way through the crowd, violence erupted all around, with the band still playing, fuelling the hatred and animosity of the pit.

Dodging the conflicts as if they were "someone else's problem", he made it back to the wings of the stage in time to be ordered to help clear the stage for the next act, as it had been advised to pull the band to calm the existing clamour of angry bodies and bouncers.

Within minutes the atmosphere changed, as John Cooper Clarke stepped out and administered much needed dry vitriolic humour against cider and simplicity, and boots and brains. The roar from the crowd signalled their agreement just as Eric was sent out again on stage to move some cables, unfortunately located behind Mr Cs swinging gesticulations, resulting in a fist coming beautifully in contact with Erics jaw. A huge burst of laughter erupted as he was sent backwards and Clarke, not missing a beat, delivered another poetic put down, to the delight of the audience.

A real lemon day.

One of the main advantages of being a roadie was seeing so many bands, for free, but Eric soon realised that he preferred to watch from out front, as it was the magic of the performance he enjoyed and not how the trick was done. He loved music, from Mozart to Zappa and often went to gigs with his mates, some enjoyable, like getting in through the Stage Door, by some other kindly bouncer, to see The Skids, or disastrous times like the Ramones.

The day started well enough. Erics rubber lipped mate Andrew, who was the bassist of the band that Eric drummed for, was an enthusiastic Ramones fan, having seen them once on his sex-fuelled exchange trip to America when only 16. Funnily, he never seemed to stop smiling. He was like a brother to Eric, the brother he never had. Both enjoyed practical jokes and would often plot various scenarios to shock or startle the rest of their friends. One time, in their local watering hole, they lit small smoke bombs and convinced punters that the pub was on fire, unfortunately the smoke generated from such small tablets filled the bar with heavy white smoke in minutes, causing evacuation and the calling of emergency services. The landlord never did find out where the smoke came from... thankfully. Many times, what seemed amusing to them wasn't always regarded the same by others.

Andrew and Eric had gone to buy tickets for a Stiff Little Fingers concert (where Todd, a stocky [muscly] not tall chap, but with a broad, cheeky smile and personality that would charm all mothers and make him somehow irresistible to women (despite his violent and wayward ways), would decide to make a clear passage in the crowd to enable him to run up to and leap and hit an unsuspecting bouncer. All hell would break loose, resulting in Andrew and Eric missing the last bus home and walking back, 20 miles at 12.30 at night, because the concert was held up for half an hour) and drove to the venue (only to discover later that they could be purchased nearer) on Andrew's bike with Eric pillion. Again, unfortunately, if they had known about purchase location or if they had watched the end of Tiswas (a raucous Saturday morning kids T.V programme) and The Bucket of Water Song finale (like they always did) they would have missed the elderly 85-year-old gentleman, with virtually zero vision, on medication, pull out in front of them causing the crash which resulted in Andrews arms and hands in cast and a bump to Erics nose. For Eric it all happened very slowly.

It was a lovely clear summers day, the road straight and clear, except for the one oncoming car, which turned suddenly across their path with no warning. The motorbike slammed into the front passenger door, front wheel pushed its way under the bike tank, while Andrews hands were crushed between the handle bars and door, gauntlets giving some but not full protection. Eric, wearing only an open-faced helmet (for the last time) had his head thrown forward, smacking his nose on the back of Andrews helmet and elegantly swung his right leg up and over the back of the bike in a manoeuvre between a pirouette and a pas de deux. His mother would've been so proud (being also an ex-ballerina).

It would take some time for Andrews arms to heal and boredom would set in, giving him plenty of time to come up with a jolly jape that seemed good on paper. Blood capsules bought and plan devised, a visit to the pub was called for. The usual crowd was there, and they settled in for a friendly evening of drinking, surreptitious drug taking and mutual banter. Eric would often recall these moments as the closest he came to having true friends and would always miss them. The session started with Eric and Andrew at odds with each other. Andrew blaming Eric for causing the motorbike accident and Eric blaming Andrew for his reckless riding. They bickered all evening, escalating tension and disharmony while quietly sniggering to themselves. It culminated with a fight outside the pub, Andrew's plaster caste arms flailing and feet kicking out while both had blood streaming from mouths and noses. Their friends rushed to separate the children, who instead of staying aggressive, couldn't help but laugh as they explained it was a big wheeze and it was fake blood, not real. None of the girls found it remotely funny and called them babies, it was the last time they, though unfortunately not Eric, did anything like that.

As for The Ramones...

The morning started with trepidation. The three bandmates were looking forward to the gig. One had already seen them before, one eager for the experience and the other...well, who knew. It is here, background on the third member needs clarifying.

Todd was much loved by all who knew him, a truly loveable rogue, you wanted to love him more, but...

Which was worse is hard to say. The violence, drink or drugs. His mum would often ask his closest friends to keep "an eye on him", meaning "don't let him drink too much, don't let him take anything". For, when he did, trouble would ensue. Break-ins, vandalism, punch-ups (a mediocre term) and general mayhem would unfold, often resulting in early morning raids by the police or tracking Todd down in hiding. Having an often-absent father and a childhood of dipping in and out of 'prove school and borstal would ultimately end in prison, after one particular innocent night of visiting his girlfriend, which resulted in him requesting "36 other offences to be taken into consideration" at court.

It unfolded like so:

Pub...lunchtime...

"Blimey Todd, you look rough, what have you done to your hand"? asked Eric.

"I'm on bail" came the reply.

Shocked, incredulous silence hit the group of friends.

"What the F..K"?

They had all been together the previous evening, and when they parted company at closing time, all seemed well, nobody too drunk or stoned.

"I went and saw 'Chell last night".

Confusion set in all round, but alarm bells started ringing. Michelle, Todd's girl, was at a girl's boarding school, they didn't allow visitors, especially by skinhead boyfriends at midnight.

Apparently, having an urge and missing her, he broke in to the dormitory, got caught by the headmistress, exposed and pleasured himself, refused to leave and attacked the police.

His friends sat agape at their grinning friend. Only Todd.

The trio arrived at the bus station to take them down to London and met with Todd's brother, one of his mates (both skins) and the unnerving Alan. Al should have had "form". The crimes he had committed seldom got reported, due to known reprisal, and because his illnesses helped him elude incarceration. If Alan walked into the bar, you walked out. And here he was now, waiting for an hour's bus journey. Both Eric and Andrew were determined, but uncertainty or awareness had dropped into their laps.

The journey started easy enough, but as soon as the cans and bottles opened, the trouble started. Complaining passengers, an abused driver and an escalating argument between the three skins and Al, with both Andy and Eric trying to keep their heads down.

Pulling into the Victoria Bus Station, passengers disembarked and an elderly gentleman was pushed by one of the drunken groups, causing everyone to scarper in all directions.

By the time they had stopped running Eric and Andy were relieved to find themselves alone and walked on to the tube station, looking forward more than ever to the concert. Rounding a corner of a leafy green square, they joined up with the two brothers and Alan, the fourth member having been detained for his callous act.

No sooner had they met up, the fight erupted. Some disagreement had started on the coach between the brothers and now was the time to settle the score. Fists and steel toe-capped (the only type) DMs flew between the siblings. Alan stepped between meting out well placed headbutts, with Andrew and Eric watching, then turning their backs on the melee, figuring there was nothing else to do, occasionally turning around to see if the fighting had stopped...it hadn't.

Both performances were the same, hit, after hit, after hit. They were glad they made it.

SECRETS & LIES

One of Erics mothers many other professing's (apart from being a BBC scriptwriter) would be being a member of Pans People (which, when growing up as a child, remembered clearly her disgust of ""that" type of dancing"), a regular dance group from the BBCs light entertainment music programme, Top of the Pops.

The "scriptwriting" wasn't discovered by Eric until very late on in Cassandra's life. He, having a need to visit her Chiropractor of 20 years, arrived to the general welcoming chit chat which was interspersed with a curious question:

"Did your mother get her typewriter"? asked the ageing practitioner casually.

"Typewriter"? came the uncertain and befuddled response.

"Yes, typewriter".

"I think you might have my mother confused with someone else". Eric said genuinely.

This was followed by an indignant look and pause.

"No. I know <u>who</u> your Mother is". Came the emphatic and terse reply.

"Er, well, no typewriter, no. I don't see why she would want one"? Eric followed.

"For her scriptwriting of course, the Beeb want her back for some specials or other" came the surprising reply, only concreting the fact that this gentleman really had the wrong mother.

Eric stared blankly, then the penny dropped. "Not heard this one before", he thought, feeling "that" familiar feeling he felt when discovering one of his mother's lies. a bit like sitting down with a sudden groan, but the groan didn't want to be sat next to and didn't know where it came from anyway. A nauseating memory of a time when Cassandra had tried to pass a children's book off as all her work. She had written it, just for him, (this occurred decades ago), an inane adventure (even to a ten-year old) of a wizard, filled with Eric relevant details. The story was quickly upturned when Eric discovered the back page for people to fill in and send off, to make a "special" connection "for you child".

"Yuck" thought the already cynical internal speech of Eric "vomit inducing".

Eric's inner voice had always been much older than him. He enjoyed listening to it and it would often give very good advice, not that he took any notice of it.

Eric remembered two special occasions when the voice had been very present. Once, when Cassandra was battering the hell out of him in the bathroom, her favourite place of attack or subjugation, where it took him to the side and talked calmy and quietly to him, taking Eric away from the onslaught. The other, when walking through the peaceful Georgian houses of Lexham Gardens (the tall pillar fronted buildings hiding so much history), with Tess, stopped by a grating in the road by the path and started dropping ha'pennies down the drain (as instructed).

"Eric" came the rebuking voice of his sister "Stop that".

Eric stopped for a moment and wondered.

"What are you doing"? she dumbfoundingly enquired.

"Dropping pennies in the drain" was the matter-of-fact response.

"Well, don't do that. It's a waste".

After a couple of moments listening, he replied:

"No, it's not. Someone might find them one day and wonder how they got there" then dropped his last coin in. Satisfied.

Eric and his "imagination" or "voice of the future" were becoming best buddies and he enjoyed taking a step back and watch the world and its people unfold in front of him, as his imagination conjured up their lifestyles and abodes and his voice explained how things worked.

The most dramatic observation, where Eric saw himself watching others (without the use of drugs or illness), was when extreme life patterns collided, when Bill and Suze came to visit. This was also a turning point for Cassandra, where her exaggerations and lies would start their journey on another level.

Many of his parent's friends and early "thesps" had stuck with acting, or such like, and some had achieved considerable success in their adapted or chosen fields, leaving the glee of envy and pang of jealousy, especially on Cassandras shoulders, and more so when awkwardness reared its ugly head.

As you know, there are many variants of people, one such are Townies. The true to life, live and die surrounded by concrete folk, who feel out of water when even not putting on their heels.

Cassandra had altered somewhat to rural life, she coped with no pavements, the geese attacks while walking (an umbrella came in handy to shoo them off) to the little post office shop that hadn't changed since it opened, tractors flicking up large clumps of muck as they drove past and the bus, running three times a week to the nearest large town. The positives were that she had done more creative cooking than ever (marmalades, casseroles, pates, crumbles and wine (the magnificent Golden Pansy, thick and syrupy, as good as any dessert wine and the truly potent Wheat and Raisin, not for the feint hearted)), learnt how to look after chickens and not "pop" as many pills as she did before (a true exponent of "Mothers Little Helper"), mainly due to her new G.P who only believed in paracetamol and chicken soup, for <u>all</u> ailments.

On top of this, there was less call for dressing to impress as the cows were more occupied with in one end and out of the other. So, when the call came of a long weekend stay by two of their dearest "darlings", the stops were pulled and drawers opened to search for the cache of emergency pinks, yellows and blues, but unfortunately knowing she would find no blacks, would have to purchase a new discovery of hers, ProPlus (which would be a standard "go to" until her death).

Another glorious day in the Dorset countryside arrived. The fresh field air, the rolling hills of time stamped beauty and wisteria, lazily draping itself, in full bloom, from the twisted limbs leaning against the thatched house, whose stone was as old as the hills that lay behind.

Both Robert and Cassandra (more so) were looking forward to the weekend reminisces of cricket, names and catch ups, though the current of, and acute awareness of how the lack of money had changed their standards echoed in both their minds. Eric had removed himself from the scene via his motorbike, tootling around the windy, narrow lanes knowing the routine of stress and ang...uish/er of his mother, that would peak moments before expected e.t.a., nothing had changed there.

Perfect timing had him coming down the road as Bill and Suze were pulling up gracefully in their brand new, prestigious Mercedes. They both looked astounding, for many a reason.

As Eric parked and took of his helmet, he noted that Bill was dressed for саж (caj). His white Yves Saint Laurent slacks were topped with a white Lacoste polo shirt, while a white and blue yachting jacket hung fabulously off his shoulders, whereas, Suze (on the other hand?) was dressed to impress. If the cows had seen her (and some neighbours did), they would have stopped chewing their cud and, even Eric thought, would have gaped in awe (or incredulity).

She looked sensational, especially to a fifteen-year-old boy. If she had been in the middle of St.Tropez in Autumn, I doubt you would have noticed her amongst the other glamour models, but in the middle of a sleepy Dorset village...

Eric saw Suze swing her legs out of the car, the six-inch stilettos trying to find solid ground under the gravel, followed by the waft of expensive living and a pair of incredibly smooth and tanned legs. Bill had already ventured to her side of the car, taking in his surrounding as he went and wouldn't have missed the accompanying smell.

Taking Suze's hand, she gracefully rose out of the car sporting a large fur, that matched her hair and large sunglasses. Eric remembered to close his mouth. F.C & N.K he dreamt and gulped. He re-introduced himself and led them up the path to the house, where they were duly greeted by his parents with genuine warmth with a hint of contrivedness.

"Darlings" and welcoming's were boomed around for all to hear.

Eric again made himself sparse and put his bike away into part of the long barn, next to the chickens, who he dropped in on to bring them up to date with events and see if they needed food and water.

By the time he exited the peaceful warmth of the softly contented birds and made his way up the small slipway to the back of the house, he heard the chattering's of the four adults out front and assumed "tea" would be served on the lawn. Entering the kitchen, he found no kettle on the stove or tray set, so made his way through the house only to be met by his mother and father coming the opposite way.

"Hi," said Eric, "Where's Bill and Suzy"? looking over their shoulders, heaving the start of an engine.

"Oh, they're not staying" they both replied "they were just dropping in to say hello". Silence followed.

It transpired that Suze had a "splitting headache" (couldn't stand the smell) and "needed to get some medication" (somewhere cleaner and more chic to stay). They were never seen again, sadly, but Eric wondered if tales would spin at their future gatherings, he hoped not but did feel sorry for his parents, for at last, they seemed to be grounding themselves in reality...or so he thought.

KNOCK, KNOCK

Eric had always seen them, they had always been there, always out of view, peeking around the corners, standing in the shadows or behind the doors, or hiding under the bed, but once or twice caught in all their glory, watching him, out of the corner of his eyes.

The bedtime ones were the scariest, for a young mind, perhaps not helped by his sister's macabre fascination with cartoon deaths, of the reveal of pictures of tombstones on eyes, when lids raised. Tess would creep to her brother's bedside when asleep and open his eyes to see if he was dead or not, her thin young fingers giving him imaginings of skeletons scraping his face, waking him in terror. The doses of morphine and such like probably didn't help.

As Eric grew out of childhood scares, he had his own experiences with things that go bump in the night, being chased by a dim light in a boarding house playground, the sounds of a body being dragged across a floorless ceiling, a piercing yell from the downstairs in a secure and empty house, the shaking of windows and doors as if a wind blew hard, yet all was still outside. Many other trivial incidents which would eventually become insignificant occurred, until the dark figure stood over him, by his bedside, feeling threatening and ominous, paralysing the older Eric in fear.

Two other events stood out, as they played out longer than the others.

The first occurs one dark and lonely night...

The bakery stood in the middle of a terraced row of businesses. An Aquatic shop at one end, a couple of empty units, a driving test centre and a hairdresser at the far end, all having separate properties above. It was a pleasant residential area and the newly acquired business was building well, despite the work needed to revive it, but was helped by the heavy footfall of examiners and visitors to the centre.

Eric had arrived at the property just before midnight (in the late 80's of the popular seaside town), and had seen the last of the drunks reel their way home on his journey there and started work as others were already far in slumberland or nestling down to sleep.

Work progressed routinely, mixing the first batches of dough and the first turns of puff pastry, with the night radio chatting in the background, interspersed with that certain quiet of the night and the thud of the dough hook. As the hours passed, he made himself a mug of coffee, helping himself to a newly baked piece of shortbread, and sat down on the stack of flour bags for a moments break. Sipping and nibbling, staring into space and listening to the drone of the radio, he suddenly leapt up, feeling a sharp pain on where his buttock met his seat. He brushed the area to see if a pin or something was protruding and checked his whites likewise. Nothing to be found he passed it off as one of those things and finished the drink and resumed work, checking the floor in case anything might have flown off. The next hour ticked by quietly but steadily, all forgotten. He was just bending over to pick up another bag of flour when he leapt a mile, thinking that one of his fellow bakers had come in early. As he was bending over, what clearly felt like two definite fingers slid into the back pocket of his trousers. He jumped and spun around. No one was there. He ridiculously called out, but naturally none replied. Totally un-nerved, he checked the doors, still locked, looked around, then made another coffee.

Nerves not calming he continued uneasily in his work, and by the time other staff arrived, another couple of hours later, no more events had occurred and nothing was said, not wanting ridicule for something so foolish…

9 a.m. came, and apart from opening time, it was also the first delivery of the day. A selection of biscuits and cakes to the hairdressers. Today the duties fell to Eric as he was off home anyway, so wandered over and walked through the door to the smiling ladies ready for their elevenses already.

The manager greeted and thanked him and asked "How you getting on next door? You settling in alright"? him being new to the area.

"Yup, fine thanks" he smiled.

"Have you met the bum pincher yet"? she said.

"What"? was all that he could say.

"Oh, the bum pincher. He's always at it".

Again (feeling a bit stupid) "what"? he replied (man of many words, bang goes his credibility).

"Isn't he girls, always at it".

A resounding "oh yes" and "always" rippled through the salon.

The "sightseers" were a very different affair and were spotted on one of the many drug-filled nights of his 30's, in the front room of a quiet residence of a seaside town.

As usual, friends had come over after work and they had

smoked and chatted and ate and drank (and smoked some more), until, as usual having to be kicked out so the day could start again.

Once gone, Eric settled down to a final smoke (or two) before retiring himself, so rolled up a couple of joints, sat back in the quiet of the large and comfortable sofa and inhaled himself away. He had quite a high tolerance. Drink, drugs, pain, he was sure his day would come though.

Lying back on the seat, staring at the ceiling he suddenly realised he wasn't alone. Not moving, pretending he hadn't seen them, he noted that there in front of him was a group of about seven figures. All different sizes and heights, all dressed differently, but they seemed to be standing behind a rope barrier, like at a cinema, watching him.

He casually got up, not paying them any attention and lit his other smoke, trying to watch them without looking or giving the game away. They were still there. They seemed to be chatting to each-other. Panic suddenly spread through the group as Erics eye caught the direct vision of one of the tourists and they were gone.

Both of his parents and siblings exhibited the feelings or awareness of other things, though his father never discussed such matters until his final days, whereas his mother was a different story.

Cassandra had always had an intuitive and uncanny perceptiveness to know about forthcoming events. The complexity of single child rearing, war shock, emotionally competitive parenting and being bred into money that was no longer there, along with the confusion that was created by "second sight" created a confused and damaged mind that would be a lifetime user and abuser of prescription drugs in all their glory.

While Cassandra was having her numerous "breakdowns" and miscarriages, enough for any single person to bear, her "episodes" would also play out, revealing themselves more vivid and traumatising in times of duress.

The mid-week late lunchtime weather was warm and pleasant and school summer holidays had only just begun for the 12-year-old, and he sat at home on the sofa, under the window, eating a crisp sandwich, watching his dad smoke his pipe (a habit that phased in when trying to give up cigarettes) and read a newspaper in his black leatherette reclining rocking chair. The smoke danced on his taste buds as he crunched another mouthful and found it more warming than the greyness of the cigs that his Dad normally smoked.

Tess was sitting, with her back to everyone else, up to the groovy, round, white table that had recently been bought from either Habitat or Harrods ("…somewhere beginning with H…" thought Eric), humming a tune to herself whilst she ate and flicked through her latest copy of Jackie.

Cassie was pottering in the small open-plan kitchen (the majority of downstairs was open-plan, kitchen, sitting room and dining area all in one) and had been experiencing one of her "headaches" lately, which tended to last a few days, so was in one of her "moods". These made for erratic behaviour, but if you kept quiet and undemanding you could probably escape any venomous retribution.

Much as Eric was enjoying his food, a drink of milk was called for (and maybe a doughnut later if they went out).

"Mum," called Eric gently "could I have a glass of milk please"?

A simple "okay" and "hang on" came in response as Robert looked out from behind his paper and puff of browness.

A silence seemed to hang in the air, as if drifted in on a breeze and momentarily froze everything. It was loudly followed by the shattering of a dropped milk bottle and the terrifying scream that came from Cassandra. Robert leapt from his seat and dashed to her aid as Tess turned to watch, rising slowly as Eric stayed sitting, figuring that "no milk today".

The screaming slowly stopped only to be replaced by:

"What…"? "…the blood", "so much blood" she shook, gasping

sobs looking around herself as if in another place, trying to wipe her arms away, all the while saying "look at the blood its everywhere".

Robert stood, his arm around her, consoling.

"it's alright darling" he said softly, "its only milk, we'll clean it up".

Cassandra looked up at him, the wildness and confusion in her eyes "What...what was that noise, that explosion"?

"You just dropped a milk bottle, that's all, don't worry" calmed Robert.

"What"? replied the more aware Cassie, now looking about her at the white liquid and broken glass a strewn on the floor.

"But there was a huge explosion and then blood everywhere and the silence, and the screams began" she said, still confused and disorientated.

"No, everything's fine" said Robert "go and lie down, rest, we'll take care of it".

"But the blood" she said again, more softly and unsure "I saw so much blood.

Robert led Cassie to her bed and made sure she took a sedative. Tess started cleaning and Eric carried on crunching, though more slowly.

It wouldn't be until later that day that the news was known. A bomb had been detonated at The Tower of London that afternoon, severely injuring dozens of people, many children, causing facial damage and limb loss and one direct loss of life.

BLACKOUTS

Being in Bournemouth had been an unexpected turn of events. It had been a few years since leaving the full-on lifestyle, which had climaxed in the loss of his stomach lining, a combination of acid poisoning and months in Yugoslavia where he discovered his second home. The friendliness and warmth of its "one" people only enhanced his desire to fully absorb the water and wine at lunchtime and the home-grown apricot brandy and coffee all afternoon and sitting with the old folk, reminiscing about German occupation and trying to compete with the chili eating sessions.

From Ljubljana to Skopje and Belgrade to Dubrovnik they travelled, visiting Milo's vast family, not once using their tent (which had been bought especially for the trip, but had been utilised journeying through France and Italy in Erics white V.W Beetle which had "Lenin" sprayed on the green, back passenger wing. Lenin served them well, though once, needing an oil change, they stopped at a small garage in France. It was a hot lunchtime and a student had been left in charge and was eager to help by putting the car on their ramps to make it easier. Once up, he pulled a portable drain system in place to catch the oil and took over task, much to the surprise of Milo and

Eric. Job done, the lowering of the hydraulic ramps needed all hands as flaps needed to be deployed and kept out of the way at the same time. With Eric at the front of the car and Milo at the back, Jean-Paul controlled the descent by means of a joystick located on the far wall.

A sudden scrunching sound of metal crumpling shot out and shouts of "Merde ! Oh, Merde"! were heard.

The oil drip tray hadn't been removed from under the car as it lowered, and now leant at a buckled angle, obviously feeling very sorry for itself.

In a matter of minutes, the tray was moved, the car was off the ramp, doors and shutters of the garage locked and they were on the way, looking in the rear view mirror at a fleeing body of a worried young man.

For their excursion across the waters, Eric and Milo had been advised to take plenty of coffee, both roasted and instant and a varying range of jeans and denim jackets to give as valued gifts to those they visited, being the most sought-after items of the then unified country.

Ironically, one storming evening in Beograd, they were taken to the cinema to see an old Warren Beatty and Natalie Wood movie, Splendour in the Grass, with mixed Croatian and Macedonian subtitles and girl that Eric sat next to, tried really hard to translate the subtitles for him, even with her broken English. He thanked her for the efforts she was making, and fellow patrons didn't seem bothered, but, nevertheless, he tried to dissuade her but failed to smother her enthusiasm and persistence, so sat back and enjoyed the film despite the constant narration, the film was subtitled true, but not dubbed.

When all was over, they said their fond farewells and vacated to the parking lot only to discover the beloved beetle quarterlights had been broken open and car ransacked. Standing in the pouring deluge, Milo and Eric frantically checked their travelling home on wheels and were amazed in their findings. The passports and traveller cheques were still in the glove compartment, though sunglasses gone. The thieves had been very considerate, only a portion of the valued coffee had gone, as had only half of the denim clothing, but what was most odd was the two half-filled bin liners of their dirty laundry had been taken. Always a silver lining.

Neither the rain or event did anything to dampen their experience of such a beautiful country and its kind and friendly people, everywhere they went strangers welcomed them and were interested in their lives, whether it was sitting on a large shared table, in a busy lunchtime café/restaurant in the capital, or at an outdoor party/festival, deep in the southern countryside. Jokingly named "prvi engleski" (first Englishman: someone who, possibly conceitingly, believes he is the first to discover something, even though he isn't, though his new friends knew he wasn't, but enjoyed the ridicule), it filled Eric with such sadness at the events that would befall the land, even though tell-tale signs were already in place and fall-outs between Serbs and Croats were not uncommon, now Tito had died, who left could hold the country together.

Returning to England was a hard knock. Arriving back in a country that was filled with unrealised aggression and selfishness was a shock to the pair and they went their separate ways, Eric to Devon, to his parent's new farm, to try to recuperate and get back on his feet.

Thankfully, for his body, being in the middle of Devon, with no contacts (and no stomach lining) and little money, he could focus again on clean living and hard manual work, milking cows and looking after the 30 acres with his father, but that would just be the eye of the storm.

He would find himself having to leave the pleasant seaside resort some years later for two reasons. One being work, the other to escape the grasping claws of heroin that were taking his friends and to trying to attach themselves with their grasp.

The opiate comes with its story of romance and intrigue, sinister yet mysterious, one of the big highs, yet as rotten as maggot filled meat.

Heroin fools you in many ways and you listen to it, knowing the lies and lying to yourself all the way, knowing the full truth, yet ignoring all, trying to block out the hurt and pain of your pathetic and worthless existence, sponging and stealing off friends and relatives when you've become too inept and only focused on your own interests.

Eric had once been shown a film of drug abuse whilst attending a Young Farmers meeting, trying to ingratiate himself into a new environment, by the local Drug Squad. The film itself was a confused affair. The first half showed the entertainment factor of various drug taking in all its glory, using "real people" in the roles followed by the sudden, in full, autopsy of one of the participants who had died of a drug overdose. Unfortunately, the message that seemed to linger was "drugs are great... as long as you don't overdo it". Not the intended message.

Bournemouth started smooth enough, slowly reintroducing his body to the pleasures of booze was quickly accepted and soon happily having a few lovely, cold half lagers at lunchtime, not too bad you say? No, not in themselves, but each one had a double brandy chaser, just to keep company. Even his girlfriend joined in, to an extent, having Dubonet and Lemonade for breakfast, not realising it was alcoholic, and finding it particularly refreshing and a great way to start your day.

*After settling in to a new job, new acquaintances arrived on the scene and with them, more and more outlets to shop at. Admittedly, the selection and availability weren't as extensive as in the Uni. City where Eric had lived, where at the time, even after Operation Julie (a big set of busts, nationwide), you could order or request what you wanted and your dealer would normally be able to supply your shopping list, though relatively clean opium itself was harder to come by. On occasions, Eric had brazenly (and worse for wear) walked the corridors of various colleges, randomly knocking on bedroom doors trying to score and succeeded.

One such evening of success, led to a heavy night's session and he woke up, suddenly and early, still sitting in an armchair of the pleasant, little, two-bedroom house he was living in, in the attractive part of town.

Being a Saturday, and still morning he would soon have his visitor, ready for her weekly fix of Tiswas.

Erics next door neighbour was a pleasant elderly gentleman, very hard of hearing, thankfully, considering the quality, quantity and loudness of music played in the household, varying from Baroque to Throbbing Gristle. One time, whilst still at school, in Social History, taken by a relatively new teacher, the pupils were invited to take a record of their choice into class in order to open up a discussion on diversity…" or some other bollocks" thought some of the kids.

Mr Chapman was in his thirties, with a wife and recent child, a pleasant chap, informative and enthusiastic, trying to pull people out of their predestined ruts and give them food for thought. He gave Eric two albums, From the Witchwood and Grave New World (the pun instantly sticking with Eric having just read the Aldous Huxley novel), both of which were taken away and played with nurturing appreciation (…and Eric sold him his woodwork project of a rocking chair, which collapsed after a few uses).

Eric never fully appreciated his width of musical awareness, it had grown with him, sometimes incidentally, from the soothing tones of the unknown harmonica player on the hot summer nights of the city and South African rhythms to Flanders and Swann and war time pub songs. Robert had attempted (and failed, due to being tone deaf) to be a jazz trumpeter, favouring Trad and Dixieland and Bing (often sung to nut no one else knew the tune). Tess was more into Roberta Flack, The Who, The Stones (which Cassie hijacked), Donavon then David Essex and Peter Skellern. Cassandra, well…she said: Modern Jazz, The Beatles, Ella and Louis, Cleo and Johnny and a bit of

Frankie boy, though plenty of 60s pop was enjoyed and popular 70s music was embarrassingly danced to. Dickie was a more serious affair. Renbourn, Fripp and Williams where the top with easy listening was left to Feliciano and Arlo Guthrie, all topped off with a plethora of classic. And Eric...he enjoyed the simpler things, My Ding-a-Ling, shaking like Elvis, Streakers in the Sun, Jerry Lee and watching The Doors concert perform on T.V. the young Eric, who already was inappropriately being given the likes of Valium, sitting there, opened mouth, as Jim Morrison writhed on the stage floor, humping the air with his microphone, telling the world he was going to kill his Mum and Dad...Eric smiled... "Wow, awesome !" he quietly mused "Mum, this man wants to kill his parents" he shouted excitedly.

Years later he would try to offend as much as possible, taking in an Ian Dury record in to class, to play the intro of a track "Plastow Patricia" to the class.

As luck would have it his track was chosen amongst a few others, being lesser known at the time. Mr. Chapman lined up the stylus to the rotating grooves and lowered the needle just as the headmaster knocked on the door and walked in with some prospective parents being given a tour of the school. Smiles dropped as the words "Assholes, Bastards..." and other profanities burst forth onto the unprepared ears, followed by, without batting an eyelid "...and here we have Social Studies, where we're not afraid to question stereotypical thinking" followed by a smile and guiding the parents back out.

Again, thankfully, Erics elderly neighbour would be spared from hearing the modern take of music and the hullaballoo that was created at the end of the Saturday morning ritual of The Bucket of Water Song, that was the ever finale of Tiswas, normally re-enacted, with gusto (and sometimes ketchup) by Eric and his chums.

Their little visitor was the gentleman's Granddaughter, who came to stay every weekend and broke into Erics house every Saturday to watch telly. As far as he knew, the 10-year-old had been doing this for a while. her grandfather had no television, so hearing the neighbours, snuck into the back garden, through the rickety fence divide and opened the window into the sitting room (this was very easy as no locks or catches were on the sash window). Once in she would make herself comfortable and watch the morning T.V before returning for lunch. Initially startled, the tenants became used to the routine and soon settled in as a matter of course, though never "partaking" whilst young persons present.

It was on one of these mornings that Eric stirred in the armchair and found the television on and company already arrived.

"That's a lot of zips on your trousers" she said pointing.

"Yeah, I 'spose. They're called bondage trousers". Replied Eric.

They were actually black Boy bondage trousers, very comfortable and bought from the Kings Road.

He'd had a notion to get some and a knuckle duster, not to do damage but it seemed like a good idea at the time. Kids! So he figured he would start in the Kings Road and if that failed he would head over to Kensington High St. and go to the basement market, which always smelt so good…

Back at Kings Road the search was proving useless and he almost gave up until he spied a small collection of alternatives, yet fashionable looking shops. Wandering around the arcade he noticed some descending stairs, so wander casually down. Bingo! He couldn't believe his luck, "plenty of leather and studs in there" thought the 1979 Eric. In he wandered and without wasting time, asked the two guys behind the counter if they had any knuckle dusters (not realising they were illegal).

They looked at each other.

"Well, no" said one, looking at his companion.

"I suppose you could use this" said the other, producing narrow leather strap with a set of studs on and fastened with metal poppers.

Eric tried it out for size, the biggest setting fitted fine.

"Is there anything else you might like" smiled the first assistant leaning forward.

A bit taken aback from such a friendly request and the strange nature of the phrasing, Eric declined at the same time as noticing, for the first time, the black and white pictures that adorned the boutique. Lots of men, with big moustaches, leather caps, naked torsos and very tight leather trousers covered the walls.

It wasn't until he was walking down the street, after a hasty exit, he pulled out his purchase, to try it on again. Fitted fine, but who would have such small wrists when done up on the tightest setting...ohh.

So, sitting in his chair, bondage trousers on, and young girl pointing.

"Are they all pockets"? she enquired.

"Well, yes, most of them" he replied.

"What's in that one" she questioned, again pointing.

Eric had to go through all his pockets, even though he knew nothing was in them as he had a faint recollection of emptying them last night, but to his surprise...

"Oh," he said, producing a small paper packet from one of his pockets.

"What's that" she said.

"Er...I don't know". He honestly replied, having no recollection of the item, though his brain was scrambled, again.

He carefully unwrapped the package, only to discover a few joints worth of weed.

"What's that" she said again, pointing.

"Erm, some seeds...for planting...my friend gave them to me... I forgot" he truly had forgot.

This wasn't unusual or seldom. Excess was his "go to" and he would frequently have recall flashes of staggering into someone or something, car horns blaring, or admiring the night sky from a peculiar and probably illegal position. One such of these events had left him confused and dumbfounded for a long time.

The evening was nothing unusual. The four elements, a combination of powder, pills, smoke and liquid had been consumed, his friends telling him ease up and to do less (except for Todd, who enjoyed the encouragement), but Eric only tended to stop when his conscious brain said bye-bye.

His hedonistic, addictive and self-destructive lifestyle was a resulting combination of many factors. A mother who showed sympathetic love, emotional fracturing, psychotic outbursts, narcissist attributes, flirtatiousness, the intelligence of B.A student with the naivety and stability of a scared and insecure child and a whiskey and nicotine addicted father who was as distant in himself as to anyone else, awkward, despite his inappropriate handling of women, in his emotional and physical connections, having being "buggered senseless" as a child by his overbearing elder brother and competing for his mother's affections with an archetypal South African alpha male husband.

His early introduction to mood and mind-altering pharmaceuticals in the mid and late sixties, undoubtably helped, with the music and colours of the time, especially the vibrancy of cartoons and comics combined and flicking through pages of the shelves of books, finding Huxley, Blake and Shakespeare, all leading to other lands, a real eye opener for a child still in single figures. It wouldn't be until some fifty years later, twenty years after deciding things had to stop, that he realised the more he imbibed, the clearer the sadness became, though not understanding what lay behind the title of that book, he had to obliterate his presence, to rid himself of the conflicting feelings, not knowing how to face himself.

Now in adulthood, he recalled standing up from his chair in the side room of the pub, where the Asteroids game, his companion, was, possibly saying goodnight to everyone, then... blank.

He woke the next morning, feeling very comfortable, on his back, in the middle of his bed, naked (he always wore pyjama trousers in bed, except when...). He sat up suddenly and looked around and stupidly called out "Hello"?, feeling as if someone was or should be there.

Being a small bedsit, there was no hiding place, but what was even more bizarre was his clothes. At the bottom right-hand corner of his bed sat an exceptionally neat, folded pile of clothes, fresh underwear included. He looked around the room again, just to make sure he hadn't missed anyone in the 20ft by 20 ft space and called again. No reply came, obviously, as it was a one-bedroom bedsit which, literally was, just big enough to swing a cat in.

He searched his memory for any hint of how he got home and got up the six flights of stairs, that would have been a feat in itself, yet alone the tidy stack, coming to the conclusion, some-one must have helped him back. He'd had quite a bit last night, even by his standards, mixing his intake heavily to prove a point, and considering, he felt pretty good...except for the total memory loss...not a hint of anything existed. Confused and befuddled, he checked the time and noticed that friends would already be congregating at the lunchtime local to pre-pare for the evening and reflect on the previous.

Eric quickly got dressed, still unnerved and still feeling re-markably refreshed, and left, jumping down the flights of stairs, eager to find out from his compadres the previous night's events.

He entered the pub under the watchful eye of the landlord, giv-ing him a look of incredulity mixed with "behave", though his wife smiled and, disturbingly, chortled.

He went to the bar and ordered a pint.

"You feeling more yourself this morning" she said while pull-ing the bitter.

"Odd thing to say" thought Eric, replying "Yup, fine thanks, never better". A noncommittal and hopefully appropriate response he thought.

He made his way through already crowded hostelry, students galore, as you'd expect to find in most places in a university city. The mix here was about 60/40 in favour of townies, though some establishments would be 90/10 in favour of the ya-ya's. The 100% of either type was never a good idea to frequent, it would result in a lot of "Oh, yuh, of course, Father had to buy the villa" or "Do you want your fuckin ed kicked in". Eric never understood the politeness that preceded the violence; odd bedfellows. He got to his group of friends who all smiled and laughed when he appeared.

"You're alive then" said Elle, smiling, causing a ripple of amusement.

"What happened to you last night then" interjected Todd.

"One minute you got up to go to the toilet" said Milo "the next, gone. How the hell did you make it home".

"Yeah" said Todd "we were actually worried" laughing.

Eric explained that it was all a blank, though did now have a recollection of forgoing the toilet, for some reason seeing the pub door instead, but then went on to recount his waking etc... to his beloved small group of friends.

When finished there was silence. Then laughter.

No one had a clue what had occurred, it was going to be one of life's little mysteries that would hang around for a long time.

THE LAW

Flouting The Law was instilled at an early age, not disrespectfully, just a matter of casual collision of cultures, sometimes literally.

Living near a major highway, leading into the centre of the nation's capital city, there were obvious restrictions and instructions for motorists to adhere to, for example, no u-turns, something Robert did on a daily occasion to avoid an extra two-minute detour, almost the amount of time it took to execute the about turn to their turning.

Always thrilling, Eric loved to get a chance to sit in the front seat of the old, two-tone Rover P4, which often had to be crank started, and watch his father manoeuvre the city's traffic at speed and to slipstream emergency vehicles up close, to get through red lights without getting caught.

A special treat was driving up the circular ramp of the West London Air Terminal, that serviced Gatwick and Heathrow, a speedy fly past of the startled doorman with a wave, whilst watching pilots and trolley dollies in all their finery, coming and going, carrying their PanAm and BOAC bags.

As the years progressed and engines got bigger, Robert's foot got heavier on the accelerator, making the most of company cars, especially when the head turning spectacle of the first Range Rover came on the scene. People stood and stared at the large, white, angular vehicle, so tall off the ground that Cassandra had to be helped in and out, attracting the wrong sort of attention she desired.

Robert was a spectacular motorist, thought his youngest child, handling the vehicle with ease, parking where he chose, sticking fingers up at parking wardens (which Eric never understood, at first, until he tried it out on a teacher at school…), the most impressive time was when the two of them were caught in a heavy London fog.

It had been one of those occasions when Eric had decided school was horrible, so threw himself out of the moving train, executing a truly magnificent double roll, he was always impressed until he felt the kick up the backside. As a result of his exploits, he had to tag along with his dad for the day, arduous meetings, waiting in the car...he learnt how not to get bored by watching, so the day passed eventfully, imagining people's lives and homes. Time came for home and twenty minutes' drive from home, the fog dropped. As thick as it was grey, visibility was zero, about a foot in front of the headlights could be seen. Thankfully it was already night, the roads were quiet and Robert knew the area well and incredibly, continued driving home, at a crawl, not hitting a single car or kerb.

Unfortunately, later in life, Robert hadn't slowed his speed to match his ability, or intake and recklessly drove as fast as possible on motorways and careered down country lanes, avoiding dusk and night driving, only to Nazi salute the arresting officers and get tackled to the ground when in his 80s for drink driving...not that losing his licence made any difference. He was even a demon on his mobility scooter, bumping into cars and crashing into shelves in the small, narrow convenience store. Cassandra had never driven, trying to ride a bike had proved too hazardous enough.

Moving to the university city, Eric came into his first contact with people who had very different views about the powers that be. Typically, at school and briefly after, there were those who professed dislike of the system, but with like so many others, confused the boundaries or painted everything with the same brush without the awareness of the many layers and angles that existed. Having had few minor and relatively innocent run-ins was inevitable, especially when riding a motorbike, wearing a leather jacket and, to be truthful, probably behaving too exuberantly at times. But he did enjoy enjoying himself, the wide openness and beauty of the Dorset countryside touched his green personality and innocent ways.

City life in the early 80s offered an eclectic atmosphere, about to be taken full advantage of by someone eager to expand his knowledge after a suppressed childhood, despite the recent freedom of the rolling hills, his two wheels and haybarns.

Despite having an easy nature, Eric found aggressive conflict quite quickly from the boys in blue. At the time, the Sus Law was still in effect, an understandable, though possibly heavy-handed piece of legislation at the time it was introduced and now utilised to its maximum limits.

Cheffing and being a roadie had one thing in common: Unsocial, actually, totally the wrong word to use, hours. Eric would often find himself walking the streets in the early hours of the morning, normally after work, admittedly, sometimes, all night sessions of Monopoly or Colditz and Scrabble (with the obligatory puff added to the mix) and get "pulled" by a pair of overly threatening enforcers, demanding information and a search. Ironically, they tended not to like the truth. When questioned about where you're going, where have you come from and what have you been doing is responded by "I've been playing Monopoly until 4 in the morning", it was pretty common to be instantly pushed onto the bonnet of their car and searched.

Eric learnt quickly to remain pleasant, something some of his friends failed to, or didn't want to grasp. Much to their expense. One evening, after a usual session at their favourite watering hole, Eric offered to walk Elle, Andrew's girlfriend, home, as And. was visiting his mother in Reading. It was about a 45-minute walk out of town to Elles parents' house, where she still lived, but that never bothered him, frequently having walked miles across the Dorset countryside to meet up with mates, when either buses were not available or having the need to stretch his legs and admire the tranquillity.

Living in a small rural village, getting to and from one predominantly relied on Shanks's pony, especially at night, walking down the narrow, sometime haunted lane and hearing strange noises from behind the hedges. At first, unnerving, but soon became comforting, hearing the wild animals of the night about their business, occasionally walking through fields as a short cut, and surprisingly, meeting a fellow traveller, normally with bulging pockets, a heavy looking sack and a mischievous smile, the wink standing out in the moonlit nights.

Walking along with Elle they chatted and laughed, making short work of the footsteps and soon enough left her safe in her doorway, silently waving goodnight. Eric jogged for a little, not only to fill the quiet, but also to cover some ground, eventually settling to a comfortable steady walking pace after about 10 minutes.

He was coming to the first main road that intersected his route and noticed in the distance a cyclist headlight heading towards him, slowing his pace to see clearer, he noted it was none other than a female police officer on her night duties.

"Excuse me" called out a soft and slightly nervous, but authoritative voice "Could you stop there, please".

Eric stopped and then checked over his shoulder, just checking to make sure she wasn't talking to anyone else on the empty street.

The slight and diminutive person, was just doing her job and Eric was impressed by her courage.

"Good evening, Sir" she said "How are you this evening" she continued.

Eric instantly decided to empty all information concerning his last hour, and more, making it clear he wasn't a nutter or a threat, noticeably, much to the relief of the cyclist, who seemed to relax a bit and laugh. They stood and chatted for a bit, finding out that she <u>was</u> a new recruit and had cruelly drawn the short end of the stick that night. They departed on their separate routes, Eric kicking himself for not getting her phone number, another trait he'd picked up from his father.

By this time Eric had already moved from his first house, though had already, usually thanks to Todd, had quite a few dealings with raids.

The evening turned to night as Eric and a couple of friends had gathered, as usual, to joke and smoke, and tonight it was

Linton Kwesi Johnson's turn to set the mood, telling it about Winston getting high, when, suddenly, Todd burst through the front door and into the sitting room, hands covered in blood, out of breath, followed by a panicky Billie, his girlfriend, clutching at a large bloodied poster. Billie shot upstairs, locking herself in the bathroom and Todd exited via the backdoor into the garden with no explanation.

The group were a <u>little</u> startled, but this was Todd after all, their main concern was hoping that no one had been attacked.

"Erm" said Milo "What just happened"? being snapped out of his sunken state.

"Er..., not sure," said Eric.

As if the shock of the bizarre interruption was enough, there came an instant heavy banging on the front door.

"Police. Open up" came the order.

Before anyone could rise, momentarily again stunned by their new situation, in burst a small wave of authoritative uniforms, instantly filling the quaint sitting dining room.

This was the first-time experience of such an intrusive encounter, though as mentioned before, not the last, especially involving Todd.

One morning, Eric would be awoken at 5, his room, which he was renting from Todd's Mum, and house filled by the raid, looking for and not finding their assailant. Apparently, Todd and cohort had broken into a supermarket in the early hours, having previously damaged a few phone boxes and fleeing with the proceeds. At the shop, for ease of carrying, only stole cases of soft drink. How did they get caught or why did the finger point so quickly to Todd?

Stacking the cases on a corner, around the back of the ringing alarm, one of the perpetrators went to an undamaged phone box and called for a taxi to drop off Todd and goods at his home address.

When interviewed the cabbie stated he did think it odd at the time, but he was convinced by the fact that they paid his fare all in 5pence pieces.

There would be other brushings, especially at parties, where raids usually were followed by violence, normally meted out by those few goers who always looked out for an opportunity. Unfortunately, normally a given if one would attend those types of parties.

To a mentally growing lad, things never seemed to amaze Eric in the complexities of life around him. Sitting in a quiet room, away from the main party, he sat with about 10 strangers, chilling back, chatting and playing pass the joint. There were definite types of tokers. Some preferred smoking other people's stuff, some hogged the spliffs (called Bogart), some were canny, and to some, like Eric, rolled quickly to override the others, just wanting to get wasted.

Everyone was friendly enough and the conversation soon ventured onto what people did for a living, and one guy caused a big laugh when stated:

"I'm with the D.S (Drug Squad)".

The laughter was free and easy, the D.S always a word your ear would be hoping not to hear shouted at parties.

"No, really" said a bloke sitting next to other "what do you really do"?

Putting his hand inside his jacket, he pulled out a small wallet and flipped it open.

"Really" he said "I work for the Drug Squad".

Silence slammed into the room as if air was no longer needed.

"Don't worry though" he said again "I'm not on duty" laughing.

That put a downer on that evening. It's funny how a few words can change the atmosphere so completely.

Paranoia is one of the negative attributes connected with a drug lifestyle, though sometimes reality can be strange enough.

Eric found himself living in a small be adequate property, a kitchen sitting room and bathroom on the ground floor, tucked away, down some steps, at the back of the main house, with a door with a single, small glass window that led up two flights of stairs to two, well sized double bedrooms.

He was sharing, at the time with his girlfriend, a trainee beauty therapist and fellow baker, whose main hobby was Karate (and trying to chat up, unsuccessfully, girls).

The maisonette had previously been rented to psychotic nurse, who, apparently, brought work home with her and had many unusual visitors, day and night (which still carried on visiting even after she had left). When they first moved in, they discovered that a good clean was in order, discovering what seemed like dried blood sprayed on the inside of the cupboard doors. The little window, in the door that led upstairs, had an unnerving nature, often catching your eye and expecting to see a face peering through from the darkness. The strange feel to the property was enhanced one evening playing Monopoly (always a favourite goes to) and each player threw about three double sixes each in turn and in succession.

About 5:30 one late afternoon, the usual turnaround was occurring.

Erics girlfriend had just returned from college, still in her purple uniform, Eric just about to leave for a shift, so garbed in his bakery whites, and their mutual friend kitted out in his Gi or Dogi, ready for a session of open hand training.

Sitting around, tea and chat, all three gasped as they saw a face appear at the little glass square and door slowly open towards them.

Frozen in amazed shock, the front door opened and again police poured in, looking rather bewildered at the three costumed figures.

A momentary pause.

"Mr Forest"? came the stern query.

"No. he lives at the main house at the front".

"Oh…sorry. We thought this might be the back entrance".

A slight shuffling, followed by "Do you know where we can find him"? Then leaving, with slight awkwardness and obviously wanting to ask, but confused about the whole affair.

As a footnote, and to complete this offshoot, Mr Forest had been involved in a car accident…of sorts. A young acquaintance, whom he hadn't seen for about a year, turned up unannounced to take his old friend out for a spin in his new car. They only managed to get to the bottom of the hill, when the car caught the corner of the pavement and rolled. The young lad then ran, leaving a bemused and confused Mr Forest to wander off to the pub, as per usual, to nurse his wounds. The vehicle had been stolen.

As was the scrumpled and bloodied film poster in Todd's girlfriend's hands.

They had been walking to Eric's, past the ever-busy cinema club, when Billie said to her beau "I like that poster".

Ever the roguish gentleman, Todd proceeded to smash the external display with his hands to win his prize. Sadly, the proprietors didn't agree with this process and decided to explain their displeasure, receiving skin on skin contact for their efforts. Todd being Todd didn't flee the scene immediately, he kindly waited until the panda cars were in sight, up for a merry chase and high jinxery.

It would be considerable years until Eric had any serious involvement with the enforcers of The Queens Regulations, apart from the occasional motor theft or accident, spending some hours in a cell, listening to the cacophony of his neighbours, one, young, continually abusing his captors, the other, older, wailing his unhappiness until silence again came to visit.

Escorted from his cubicle, passing the "other"'s open door, he saw him still and lifeless, surrounded by activity, trying, uselessly, resuscitation.

"Move along. Nothing to see here Sonny" came the order.

NEAR MISSES

In his first fifty years, Eric had been considerably lucky in avoiding serious injury, considering the risks and foolhardiness he partook in.

Apart from his mother's attempt on his life, he had almost drowned on a number of occasions, once, at a crowded swimming baths where he was dive bombed by accident, a couple of times at schools due to cramps and broken toes and again at a primary school friends country house, a party left him pushed, literally, into the deep end, leaving him out of his depth, physically and emotionally, possibly for the last time.

Evel Knievel became a big influence on his desire to become a stuntman, with Tess and friends putting on shows for the family, or anyone else who could be persuaded to watch, and Eric being used as the clown or acrobat, falling over invisible hurdles, pratfalling into walls and doors and spectacularly falling off chairs, much to the alarm for the onlookers.

As age progressed, his desire to outperform previous exploits also grew, learning how to jump of first floor school windows, blazer flapping in the upcoming draught like Batman, climbing towering T.V masts that swayed in the lightest breeze, then onto activities such as abseiling and rock climbing, parascending and parachuting, but the thrill of motorbiking didn't need speed in the quiet, narrow Dorset lanes, just the meeting of a milk tanker coming the opposite direction was sometimes enough to get adrenaline racing. The large, unforgiving lumps of metal, carrying liquid which would push the brakes to their limit and taught Eric the ability to make friends with hedges.

The freedom he experienced at such an important time in his life, was, perhaps, unfortunate and well timed (though perhaps the real unfortunate thing was the tight rein that he had been leashed on for his first twelve years), the subsequent "knee-jerk" reaction would take twenty years of experimentation, resulting in dramatic weight loss and homelessness (being saved by a £10 note and a small bible verse, the only things found in a wallet, discovered in a phone box late one night, wandering the streets for warmth and distraction (saviour indeed).

That event was a pivotal change, instrumental in getting him back on his feet, though, at the time, probably not taken full advantage of, as his habits wouldn't be dissolved for a long time yet, but, nevertheless, it was instrumental in many ways.

Things escalated quickly from the turnabout. A job came first, mobility and relationships followed and the passing of his driving test gave a renewed sense of independence.

Italy was an exciting country to drive around. Banked corners were a delight to speed around and every driver was in a hurry, honking horns and gesticulating and where there were two lane roads, the motorists would turn it into three, and no waiting for your lights to turn "GREEN", but "GO" when the opposing lights turn "RED".

Milo and Eric had been advised to go to a certain Piazza in Roma, for substance purchasing, if needed, so after a couple of days sightseeing the spectacular ruins of ancient history, went in search for the advised beautiful square and statued fountain. Rome, like many other early cities, offer breath-taking architecture, from the magnificent giant buildings, to the smallest, unassuming courtyards, that can be found hidden about the small back streets, unlooked on by tourist's eyes, but lived with like an old acquaintance. Even visiting an Italian bank could be an experience. Housed in some archaic marbled building of a senator, now repurposed, but still as casually masterful in its simplicity yet effectiveness.

Milo and Eric stood in the piazza and looked around for a likely target for their need. A group of seven likely suspects lurked with darkened eyes by the entrance of an alley way, a more residential part of the square and after several minutes of discussion, Milo drew the short straw of contact.

They strode towards the like aged youths and waved with smiles.

"Ciao" they both said.

"Hashish"? came the response.

They were a bit taken aback by the reply, but were relieved at the same time.

"Er, yeah, Prego". Said both Milo and Eric in unison.

"Opium, heroin…"? came the further question.

"No, no, just some hashish prego". Again, in unison.

The Italians looked a bit disappointed, but the older and taller one of the groups, who had not spoken yet said "you, come with me", turn and started to stride off.

Milo turned to Eric.

"Stay here, I'll be back soon" and trotted off after his quarry down the dark alley.

Eric stood, feeling like a little kid watching his balloon blow away with the wind, unsure of what to do next.

The diminished group dispersed themselves in various directions, leaving Eric totally alone and uneasy. Something didn't feel right. He felt immediate concern for his friend and realised that him, being the more physically toned of the two, should have gone in his place.

He found an old stone bench and sat and waited.

Time passed.

Then some more.

Too long for a simple deal, Eric started working out plans of action and possible scenarios.

Eventually, a couple of hours later Milo returned and both were relieved.

They had topped up for their journey out, confident that no checks would be made on a ferry from England to France, and had even obtained a couple of tabs (thin cardboard-soaked LSD) from a magnificent and an impressively filled old mansion that look like it belonged to Miss Haversham, but was owned and housed by Hells Angels, one of who sat on a raised throne in a darkened ballroom, next to the hallway an impressive staircase, all of which exuded the danger and paranoia of excess intake.

The acid had been consumed whilst camping, out of season, at Lago di Como, a beautiful lake in Northern Italy, the backdrop of the still mountains reflecting in the calm waters, which was only disturbed by a large fish which, Eric and Milo considered, insisted on messing with their heads, as it kept swimming onto the nearby bank from where they sat, getting extremely sunburnt, flounder around for a moment and then disappear back into the water, only to repeat this process many times over a couple of hours. Fortunately, the acid was weak and the fish became a joke instead of a concern.

They had not intended to stay at this campsite, which they were the only visitors at, but as Eric had decided to almost cause a multiple collision on a mountain road, overtaking three cars and a van, a hair breath away from colliding with an oncoming vehicle, sending many to their demise down the drop of the side of the road, Milo, not for the last time, said "Enough".

A brother and sister owned the campsite, situated on the banks, with the other main road blocked by a rockfall, that had buried a small factory some years earlier, but was not allowed to be cleared, by orders of "Mafiosa".

They set their tent up on the back edge of the site, in front of a spindly wooden fence, with a wide view of the vast countryside and hills. Evening came soon enough and an invite for beers came with it and for the first time, Milo and Eric felt that they had begun an adventure.

Returning to their tent after the fish escapade and slightly sore from being burnt, both by the sun and metaphorically, they spent the rest of the eve eating tinned ravioli, listening to their collection of tapes, Sandinista and Dr Hooks Medicine Show tonight, and smoking and glad they had decided on this excursion. France had been France, but Italy, well, after all, all roads lead to Roma. They settled down, happy and peaceful and sleep came quickly.

Erics eyes flicked open, instantly alarmed. A hand, not his, covered his mouth and in the dimness of the tent, the bright full moon outside, could see Milo raise a finger to his lips, signalling silence. At that exact time, he heard it.

Raising his head, milo removed his hand and they listened.

Outside of the tent, someone circled. They moved stealthily around the tent, checked the car door and carried on moving around in a clockwise fashion, stumble over a guide rope, then resume. Being stuck inside a tent was a dilemma. It would take some effort to get out quickly as there was an inner and outer zip on the small four-man tent, and could easily be trapped or overcome without defence, not knowing where the attacker, or even attackers might come from. So, silent they stayed, listening to the heavy, deep, erratic, yet calm breathing, as theirs had ceased.

A sudden cracking and snapping emanated, as whoever, must have climbed the spindle fence and then silence.

Staying in the tent for a few minutes that took ages to pass, not hearing any sound, ventured, carefully out.

Clouds had started covering the moon, but no one could be seen and no damage had been done, so cautiously they returned to their shelter and spent the rest of the night half awake and vigilant.

The morning came soon enough, and the previous night's experience was behind them, as now was the broken wooden fence. What startled them though, was what else they saw. The foot trail could be seen clearly in the long grass, leading off into the distance and up into the uninhabited hills of the countryside. They didn't stay another evening, just in case, though mentioning the events to their momentary incredulous hosts. They say a cat has nine lives. Eric grew concerned, as he touched his 60's, that he had spent them all many times over and then some. Whether it had been falling through a roof and managing to clutch a beam on the way down, only to find the six inches of a nail grazing his upper torso or falling through a skylight of a factory roof (… whilst with Todd), only to land on a huge pile of recycled clothing. The list was extensive. Staggering into the road, in flashback, hearing car horns and lights, snorting unknown recipes of stolen pharmacies causing blindness and pain, the drownings and fights, the psychotic and schizophrenic, the undesirables, and not to mentioning the innumerable car accidents, for the moment.

Everywhere has its toilet. Wolverhampton in the mid-90s was no exception. Following his future wife, Eric found himself working for a company, under a pseudonym, by accident, and couldn't be bothered to change it.

One day, Big John and Bob, his co-workers, were assigned a job in Wolves territory that had a reputation. The previous year, Big John had parked the Land Rover and secured all the equipment in the back cage, and walked along the canal treating unwanted plant growth, spraying from his knapsack. All was going well as he crossed the bridge to return to the vehicle for a top up when he was approached by a stranger in his late 20s.

"Give us a hand with that," said the male.

"What"? said Big John, a bit confused.

"That cylinder, there" he gesticulated to a large gas cylinder on the back of BJ's wagon.

Still uncertain as to what was going on, Big John replied again "What"?

"That cylinder" pointing "Give us a hand with it over the bridge. Its mine" came the reply.

"No' it's mine".

"You're mistaken mate" pulling a machete from his loose jacket "it's mine".

"Alright then" said Big John calmly "Keep your shirt on".

Having re-laid the story to their new fellow worker, they were advised to work in groups and not leave the van unattended, for any reason.

They drove for a while, through the estates which had walk ways over the roads, where you could see debris scattered all round, broken bricks, bottles, even smashed toilets, unsuspecting cars being target practice for those above.

Arriving at their destination Eric was confused. Why were they working here? The whole estate looked deserted, only the occasional car moved by, and sizeable as the area was, shops and house alike were boarded up, not with wood, but steel shutters, punched with holes, covered every door and window, on every building they saw.

He queried Big John.

"Daft bugger" he said "Course people live here".

Naively Eric questioned again.

"Stops them from being petrol bombed" Big John said, pointing to scorch marks on some of the walls.

"Even the police don't come here" he continued.

Eric considered himself an aware person, he knew about poverty but this, this was in the heart of England, at the end of the 20th Century. A supposedly enlightened and civilised country, rapidly going to the dogs. A country who was turning their backs on growth for cheap distractions, whilst the wealthy grew at the expense of the masses, most of which who were too blind to see, too deaf to hear and too dumb to speak.

The full sentence by Karl Marx, that is often misquoted, as so many quotes are, is such:

"Religion is the sigh of the oppressed creature, the heart of a heartless world, and the soul of soulless conditions. It is the opium of the people".

In the last fifty years, Christianity has been replaced by a new idol in the so-called United Kingdom, a new love, many seeking its glory and shallow rewards, never finding answers, only emptiness, money.

Now opium, cocaine and money are the most popular new religion and the big wheels of the machine keep turning.

Eric had been on the start of his journey when he first tried opium, the sticky brown substance smeared onto cigarette paper and sprinkled reverently with tobacco or grass, rolled, smoked and enjoyed. Though his dealer (who Tess had a major crush on, a blonde version, though more chilled and hippy type, if such a thing can be, of the character Mack, from Green Wing) refused to supply on a regular basis, conscientious in his dealings and responsibilities, a very rare commodity in dealers.

On his second leg, he lost his first in Oxford, of his existential journey, with the Mondays and Roses in full bloom, heroin and its abusers were growing more common in his life and the gap between refusal and acceptance was getting narrower all the time.

Bournemouth, more notably Boscombe, was a bedsit land for a large population of Scots and Scousers, winos and skag heads (not saying they go hand in hand, but a lot of them did), most trying to make a deal or score, to escape the misery that haunted their minds and chased their souls.

The winos normally littered the attractive public garden benches, cadging change or selling petrol-soaked hash, the discarded and failed smuggled goods, whereas the Scousers could be found shoplifting to order or selling Aunties best china.

Driving around the area also had its hazrads, especially at traffic lights.

Pulling up in his old, dark blue Triumph Herald, a wild haired, leather jacket Charlie Manson look alike stepped in front of Erics car and signalled a thumbs up.

The gesture was reciprocated, as a matter of goodwill, but not as a signal of "yeah, come on, bring your mate with his massive German Shepard dog. They can get in the back and pant over my shoulder, while you get in the front and stare at me". Which is exactly what happened in a flash. Before he knew it, the lights had changed and he had three new passengers. He was as surprised as the onlookers.

Eric didn't mind hitch-hikers. It was, after all, one of his favourite books and he knew what it was like not having a car, but this was...unexpected.

"My names Mantis" said the front passenger.

"I've just out of jail and I'm going to do the bloke who put me there" he continued.

"Ah...right" responded Eric, unsure what else he could say, talk about sensory overload.

"You're not going to tell the police, because I've seen you and I know your car. Otherwise, I'll kill you too".

"Man," thought Eric, "why do I have to always get the weirdos" thinking back on all the occasions, flickering across his brain, like that other guy in the cinema who tried to pick him up, or that other nutter, or...

"Turn right here" came the order.

"Yeah, no problem" came the slightly stoned reply. He wasn't that bothered and offered his now companions a smoke.

"I don't smoke" said Mantis "it doesn't help my head".

The guy in the back did though, not sure about the dog.

After several minutes of left and right turns they got to their destination.

"You never saw me, right. I don't exist. Right" came the emphatic order.

"Yeah, okay" stupidly "Good luck".

Many lessons were learnt in that area. The biggest was another life changer. A realisation that would take almost five years to fully implement and almost twenty years to be fully clean.

They were out on a trip to score some gear. When you're in the thick of it, you don't see what could be construed as sad desperation, trawling from house to bedsit, especially in dry times, where had become easier to pick up heroin than any other substance. Horse was for Matty, a female scouser friend who was getting deeper and deeper into it, and something special for the weekend (normally Whiz/ George (speed/amphetamine sulphate) or, if lucky, some acid) for Eric. All the "stuff" had different monikers, and depending on who you talked to and whether on the phone or out and about, might have extra aliases, depending on the real likelihood of phone tapping (as some had already got extensive form) or just plain crazy paranoia. Even for the most up to date and on the ball addict, name changes could get confusing.

"Hi Bob (Frank) is Terry there (do you have any grass)?"

"Hi Helen (Matty/Matilda), Terrys out (no), he's gone over to Asda (getting some later, good deal coming)."

"What's Chuck (Charlie/Skag/Heroin) doing (how much £) this savvy (afternoon) as I'm coming over in a bit (get some gear ready as I'm gagging for a hit)".

"Wha'? Who the fucks Chuck!"

You get the drift.

After a few calls and drop ins, Matty decided to call on her brother Matty (Matthew) as a last resort, but also knowing he would give her a better deal, if only slightly, than any other.

Whatever you call them: Druggies, Junkies, Addicts, Skagheads (specifically reserved for the dross of heroin users), a lot of them have issues and a lot of them...let's face it, can't be trusted. In order to get their fix, the majority turn to either theft or sex, selling both for a bag or wrap and while they're literally chasing (inhaling) their dream, their life decays around them.

Eric hadn't sunk that low...yet, but he was beginning to notice the rot getting closer and closer in more of his socialising circuit, whereas his work life was a totally different cuttle of fish. By day Delivery Driver and Baker, by night...

He was enjoying his work. The driving was fun and he got to see most of the South of England countryside in a time when traffic wasn't excessive and road surfaces were well maintained.

Accidents were an ill-fated side product of covering so much mileage, encountering the variety of other road users and the diversity that was offered by the conurbation and rural highways.

Whether it was reversing into a forecourt petrol pump, that jumped out behind him, from nowhere, crumpling like a carton and gushing fuel over the petrol station, much to the amusement of a couple of lads in a mini. Or buckling up, in a fully parked, large white Mercedes van after a delivery only to suddenly leap three feet forward, and on inspection, finding a Mercedes car had decided to wedge itself under the back of the van, crumpling its bonnet, whilst its driver and passenger removed themselves in an alcoholic ether that was still lingering from the night before at 9:30 in the morning. Or even driving into a yearly family outing, including Grandma, while sightseeing. The most dramatic was one of his luckiest escapes.

Eric picked up Betty from his parent's house, on an estate on the outskirts of Bournemouth, having a chat with the parents while Betty finished his Breakfast (6pm). They climbed into the works Citroen pick-up and headed off, chatting. It was a pleasant evening; no hurry was needed to get to work and the back roads into town were always quiet. A sharp right-hand bend loomed, but no concern was needed, as their speed was steady and not at all excessive, so cornering was at ease without any thought, until the van decided to go the opposite way from which it was being steered.

Without hesitation, Eric compensated, but again it had the opposite effect, again and again the van careered on its own course, zigzagging into the path of oncoming car, when suddenly off it shot.

It hit the low hedge and flew into the air, twisting as it went, landing upside down in a field, where the new momentum of height kept moving, windscreen popping out over their now upside-down heads and watching grass flick the roof to a standstill.

The loudness of the silence had been deafening. Ears ringing Betty and Eric looked at each other.

"You okay?"

"Yeah, you?"

"Yeah" smiling "Fine" …" better get out then"

In these moments of life, one isn't always quite aware as one should be. The seat belts were very stiff to release, this is when the first minor injury occurred. Not thinking, they both dropped, simultaneously about 6 inches onto their heads. Realising that the doors were buckled shut, they had to clamber out of the back, tripping over a tangle of brambles, second injury, and looked at the snapped chassis and driveshaft.

The woman, from the before mentioned oncoming vehicle was running towards them, shocked and relieved to find two living people. The police eventually arrived and were likewise amazed, a couple of feet in either direction and the trees or telegraph pole would have claimed lives. On closer inspection, it was discovered that, probably a kiddie prank, a large nail must have been leant against the tyre, when stationary, sticking in when pulling off, intending an instant flat, but not actually coming into its own until a sharp corner hit.

It gave Eric a new respect for the road and its hazards, realising he had to take a more defensive stance when behind the wheel.

The same was to be said for his visit to Matty with Matty.

They pulled up to the Victorian block of red brick flats. Eric had always wondered what they looked like from the inside, having passed them many a time, and now his curiosity would be peeked.

Entering through the well-maintained, tiled communal hallway, they climbed the concrete stairs with wrought iron banister, up four flights of stairs. They knocked on the wooden door and waited.

Matty's brother's girlfriend, Sharon opened it slowly, with caution, letting the rancid odours escape from their captors. Her lank, long, straggly once blonde hair draped her sallow[PK1] and gaunt face, sunken eyes and dirty yellowed teeth.

"Oh, hi matty" said the flat voice "c'mon in". opening the door, a fraction wider.

Matty and Eric entered. The darkened room was not dark enough.

Rubbish was strewn everywhere under the dirt and filth. No surface was left untouched, even old needles could be seen amongst the debris. The walls stained and damaged, as was the ceiling and the carpet, what there was of it, torn, pulled up, once a vibrant green, now browned and burnt. Curtains hung torn and nailed in place, furniture broken and sparse as the two tenants walked in circles, trying to remember if they still had a stash.

A noise came from behind Eric as he stood near the front door. He turned his head to see a young child standing in a cot behind him in another room. The occasional pink splotch looked out of place on the grime covered and soiled child, like badly applied camouflage, he would have blended in perfectly with the shit smeared walls had his tears not cleaned part of his face. He couldn't believe he had just stepped into this pit of squalor; the contrast had been so extreme and sudden.

It was then he knew he had to change his life.

OOH, OOH, OOH…

The leaf lined lane, bushes along the sides and trees bending overhead, ran quietly down to the waiting canal and moored barge, waiting for its passengers as the water gently sploshed and lapped when the occasional boat passed by. Ducks quacked and moorhens hurried about their business with the warmth of the summer air flowing idly along the green tunnel of foliage, as Eric skipped along beside his mother, Little Ted in hand, wearing matching red shorts and his favourite striped T-Shirt.

Today was definitely a good day. Not only did the excursion by longboat beckon, but the destination would be seen from a distance, the towering, curved metal frame and, if lucky, some escaped inhabitants might also be spied.

Eric knew this much, and had been taught it from his early steps.

Living in London, he was very fortunate to have so much around him.

"Many people have very little" Cassandra explained to her youngest son.

"Some people live in smaller houses than us, can't afford nice things and can be very unhappy." She told him.

"Can't we help them, mummy," said the little voice.

"Sometimes, but we don't have much to give ourselves, that's why we hide when the milkman comes". Cassie continued.

Eric enjoyed hiding behind the sofa, but sometimes gave the game away by popping his head out over the top to see or by laughing too loudly.

There were many free things to do being in the centre of the metropolis. The nearby park with its round pond (to exhaustedly run around or lose your little boat in) and the tranquil and fragrant orangery of Kensington Palace, or a further walk, deeper into the park, to enthusiastically run up the steps of The Albert Memorial and run your hands along the statues that surrounded the plinth. There were the museums too, the Science, with its rockets and physics displays, the V&A, housing memorabilia of all societies, but the most visited being the Natural History, which was as silent as a library and as reverent as a chapel, only a gentle cough being heard, normally by one of the suited attendants, signalling a dislike of behaviour.

The marble floors, brass hand rails, wooden panelling and large glass fronted displays all held their occupants frozen in a snap shot of time, the many forms to marvel at and wonder of the times they all moved in, with the mighty blue whale suspended above the visitors' heads, exhibiting its vastness and sleek design.

Erics favourite museum though, and one not often frequented due to its further location, was the magnificent British Museum, with its Roman-Greco style entrance already issuing a statement of what was to be found inside. Treasure abounds lay within those walls, Egyptian, Aztec, Mongolian..., mummies, statues and jewellery, the spectacular to the humble, each having had its place in human history and to Eric, each touched by another far distant hand, maybe a simple person had reached out casually, whilst walking past and touched a smooth porcelain monument, or a lover had handed over an amulet to his to be wife. History in its entirety. That is what the beauty he saw, the stories that lay behind the stories, the tales of the unnoticed.

There was a greater prize to be had than a visit to this monumental location. An ulterior motive to persuade his mother of the distant journey. This treasure did not play within the confines of the grandiose or among the throng of tourists.

Sitting quietly, but always enticingly, stone's throw from the front gates of the museums entrance, stood a small fronted, wood and glass shop, with the words Alan Alans written clearly above.

Entering through the ping of the doorbell, you were accosted with amazement and spectacle.

A glass counter ran along the right-hand side and end of the shop, but the walls were covered with small wooden, shoe box size draws, each with a brass curved handle and a label. But what was truly magical, was the festivity of colours and shapes, ranging from a large red and black, imposing disappearing cabinet to multicoloured knotted hankies, bunches of collapsible flowers, pointed wizard hats and gowns or plastic flies to scatter on your mother's sandwich (snigger snigger).

Every trick under the sun was to be evident somewhere in your vision. Escapology, mind reading, sword swallowing, juggling, everything there to be bought, whatever your trickster needs and whatever your budget. There was one strict condition for purchase. You could only buy if you knew how the trick was done.

However, for those who had aspirations and were new comers to the trade and showed awe and enthusiasm, the diminutive, yet fully skilled Mr Alan, and assistant, would encourage observation. While serving the average punters, who might have called in to buy snapping chewing gum or the ever-popular whoopee cushions, the sales team would be performing sleight of hand or prop ridden tricks, astounding those directly in the frontline, but being a huge sense of amusement to the side-liners.

There was other daytrips Eric looked forward to, but, most especially, the yearly event of November 5th and not just because of the obvious. He did like fire though. Whether it was a chance to try and toast bread on a fork in front of the sitting rooms gas heater, or "accidentally" lighting a whole box of indoor fireworks with his cousin, both gleeful at the fizzes and pops and ever-increasing flames.

The days and evenings leading up to the date in question was spent in dilemma, mainly because of the making the Guy. A pair of old trousers and tights would be found, tied and stuffed with scrumpled up newspaper, as was a shirt, which would be stitched to the legs and a head fashioned by covering a blown-up balloon with papier mache. The quandary was (something he had learnt from school and his from his rebellious father) thus:

1) Guido Fawkes was only one of a group
2) The only one caught
3) Was probably innocent of the accusations
4) Died horribly
5) Those in power probably deserved it

Having all this information to hand, and more, Eric felt sympathies to the yearly ritual of burning this unknown effigy and made sure that everyone attending knew it, not that it stopped anything.

The car would be loaded with attending personnel, poor old Guy being relegated to the boot with some fireworks (away from his father's incessant smoking, unless Dickie wasn't around, then Guy could be safely placed between Tess and himself for company.

Robert's smoking could be a pleasant and familiar smell, particularly when blended with au de whiskey, but when trapped in the confines of a car, played havoc with Erics travel sickness. On most journeys the scenario was the same, despite the known and impending results.

About two hours before a major (over half an hour) journey was to be had, stress levels would start to rise in Cassandra which would be the same time as extra pill popping and a short rest was needed. Once the meds had kicked in, she would rise, a relaxed, more confident persona, organised and prepared, but not yet dressed for the occasion ahead and the fragility still lurking in the closet.

"Come on Darlings, you have to get ready. Don't forget it's going to be cold tonight, so get something warm to wear" Cassie would say, nurturing her children.

"Ooh, I might wear my purple corduroy dress" said Tess, thinking aloud.

"Don't be such a stupid girl" Cassandra snapped "I'm wearing purple. Honestly." Walking off into a dark brewing cloud.

Once costumes had been selected and greasepaint applied, the character was ready for the performance, as were the chorus line.

The drive to Cassandra's grownup school friend, Connie (one of the so-called 3 Witches), was an hour drive over the Surrey Hills, always fragrant with bonfire smoke wafting through the cars ventilation system or the smallest open crack of a window that Eric would keep his nose near, rather than face the full and overpowering air of the interior, where Robert chain smoked, insisting windows be shut.

"It'll stop you from smoking when older" came the reply from pleas of air.

Eric would rather have not had bouts of bronchitis and travel sickness, if he had known the consequences of his dad's incessant puffing and nicotine intake. Ironically, all three siblings smoked at one time or other, Eric the most intense, Tess the longest, Dickie the least, this was also the same for their alcohol intake, with Tess never managing to unshackle herself from her prison.

Reaching their destination, the family bundled out of the car being greeted by the other family, Eric dashing off for a fight with his equal, while the others greeted each other with casual luvvie (acting term for "Darling, how lovely to see you... mwah, mwah" etc, barf) friendliness and relaxed charm (yuh, whatever).

Bill, also the youngest of the family, a stocky powerhouse that took delight in inflicting powerful headlocks, showed Eric the tall bonfire waiting to be lit at the end of the garden, through the large lounge windows, only to suddenly choke Eric from behind and pull him to the floor behind the sofa. The games had started. After several minutes of mutual punishment, the Gladiators were told to get up and both behave themselves.

Suitably reprimanded, though still subtly issuing an occasional kick, the visiting family were invited to say hello to Connie's parents who lived next door, who had known Cassie ever since little.

A stillness came over the red faced and sweating Eric. That meant...

The houses were connected by a large garden that had not been divided, so following the gravel path, lit by the large military torch, they made their way to the neighbours. Eric was silent with anticipation. The greetings were standard and short, and to Eric frustratingly long, he just wanted to go and see.

"Hello Eric, and how are you" not waiting for a reply the kind, odd looking gentleman said "Do you want to come and see them"?

"Yes, please" the quiet voice spoke...not forgetting his manners.

"C'mon then, let's see if they're awake". Leading the way.

The door opened to a large, dark room, only the faintest outlines could be ascertained. The flick of a switch sent a jolt of mixed emotions through his young body. Childhood fear, intrigue, nervousness met smiles, leers, eyes, teeth. He was sure, that if they weren't looking at him, then they wanted too.

All about the room, the shelves on the walls, on top of and in cabinets, on the chairs and most alarmingly hanging and dangling from the ceiling, like Vlad the Impaler's victims, were puppets. Every type and colour of puppet you could imagine. Hand, marionette, finger, glove, rod and arm, even the exquisite Malaysian shadow puppets, amazing in their intricacy and simpleness, the favourite to the small eyes that beheld them. For in those shapes, he could clearly see which were the monsters and which could be trusted, something he didn't feel with the painted masks. A cacophony of stories and movement waiting to be told, yet hanging lifeless and macabrely still with eyes straining to see their visitors.

Eric stood and marvelled at the beauty, the sinister, each already belying their intentions, as this elderly man carefully handed Eric his friends, introducing them and talking to each of them as he went, sincerely saying:

"We have a guest. Would you like to come and say hello"?

"Oh, I see, dear me"

"No, I haven't and you don't either"

"Sorry dear"?

"That's frightfully rude of you"

...and so on, all the time, until maybe one or two came to briefly rest in Erics open arms, only to be whisked away again, being told...

"They don't want visitors today, they're a bit unhappy".

The same couldn't be said for a certain well known puppet, with whom its owner had flat shared with Robert, in the days of being jobbing actors.

One of the other yearly rituals would be a visit to the pantomime. A time when the public would put on their finest for cinema and theatre alike and would stand in silence for the national anthem at the end of the night's performance.

The most magical of pantos was undoubtedly The Wind in the Willows, with Moley busily spring cleaning, Ratty being Ratty and Toad...oh, Toad, you are so troublesome...Toot, Toot.

Many a visit to the theatre would involve a boring back stage visit for Robert and Cassandra to catch up with an old luvvie or two, but coming face to face with the fur snouted gagster was something Eric was looking forward to.

Opening the door to the dressing room, they came face to face with Basil in the arms of his handler. A curious situation developed.

Eric knew, as surely everyone did, that this was a puppet, not real, but instead of being shown the furry figure and all its mechanisms, it persisted in behaving like it did on stage, which only made Eric feel embarrassed and uncomfortable. He was 8 after all.

The fireworks after the puppet visit were a good way to end the evening, the fire and guy having already been consumed and would have to wait until next year, but for now the canal was only steps away.

Climbing in, at the back of the long, narrow vessel, the warmth of the sun dappled its way through the trees above and flickered its light that had travelled the millions of miles on a young boy's arms, unaware of the vastness of the cosmos, only concerned with the smiling faces about him and their mutual destination.

The boat chugged easily along, with gentle warm diesel fumes tickling his nose, making his tummy rumble and think about Winnie-the-Pooh type elevenses. Eric watched as houses and roads sailed easily by, all filled with others dashing about here and there, shopping and meeting, working or cycling, a never-ending stream of busyness and variances.

The slow curve in the canal came into view and Eric knew that soon the boat trip would be over. Nearing the end, Eric's thoughts turned to what lay ahead.

"What to see first" he pondered "Hmm..."

"Maybe..."

"Or…"

"Hmm…"

And no soon as these few little thoughts and imaginings had come and gone, the boat was mooring up, and passengers alighting with help.

He was a little annoyed at himself for drifting off into his imagination again, as he missed the towering structure that he liked so much, but walking up the rampart to the main road, he saw the familiar large black, metal ironworks of the turnstiles with the unmistakeable signage saying "London Zoo".

Excitement raised in the young boy's veins with the hearing of macaws squawking their calls and the familiar warm, earthy yet tangy smell of all the animals drifted across the concrete path that led into the myriad of pathways leading off into all directions.

There was never enough time to see all that he wanted, he thought, staring up at the signposts. He mused. A visit to the warm and dark reptile house, with light spilling out from the glass fronted cages, where the inert and docile inhabitants lay, only relishing the chance to strike. The insect house lay nearby too, but held little fascination apart from the industrious ant farms. The penguins would be excellent fun, watching them waddle and splosh would content him for hours, though they were situated far from other possible enclosures and he was unsure whether he could persuade his mother on the venture. "Hmm" he pondered to himself "where first"?

As if reading his mind Cassandra suggested "The giraffes might be a good place to start. Come on darling".

"Oh, okay" he replied, a bit disappointed "Hippos would be more fun" went unheard.

Strolling along to the enclosure, they passed the restaurant and Eric gently made a hopeful observation which was abruptly rebuffed with "You can't have everything you want; besides we haven't got time. Hurry up, don't dawdle" from his mother.

Eric did enjoy the Zoo. He remembered how, on previous visits, he liked the crocodile, who would sometimes give him a salacious wink, and the furry wombats, but felt sorry about how unhappy they must be, especially as they and the lions who paced up and down their cages, Eric thought, possibly looking for a way out.

Wandering in his thoughts, he noticed they were passing the chimpanzees and long armed gibbons cages. The tall iron bars were all that separated the out reaching arms, humans and apes alike.

The gibbons were happily swinging about, looking about them, but generally unconcerned and unamused by the outside life of their domain.

The chimps on the other hand were quite the opposite. Their antics were running rings about the two keepers who had entered the enclosure. Running, rolling and hiding under sacks and bins looked like the high light of the day. Treats were being offered for good behaviour and compliance, but as soon as one feigned submission, another would prank their handlers causing others to scarper with much hilarity, apart from the gaolers.

"Where have you been, horrible child" snapped Eric out of his absorbment.

"What"? "Watching the monkeys" Eric said.

"Don't answer back to me you rude little boy", slap, "You're going home straight away" insisted Cassandra, yanking Eric arm.

Tears burst into his eyes and unhappiness shook his body, as he watched distantly from inside, his grown-up voice quietly conversing with him, only to turn, while being dragged away, to see a gibbon making eye contact, directly with him.

"Maybe one day we'll escape our cages".

DULCE ET DECORUM EST

Robert lay in the hospital bed, not for the last time, pipes and wires leading to "machines that go ping". Eric had been warned of what to expect, but found himself unstirred by the sight of his father, lying helpless and vulnerable with the equipment breathing and pumping his blood for him whilst placed in an induced coma.

The whiteness, functionality and sterile surroundings generated their own version of white noise that hissed in Erics head as he leant over and kissed his father's unresponsive temple in greeting.

"He can't hear you" his mother said "though the doctors said to talk to him. It helps apparently"

Tess was sitting in a chair nearby, angrily crying, while Dickie, standing behind her, rested a hand on her accepting shoulder, looking grown up, in charge and in control, yet exhibiting his professional and detached demeanour.

"Poor old Dickie" thought Eric "I wonder if he'll ever be able to get off his high horse".

Dickie had always separated himself from the family. There were only two years separating each of the siblings, so when an 8-year-old gets attacked by an irritating 4-year-old it takes nothing to swat him aside.

At the time of when they were growing up, Eric had thought Dickie had enjoyed his boarding school days, but years later would only partially discover his turmoiled times, but preferring the isolation and neglect than the beatings from his father and lack of parental empathy, consequentially making him call his parents by their names rather than terms of endearment.

Dickie had been an angry brother, developing a detached behaviour towards his family, wanting less and less to do with them, all the while nurturing a serious and proper disposition, buying tickets for the family to attend classical music concerts for etiquette improvement and introducing them to more socially acceptable standards of living and to acquaint them to people of a better class.

Robert and Cassandra were more than happy to oblige their son's behaviour, having both heritages of coming from wealth and the knowing of how to put on the airs and graces, yet having capital little of their own, Cassies money coming mainly from her aunt and a steady stream, of varying amounts, of mismanaged monies from archaic trusts, for her to spend. To Cassandra, keeping her looks were important, neither she nor Robert liked the idea of getting old, so spent on heavily on expensive make-up, potions and pills, haircuts and dyes and regular visits to massage parlours (...). Robert, similarly had trusts, though with lesser investment, and was canny with his expenditure, though experienced a dyslexion of figures in his proficient attempts to keep the books.

Sirs lay on both sides of the family, family crests on notable public buildings and sizable portions of the City of Westminster belonged in the purse strings, all lost to individuals bad and possibly unscrupulous dealings, but leaving the echo and scent of better times, each generation having their own viewpoint and crumbs to what was left.

The money might have gone, but the behaviour hadn't.

Though he, sister and brother were born of the same pod,

the views and behaviour of each were as different as calcium-based products, the divide increasing over the decades, however, Eric would always be treated as "the little brother". Assuredly, as children grow, they will gladly define their ages, with importance:

"I'm 8 and a three quarters and Timmy is only 7".

"I'm actually 7 and 2 months" Timmy would think.

Admittedly, the difference between a year and a half can be huge to pre-teens, especially girls and boys and if you're a pro-active parent, but by the time you're all in your 50's...

Their mother was dealing with her husband's possible demise, with, what seemed, great strength and fortitude, something never seen before and somewhat disarming.

She calmly organised her grown children, asking them for unified cooperation and realistic setting tasks for each, while her husband of 30 years lay in a possible terminal state.

Professional prognosis was less than good and each prepared for the curtain call. Tess in tears and turmoil, Dickie with adult thoughtful detachment, Cassie in quiet solitude, possibly performing her finest role, not knowing how else to really behave and Eric, not believing that the time was now, but persistently being told it was and there was nothing wrong with denial. But, no matter how he tried, it didn't feel like the right time to say goodbye.

Sitting by his father's side, alone with the machines, Eric talked.

"This is the first birthday of mine you've missed" he said, his hand resting on his dad's forearm, thinking how lucky he was to have had two present parents, unlike some of the kids he had gone to school with. That rare few who saw their only parent for maybe two weeks the whole year; who knows what complex issues would develop in those later lives.

He tried to talk more to his father, as he would in Roberts final days, but felt self-conscious and lacking ability, and besides, he was confident his dad was going to be okay, he was sure his time wasn't now.

Two days later, Robert took the first steps to recovery, signalling the future of how he and his wife would take hospitalised turns. Broken limbs, lung cancer, mysterious illnesses (probably drug or alcohol related), were just some of the reasons for the inductions to ward life; some would be treated as life threatening, only for Death to be cheated again and again, eventually, when being told of another grave ailment would sigh and roll his eyes.

It would be some months before Cassandra would take her turn in being administered to a ward, and with each turn, a step would be taken closer to the mortuary, never fully regaining the health they had before, the slow spiral down.

On one visit, Eric accompanied Robert, who, still not totally in tune since his coma, needed to verbally transcribe his experiences of being in his stoic state. He related the intense fires that burnt his skin, and the screams and torment he suffered, remembering the first thing he saw was, what he thought was, his watch, pinned to a nurse's bib and tried to claim it.

"Probably an excuse to try and cop a feel" thought Eric to himself.

They stood together, alone, in the lift to go up to the wards. The doors slowly shut and a hand pushed itself into the gap, causing the sliding shutters to reopen. Two orderlies and nurse wheeled a bed, complete with drip and patient into the now snug confines of the metal box. The prostrate, semiconscious male was of the same age and appearance to Eric's upright and unfamiliarly, nervous looking father, who was trapped by the side of the stranger's forearm.

The doors re-slid shut, trapping all in their journey, Robert looking down as the prone man reached out to touch his hand.

Robert dramatically flinched in sudden disgust and terror, a behaviour his son had never seen. This tall, no-nonsense Afrikaner, who had never shown a weakness (except for the bottle…and tobacco……and women) was afraid of decay.

This was a common factor in both husband and wife, each having the dislike of getting old and neither recognising when they had done so, sometimes with amusing results.

Cassie would regularly visit the hairdressers as part of her regime, insisting that she never dyed her hair, and the stylist only ever touched up her roots. As for Robert, at 80 he would attempt to put his fingers down a shop assistant's blouse for a better look and shout out at a bandaged patient that shared a ward.

"Look at that old bugger over there" pointing, not realising that the entire wing could hear him "looks like his wife gave him a going over, he looks in a bad way".

To which the lady sitting next to the assailed said.

"I'm not his wife. He had a fall" too quietly and not with enough conviction for Robert to take any notice of.

Eric had been fortunate on his personal record of infirmary visits, his illnesses mostly treatable at home or school sickbays, where he would rattle like a battleship because of the amount of various medication administered.

Only one did he recall actually staying in hospital, which was for the removal of his adenoids and tonsils, and while recovering from the anaesthetic, told his mother that he didn't like the lions.

"There's no lions here darling" she tried to soothe.

"Take the lions away, I don't like the lions" would reiterate, if he knew what the word was, "Take the lions away".

Cassandra eventually twigged. Eric had been placed in a cot type bed; bars raised to prevent falls. Bars, lines, lions.

The only other time in his young life that Eric experienced the pleasures of the medical system was for a tooth extraction.

He had suffered a catalogue of bad dentistry practices, now needing to be pre-tranquilised before treatment. The worst had been a visit to a Great Uncle whose hand shook, not steadied by the glass and bottle on his desk, who extracted a healthy tooth (forgetting to numb the area first) instead of applying a filling.

The next tooth removal would be done under gas at the local day clinic, who specialised in child mouth care.

Cassandra and her youngest arrived on foot, one reason because it was so close to home, the other to speed up Valium into his system.

They were led into a colourful waiting room, painted greens and blues, to look like the sea, full of painted fish, seahorses and octopuses and "very childish and rubbish painting" thought the six-year-old.

A nurse came in and talked to his mother as his spinny eyes played whirly games with the tangle of seaweeds and the familiar, comforting, dizzy numbness crept along his body.

"We're going to take you into the room now Eric to see the doctor, okay"? she said in a patronising way that Eric knew was patronising but didn't know the word for it yet.

"Stupid nurse" he thought, smiling happily.

The room was a room. Sparse with plain, pale-yellow walls and a black, raised, operating bed in the centre with the head tilted slightly up and large gas cylinders set behind.

"Here you go" said the stupid nurse, lifting him up to sit on the bed "just get you comfy".

Eric watched the grown-ups wandering around on their business as stupid nurse said:

"I'm going to pop this mask on you, it'll cover your nose and mouth for the gas, and then we'll lie you down".

As she placed the triangular plastic over his face she added "Don't speak when the gas comes on, just breathe deeply, we don't want you swallowing any gas" with added smiles.

"Just lie you back" she said again, helping him into position.

Three large, hard rubber rings, the type a dog might like, had been taped together and served as a head rest and were placed under the back of his head.

He felt like an astronaut. Mask on. Check. Helmet on. Check. Ooh, Gas on. Che..

"Do you like Andy Pandy"? came the interrupting voice.

"Uh" grunted the response.

The gas was cold and smelly and he didn't like the hissing noise, it was the same noise he heard when he would pass out.

"What do you like to watch on T.V"

"Uhuh uh" came the reply, not wanting to talk and swallow gas...LIKE HE HAD BEEN TOLD, he wanted to say.

"I said what do you like to watch on T.V"

"Cartoons" came the answer

"OOH, which ones"? still with the patronising tones.

Eric had to think and concentrate hard, short answers he thought, trying to comply with both directives.

After a sentence or two and more questioning he started to feel the rockets ignite. The rumbling increased and the ship shot into space, the pressure pushing his body down as the stars came into view.

"Wow" not for the first time "if this is what gas is like..."

He woke up a while later in another room and saw his mother sitting, reading a magazine, started to sit up and didn't stop vomiting for almost an hour.

"The nurse told you not to swallow any gas" she said.

LAPSANG OR DARJEELING

Andrew and Eric stood in the middle of the freezer section at the local Co-op supermarket. It was a quiet afternoon; the stores security guard was upstairs and Eric had been given his instructions.

And. was doing his weekly lift, a habit he had adopted as he disapproved of any company taking his hard-earned money and, besides, as far as he could see, if they didn't want it pinched then they shouldn't put it on the shelves.

The whole affair made Eric very uncomfortable. Stealing always had.

In pre-decimal days, when pennies were worth ought, he could buy a comic and some chocolate white mice for four pence and still possibly have a ha'penny change.

The comics need a whole mention of their own, too extensive and more worthy, too varied and colourful than I could possibly manage. Let's just say that Eric had a love and fascination for the small piles of paper, such as Buster (and Jet), Whizzer (and Chips), Topper, Shivers, Weird Tales, Astounding Stories, Marvel and D.C., Mad and eventually leading to the likes of Strip and Toxic, all the while being captivated with the likes of Crumb and Shelton, enjoying the kooky and intoxicating images and colours.

On times, when an interesting serialised story line reared, Eric would scour the local sellers, whether it be the train station kiosk, newsagents or paper stand, to find the continuing story, depending on the number of coins in his pocket.

Robert always kept his loose change in a leather tray, next to his side of the bed, on his cabinet with light. Rising early, long before others stirred on a Sunday morning, wanting to catch the only cartoon on television, The (dreadful) Tomfoolery Show, Eric would invisibly move across his sleeping parent's room (like The Vision), around to his father's side, and see how much treasure was available. Sometimes, if lucky, a collection of coinage lay recently strewn, and at other times maybe a crumpled note. Being careful, he always tried to be discreet in his selection, never taking the only coin of one type and never of high denomination, looking at the pile and its design was just as an important move for selection as anything else. Everything had to be taken into for consideration, even listening out for the breathing patterns of all (after all, he didn't need to breath as he was The Silver Surfer).

Once the haul had been secured, Eric would light footedly fly from the room (on his trusty board), down the stairs and out the door, in search for the pesky Bash Street Kids.

Depending on which shop he would call on today (unlikely visiting more than one due to limited finance and carrying purchases from one store to another unsettled the keepers, creating awkward conflicts), was decided upon which comic was needed and which route he wanted to take. Quickness, less public contact or sightseeing.

Today, he had his glove on him, so opted, as time permitted, the more public and longer route. The plan was thus. Glove would be worn on his right hand, no, left hand, just to confuse them more and it would look odd, wearing a righthanded glove on his left hand. "Even better". Thinking to himself "Hopefully, Charles (sounds like a good grownup name, or should it be Frank...hmm, stick with Charles for now). So, hopefully Charles will be asked "What happened to your hand" or "why are you wearing one glove" ...hmm...good". He continued in his thinking "then I can say "oh, I lost it in the war (it's a shame I don't have a sling as well). That'll really get them". He finished, satisfied with his plan. Unfortunately, no-one seemed to look, be bothered or ask, much to his disappointment, so fortified himself with the thought of next time he went out with Tess, he would make an extra elaborate attempt at his walk (perfecting a style in the manner of someone with extreme cerebral palsy).

Nearby one of the newsagents, a couple of doors down from the magical sweet shop, (with its counter filled with coloured sugar mice, babies wrapped in blankets, foil wrapped chocolates that looked like cars, ladybirds and spiders, bright swirled lollipops...and an endless amount of glass jars, all shapes and sizes filled with an assortment of drool inducing confection, as well as the latest gimmicks, like jumblees, pez and tictacs) stood the toy shop.

The large Lego pirate boat stood in the window by the door, surrounded by an assortment of other glorious possibilities to buy, just as exciting as the range next door.

Entering, polite greetings made, Erics eyes were always drawn to the shelves of models to build, rarely interested in the military range, unless odd or protype planes, but preferred instead the monsters of film with luminous parts.

He had a love for all things luminous. Stickers and putty were his favourite, hiding under his covers, entranced by the ghostly green light which he found comforting and reliable.

Lower down, under the boxes of tanks and figures were the shelves of novelties and new comers. A glut of potentials, each seeking tactile recognition "Play with me" and "No, play with me" could be heard.

Erics eyes landed on one particular box, something new, never before seen, something he loved drawing (even on the wall).

A box of rubber monsters. Oh, the delight, as he searched through the box. Each one could fit on the end of your finger, but each was a different size and different colour. Blue with yellow bug eyes and green tongue, another was orange with antennae for eyes and sharp red teeth, another...oh, the joy.

"Problem. No money. How much were they? 2D..."

Eric turned his head to see the shop owner busy with a customer, his hand went into his pocket. He turned and left with a smile, a bye and something he hadn't come in with.

The walk home was full of shoulder conversations. The left one telling him not to worry and it was no big deal, with the voice in his right ear berating his behaviour. By the time he arrived home, he confessed all to his mother who gave him two dence and told him to go back to the shop and pay for his deeds.

The shop bell rang and the he was greeted again with politeness and a professional greeting. Eric walked to the counter and produced the coins and stolen ware, explaining his actions and consequences.

He did not expect such a furious response, he had not expected any response, but was sent out, tail between his legs, only daring to return on occasions, behind his mother's coat tails.

The short, sharp, shock worked at deterring Eric in further thievery, so feeling ill at ease with his friend's exploits was understandable, though he had been given the task of look out, Andrew insisted the deep pockets of his trench-coat would come in handy.

An elderly pensioner walked by as Andrew was attempting to secrete four packets of frozen bacon down his trousers, as Eric, uselessly was looking the opposite direction.

"Honestly, what shocking behaviour" she said as she walked off.

Andrew hurried his selection, disgruntled with his friend's inexperience and incompetence.

Laughing at his mates' serious endeavours, Eric failed to notice the encroaching security guard, stealthily catching him in the act.

The words came emphatically clear and loud.

"Put that back".

With a nonchalant shrug all contents were ditched and scattered on the floor and despite the insistence from the officer that Andy should be escorted to the manager, he turned tail and ran, leaving Eric befuddled as to what his actions should be.

This behaviour had a familiar pattern.

The instance of when his motorbike was moved, whilst locked, during his visit to see the new film from John Carpenter, Halloween, leaving him to walk 6 miles home down dark country lanes. Not that he was particularly spooked, it was more of an inconvenience (he found it later the following day...a "friend" told him where it was), walking down an enclosed by trees lane, at midnight, with a moonless and cloudy sky...Close your eyes, walk around where you are for 5 minutes (you might look a bit silly if on a plane or train), it's a lot quicker with your eyes open, isn't it, miss calculating the curve in a road can prove prickly.

Another instance was when Eric's motorbike was actually stolen, for real...by another "friend".

They had been working together for a number of months in a pizza restaurant, a popular and busy bistro for local office workers at lunchtimes, split levels supplying different needs.

The manager was an agreeable chap, allowing Eric to take in mix tapes of his making, something he relished compiling, as long as nothing too heavy or gratuitous was played. Regrettably, some of his favourite vinyl had suffered from exuberant behaviour, such as dancing on tables or slam dancing, which resulted in a sticking point caused by a minor scratch. This didn't deter the recording however, knowing where the glitch might be, Eric would poise himself over the rotating disc, waiting for the "yeh mun (tick), yeh mun (tick), yeh mun (tick), only for kicks...

The amusing part would come when playing back at lunchtime and a helpful customer would point out that the record was sticking sometimes, only to leave them confused when told that it was a tape.

Erics workmate, we'll call him Knobby, occasionally borrowed Milo's (reluctantly, apparently, they had been acquaintances for a couple of years) dirt bike, to visit his (Knobs, not Milos) sister, who lived the other side of town.

During one of their shifts Knob approached Eric, who was busy prepping jacket potatoes.

"Hey Eric, can I borrow your bike tonight" the knob asked "my sisters having problems with one of her tenants and I've got to go and sort them out" ...being a body builder and martial arts expert.

Being the first time, the knob had asked him, Eric was reluctant.

"Not really sure, I don't like lending my bike" Eric honestly replied.

"I'll only be gone a couple of hours. I'll definitely be back by 8".

Eric thought. Knob had known Milo for a while, seemed trustworthy and had borrowed Milos bike a number of times. Besides, he was working with the band tonight so wouldn't be using it.

"Okay," said Eric "just drop the keys through the door when finished, I'm gigging tonight".

"Great, thanks" he said, taking the keys.

Fast forward to 3 in the morning when Eric got home to find no bike or keys. Concerned and annoyed he figured some good reason must have occurred and half-heartedly went to bed, knowing he would see Knob in a few hours at work.

Bleary eyed, despite the doughnuts and coffee, sometimes they just don't work, Eric stepped through the door to work to be met by a commotion.

Ohan, a fellow worker, a 6-foot 6 muscle bound 21 year old from Turkey was smiling, like he always did (especially after eating 3 pizzas) and said "The place was robbed last night" grinning even more "Knobby took wine, till trays and the safe contents". His smile really couldn't get any bigger as he casually leaned against the wall...or was the wall leaning against him?

"How do you know Knobby did it"? Eric puzzled.

"No forced entry and he had the only other set of keys. They've (the manager and police) already been to where he lives. Landlady says he's stolen her cutlery and owes her 2 months' rent. Ha" ...still, smiling.

Eric felt his knees weaken; he felt a bit pale.

"I leant him my bike" he said wistfully.

"Ha. Last you'll see of that" Ohan said, cheerily, heading back to the kitchen. Afterall, it had been 10 minutes since he last ate.

"Shit".

Eric walked down to the police station, he couldn't ride, to report the additional theft. On entering, he was met by a very abrupt desk sergeant.

"What do you want"? came the query, making Eric unsure if he had done anything wrong.

"I've come to report a theft" he said, genuinely perturbed.

"No, you're not" came the reply.

Confused, Eric stupidly said "Yes I am, my friends stolen my bike" feeling like he sounded like a school kid.

"Look, Sonny" said complete with sneer and venom. "You're not coming in here to report anything...dressed like that" pointing hard to Erics chest.

The penny dropped. He tried to explain that it was a religious symbol of peace, the Buddhists use it, and besides Sidney wore it, it didn't mean that...

"Fuck off and don't come back until you've changed". Came the demand.

It would be three years until Eric got his insurance pay out for his bike and he never wore his swastika t-shirt again...it was stolen...by a "friend".

Friends helped Eric lose many things. One time, when letting a friend crash between accommodation, a couple of days turned to a couple of weeks. Having not seen them due to work, he popped his head into the bedroom to touch base, only to find six other people smashed out of their skulls on gear and had been so for days. He wondered where things were disappearing to.

Sometimes he lost more than possessions.

Being young and impetuous, Eric jumped from job to job, trying to find his footing, but more importantly, trying to make a living while committing himself to the blossoming music career, which he felt dedicated towards.

The varying stints would lead him to cross paths with many a varied person, sometimes finding links to people he already knew. One such person was Matt (a different one from before, though those ones were after...). Matt (do we call him #1, being the first in chronological order, or #3 as in reading order...I'll leave it to you), worked in a record shop that Eric had recently been employed in and found that they both socialised, at different times, with the same circle of friends, so received an invite to an afternoon session that was occurring at the weekend at his pad.

Matt's pad was actually a glorified bedsit attached to his wealthy parent's house, who had little to do with their son, and smoking soirees of different sizes were a fixture on some people's calendar.

Eric arrived, not knowing what to expect and was surprisedly greeted by Elle, Andy's girlfriend, with her usual mischievous smile and warm hugs. She led Eric around the back to where he found at least 10 people crammed into a tastefully decorated bedroom, with 60's Americana rock blasting from the speakers and pungent smoke in the air and professional disco lights mixing it up.

Eric waved to the familiar faces and gave a smile and nod to the unknown ones, all of which was reciprocated. Settling down on some spare cushions, of which there were many, he produced his doings and started to roll. Before he had finished, someone had already passed him a joint, which he toked a couple of hits from and passed it on, never wanting to be accused of bogarting (keeping it for yourself, he had been brought up with good drug manners after all).

The room continued to fill with music and a green tinted cloud, even though the number of bodies decreased. The afternoon wore on and as usual, no sooner had one spliff had finished, Eric felt like another, and another. The music started varying more, not always to his taste, until Matt passed over the next record. Eric couldn't believe his eyes. The colourful album cover was undoubtedly the work of Robert Crumb, an adult cartoonist extraordinaire from his childhood, ones he wasn't allowed to read. Cheap Thrills was the title, with Big Brother (and the holding company written beside). It all clicked in place for him. Cheap Thrills is what he searched for, missing out on reality. Big Brother, from George Orwell, a book he had just finished, everything coming from the past, the answers had always been there, needing to be found. The room started to move slowly. Janis started to sing. Eric started to feel very hot and suffocated. He smoked some more, unsure of where the spin was taking him, the ball and chain being sung about hung heavy on his neck, pulling him down, he tried to stand but the floor slipped onto the wall, so he crawled carefully to the bathroom nearby, resting occasionally in the swirl of sound and feeling different textures as he went.

He made it into the cool, oh, that's nice, clean, bright, so bright, bathroom and managed to climb on the toilet. Sitting in an upright...ish position, slumping against the cistern, Ah, that's better. A small sink was at his side so splashed some water over his face and arms, ah, nice he said.

He breathed in deeply his new environment and was at a new peace.

He gently closed his eyes.

Suddenly.Knock. Knock.

"You alright in there Eric" came the familiar voice of Elle.

"Yeah fine," replied Eric, "just needed the loo".

"Well, other people need it too".

"Well, yeah," thought Eric "it's not like I'm going to be long".

He stood and splashed a bit more water on his face and opened the door.

"That's odd" he thought, looking.

"Where's everyone gone" he asked Elle.

Noticing that almost everyone had suddenly disappeared, music stopped, windows opened and aired, wondering what drama he suddenly missed.

"They went home ages ago," said Matt.

Eric obviously looked confused.

"You've been in there for over an hour" Elle said laughing.

"What? No?"

"Yeah, everyone went ages ago".

Eric felt he really should do something about all this time he kept losing. So, he went home to have another smoke to help him think.

SICK

Eric couldn't decide which was making him feel worse, the ear infection or bronchitis. One aggravated the other. Sitting up in bed in Sick Bay, the room used for poorly waifs at boarding school, he vaguely watched Open University (the television set only being allowed on for one hour in the morning and one hour in the afternoon), not understanding it all, but becoming absorbed in the comforting tones and the reassuring neutrality. He especially enjoyed the lecturers who were excited or fully immersed in their subject, their infectiousness grasping the viewers attention, despite how ill he felt.

Matron had already done her rounds, issuing medications and instructions in equal measure, so Eric was left alone, no other occupying the other 3 beds, in the plain white room, window too far to see out of, with a pile of homework for added companionship.

He yearned for a comic or jigsaw puzzle, more for emotional support than actuality, but he wasn't at home now, nor would he be for some time, he had given up counting the days, as some others did, and tried instead to occupy himself with distractions. Regrettably, these ventures usually attracted the unwanted attention of either a teacher or a school bully. A real lose/lose scenario.

He recalled how, before the recent snow, out in the nearby woods, a tree had partially uprooted, making it lean, propped up only by trees around it. An excitable queue of kids would form at the tilting tree, waiting to take turns, with the main despot issuing orders and guidelines, sometimes demanding sweets, but always dictating who can or can't have a go. If some outspoken child refused to be dominated then the consequences could be swift and accurate.

Normally, cohorts would be nearby, waiting for crumbs to be dropped by their master or to do their bidding, and for the disobeying, the made-up rules could be brutish. Tear inducing headlocks, dead legs galore, punches were the favourite, with hangings and body slams (being picked up and thrown to the floor, normally by two assailants and on your back) being left to the more opinionated or smaller targets.

Once you had manoeuvred the gauntlet of the line, the next trial begun. The Leap.

This was split into sections. Firstly, you had to complete the climb of the damaged tree, not an easy task for the smaller child, but fun in itself. It was important to get as high as possible in your climb, not because of what you were attempting, but so as not to get rebuke from your piers or the wolves who circled below.

Achieving optimal height, the sway of the tree could now be felt in the light breeze, its roots wanting to give way fully, only supported by its close-knit colleagues. Eyeing the gap carefully, assessing the distance from tree to tree, branch to branch, heart pounding loudly as calculations for swaying and foot slippage was taken into account. The trunk of the adjacent plant seemed too far to grab onto, but a fall was more preferable than facing the group below with retreat.

"JUMP. JUMP. JUMP" came the chanting shouts from below.

The gibbon swung, jumped and clasped the new friend the other side.

The exercise was however far from over for the performer, though the crowd had moved on to the following possible sacrifice.

Next was the task of descent. Manoeuvring down the upright tree was no easy task as various branches and limbs had been damaged and were now missing, leaving the hapless doer to cling tightly to the bough and attempt to slide down the bumpy surface, scraping arms, legs and face in the process. The most unconsidered part, despite seeing previous victims, the last eight-to-ten-foot drop. Weary from the downward progress most youngsters would just drop, like surprised bricks from a tree, hitting the ground with gentle thuds and, if you looked carefully, bounces.

Minor injuries, cuts and bruising aside, rarely were anyone hurt, more pride damage from laughter of the onlookers than anything else.

The snow fall had cut short climbing activities, replaced with snowball fights and igloo and snowman building, always keeping a watchful eye on bored human trolls, mentally dragging their knuckles while looking for the next target to alleviate pent up angst.

Today was Erics turn.

The pack of juniors rolled and played in the fresh fall of water ice, like young otters enjoying their first taste of freedom, while some flakes, still wafting gently about, looked for suitable landing spots. Eric had dropped his guard, having been distracted by a handful of snow shoved into his face, when the punch came swinging out of the blue cold air and contacted squarely with the side of his head, the blinding black and white light lit up his brain on one side as hit head hit the soft (though not as soft as it should be) ground on the other.

His assailant jumped onto his prey and proceeded to ensure that all visible orifices and clothing were fully filled with clumps of whatever was at hand. A few hefty kicks finished off the ordeal, just for good measure, as Eric remembered winning a fruit cake at this exact point in the playing field only a year ago.

Sated in his glory, Blubber strode off to look for his group of passing friends, eager to retell his exploits, unaware and uncaring of how his actions would not only affect his goal but also of the witnesses.

E.N.T was a weakness for Eric, always coming at an unhelpful or inopportune time.

Great Aunt Janes death came days after the birth of his youngest child, which had been an outstandingly long 9 months pregnancy.

The night was dark. The sparse streetlights in the village themselves giving little light to the distant windows that lay about, with residents, bar one, sound asleep in their imaginary worlds.

Anne knelt beside her husband's side of the bed, hand softly shaking his arm.

"Darling…, Eric…" came the quiet words, but with a hint of concern.

Eric stirred, though was instantly awakened by the unusualness of the events.

"Are you okay" he said, noticing the paleness of his wife even in the darkness.

"I'm not feeling too good" came the reply and as if the last effort had been spent, collapsed, unconscious on the floor, sadly not for the last time.

Eric, wide awake, motor running, grabbed the phone and called the emergency services, making his wife as comfortable as possible and trying not to disturb the sleeping children.

With the bedside light on, he could now see the blueness of her lips and hear the shallowness of her breathing. The slow uneasy thud of her heartbeat was no match for his own.

Despite the distance for the crew to travel, the wait time was impressive and soon enough questions were answered, pressures checked and patient dispatched to hospital for immediate attention, where they discovered internal bleeding and issued a 50/50 nights survival.

The following days of hospital stay was filled with an operation to stop the bleed and an abundance of tests. They were given the news. Anne had been pregnant but had lost the baby, commonly called an ectopic pregnancy, the rupture had been severe. Stunned by the 5 second sentence, the complexity of being blessed with the opportunity of giving life, only to have it taken in an instant was beyond words. Happiness to sadness, relief to grief all in a single breath.

Anne was sent home, needing to report for more tests to check on her progress and ensure healing was going well.

The rollercoaster was along ride, spectators, few, time moved, but normality was not yet in reach.

Returning for her run of examinations, needles and samples everything seemed to be going in the right direction except for the hormone levels. They didn't want to correct themselves. Days passed with worries, more tests, backwards and forwards to the department. Until one day.

"Well Anne, Eric…what can I say," said the doctor.

They looked at each other quizzically, not wanting bad news… it didn't sound like bad news.

"You're still pregnant."

(the sounds of chins hitting floor)

"It seems as if you were going to have twins. One ruptured and the other...well, seems to be carrying on". he said with a smile.

As you can imagine, it was a long 8 months.

Even up until the night of the birth it was eventful.

Their little car broke down about five times on the drive to hospital at 2 in the morning. All the time, Eric checking on Anne and keeping an eye out for houses with lights on...just in case.

For Eric, the delivery was relatively quick, but the hidden stress of the months, the hiss of the gas (and the need for the toilet) was almost too much for Erics body to handle...there was a definite sparkle of black lights and the weakening of the knees as his youngest daughter came into the world x

He was no stranger to passing out. The kick in the head playing rugby, being pushed over in the playground or hit with a climbing frame knotted rope had all had the same thud sound, just before blacking out. But the ones that were annoying, were the ones that crept up on him slowly.

Over time Eric learnt how to deal with the intrusion, though sometimes they got the better of him.

Sitting at the hexagonal school desk, listening to their Divinity teacher fantasise about Mrs Barrett's (a short, hairy bespectacled elderly teacher) "pendulous breasts", while introducing the class to Derek and Clive, the lads were seeing who could "stab between the fingers" quickest. No knife available, sharpened pencils would do the trick and Eric was doing quite well, much to the annoyance to his mate Dave. So much so, as a joke, Dave snatched the pencil and stabbed Eric in the hand. Being a pencil, the lead snapped of and lodged under the skin and immediately the whishing sound started.

His head sank to the table as the ringing got louder and the beads of cold sweat covered his hot face.

"Sir" said Pete, hand raised "I don't think Erics feeling well, Sir"

Mr Powell strode over and inspected the situation.

"Hmm" he said jovially "you boys better take him to see Sister" sounding like he was relishing the event, perhaps Mrs Barrett was still on his mind.

Peter and Dave helped Eric to stand and started to drag him out of the class.

"Don't walk so fast" came the murmur.

"You're not walking" came the reply.

The incident of being "glassed", smashed in the face with a handled pint glass for bumping into someone or dislocating his shoulder and breaking his thumb, didn't go the full distance of unconsciousness, but almost. Whereas the day operation on his mouth was a surprise, even to him.

With local anaesthesia applied, the operation started well. No nerves were had on the lovely sunny day and the operating chair was comfortable, with surroundings fresh and clear.

So relaxed was he feeling that torpor was creeping in, when suddenly the familiar tingling sounded in his ears, getting louder, washing over him like shingles on a beach. Before he went down he was slightly aware of concern, replaced by activity and his name being called. Then he was gone.

The blackness was fine, in fact quite comfortable.

"Eric. Eric. Can you hear me"? said a voice, loud and clear.

He thought for a while in his own little world. Hear? Yes, I can hear. Seemed like, odd...words.

"Mr Strong. Can you hear me"?

Hmm...it was cool and dark where he was, everything felt fine thanks.

"Eric, you're perfectly safe. You're in hospital"

His eyes flicked open immediately.

What the hell was he doing in hospital? Had he had a car crash or something?

The nurse handed him a small square tablet.

"Pop this under your tongue, let it dissolve. Its glucose" she said, with Eric still unsure what was going on.

His lip was very numb, he thought, and the tablet fell out on first try.

"Hello Mr Strong" said a voice "you're back with us then" said the amused doctor "do you pass out often"?

Eric smiled back and proceeded to explain how his body liked to misbehave sometimes without consulting him first.

It was similar to when poisoning was around.

Many people use the excuse of eating something dodgy the day before to get off work, but when food poisoning kicks in... you can kiss your ass (not literally of course, especially during these extreme conditions) goodbye for a week.

Having eaten a warm corned beef sandwich on the National Express, Eric certainly enjoyed the pleasures of voiding his body, from both major orifices, at the same time for the first few days, amazed at how much could still be in there.

Though there are, obviously, other types of poisoning, one such... acid.

Eric had imbibed some LSD from a dodgy source, that had proved flat, so went to visit his sister, Tess whose old friend from their Oxford days was visiting.

A spread of vegetarian food lay on the table, mainly hot and spicy curries of various descriptions, tomato and onion salad, cheeses, bean dishes...an array of non-alkali sustenance.

By the time the meal was finished, glugging down a glass of orange juice, the negative effects of the bad lysergic was crawling its way through Erics body.

Excusing himself, he went upstairs to the bathroom to was wash the sweat away, only to reveal the shakes that wanted to come out to play.

Staggering to the top of the stairs, he fell into the spare bedroom and landed on the small mattress groaning.

The impact was sudden. The pain jolted through his entirety, which decided to convulse his limbs at random, no position alleviating the discomfort he was experiencing.

How long he had been there writhing in agony and hot and cold sweat he was not sure, but the doctor was attempting to take his pulse, with Cassandra standing in the background.

He always did like the song "Fool on the Hill" by the Beatles, now he knew why.

COME OUT, COME OUT

He couldn't decide which to play.

"Hmm" Eric pondered, tapping his chin.

"Hmm, which to play" he thought, looking down at the two boxes.

"Flounders or Magnetic Fish"?

Sitting on his blue and red tiger pouffe he looked down before him trying to decide which he wanted to play.

"Have you decided yet" called over Cassandra from the small open plan kitchen.

"I can't decide. Which would you like to play"? asked her son.

"Oh, I haven't got time to play I'm afraid" she said, hearing a small sigh in return.

Eric concentrated, thinking of his choices, but also playing through a game of Flounders on his own…it didn't quite work. All that dice throwing and you really needed at least two people to make it exciting.

"I guess I'll play fishing" he half dejectedly said, hoping his manner might persuade his mum to join in.

"Okay, you carry on darling" she replied.

Eric started setting up the underwater scenery frame and dropped the coloured plastic fish into the square, all the while pondering which rod, he was going to use.

"Blue" he unquestionably agreed upon. It was always blue.

He led down, head resting on the floor so not to be able to see where his targets lay and dangled his rod, with magnet attached, for the littles fishies to click onto. He liked games, but did prefer to play with someone else rather than on his own.

His love for games was equalled for his love for practical jokes. Whoopee cushions, fake chewing gum and the fake nail through the finger were all good main stays, but enjoyed plastic flies, ping pong eyes and guillotines more. The more sophisticated the better. Jumping out from behind doors was a great routine, never failing, learning that timing was everything, but playing dead (unconscious) was also a fantastic ruse, but one that people didn't react so favourably towards.

He rarely was without some trick or two in his pocket (as long as it wasn't filled with rhubarb crumble) having an affection for chattering teeth (that got confiscated at a school church service) and googly eyes on springs (which were a turning point in his escapades).

Having moved to the expanses of the countryside and all the ooh-ahhs it had to offer, fuelled his once inhibited exploits.

As a trial, the local comprehensive was offering an O'Level in Photography, but it was soon highjacked by the new movement of punk influenced youth who instead of wanting to learn about the formalities and structure, decided to push the practical uses of being given a cine camera, now all common place.

They revelled filming pranks on unsuspecting victims, making short idiotic films and producing general mayhem with the patience of the headmaster being sorely tested.

Most had been reared on Candid Camera, a popular 60s hidden camera show, and doses of Milligan, The Goodies and Python and now, with the help of anarchy in their blood, it was their turn.

Eric enjoyed being one of the instigators of the plans, having had years of unbridled restraint, plans a many stored, and brought back memories of a little boy hiding in a cupboard waiting for the ultimate moment to jump out on his unsuspecting prey, sometimes wanting to stay hidden longer, but the need to go to the loo being increased by the suspense.

He realised his true talent in his mid-teens at Halloween.

The peaceful, unaware Dorset village had plenty of good hiding places to jump out of, but Eric decided a more reserved approach could be called for.

The village had a small population, so waiting behind shrub on the upper bank of their front garden, that overlooked the only road, he was going to have to be patient.

An elderly farmer, wellies clopping as he went, came walking down the road, off to his nightly session at the local.

Eric shook the shrub subtly and gave a low growl...trying not to laugh.

The farmer poised momentarily and looked.

Eric growled lowly again.

"Fuck off, you twat". Came the farmers answer as he strode off...Eric thought with a little quicker pace.

Not bad. Must try harder...as all his school reports read.

Silence and waiting resumed.

Payoff.

Down the small country road, out of the darkness, into the light of one of the three streetlights in the whole village, Eric spied Mrs Tate walking with her six-year-old daughter.

His heart kicked into gear immediately, with that old familiar feeling of needing a wee. This was going to be a good one.

Scenarios of how to deal with this one flashed through his mind, like a shuffling machine, sorting for the best possible set of circumstances.

Before they got to close, he emitted a low growl and rustle, just to set scene, just faint enough for them to hear.

They stopped.

"Mummy, what's that noise"

"Probably, nothing dear" in a broad Dorset accent, listening to what sounded like soft, heavy breathing coming from somewhere.

They moved on with definite trepidation, mother scanning the dim darkness, daughter now firmly in hand.

Eric eased his breathing, reeling them in...

Wait......wait.........

The mother and daughter were almost in line with his bush when Eric screamed a yell as loud as he could. A blood curdling mix of snarl and pain.

How high off the ground the ladies leapt he could only marvel at, but their scream echoed his as the fled off into the night.

He smiled, broadly. That was a good one. He thought triumphantly.

Not realising how his actions might be having unwanted implications, he carried on the years coming up with new schemes, until decades later, the penny would drop.

Still at school, another idea grew and blossomed.

Their drama teacher, who shall be made nameless, not that we're using real names as it is, agreed upon an experiment of social reaction within his younger class of pupils.

The small group if Year 6's, 5 in total, would disguise themselves with padding, balaclavas and stockings (for over the head, we're not at public school now), and burst into the drama lesson and pretend to be bank robbers.

Armed with artificial guns and setting off some rook scarers before entering, the band of desperados burst in on the unsuspecting class, shouting orders to lie face down and tied up the teacher (giving him a gentle kicking for good measure), just, by good fortune, a police car with sirens blaring went past.

A couple of kids were immediately distraught, so were taken to the attached foyer, away from prying eyes, an explained what was really happening, with the responses of:

"Ah, we knew it was you all along" and such like.

The event lasted a full half hour until the final reveal, and was hailed as great success and more enjoyable than the usual type of lesson.

However.

The fan got rather splattered.

The following day, the teacher, who shall not be named, received innumerable complaints from concerned and annoyed parents, calling for apologies and resignation, something he skirted by the skin of his teeth. Apparently, some children had wet themselves with stress and others had a sleepless night.

Eric and his mates all thought it had been rather good.

The more routine japes would be driving around Bournemouth years later in the front seat of Bettys home-made car, disguised as a dummy looking like a werewolf, only to surprise people crossing at traffic lights or hiding under a tarpaulin in the little open topped car with hand puppets of Mickey Mouse and Donald Duck...doing things.

Another successful rouse only came into being on the pivotal success of getting a letter printed in the girl's magazine/comic Jackie.

Being a roadie left a lot of time on your hands. Normally sleeping in the back of the van on top of the sound equipment was one way of dealing with a couple of spare hours as the band partied with celebs, besides, someone had to look after the kit.

Eric only attended a couple of the after-gig doo's and frankly found them pretty tame and boring, mainly people pretending too much. Not the type of climate you want to be taking drugs in.

So, lying on a stack of speakers, trying to find the right position, his mind would bounce around new ideas.

An inkling came and the next day, having a communal smoke with his house sharer, the plan developed.

The lead singer, of the main band he worked for, had a brother (the drummer) and girlfriend.

They shared a house and that house was also the recording studio.

Girlfriend read Jackie.

When finished, drummer read Jackie.

Drummer LOVED problem page.

Drummer FANTASISED about teenage groupies.

So, with great dexterity a letter was penned to Cathy and Claire about two girls, Tracy and Sharon, who LOVED the drummer of a local band.

Amazingly the letter was printed and advice given. The girls should stop being so shy and go and tell the drummer how they feel.

As luck would have it, the band was playing in town the weekend of the published letter and our dear drummer man was... excited is an understatement.

"Now Eric, you understand," he said "if any girls come up to you and say they're Sharon or Tracy, you bring them to me. Understand".

"Der".

The band played a great gig and afterwards, when Eric was packing the gear away...

"No girls then? They didn't show" as drum boy.

"What? Girls"? replied the nonchalant roadie "Oh, yeah, there were a couple of girls, but they said they were too embarrassed".

"WHAT? Where are they? Why didn't you tell me"? came the incredulous torrent.

"Sorry, I was busy".

Eric found it really hard not to give the game away, but they were saving that for another day.

The googly eyes on springs were worn with a small plastic moustache in Maths class, much to the annoyance of the teacher, who, wearing glasses herself, took it as a slight, despite the insistence that Eric needed spectacles himself for long distances,

They were confiscated and secured in her small office, with the instructions that they were only to be returned at the end of term.

Upset by his loss, Eric consoled himself with the small brown mouse (not a real one) he kept in his pocket.

That evening, after prep (enforced homework) Gary, a boy from his maths class came rushing up to him.

"Hey Hunter (no kid at boarding school gets called by his first name), here's your glasses" he said in a puff.

Surprised at receiving the gift so soon Gary added.

"Miss said to give them back to you" and dashed off, obviously in a hurry for something.

The following day, another Maths lesson and to show how stupid he could be was wearing his boingy eyes when teach walked in.

Visibly shaking the shout burst out

"Where did you get those glasses from"?

The pin was heard dropping.

"Go and explain yourself to the headmaster this instant".

The squeak of the chair sounded embarrassed at breaking the atmosphere in the class. Now Eric was trembling too.

It was a long walk to the study and he took a seat by the closed door after knocking and hearing no response.

The door eventually creaked open with the instruction "IN".

The Head seated himself behind his large oak desk as the 12-year-old Eric stood the other side. Hands behind back.

"Well, boy"? he really didn't mince his words.

Eric briefly explained the events, omitting key information, like, names, but it certainly wasn't him who had broken into the locked office and removed various items. Though he did wonder what else had been taken…he'd have to find out later… he was very interested.

"Well, boy, what are we going to do"? said the Head rising from his seat, picking up his swishing stick.

Eric knew full well what he was going to do. Regardless of guilt or innocence. 6 strikes later he was dismissed and glad he was wearing his trousers.

And by the way, he was made to apologise for his behaviour that Halloween.

THE JOURNEY

The knight knelt in the throne room awaiting the presence of his queen having completed his tasks that had been set before him. He was weary, bloodied and filled with demons from the deeds of past and the multitude of ventures he had performed for his highness, though gratitude not came from those tender hands he sought. He wished only to break the spell that she was under and free them both of the evil that lay within the protected caves, though anger and violence, as to care and patience, were no match for the witch's power. So, hoping to prove his worth, he carried the burdens that were put upon him, knowing not where the answer lay, for it was hidden deep.

All he sought was to be clean again. Fresh and hopeful. Unburdened of guilt and the weight of the armour he had to wear to protect himself from dragons and use as an excuse for the lack of the ladie's touch.

And so, he knelt, hoping that perhaps, this time, the curse had been lifted.

Descending the stairs, with muted dignity and innocence of her crimes trailing behind her like a gown of broken gems, the fragility of the knight's bones splintered in his mind, cracking and braking, all barriers failing, as he lunged in a possessed frenzy at the imaginary creature that stood before him, wishing to extract vengeance for the multiple scars that lay upon him, even though many were from times of old.

Harm inflicted, the courtiers pulled him from his clasp and dragged the stunned man who lay inside his once shining chainmail to the waiting dungeons, leaving his love behind, more damaged and retreated than before, consoling herself and children of the wounds that lay unfathomable.

No light shone through the narrow slit of his cell, save the flickering of a burning torch, casting its eerie shadows, jumping too and hither, mockingly dancing on wall and floor, not realising that they were as trapped as he. Despair clutched at his very being, for as he had lifted his hands in anger that final time, it was as if he were striking at his own very soul, though another had been harmed, and fought in a tumbling spiral the eternal fight of good conquesting evil, leaving him void and clear, vanquishing his past conducts, though now endangering his future.

Coldness gripped his form, no escape could there be and the shouts and screams of fellow captors echoed round the chambers.

The queen sat on her throne, still shaken by her ordeal, servants tending to her wounds, while she could still not fathom why the reasons for her gallants actions had unfolded, confusion lay all around, and fear lay in behind, laughing at her frailty and ridiculing her every move, controlling her actions and thoughts, just as they had done so for countless years, ever since the spells had been cast.

She had been a fair maiden, happy in her own world of books where she hid from the rejection of parental love and care and the strict guidelines of conformity set out by the priests, who tried to force her into an unachievable icon, doomed from the onset, when nurturing was all that was required.

The dark cloud grew within, covering the nature of her conflict and becoming a force of its own, separating her selves from each other, causing disagreement and conflict that she desperately tried to flee from, only for the monster to pursue her at each turn, easily following the scent of decay.

The Lady fled from land to land, many lords attempting to take her hand, yet none succeeding in holding on for many a length of time, save the first, whose actions, cruelty and love combined, struck hard at the very heart of the maiden, and that the cut, inflicted with poison, failed to heal properly, leaving an open sore to be infected once and once again, nourishment for the creature within.

Time passed for all in the kingdom and the knight was exiled for his acts, so roamed he the lands, seeking out, instead of fair ladies to be saved, for which there had been many, and ventures to be had, seeking instead answers for his crimes and reasons for the manner in which he acted.

Over hill and over dale he searched, his path leading back to his family fold, though there he found no solace or rest, for his parents were now with age, mother succumbed by her own torments and father in the early clutches of madness.

Not able to contain his distress, he fled, determined to end the suffering afflicted on all, only to be halted by his father's speed.

"Son" he said "Where do you fly so fast and where do you go, so to as assail our love and care for you"?

"Father" saith the knight "I cannot stay in this world with the pain on all. I cannot bear this final task".

"My son, you can endure much. More than you know. Your life is not yours to take, it belongs to God above and he wants you to overcome your trials and tribulations, as did his son".

The simple words struck true to the knight and he spent many hours meditating and praying for guidance and forgiveness, which was answered by a storm of unparalleled animosity in the quietest moment of the night.

The days past as the flowers withered under the coldness of the season, as the path delivered him back again to the land he was once banished from.

The path lay clear to the castle cited through the cobbled streets, resting solely in the middle of the citadel, soldiers standing, turning their backs as he stepped up the stairs to centre court.

No longer wearing his dented armour, nor no longer needing its protection, he felt exposed though reassured without the bulky steel.

He knelt again before the throne and waited...

FRACTURES

Now Mum had died, Robert's dementia came evident for all to see, having been covered up by his wife, either not realised or acted upon, though excused, for at least a few years.

Cassandras habit over hoarding medication and hiding bills (both found in every draw and under every surface) became evident, as Tess took over the unwanted role of her mother, creating even more friction than before between father and daughter. Robert being an independent type (not able to make himself a cup of tea and sandwich, choosing instead whisky and wine and packet of fags) and Tess being the controlling type (though unable to limit her alcohol intake or have an organised house).

Resentments lay deep in Tess, the screaming torrent hindering her daily life, with memories of sexual inappropriateness instigated by her father and possibly mother, climaxing in the almost abuse of her own daughter committed by the figure who should have been the archetypal protector.

The duties of their father's care were split in the usual manner and style between the three siblings. Dickie taking control of the Power of Attorney, as he lived "too far away to be of practical use and was always busy with work", though never liked to dwell on the subject of illness and his ailing partner, remaining a private character at most times.

Tess elected herself as Roberts main daily carer, despite having three visits a day from an external service, even though she was advised against from professionals and family alike, but the handiness of a washing machine, extra money and a free supply of booze was too hard to refuse.

Eric was left with the bits in the middle. He would eventually be left with the weekly shop, general repairs and social visits, though living an hour drive away, with a low income and unreliable transport proved testing at times.

Tess resented both her brothers lack of involvement, which she took personally and often vented her frustration in an aggressive manner towards any male in the vicinity, innocent or not, one time calling Eric a "sexist twat", for not agreeing with a decision and refusing to talk to him for two weeks.

But they muddled on.

Roberts virtually constant chest infections were encouraged by his eating in bed and coughing, sending bits of food into his lungs, which he only had one and a half of, since losing some to cancer some years before.

The diabetes didn't help either, though it was a lot better than before, in fact, virtually non-existent, due to his huge increase in scotch, almost burning it out entirely, stunning the doctor into silence.

Robert was quite happy in his own way.

He decided he was going to buy a car, having had his confiscated by the police at the same time his licence was revoked, and visit all his old haunts and possibly a trip to South Africa. Unfortunately, he could seldom make it to the bathroom to urinate, let alone get out the front door. A 3-hour session in the bath was quite a norm. refusing to budge, waiting for the water to reheat.

When he first lost the car, a mobility scooter was a compromise. Not much of one, true, but he accepted that rather than a Zimmer frame and it gave him a bit of freedom...

Robert decided, "Shop or pub"? so off he went.

He hadn't bothered changing his trousers, "...pyjamas will

do and besides, slippers are much more comfortable..." he thought as he weaved down the pavement on his scooter, bumping into the occasional car "...really must get this steering fixed..." almost toppling sideways on the edge of a kerb, only to be saved by some builders chatting, admiring their mornings work.

He paused briefly to cross the road and carried on regardless of the horns "...fucking drivers, why don't they look where they're going..." as he bumped up the other kerb by the local convenience store.

He stopped momentarily and drove in, clashing into the pile of neat baskets by the entrance "...only wanted one of those blasted things..."as he sped on down the narrow aisle and honking his horn. Fortunately, not many people were in the shop and luckily no other pensioner or slow on the uptake person, as he came to his first of two corners. He eyed it carefully, working out if he could take the double corner, effectively a U-turn, in one move, though instead, as his mind was working quick enough, ploughed into the ice-cream freezer with an almighty dong.

Shaken, not stirred (...have I told you dear reader of one of his earliest auditions?) he proceeded to back up, beeping as he went, still determined on a few extra bottles, went forward, backed up and so one for quite a few minutes, while shoppers and sales staff alike tried to assist, but were met with oblivious looks and utter determination.

Eventually, mission accomplished, Robert headed for the till, for that is where the real treasure lay and he could see that the girl had already selected his usual choices and was at this very moment bagging them up. He licked his lips and swallowed. Hopefully, he was thinking of the drink.

"That'll be £53.60, please" she said, smiling.

Robert looked at her for a moment, blanky, reaching out his hand.

He stopped then patted his dressing gown.

"Erm, I seem to have lost my wallet" he said.

"Oh, I see" she replied concerned.

"I'll take this now" he said "and I'll pay for it later" reaching out again for his prize.

"Sorry, you can't do that here" the young assistant said, looking a bit nervous and ringing her bell for assistance as the queue built.

"What do you mean "I can't do that here". I shop here all the time" emphasising the "here" with incredulity.

"Sorry" she said getting more nervous "but I can't let you just take your shopping without paying for it" (ring,ring,ring).

"You CAN. YOU just don't want to" he shouted wagging his finger.

"Hello Robert" said a voice, causing the scooter to go into reverse, running over somebody's toe. "...shouldn't stand so bloody close...".

Robert looked around and saw the store manager, she was a pleasant lady, he'd known her for years...he licked his lips again.

"Having problems"? she enquired.

"Seem to have lost my wallet. This (pointy, pointy) girl, won't let me have my shopping".

Whether it was good luck or not, Tess came in through the doors and noticed the commotion, her dad and instantly considered whether it would be possible to vanish into thin air. Instead...

"Hello Dad" she said tiredly, trying to smile at everyone at the same time instead of just scream "can I help"?

Tess paid for a quarter of the shop, enough to keep him going for the afternoon, but he did say "I'll be back later, for the rest" leaving the girl hoping she had finished her shift by then.

Eric would have loved to be able to visit more often, that was one of his reasons for moving back into the area as it was, though work and money was an issue, Robert was...a man who...

...happily, travelled 110 mph on the motorways, he knew his limit. Liked to smoke when and where he wanted, setting off fire alarms in hospitals because he had decided to smoke in the ward's toilets, regardless of being told how dangerous it was by oxygen cylinders. Gladly stood up to anyone, particularly what he viewed as fascist police. Refused, point blank, to be told "you have to" always replying "I don't have to do anything". And the list goes on.

Nicotine became an encapsulated example of all things Robert. With the ban of pleasuring yourself in public, know what I mean (nudge, nudge, wink, wink), with pubs, shops, taxis etc banning the exhalation of possible noxious fumes, don't worry about the factories that are predominantly responsible for the world's pollution and people's health or the production of heat and electricity that contributes to over 25% of greenhouse gas emissions, instead focus the public's attention on passive smoking and the dangers of the little white (or brown) stick.

Robert never liked big companies, preferring to deal with the more local concern, partly due to his time in marketing, so it didn't surprise anyone to his response to "You can't smoke in here".

Eric went around for the weekly shop event and sadly prepared himself for the possible conflict with his sister, breathing relaxing breaths as he exited the car, feeling the ground under his feet, letting tension slip from his body, seeing the beauty in the flowers (remembering a round, side plate sized plaque he had bought his mother when young. A picture of a smiling frog with the words "Don't worry, don't hurry and don't forget to smell the flowers"), smelling their scent and wishing he wasn't here.

Much as he loved all of his family, despite the fractures that had occurred, home life was difficult, money and time was always short, the car not happy and time with Tess, not matter how short, had to be handed with patient diplomacy, tact, and sympathy. Not the condescending or patronising type, that would be quickly picked up on, shooting yourself in the foot and getting nowhere, learning how to deal with things accordingly was about being true to the moment.

The front door was ajar, signalling that Tess was definitely here and the smell of disinfectant and the sound of the washing machine going were also signs of activity.

"Hi Dad" Eric shouted, respecting that it was his house after all, but knowing he'd probably still be asleep.

"Hello" he shouted again.

Tess appeared, glove on, arm of damp tea towels.

"You're late" she said in an unharsh but enquiring tone.

"No, usual time" Eric replied.

"Are you doing anything useful today, or are you just shopping and going" Tess said, obviously feeling terse.

"I'm not sure, is there anything Dad needs doing"?

"I don't know" she snapped "Why not take him out somewhere? He'd like to go out. Take him for a drive somewhere. Why not take him to the pub"? she finalised in exasperation.

Erics brain quickly worked through the ramifications of the brief tirade.

First, he'd have to check on his father, see if he was awake, fit enough to go or even wanted to go, let alone able to. It would take at least an hour, maybe two, to get him ready. He would want a bath and shave first, then a coffee, then another cigarette, which Eric would have to go and buy first, so may as well do the shop at the same time. Robert's cigarettes were cheaper at the supermarket and Eric had a limited budget for them, the booze and food...prioritised in that order.

That wasn't the end of the decision making or thought process.

Robert's mobility was an issue, the journey from bed to sitting room arm chair, via the bath, would be exhausting for him, a nap would be had. Then the car journey. Robert would refuse help getting in and out of the car. "I'm not feeble" he would exclaim, taking at least 10 minutes trying to get out of Erics low ride.

On one occasion, after he lost his driving licence, but not his car, he had fallen asleep behind the wheel, after parking in his drive, woke up, fell out of his car, then fell asleep again, on the ground, only to be found by a neighbour in the early hours, cold and sore.

And after all that. If all that was achieved. His father would want to smoke in the car, which Anne, sensitive to odours, disliked, but the worst would be the pub. Robert would go to the bar and have to be assisted in ordering drinks as he flirted with the barmaid, sometimes offering his bed, scaring the young girl into nervousness as the 87-year-old lit up.

You could hear the looks customers gave him.

"I'm sorry Sir" the bar staff would say shocked by this defiant action "you're not allowed to smoke in here".

"Not allowed? Who says I'm not allowed"? came the usual challenging response.

"It's the law" the landlord would intercede "Sorry, but you can't smoke in here".

"Can't"? would come the incredulous reply. "I can smoke anywhere I like" and so on, until defeat, being asked to leave or showed where he was allowed to smoke. Always a show.

All this flashed before Eric's eyes when his sibling made her suggestions rather than the usual greetings, signalling how the day would unfold if discretion and tact was not employed.

As it was, Robert was fast asleep, half eaten bowl of cornflakes balanced on his chest, flask of coffee and urine bottle by his side and a fresh ashtray by his lamp, not that he used it, preferring his mug, food plate or bowl instead.

Eric kissed his father's forehead and gently shook his shoulder.

"Hey Dad, its Eric" he said, loud enough to penetrate the deafness.

Tess came in.

"Honestly, he hasn't eaten his cereal" she exclaimed.

Robert stirred and smiled at seeing his son, annoying Tess even more.

"Why didn't you eat your cornflakes Dad"? she shouted.

"They'll be okay, I like them soft" he said taking a spoonful.

Whilst munching he patted his son's leg.

"Lovely to see you" he said as Tess huffed and left the room to carry on her constant cleaning.

"Hi Dad, Anne sends her love. How you feeling"? saying it to guide as to how his afternoon would plan out.

No response came. Robert was back in his safe imaginary land, eyes already flickering in dreams leaving Eric to hope that they were pleasant and peaceful ones, away from pain and solitude.

He rose and went into the kitchen to find Tess cooking herself some food and munching on a chunk of cheese, her mood seemed to have changed, though Eric wished he could help her untangle her worries and let her reclaim the life she lost long ago.

He talked about childhood memories, swimming in the basement of the Kensington hotel, the hot, steamy changing cubicles, the warm stamp of chlorine and the mangle that stood in the corner.

For a while it distracted Tess from her daily torments, but no thing lasts forever.

The shopping list was subtly compiled while in conversation, making especial care not to forget essentials and see, if budget allowed, a small bottle of whiskey might be purchased.

By the time Eric had returned from the unexpectedly arduous task of the supermarket, dodging the shufflers and mentally blind, Robert was still in bed, though now awake, just, at the insistence of his daughter.

Unloading the bags into the cupboards Tess enquired again.

"Are you going to take him out"?

"I don't think he's up to it today" Eric said earnestly.

"That's typical of you isn't it"? Tess said in a raised voice.

"You turn up once a week, don't do anything, stay for an hour, then go".

There was little point in dissecting her sentence. It was true he only came once a week, but he didn't live just around the corner like she did, apart from other details, and besides, Tess didn't want answers. Part of her needed justification of her actions and the access to her father's bank account, of which she felt entitled to.

BEING BLACK

The Sixties, full of colours and patterns against the back drop of grey, the music as varied as the spectrum it blossomed from, giving birth to long tendrils that reached forward in space to a time that would forget its roots.

Large brimmed straw hats, kaftans, beads, joss sticks, funny feet, gonks, tassel waistcoats, groovy lava lamps, peace and love, splattered over the top of existing structures, trying to show how a world could be before the corporations took over.

Life was burgeoning everywhere. Television, fashion, politics, psychology, all expanding into the publics view, with many failing to connect with the fast changes, always lagging behind like the preoccupied child not looking at where it was going.

The speed of the alterations would only quicken, mankind being left in arrears, easily being outsmarted in the end.

The family would attend church each Sunday, until Dickie left for full time boarding, when Robert carried on the task with his two youngest children, normally leaving Cassie to rest.

Eric didn't mind the routine, the church was attractive, old and set in a quiet leafy spot and he enjoyed some of the songs, but didn't like it when they changed the tune or sang a hymn he didn't recognise and would tap or jiggle along instead, surrounded by scornful eyes in the busy pews. He never questioned the way things were until one day.

He already had an awareness of world music, liking the Kwa Zulu sounds of his father's homeland, but never connected the dots.

Watching television, as he always did, being littered with old westerns, the native Americans tribal music, regardless of authenticity, tickled his tastebuds, but one day was shocked at a discovery.

He had seen the blues songs performed by toiling workers on plantations, sea shanties by old sea dogs, top hat and tails, but nothing compared to the energy of Gospel.

Turning on the small TV set, sitting under the stairs, the black and white images suddenly burst full of vibrancy and excitement, dancing, clapping, with a wall of sound backing the emotional singers spread "the word of the lord".

Why didn't they have this at his church, why wasn't he allowed to wobble, why were some people so…stiff?

The first of many questions about the hypocrisy of some of the congregation, ending with him walking out of midnight mass one Christmas Eve, not to return for decades.

Having a South African father was a good source of ammunition that was to be had in general conversation at school. As kids do, talk would turn to families, and having a foreigner among the ranks was a too good an opportunity to miss.

"We're half Scottish, because my father comes from Scotland". Says one child.

"Well, I'm a quarter Spanish, because my grandmother came from Madrid when she was younger". Says another.

"Where's Madrid then"? says a third.

"Don't you know where Madrid is? Its in Spain" says the first.

"Erics dad is black. He's from Africa" says the third.

They all look at Eric.

"Why don't you look black"? asks the first boy.

"I am a bit," said Eric examining his arm "See".

To be met with a mixed response. It never got old.

His father was an unaware font used by his son as an aid of mischievousness.

Years later, when Eric was discovering how to be successful in conquests, he would casually mention to his latest part-ner (when an imminent visit to the family abode was on the agenda) that not to pay attention to his father. If they should feel movement against their leg (while sitting up to the table), it would be his dad and his lecherous behaviour. Half the fun was in the telling of the tale, the other half reserved for the look in their eyes when actually Eric himself brushed their legs.

ANNE

A nervous anticipation was building up in the young girl as she got out of the car, making her way to the main hospital entrance, once used to treat infectious diseases for the Wir-ral's workhouse poor. Now, a general infirmary, Anne and her father were going to the geriatric ward, as usual, located near the mortuary, housed on the outer edge of the building, to meet up with fellow church goers to sing to the elderly.

As usual her father was his strict, domineering self, issuing commands about behaviour "Sit still", "Don't fidget", "Stop humming" were just some of his favourites.

The pale and faded mustard yellow walls of the ward came into view as they met up with several of the more devout congrega-tion outside the open doors of the ward, a familiar smell of dis-infectant and urine-stained armchairs wafting out.

As they entered in, Anne's eyes took in the scene with discom-fort and uncertain fear, having never seen, or unprepared, for a gathering of old, gaunt bodies and faces sitting and lying alone waiting for either the healing touch or the hand of death to release them from their temporary prison. One way or other, they would be leaving.

She noticed the nurses, being directed by matron, busying around in their duties, preparing for visiting time, with trays of pills, various sized pans and cardboard trays, curtains being pulled open and closed and hearing the murmurs of gentle re-assurance or discomfort, with the senile jabbering of two pa-tients at the back of the room.

The doctor completed his rounds and left with a silent wave to all, his white coat whishing with a gentle flourish past Annes face, the breeze making her blink and refocus her mind.

She noted that now, more patients were sitting in their arm-chairs next to their cots and beds, dressed for the occasion, some chewing aimlessly on their gums, staring blankly into space or eager, deep-set eyes searching out to see if perhaps today they might have a visitor.

As if on cue, a momentary silence signalled the beginning of visiting time and the expectant looks of seeing the loved ones resigned to sadness, knowing, foolhardily, that today would not be their day...maybe tomorrow.

The small group of Christians, who had been ignored until now, started singing, the sound instantly filling the room with a different atmosphere, distracting the patient's thought pat-terns, for many reviving old memories of younger days, where life was full of comings and goings and vibrant in unrealised love.

As the songs continued, Anne saw all these changes occurring, her young mind recognising that agedness was just a few flights of stairs away for her parents, and that all these bodies had lived full lives, just as she was about to.

WORD

Having relocated work, to one of England's smallest cities, aiding his escape from the clutches of the dark squalid depths of drug life in the seaside town, Eric found himself searching out new contacts to fuel his existent habit. Fortunately, though unrealised and unappreciated at the time, life was not being forthcoming and he was having to rely on old haunts to get his fix. Though he knew that all things must pass. Over the years he had heard enough hints and shouts of how he should be conducting himself or how there was a better way of living, though often had failed to listen to the call.

His biggest shortcoming was The Chase. Whether drugs, money, sex, everything came down to the chase. Stringing one partner along after another, being duplicitous (even quadlicitous at times) and rambunctious, burning the candle heavily at both ends, finding less and less satisfaction driving him further and further on.

In the back of his mind, he knew he had to change. He had to stop all his tomfoolery and create a better life. He knew what had to be done, but shedding his past, losing everything he had, that was the only way he knew how to move forward. Clear out the desk and start again, hopefully not cocking it up...this time.

Life doesn't give you a clean straight forward path, it wants you to learn and develop. Only by trial and error do we truly acquire new skills, the pains and sorrows can be the gum stuck to our shoes or blocks of stone to help us build, placing them in the right place on our journey.

Eric was seeking answers, help from the universe, as no person he knew seemed to be succeeding fantastically, so turned to a little book that had presented itself to him not long ago.

The Tao (pronounced dow, as in d ou(ch)) of Pooh, was a friendly introduction into Taoism explained using the characters of Winnie the Pooh, one of Erics favouritist stories from childhood. Having enjoyed the aspects of the uncarved block, the next logical step was to read the Tao Te (pronounced: day) Ching itself and understand The Way, as it is loosely put, and in turn, study the I (pronounced: Ee) Ching itself, an ancient book of divination, using hexagrams to answer moral dilemmas and decisions.

Ever since his early days, watching psychedelic rock and pop, shaking his butt like Elvis, Scooby Doobiedoobiedoos, Biba and mogadon, he knew that all things can be answered, but like Douglas Adams pointed out, it's great to have the ultimate answer (42), but what's the ultimate question?

Questions have been asked for millennia, in every culture, from South American Shaman to Indian Fakirs, seeking guidance from departed ancestors or trying to reach Nirvana. The act of Zen and the peace of Buddha, all seeking answers from beyond for the understanding of life on earth.

Eric was no different. A life time of influences and experiences, from music and T.V to things that go bump in the night, from Zapata to Archimedes. He made connections to times gone by, having had a grandfather who showed him a map from the First World War, a mother who loved history, a father from another country and seeing men, disfigured from bombs and warfare, walking around old London town. This wasn't only his life.

Casting the coins, focusing on the dilemma and opening himself to the universe (normally while stoned), he built his hexagrams, searching for the answers he already knew, but lay slightly hidden behind the veil of blindness.

On consultation, sometimes the answers fitted, sometimes not, probably because the universe was trying to tell him something he wouldn't listen to.

Before his relocation, promotion and onset of divination, he would sit in quiet contemplation, trying to seek out his hidden demons and vanquish them, that's when he heard his voice. In the stillness. Meditating on life. Knowing he must change. It spoke to him.

He hadn't heard his voice for years, drowned out by his constant excess of work, sex, drugs, drink and music. The cacophony noises.

But now. It spoke.

"You must go west" it simply said.

"Logical" thought Eric, unsure of what he had heard, but knowing his parents lived west and were probably in need of help on the farm. Just his thoughts making themselves known, but next came the unexpected surprise.

"You will be with a curly haired female with two children and talk to a vicar who is not vicar".

Shocked by the sudden sentence of specific information, clearly encapsulated and precise, almost loud enough for anyone to hear if they had been presented, his mind spun.

As if answering his next question before he could say it (which was going to be "Anything else"?) came the statement "Where the trees are".

Then it was gone. He was left with four events and he had no clue as to what just happened. The last most cryptic yet simple of them all, but all puzzling and intriguing.

Time passed, but the seeds had been laid and bounced around, piquing his curiosity, feeling impelled already to try and help his parents, but the thoughts slowly drifted away, stored and almost forgotten until one day...

Leaving the office, located at the back of store, Eric floor walked, checking displays, promotions and tidiness, when his eyes fell upon a lady pushing a child in a buggy. Sleight and attractive features were topped with a mass of noticeable very light brown curly hair and he smiled a greeting as he passed, not because of what he remembered, besides she only had one kid, but because she was attractive and looked like she needed a smile.

Anne walked past, ignoring his salutations, and carried on her way.

Eric was somewhat surprised and intrigued, most customers were convivial, but perhaps this one was having an off day.

Again, time wound on, and he rarely saw her again, but his business reputation grew, eventually being offered managerial prospects with a large brewery company that held retail units opposite where he worked.

Accepting the challenge, to his surprise, he found that the young mum who ignored him worked there as well.

They chatted easily, Eric enjoying her confidence and forth-rightness, amazed to find she had an older child that she had given birth to when she was just 17 as, he ignorantly thought, she didn't look like a mum of two.

Though not seeking involvement at the time, they inevitably and slowly grew closer, Anne joining him on deliveries and enjoying each-others company. Their paths became entwined and Eric was advised by Anne to think carefully on his next steps.

"Before we get into a relationship" she said "you need to consider what you're doing very carefully".

"How do you mean"? he answered.

"You're not just taking on me, but also my children". She said earnestly "You're going to have an instant family. It's a lot to take on".

Eric had already been thinking of this, but now was prompted to be more conscious, now it had been spoken aloud, so thought deeply on the implications, though few could imagine what would transpire and how it would affect the next ten years and then the next ten after. Dominoes would fall, knocking one into another, rippling across the years, touching all involved, passing the legacy onto the children, children's children, and possibly further. Eric would be filled with sorrow with how his kinfolk had been touched, wishing he could wipe their slates clean, amend his errors and give them the lives they deserved, rather than the influences of his faults and ineptitudes.

It would only be a few years later, from when they first met, that he would experience a simple, innocent touch that would mean more than anything he had experienced in his life.

He sat on the edge of their sofa, the sun coming through the sitting room window, their young son taking steps in his pale blue baby grow, clutching a small toy car. Eric was checking instructions for a bookcase that needed putting together, judging how much space was to be needed and which extra tools to get.

His son waddled up to him reached out his hand and rested it on his dad's knee to steady himself.

For the first time in Eric's life, someone showed how much they trusted him. This simple act, without word, meant so much to him.

He then realised what responsibility was really about. He had wasted so many years, time, tears and money…

MOVING HOUSE

The call rang out through the house.

"Anne, Vinnie, sitting room, now" the direct order came from their dad and nerves immediately kicked in, making the kids wonder who had done something wrong.

They had only just got back from their day at school, only just mid-term, leading up to the summer holidays, with the new school year not yet being thought of.

Settling into their usual seats the bombshell was dropped.

"Right kids, we're moving house. Not far, but you're both going to have to change schools as I can't be driving you to and from and having to pay for buses all the time".

"But I've just started my C.S.E's" said a shocked Anne, realising that it would also mean leaving her friends behind, just as she had started to feel less disliked for having a preacher for a father.

It had been a hard road to travel, kids could be really cruel.

"Ew, stay away from her" some would whisper behind her back, "...her dads a vicar..." or "...look at the clothes on that..." and "...don't get too close..." thinking that they might catch religion. The parents didn't help. Noticeably pulling their children away from the innocent young girl who might poison their darling offspring, but who actually only wanted to laugh and run, be free from her bonds and feel the freshness of youth wash over her skin.

"It's happening and that's all there is too it" said her dad emphatically, already getting short tempered with her brief remonstration, signalling to her that a conversation, as usual, was not going to be had.

Ignoring the silent threat Anne pushed on.

"But what about my friends? I'll never see them again"? she said, raising her voice, but not too much, calculating how much to go so as not to trigger the full wrath, though for possibly the first time in her life, needing to find her voice and stand up for something that belonged to her, something she had worked at and something that had been out of her parent's control.

Within weeks, with only about thirty days of the summer term left, Anne found herself at a new house and a new school, an all-girls school. Resentment and anger, that stayed lurking, unresolved for decades, were her only friends in her new environment, the girls already having already well-established cliques, which were difficult for a total outsider to infiltrate. Anne again felt like an outsider looking in, after all she had been through, and instead of having sympathy and understanding from her parents, was instead met with rebuke and intolerance of her demonstrations and upset.

The thoughts continued to whirl, unchecked or appeased, within, trying to come to terms with the transition and understand why the move had occurred at all.

"It's not as if dad needed to move to be closer to work" Jubilee (the inner child, wanting only peace and love) cogitated to Storm (her outer child, who was slowly gaining power, controlled by whatever lay behind the dark cloud).

Her two brothers, a lot younger as they were, had taken the move in their stride. Vinnie was changing schools anyway and Frank was still scribbling on paper and learning how to use a toilet, both always getting preferential treatment and Anne getting the blame for their errors.

The church community had its advantages. Having a wide network of associates meant that holiday time could involve visiting far afield locations or outings organised for large groups to attend, which for Anne meant escaping the confines of the vice type grip and an opportunity to discover a small bit of freedom. To be able to listen to another child's radio or watch a communal television without being told that it was the devil's work.

At the end of her disastrous part-term, Ann's mother decided that they were going down to Somerset for a week, visiting a member of the church, a much-needed break for all after the turmoil of the move.

The four-hour drive felt long, but looking out of the car window, watching the scenery change from grey to green helped ignore the elbows and wiggles of her younger brothers on either side of her.

They arrived at the large red bricked house with a pointy porch and gravel drive, the tall windows looking easy on the eye, and instantly Anne felt relaxed and calm, ready for a break and be able to take a breath.

The week flew by, especially as there were two children, a girl and boy of similar age as Vinnie and herself, and having room to roam and her parents distracted with their work, Anne started to forget her worries, putting it all behind her, resigning to her new path and determining that she would make it work and not be defeated.

Unfortunately, time waits for no man (it's got a bus to catch), no sooner as Anne had got into the swing of things, it was time to go home…though it still wasn't, in her eyes.

They packed the car, said all their goodbyes and took their prospective seats for the return journey.

The silence of the drive was broken by Annes father.

"We've decided to move to Somerset" came the bombshell.

Anne couldn't believe what she had just heard. "WHAT"? she uttered.

"I've decided we're moving to Somerset, probably in October".

Anne was stunned. They had only just moved and hadn't even got used to that. But Somerset! That may as well be the other side of the world. It would mean leaving her Grandad behind, all her aunts, uncles and cousins (and there were a lot of them). It was nice coming here on holiday, but to live! She would be leaving everything she knew behind. Her mind reeled.

"I can't move. Not again. Not now." she implored "We've only just moved. I'm in my final year. I've got my exams" the torrent of reasons spilled out, begging her parents to let her stay and finish off her last year of school, she didn't want to start all over <u>again.</u>

"Please Dad, please let me stay" was answered each time, more and more abrupt than the last.

"No, you're coming with us, final".

And that was that. End of. Years of doing as she was told. Years of being pushed into a tighter and smaller mould, years of hearing "You can't watch this", "you can't watch that", "we know what you're doing", "God sees everything", "don't lie", the fear and punishment, never being able to learn for herself, make her own mistakes, hand-me-down clothes and broken promises.

At that moment…Anne hated her parents. This was one step beyond. She would never forgive her parents. To many the school move is normal transition, but for Anne it was the final insult to injury. The years of carefree suppression, the lack of care and respect, she felt like her identity was inconsequential, only there to do their bidding.

Why, she thought, the vortex pulling her into its clutches, why would any parent do that to their child. 3 schools in 6 months. The anger lay brooding deep inside, plotting and gnawing in the pit of her stomach.

They moved in the October half-term, school break, and the culture shock of the north-south divide was probably more difficult to cope with than the school itself.

Compared to Liverpool, Bath truly was a world apart.

Now she didn't fit in for other reasons. Classmates were of a different breed, had different habits and different attitudes compared to her early estate life style. Her hatred for the airs and graces, innocent they may have been, didn't sit right were her down to earth, no-nonsense approach. Even the lessons themselves seemed alien, led by teachers who spoke a different language and dressed a different style.

Storm became bored of all the stupid behaviour and decided, at times, not to turn up for lessons, preferring instead to sit in the toilets or cloakrooms, only to appear for lunchtime, then resume her disappearing act after registration.

Even this became tiresome, so Anne would wipe away her hours in the park or wander the shops, only visiting school for games or registration again, making sure she was around for home time. On occasion, after registration, she would go home, claiming to have a special study period and shut herself in her bedroom for the rest of the day. Her parents never queried and the school never questioned, Anne made sure of that.

Exams came and went with inevitable failure, due to lack of interest, except for the subjects she enjoyed and had genuine interest in. But the hurt of that year stayed and became pivotal in many decisions, impacting for years to come.

It would be almost thirty years for Annes father to acknowledge the harm he caused to her schooling, but the damage had been done.

Anne would often look back at what could have been, even at the age of 50, only then being able to start to address the long-lasting impact of, what she saw now as, an abusive childhood. The shadowy curtain starting decaying, revealing the truth of what occurred, leaving it up to her to heal.

BITCH

"Get that BITCH out of here" Cassandra shouted at her youngest son.

It was the first time she had met his new girlfriend, having been away in South Africa for a couple of weeks in the wake of Roberts mother's funeral and Eric had been looking after the farm, with Tess attempting to tend to house duties.

The bleach had helped to keep the toilets clean, but Eric could still smell the unmistakable tang of her bulimia, even though she was still in denial.

"I want her out of the house now" Cassandra ranted, even

though the area had already been vacated.

Eric noticed that his mother was evidently going through another, for want of another word, breakdown. He thought that time away might have helped, change of scenery and all that.

Instead, quite the opposite was true, hopefully it would settle down and fade away without erupting into a too fierce a storm.

The horses in the neighbouring fields had settled down, now that his mother had stopped throwing stones at them, but the dog that trotted happily, up and down the road on his daily jaunt, now steered clear of the gated drive, fearful of being attacked again by the crazy lady with the rake.

The sudden snap that could occur was as uncanny as the look in her eyes. The madness would take her, despite the incompetent psychologists giving her a clean bill of health, and her eyes would sparkle with malintent as her mouth twisted into a satisfied sneer, with words misinterpreting actual events.

As he grew, his early allegiances shifted from maternal to paternal, understanding more and more of his father's habits, sympathising for both his parents lives and how one supported the other in destruction and aid.

Life, nature, whatever you want to call it, like water, has its own path. Try as you might it will do what it does. Mankind is but a blip, lost in its importance, though many cultures found themselves on the right path, they were diverted by other humans to destruction, themselves seeking answers that already lay at their feet, just as man cannot smell his own bad breath, though his mouth is right under his nose.

The small shelter sat on the sea front, large crashing waves throwing up spray, signalling how the weather was further out into the deep blue. It was a favourite spot for Eric to park up his bike and sit, watching the lightning hit the water miles out, undisturbed by the natural madness, feeling that it was nothing compared to what he was used to, but found its ferocity and power comforting. It offered no spite, it was what it was, as all nature, if you bathe with crocodiles, you're gonna get bit.

Every time he witnessed the white forks of unbridled power, he would momentarily recall his seat, whether it was driving in a car, seeing it spark on the road in the empty distance, late at night, anticipated stillness holding its silence, or standing in a back door porch, feeling the air charge up for an imminent strike.

The natural world was the home that Eric always wanted, the desire for hermithood with the uncomplicatedness of the man-made disasters, dealt with such disregard to fellow humans and the ground on which they walked.

Driving, one day, in the depths of winter, with Anne in the front and the two youngest at school, the other two having already left home to seek their own paths, they noticed how the road condition was deteriorating.

Works hadn't been implemented for some time, and the snow, rain and ice, along with lorries and heavy tractors, were not helping the situation. But looking closer at the pattern of damage Eric noticed something quite clearly.

"If you look at the main damage of the road…" he pointed out to Anne "…its where the trees are…".

The words jumped out like a flag and he explained to his wife what the phrase meant to him and how he had been wondering for almost 15 years. But now he knew, maybe. Maybe, he was meant to be here. Maybe this was the place. He would have to wait and see, he had not received any messages since, in fact, not since:

"I'm sorry, I can't be your guardian angel anymore".

THE END

The knight still knelt, though his long hair of grey now shone in the light of the moon, that lay full in the sky, as bright as his once tarnished armour and as cold as the pain in his knee.

He had vowed to await his lady, knowing the ice that imprisoned her heart would one day melt, and on that day, she might be in need of his warmth that once shone brightly, though now was a flickering shadow of its former self.

This had been his greatest errant, his chivalric virtue tested to the utter most of any courtly love.

He had knelt as his lady had passed him by, at first ignoring his expostulations and pleadings, until her anger fired so, refused to even acknowledge his being, as if some unwanted piece of furniture there he stood.

The castle stood in quietness, it too waiting and watching, the dust settling on ageing ledges, that soon might crumple under the sadness that also landed on their sills.

Days and nights fell into months, then years, as the knight watched the queen, still wracked by the spell that had been cast upon her innocent body, ignore his love for her.

Time passed, as her own children grew of age and left the safe confines of the castle's walls, each unknowingly carrying a small piece of the evil enchantment, laying dormant in the recess of their souls, hoping to be fed and nurtured so to blossom again, but as a different flower.

The knight pled with his love to hear his voice and words as they were, not as she imagined, not slighted by her childhood nightmares that sort to control her innermost thoughts and deeds, but free her to become the person she was.

The dragon twisted in her gut as it writhed against what it thought was a spell being cast, not wanting to leave the safety of its cave and lonely prison.

The haze that once gripped the queen faltered as she saw the beast yell in pain and anguish, startled she became.

"How can this be so" she softly uttered as the clearness shone its light in the darkness of her soul, protected all this time by tattered shrouds and webs of creatures long since passed.

The light grew stronger as she felt its warmth against the bleakness which beckoned her back, yet she fought the gnarled claws and rejoiced in the new found glory and all that it promised.

Too soon came the end of the moment, that brief glimpse that she had espied, like an echo she could sense that feeling still, as if an eternal fire had been sparked and though dim and flickering as it was, just needed sustenance and tending to grow as it should.

Aghast at her findings, she stumbled slightly so and was caught in the arms of her waiting knight. They stood, both unsteady yet with renewed strength, just as the castle stood, knowing that change had become and in each-other's arms they kissed again for the first time and lived ha...

ACT 2

THE OUTSIDE
ON THE INSIDE
IS
THE RIGHT SIDE

BARBED WIRE LOVE

Night had fallen and the rain had stopped and the full moon lit up the ruined land, glistening off the pitted mud with its still silvery glow, darkness mimicking shadows, creeping in behind the fallen, hiding the full horrors of the battles that had been held.

Tommy called out, but no reply came, save a gentle dripping from the trenches torn apart structures, plopping into the puddles forming in the small craters or footprints left behind by the once living, only now torn and damaged, eyes left open, staring with their bloodied emptiness, contorted bodies and mouths agape.

The bombing had ceased sometime before the rain, but Tommy had been trapped under a collapse of one of the bunkers and had tried in vain to free himself, until saturated from the downpour, was able to claw through the claggy ground.

Standing upright he conveyed the scene and called out once more, stumbling, still shaken and dazed, he made his way along the broken, slippery foot boards, listening for an answer, but none there came.

On one stumble he noted a minor wound to his leg and another to his torso that lay under the singed tatters of his jacket, that had been tailored out of old hessian to protect from the freezing nights.

Staggering on, finding none alive left behind, he pondered as to whether they had moved forward or fallen back from the front lines, remembering nothing of instructions or signals.

Ahead of him, part of a rampart had been blown apart, so he scrambled slowly upward over the wet mud to tentatively peer out on the scene beyond.

Annihilation met his eyes. Once, fields of vibrant green gave way to the blackened wet earth of the silver night, the mighty trees now bare stumps, unbelievably recognised and the gentle beauty of the rolling countryside turned into hurt dark blemishes against the watching sky.

No bird flew and even the plumes of smoke from the still burning insignificant fires appeared uncomfortable in their movement. All was still and all was quiet, not revealing any clue to which the fighting had gone.

Tommy searched the horizon, of what he could see and called again for an answer. He paused, motionless, craning his head, had he...

He called again. Yes, a shout, somewhere distant, far off, yet he couldn't discern from exactly where?

Suddenly a single whizz shot past his ear, as if a fast and angry dragonfly had flown straight by, to embed itself in the bank behind.

It had come from a different direction of the call, so danger still lurked in the depths of the bright night, but at least he knew now he was not alone.

He started crawling amidst the muck and the filth, trying to avoid his fallen comrades but keeping his head low, not wanting to make noise as he went for fear of becoming an easy target, though eager to catch up with his own and find some sort of relief, especially as now he was starting to feel the cold of the damp night and judders of shock starting to shake his body.

His progress was slow, rarely being able to stand fully upright, but at least this was better than staying in the putridness of the trench, possibly just waiting for deaths hands to take him, whilst he sat thinking of nothing but his loneliness and fear of every movement or sound.

He paused for breath, weariness and hunger making itself known, and admired, that even in this desolate landscape, beauty was to be had. The sereness lay bare for all to see. Amid the death and destruction, the shapes, new and familiar, had form and being of their own, once living, created out of violence, one could not help but marvel at the landscape ahead.

The stars continued to shine, as if watching eyes staring back, though as far as any man could touch and would never know how its land looked.

Tommy called out once more. "Hello".

He waited. No shot came this time, but a reply sounded closer.

"Over Here" came the distinctive, yet still far off familiar voice.

His heart started to beat faster, but daring not to make another noise to alert his predator, he channelled his renewed energy into movement, focusing on the direction he thought he heard the cry come from.

Inch after inch he continued through the light of the moon, only daring to stand when down in a bomb crater, though despite his posture, it still was not an easy path, having more dead souls to climb over or manoeuvre around water pits that were waiting to swallow man and beast alike.

In the near distance ahead, he could see what looked like fallen walls and part of a roof, obviously once being a small barn or house, though now having been hammered by heavy shells was a poor example of shelter itself, but might prove a good resting point.

Scrabbling on, Tommy noted that the moon was going down, it too tired from its travels across the heavens, going home to rest, to allow its brother to awaken and take centre stage and view the proceedings, unable to assist but always watching.

He heard a shot ring out. It too closer than before. But whether it was directed at him or not he could not tell, save for the fact that he heard no bullet or received no wound, he figured that a different target had been selected in hope and failed.

Time crawled, as he did, making his journey to the building, but eventually, exhausted, muddied and wet, he clambered over the rubble, as softly as he could, and sought a corner to huddle against and rest a while, hoping to feel refreshed when wakened, ready for his next push.

Sleep came quickly, eyes closed, though his ears stayed alert to his surroundings, while he dreamt of home, of family and the farm. He dreamt of Bess and the walk through the fields they would take and the small copse at the end of the lane, where his dad had taught him about catching rabbits.

A chink of light, the first rays of the morning sun, touched his eyes, a gentle call to stir and move and it was then he realised his mistake,

He should have pushed on. Ignored his pain and tiredness. For now, though he could already feel the difference of night and day temperature, he would be clearly seen. No longer having the aid of shadows to fall into and cover his movements.

Slowly and carefully, he moved to the opposite direction he had come in from and saw, to his horror, the tangled mess of barbed wire coils, scattered by the bombs, though still recognisable in their twisted forms, waiting to catch hold of their victim and help that hidden hunter in his task.

Daring not to make any more noise than necessary, he slowly studied his horizon, trying to ascertain the best route to take, in shielding and ease, and which direction the last call out came from.

Realizing that not all options could be ticked, he started out on his journey, heading for the most promising way ahead, still having to keep his head down, though noticing now more flies buzzing on the corpses as the day started to warm up the feast as well.

Struggling slowly through the first set of confusion, he moved too fast and without enough care, causing him to slip in his haste catching his ankle deeply with the sharp spikes, instinctively causing him to pull back and yelp in pain, suddenly motionless, waiting for the smack of the bullet. But none came.

Instead, he heard "Hey, over here", still weak.

Not daring to move unnecessarily and inspect the damage, besides compared to his other wounds this was minor, he focused again on his hopeful destination, determinedly pulling himself along under and through the maze, ignoring the little scratchings, willing himself forward.

The sun was trying its hardest to dry up the land, unfortunately it was also helping with the process of the decay that lay about and a sickening rumble growled in Tommy's stomach, reminding him that it had been a while since he last ate.

Pulling himself carefully along he came to an impasse. There seemed no way forward and going back was not an option, wood and wire blocking his way, the only alternative was to try and jump over. It would have to be quick. He turned his head to try and see whether there really was no other route to be taken, but could see none.

He mustered himself, readying to the hurdle, thinking just of clearing some distance, willing not to be a target, aiming his jump carefully.

He slowly bundled himself into a crouching position and thrust himself with all his might, reminding him of how the frogs at the pond took off with self-abandon.

He heard the explosion of the powder and the bite striking his hip, that sent him sprawling across the ground, catching barbed points of steel as he went, though this time he did not cry out in pain, determined to complete his self-appointed mission.

He lay, inert and unconscious. Finally at peace, until he heard his name being called with renewed effort.

"Tommy! Tommy! I that that you Tommy" called the broad Scottish voice. Unable to talk, pain so intense and effort being saved, he untangled himself from the wreckage, he was surprised not to hear another shot, but winced with the extreme pain at every movement, noticing the blood coming from his wound, but was more determined than ever to reach his quarry.

He struggled forward, now having to drag his useless legs, grit and purpose driving him on until he came to the ridge of a long but narrow trench.

He fell down the side, landing too hard, but the noise signalling to who heard it, to feebly utter "Who's there"?

The sound brought immediate joy to Tommy.

"Stevie? Is that you"? he yelled.

"Tommy? Tommy?" the reply came back, frail and amazed.

Tommy dragged himself through the still wet and cold trench, leaving the trail of life-giving blood behind him, desperate to find Stevie nearby, knowing they would never leave eachothers side, they always had been together in life and now, probably, in death.

He pulled himself along, inch after agonising inch, until he found Stevie, propped up against a fallen plank of wood.

"Tommy lad" came the rasping voice, tears streaking his muddied cheeks.

Tommy crawled with a final effort and rested his head on Stevie's lap, wagging his tail. At least they were now together.

MR WICKS

His watch vibrated on his wrist with a gentle tinkle, signalling seven o'clock, exactly. He would have liked to be woken at least quarter of an hour earlier, but he much preferred round numbers, they were neater and tidier to deal with.

No soon as his eyes were open, he was awake. No point in lying around in bed, things always needed to be done, so swung his pyjamaed legs around, sitting upright and tucked his feet into a pair of awaiting slippers.

The reached over to the small bed side table and located his thick, small, round lensed spectacles, exactly where he left them, which had been cleaned and folded before going to sleep.

"Cup of…" he said, cutting himself short, remembering his wife had gone on holiday with her friends, a yearly exercise. He couldn't blame her. She was a magnificent lady, in every way, full of life and vitality, and married to him.

He would give anything to be more like her. To be able to let his hair down, not that he had any, though sometimes he did resort to wearing a wig at business meetings with clients who he had not met him before, it gave him a certain anonymity and a feeling of more confidence.

He often thought how wonderful it would be, to be more adventurous and carefree. He sometimes imagined himself parachute jumping from buildings or deep-sea diving with sharks. He would have loved to have been a pirate. Instead, Mr Wicks was an accountant. A very good accountant, exceptional in fact. He had a natural flair for numbers and worked very hard for the company, though was always

a little saddened of how underappreciated he felt.

His wife would always try and raise his spirits, tell him how wonderful he was and how grateful she was, but sometimes… well…sometimes it wasn't enough, he wanted more.

Admittedly, he felt a bit guilty feeling this way, he did get yearly bonuses, but what about the rest of the year. "Perhaps," he thought still sitting on the edge of the bed "perhaps, I should start taking some dance lessons". The thought made his eyes roll to themselves; he was glad he hadn't said it out loud.

He stood up and put his dressing gown on and knotted the belt up as he went downstairs to the kitchen.

"Hmm? Toast or cereal" he said while rinsing the kettle and putting it on for a cup of tea. He had heard that coffee as a first drink of the morning is bad for the metabolism, so tea it was from now on. and why he bothered asking himself toast or cereal for breakfast never ceased to amaze him. He always had toast. Reaching for the bread bin or realised he missed his wife on mornings like this, more than usual, he loved her company, she would know what he should do.

He looked at the phone as the kettle boiled and the bread went down into the toaster.

"I could always give her a ring" he mused.

No, that would be unfair to interrupt her break, besides, she's probably still asleep. They probably were out late as well, he thought as the toast popped up.

He took his tea and toast over to the kitchen table, which he had prepared the night before, laying out a small jug of milk, plate, knife, a jar of peanut butter and a spoon (with a piece of neatly folded kitchen paper to rest it on and wipe the crumbs with, mouth and table).

"Why was he so organised"? he thought, slightly annoyed with himself.

He checked the clock and realised that he was running three minutes late, "…it must've been all that thinking I've been doing…" he thought, again berating himself for his lapse of concentration but also for his exactitude.

Suddenly, the phone rang, sending little flutters through him, hoping it was wifey.

Momentarily flooded by the idea of not having his tea and toast at the right temperature and that the call was going to set him further back, he did like to be at work at least half an hour before official start time, he stood and walked over to the ringing machine.

"Hello"? he said in his usual monotone and wary voice.

"Hello, darling its me" came the flourishing of warmth and tenderness to his soul, as if a mountainside of flowers all bloomed at once filling the air with fragrance and colour, love seeping into his very bones.

But all he could manage to express was "Oh, hello dear".

"Darling I'm missing you so much, it's never the same without you". she sincerely said "Why don't you come out and join us, the girls wouldn't mind, I'm sure you could get some time off, you always work so hard". Her voice was making him giddy, like a young child spinning round and laughing on a summer's day.

"I'm sorry dear" he said gently reserved "but I have to finish this quarters projection before next months budget meeting. Besides," he continued, a small voice complaining to him from inside "I'm sure you'd have much more fun without me".

("Please come and get me and take me away" he silently begged)

"Oh, alright darling" she said, saddened and crestfallen, though knowing that she should not have gotten her hopes up. "The girls have decided to go on a tour, we're going to be away for a few extra days. Oh, why don't you come. You'll love it". She added.

"I'm sorry dear, you know I have to work" he said, his small voice getting louder inside, stamping about, waving its arms in the air, telling him what an idiot he was.

"I have to go or I'll be late for work dear" he said, not believing that he had just said it.

"Oh...okay darling...well...I love you lots" she said, blowing kisses down the phone.

And with that...she was gone...gone for even longer...

He put the phone back on the cradle harder than he usually did.

"Damn it" he said allowed, surprised at the volume and language.

"Damn, damn, damn". He shouted angrily at himself.

"What I would give, to just for once, not be such a..."

Ping-pong. The door-bell rang.

Mr Wicks strode angrily to the door "What now"? he thought as his hand yanked down on the handle.

He stared, frowned brow turning to puzzlement, mouth

slightly ajar from all his swearing, caught in mid action, now not quite believing in what he saw. For there... in front of him...on his doorstep...at approximately 7:25a.m (he knew that because he had just done a time check, but it had taken him about 12 seconds to answer the door, checking his knotted dressing gown on the way) ...was...himself.

"Er...hello..." he said to himself, feeling unnerved at the red horns that sprouted from "his" forehead.

"Ah, Mr Wicks," he said, in what seemed in a slightly sardonic manner "delighted to meet you, I'm sure" he said to himself, grinning with pointed teeth and blackened mouth.

Not one to be put out of stride or be accused of rudeness he replied, with a bit of confused curtness himself "Delighted, I'm sure. May I help you"? he enquired, not really knowing what else he could say. It wasn't every day that you met your counterpart, while missing your beloved AND making yourself late for WORK.

"Yyess," smarmed the other Mr Wicks, who also had the same briefcase tucked under his arm "I've come to give you your secret hearts desires" licking his teeth with a forked tongue that came from the depths of blackness.

"Well, not today thank you," Mr Wicks said curtly, starting to close the door "I'm going to be late for work, thank you again, goodbye".

Before he could full close the door, he noticed a cloven hoof had wedged itself in the way.

"Now, please Alistair," he smarmed "it was you who called I". he completed, pushing the door open, followed by his pointed red tail.

"Now see here" Alistair tried to protest, though his voice got lost in a choke as the foul stench of sulphur flowed in behind his visitor.

The newcomer Mr Wicks sat himself down in Alistair's armchair, grinning and surveying the room, legs crossed, having placed his briefcase on the floor beside him. It seemed the gently wriggle and moan as if it quietly carried a thousand souls.

"I take it the lady of the house is away on her usual holiday" the Devil inclined with non-interested casualness.

"Er, yes" Mr Wicks replied, pushing his glasses back up his nose, noticing that the room was feeling a bit hotter than normal, though he knew that the thermostat was set correctly... he liked to check it daily. 18.5 degrees as normal.

"Well, let me come to the point," the creature from hell said "Oh do sit down, please Alistair my dear," pointing to the sofa "then we can really talk. I know how you hate to be late for work".

"Work"! thought Alistair, he had forgotten all about work, so immediately sat down, his mind reeling with the intrusion and wondering what his wife might say.

"That's better, now my dear boy" the demon spawn said, leaning forward and picking up the oozing briefcase and extracting a neat pile of paperwork.

Alistair Wicks' attention was annoyingly peeked by the white sheets of documentation, wanting to know what was written, whether it was correct, but at the same time eager to get on.

"Now, then," the devil said, looking down his nose at the writing through his glasses "let me see...hmm...hmm...yes, well, it clearly states that you would give anything" he finalised with a hungry smile that ran shivers over Mr Wicks' back.

"What would you like...for...anything"? he concluded.

Alistair Wicks sat dumbfounded at his morning, he really didn't like to be put out of routine...but...he did like the idea of sky diving, he thought to himself.

"Skydiving perhaps"? the sinister Mr Wicks inclined "Or perhaps an astronaut or famous rock star...my dear boy, you could have anything" he said eyes burning with a hungry fire in the blackness.

"Well," said Mr Wicks in his usual restrained manner.

"Yess" leaned forward the other, tongue snaking out.

"I've always fancied..."

"Yesss" leaning ever closer.

Mr Wicks paused, thinking of the best possible way of explain his desires.

"I've always fancied being an explorer" he burst out, as if a torrent of expeditions had been damned up behind a crumbling wall.

"I want to discover everything" he said standing up, his dressing gown knot coming undone, though quickly rectified.

He struck an almost heroic pose and splurted out:

"I want to be able to travel to worlds unseen, to times unknown, discover the universes mysteries and uncover the secrets of life that has gone".

The outburst exhausted him and silenced the room, as if even the furniture stared in shock.

"Excellent, Mr Wicks, thank you for your business" the devil rose, putting the paperwork away "I'll be in touch soon" thrusting forward a clawed hand.

"But...I didn't sign anything" the crestfallen words came out.

"Oh, you don't need to my boy. Your words are good enough for me. Be seeing you". He said striding to the door, holding back an evil chortle.

Panic suddenly erupted in Alistair Wicks. What would his wife say? What would all the workers at the factory say? He would be the laughing stock.

Turning quickly, he shouted "Wait, don't go". He pleaded.

The Devil paused and turned, looking at Mr Wicks with contempt.

"What is it" he snarled, unhappy about being stopped, so many humans behave like this...he wished...just once...

"I've changed my mind" Alistair said definitely, pushing up his glasses again.

"Sorry, my dear boy. No can do" the ever-growing figure said.

"There must be something in your contract that lets me change my mind" the work side of Alistair Wicks said, taking over and letting gears kick into place.

"No. Nothing," said the gleeful monstrosity, hoping that this pitiful human wouldn't ask him to let him have a look at the contract. He did so hate wasting time, but hey ho.

"Let me see my contract" Mr Wicks demanded, with out-stretched hand.

"Oh, very well" came the exasperated reply, with much mutter-ings and scrabbling around inside the briefcase. "Here" thrust-ing the hand full of papers at the mortal.

Mr Wicks took the papers and sat down on his chair at the kitchen table, adjusted his glasses again and mulled over the agreement with much "Hmm"s and "I see"s, with the occa-sional "oh"s. Until.

"What does this say here" enquired Mr Wicks, pointing to some extra small writing.

"Oh, that, that's nothing for you to be concerned about" boomed the Devil "that's just a standard subclause. You'd find it in most contracts" he stated "That just says "...if any of the participating parties in this agreement are shown not to be of sound mind, the entire contract is automatically nullified"".

"Subclause..."? Mr Wicks smiled gently at the irony.

"Yes, yes, its alright Alistair my dear, its in every contract" the Devil replied, getting a bit frustrated at being kept from busi-ness elsewhere and short tempered with this little, inconse-quential man.

"It's called the sanity clause" he finished, snatching the papers back off Mr Wicks and rolling his eyes.

Alistair Wicks let out a small chuckle.

"Honestly my DEAR man. What now"? The Devil said, infuri-ated at his waste of time.

"Well..." Mr Alistair Wicks said gently "its just that my wife is Santa Claus".

Fury filled the room, shaking the walls and rattling the win-dows. "Now don't be ridiculous, we all know Santa Claus is a man and besides..." the evil snarled, faltering.

"Santa is a female title you know, not male" the timid voice interrupted "and besides any court would claim me mad if I de-clared I was married to Mrs Claus".

"Bah, little man..." the devil shouted raising to a monstrous height of flame and agony "you can't fool me. There's no such thing as Santa Claus anyway". He yelled.

Mr Wicks sat and raised an eyebrow with a wry little smile. When you make toys for all the children in the world you have to be well organised or at least have a good accountant.

SHOPPING DAY

"Oi Sha"! Gavin shouted "What time is the delivery coming"?

"Blimey, can't you wait for yer biscuits"? Sharon shouted back from the kitchen.

"No. Yeah". Gav shouted back "I just want to know what time the delivery's coming".

"I've only just told you what time it was coming" she shouted back.

"No, you didn't" exclaimed Gavin loudly, tapping furiously on his controller.

"Yes, I DID"!

"NO. YOU. DIDN'T"! he hollered in return shooting at the swarms of aliens.

Sharon rolled her eyes at her boyfriend's lack of paying attention.

"FOUR THIRTY (dick)" she called back…except for the last bit.

"oh, yeah" Gavin said quietly to himself.

"Bit of a late one innit"? he retorted, putting his controller down, forgetting to put it on pause and standing up.

"I told you, it was the only slot left because of… Aargh" she shouted back, jumping out of her skin when Gavin crept up behind her.

Shaz turned round and swotted him on the shoulder "KNOB" she declared.

"What were you saying"? Gav said chuckling, rubbing his arm.

"It's the driver shortages. It was the only slot I could get".

The virus had hit about 2 years ago, turning into a pandemic and causing countries to instigate total lockdowns and guidelines of masks, handwashing and social distancing. Panic buying was a common knee jerk reaction, especially with toilet rolls, of all things, but as time progressed things evened out, though the virus was here to stay.

Vaccinations were developed, which helped to an extent, but for the U.K, Brexit, the leaving of the E.U, loomed on the horizon. The British government had asked the people to vote on an exit or not, and despite not actually not knowing what the consequences would be, a majority vote to leave was secured.

A new norm was evolving, everyone was having to adjust, but there were going to be plenty of ups and downs to deal with when it came to the complexities of modern life and if that wasn't bad enough, the supermarket company they dealt with were selling, leading to cut backs and shortages on top of shortages.

"Fuckin' blood suckers" mumbled Gav, all out for their pennies worth, stuff the people underneath.

"What did you call me"? Shazzer glared.

"Not you. I'm just fed up with it all" Gavin glumly said "it would just be nice if…" he mused for a moment reflecting on everything that had happened in the last two years and realistically it was going to be another two for things to balance out…at least.

"It's just that big businesses don't help much, especially the ones who make millions if not billions of profit a year. All for the shareholders" he said waving his arms "and people just follow suit, bunch of stupid sheep, if everyone was more careful…"

"Shut up Gavin" Sharon said "you're doing it again".

"Well, I mean…"

"No, Gav. Don't want to hear it for the sixtieth time. Alright" she said giving him one of her looks.

"But they're parasites. Selfish fucking parasites" he continued. "Just thinking of themselves".

"GAV! Enough"! came the final word.

Gavin went to the sink and poured himself a glass of water and was about to mutter when his beloved interjected.

"No Gavin. Don't want to hear another word".

So, he took a swig from the glass and went back to shoot some more aliens, mumbling to himself.

"Oh, that's great" he heard Sharon say about an hour later, obviously loud enough for him to hear. Feeling obliged, he called out, dropping a drone bomb on a hoard of burrowing alien termites intent on world domination.

"What is it hon"?

"They're going to be late" she called back "could be anytime up until 11".

Gavin got up and trotted back to the kitchen where Sharon was sitting at the table reading her messages on her phone.

"Ha" he laughed "you do realise they won't come now. "You're just being fobbed off".

"No, it says they're still coming, just don't have an exact time" Sha remonstrated.

"Does it say why"? Gav enquired.

"No. Probably broke down or something. You know what it's like" she answered.

Both he and Sharon had worked in retail, so understood full well the excuses that could be dished out to cover situations.

"I did hear they stopped paying overtime" Shaz continued.

"And whys that" he said raising his eyebrows, about to go on another rant "Fucking. Blood. Suckers". He was about to go on a full-on spiel, when he was interrupted.

"Will you stop saying that" Sharon shouted "Why don't you go back to your game" she said, pointing.

"Well, have they reimbursed your delivery charge"? Gavin asked

Time suspended itself while Sharon quickly checked her bank account.

Looking up with warning in her eyes "No".

Gavin pulled one of those "See! Told you so", the type she would love to slap, but he turned and left, probably feeling very smug with himself.

Sitting back down in front of the T.V he noticed that he hadn't pressed pause, instead the H.U.D was on full screen mode and by the looks of it, was getting eaten alive by some weird looking zombie type aliens instead. He had lost the enthusiasm for alien annihilation, so powered off the console and sat and thought for a few minutes.

He got back up and went back into the kitchen where Sharon was scrolling through social media, tutting and pulling faces.

"Shaz"? asked Gavin "what happens if they don't turn up"?

"What"? answered Sharon.

"The delivery. What do we do if the delivery doesn't turn up"?

Sharon looked at her boyfriend, trying to comprehend whether he really was that stupid and whether he had said what he had said.

"Well, "Mr I'm going to put the world to right with my big ideas", I guess SOMEONE, is going to have to go shopping" going back to her phone.

"Aw, do I have to. You know how much I hate shopping" Gav said getting his knickers all tangled like a big girls blouse he was.

"It's either that, or we wait until next week, you decide" Sharon finalised, not bothering to even look up.

"I'm not going tonight" Gavin said, attempting to lay down the law and be all grown up.

Sharon looked at her boyfriend. She loved him very much, but he could be such a dick at times. I mean, who said anything about going this evening. Besides, they lived at least 10 miles from the nearest supermarket and it wasn't as if they were really short of anything, well, not too short of anything. She was sure they could manage until next week if needed.

"Gav". Sharon said, explaining to Mr Man. "You don't have to go tonight…or tomorrow…or the day after if you don't want to… okay"?

"Anyway" she continued "the delivery will be here this evening and you're getting yourself worked up over nothing".

No sooner as the words had left her mouth, her phone pinged.

"Bollocks" she said.

"What's that"? Gavin enquired moving around to her side of the table.

"They've cancelled the order. Dickheads. They're not coming until the day after tomorrow now".

Gavin smiled, to himself, and gave himself a congratulatory pat on the back.

"Never mind" he said "Could be worse" he smiled and decided to go and put the T.V back on.

He was just getting comfy, flicking through the channels, trying to find something to watch, something that wasn't gossip, scandal, American drama (oh, how they did drama: "Oh my God" "What is it Dolores" "Larry's DEAD" "Dead" "Yes, he's DEAD" "My God" "I Know" "How did he die" "He just... Died" "My...God... and sooo on), American Documentary (full of dramatic music), in fact nothing American, comedy was the worst, though modern British comedy wasn't much better, when Sharon walked in.

"Honeyy," she crooned "you know how much you love me"? she asked, giving him one of those "I'm going to ask you to do something for me looks".

Gav knew straight away what she was going to ask, so decided to go along with the charade rather than cut to the chase, hoping that she wouldn't ask.

"Yes" he replied.

"and you know how much I love you" she continued.

"Yess" he replied again.

"The thing is..."

"Yes"

"I forgot"

A mutual pause was between then. Sharon wanting him to ask what it was that she had forgotten and Gavin not wanting to ask, knowing what was coming next.

Stalemate had been reached, eventually it was Gavin, as usual who crumbled, his resolve was a lot weaker than hers.

"What have you forgotten, my love" he enquired.

"We've got no milk" she said.

"Bollocks" he said, knowing that he had just lost the game.

"Well, I didn't know we wouldn't be getting our shopping delivered, it's not my fault".

Gavin's mind raced through all the possible scenarios that he could go through with the milk dilemma.

1 They could wait until the morning, but he'd have to go shopping anyway.

2 He could go now and get it over and done with.

3 Go without milk, no biggy.

4 Bollocks. He was going to get it over and done with. Besides it wasn't that late and then he could have a bowl of cereal when he got back. He could but some Sugar Puffs at the same time. He hadn't had Sugar Puffs in ages.

"I may as well go now" he said gloomily, not letting on about his plan for Sugar Puffs.

"Oh, thank you darling" Sharon said giving him a big hug, looking forward to her hot chocolate later.

he put his boots on and went to the downstairs loo, just in case, calling out "Is there anything else you want me to get whilst I'm there" he called in mid flow.

"I'm writing a list" Sharon called back from the kitchen.

"Hey ho" he thought, doing his flies back up and flushing.

Shaz met him at the door.

"Here you go, don't be too long and take care" she said "have you got a mask"?

"Yup" Gavin replied, slipping it on and clicking open the air lock, the depths of space visible beyond the hatch.

He had already cleared the area of the alien vampires, so didn't expect any trouble for a few miles, but he had his double laser guns fully loaded and ready.

THE FLOWER LADY

The gates to the park, with their high ornate spiked bars, were still locked, having been closed, regularly, the night before. A frivolous act, considering how low the railings beside them stood and how easy it would be for an inclined person to climb over. The flower lady arrived half an hour before opening with her small homemade, wooden barrow, complete with shelves to display her daily selection of buttonhole flowers, trimmed and wrapped ready for gentlemen to buy on their way to work.

Little posies of fragrant blooms entwined with scraps of ribbon or cloth sat perched in miniature jam jars of water, that, despite their size, wouldn't look out of place in a dolls house. All seasonal colours had been chosen with natural care, complimenting each other with size and scent, always offering something for young or old, happy or sad, there was a flower for everyone, if they stopped to look.

The flower lady pulled out her three-legged stool from under her stall and carefully checked and gently tweaked her flowers, whispering gently about what a fine day it was and how lucky they were going to be to brighten someone's spirits, making them glow with inner radiance.

She had been selling flowers at the gate for as long as she could remember, well before the turn of the century, when she was a young girl.

Back then she just had a basket to sell from and would walk up and the railings of the park, catching the men's eyes with the swaying of her hips, her long flowing locks and sparkling eyes. She made a fair fortune with her smile and complimentary words, even ladies on their constitutional were pleased to see an innocent with a smiling and welcoming face.

Her mother used to say that she had been granted natural grace from the good lord, hence her name. He had seen fit to bless her with a good heart, but it would come as a price.

"You can't have one without the other" Bonnie would remember her mother saying.

It had been a hard childhood, not as some others had though. They hadn't lived in the slums but were always one step away from, both her parents having to work hard from dusk 'til dawn, her brothers the same and luckily for her they had a little patch of garden out the back of their house where she grew her flowers from wild seeds and shoots.

It had started by chance, a lone plant taking root in the wall, the little blue periwinkle spreading fast, but mixed with buttercup and daisy made a fine posy when tied up with a leaf or two.

No one round the area wanted, or could afford such luxury, though some would except the generosity of a small bunch at the end of a day to brighten the ramshackle lives. So, she ventured further afield, walking miles to find a suitable location and that's when she found the palace that stood in the park.

It felt like home straight away. The gentle paths that wound themselves around the more secret and discreet walks for lovers and newlyweds to stroll. The low overhanging trees that leant gentle protection, the open stretches of grass for little feet to run and skip on and the mighty oaks with arms outstretched, having stood for years, watching, like she unknowingly would, the changes that occurred.

To her surprise, the first day of selling her wares, she sold her whole basket in one go to a footman from the palace. He had been sent out to find some token items for the children's game Hide and Seek, where items were to be laid around the orangery for attenders to discover, and on meeting Bonnie, offered a princely sum of a shilling for the whole basket, which she gladly took, returning home with a smile as bright as her coinage.

The flower lady sat on her stool and checked her large dark grey coat and scarf, her hat already neatly pinned into place, it looked like it was going to be a cold day, but she didn't mind the weather, though she did cough more than she used to.

She sat, her eyes fixing on a point in the past, where Hansom cabs used trot by too destinations a many, comings and goings, the genteel in their finery and horse and carts delivering their goods from out of town, unloaded at either canal junctions or railway stations or even some delivering exclusively to large haberdasheries and stores.

A car horn brought her back to the modern times, the vehicles already rushing backwards and forwards on their endless journeys, only stopping when the lights turn red, never halting to greet a time of day or talk gently about the beauty of life.

A business man, with bowler on and case under his arm, strode down the pavement with purpose in his gait, his umbrella swinging in military time of his step, halted before her and scrutinised the selection.

"Good morning, my dear lady" he addressed her with precise informality.

"Good morning, Colonel" she replied back politely, slowly standing. She hadn't known whether this was his rank or not, when they first met, but suspected, not. He had been a regular visitor for years and she had recognised his military persona straight away and had opted for a complimentary stance, and was duly accepted, though something which he had never confirmed nor rectified.

"What shall it be today" she said more to herself and he flowers than to him.

"A rose, I think" she said, spying the little yellow bud trying to hide itself.

"Not today, my dear lady" he replied "I seem to have come out without my wallet" he said patting his inner jacket pocket.

Bonnie smiled, not for the first time at The Colonels "forgetfulness".

"Well, never mind dear" she said pinning the flower onto his lapel with care, smelling the warmth of his shaving lotion, which had gotten cheaper over the last two years. "If you find it later, you can always buy a box of matches on your way home" she said, tapping her flower goodbye.

The Colonel smiled genuine gratitude, they understood each other well enough by now. The old man at the tube was another soul who touted his wares, of matches and shoelaces, and could always do with a helping hand.

"Good day, my dear lady" he said as he strode off with renewed vigour and an extra zip in his swing, ready for the unappreciated and meagre work he would do, for people half his age commanding his actions, where one time…

The flower lady checked her stall and stretched her legs, even though they got stretched enough with her daily walk to and from home, pushing her barrow, wrapped in her thoughts of time gone.

She sat back down, adjusting her stockings as she went and remembered the day a little boy got his head stuck in the railings. He was with his mother at the time and they had been strolling along the park side of the pavement, an unusual way to walk, she thought as she watched. She noticed that words were exchanged, the mother distracted by nothing that she could see, as the young child pushed his head firmly between the iron posts and became wedged, much to the amusement of a milkman going past.

Firemen had to come and cut free the trapped youngster and the flower lady was surprised that no rebuke was dealt. If she had done such a thing in her day, she was sure father would belt her so hard with his belt, that she wouldn't be able to sit down for a week.

She smiled with the memories of her family. All gone now. Even her dear Albert had passed. Just her and her flowers left… and Tibbles.

The morning passed slowly, with fewer and fewer people buying flowers these days. She would leave at about 2, after lunch when ladies and nannies would bring the little mites for a stroll around the park and, by which time, Giuseppe would be here.

Giuseppe was a nice young man, who looked older than he was. His curly black hair and large moustache, all hidden under a soft peaked cap, never gave away his age. It was also in the way he dressed; in a tatty dark suit, that could easily belong to a tramp, but nothing was lowbrow about his conversation.

When he talked, the air came alive with fun and laughter. His loud Italian expressions and gesticulations were all part of his performance that sold the balloons he carried around. An assortment of shapes and colours bounced together on bits of coloured string. Some balloons had pictures on them, others had smaller balloons in them, long tall ones or star shaped, even rockets and car ones. Just the sight of a bobbing balloon could catch anyone's imagination.

Bonnie was feeling tired today. She leant down behind her barrow and produced a paper wrap of sandwiches and a small thermos flask of tea. She had never liked coffee. Her Albert had. He could have drunk coffee until the cows came home.

She poured herself a metal cup of still steaming liquid, screwing the lid back on tightly and took a bite out of one of her egg and cress sandwiches, chewing thoughtfully as she went.

She thought of the time she had met the king, when he had come visiting his daughter at the palace. A fancy carriage had pulled up not feet from where she sat now, and out he stepped, as bold as brass, right before her very eyes and tipped his hat... at her. Well. She could hardly believe it herself. Her. Miss Bonnie Nobody being greeted by the King. He bought a beautiful red rose, not one of her finest, but a beaut nonetheless and paid her the exact amount...from his own pocket...though she tried to refuse payment, he insisted, pressing the coin into her very own hand. 'Course, mum and dad didn't believe her at first, took a few days of convincing mind, she remembered.

"I said, how much for the freesia" came the voice of a lady.

The flower lady snapped out of her daydream, realising she still had hold of her tin cup and unchewed sandwich in her mouth.

"Oh, I'm sorry ma'am" she said, organising herself "I was a million miles away" the thoughts still lingering in the background.

"Oh, never mind" came the curt response, as the lady turned about and walked off.

Bonnie sat and watched for a moment, surprised by the event, then took another bite of her sandwich and resumed day dreaming of days gone by.

When she awoke, she noticed the flow of traffic was heavier in the wrong direction and the shadows had already turned. Fumbling for her uncle's pocket watch she was amazed to see that she had been asleep for hours. Her back was sore, her legs were stiff and her bum was as numb as a...well, it was very numb. She stood and groaned at the discomfort and realised that she had never done this before. Never in all her days. She could see that the light was changing and Tibbles would be wanting food, so she slowly packed up, cursing herself for her old age, picked up the smooth handles of her barrow and started the push home.

"Mummy? Can we buy some flowers from the flower lady today"? the young lad asked the next morning, hopping along next to his mother while trying to miss the crocodiles in the cracks of the pavement.

"Not today, Eric darling," said his mother.

"Aw, how about some bird feed" he asked, knowing it was only tuppence a bag, he had one penny in his pocket.

"No, not today" came the reply as they carried on walking up the hill towards the gates for their regular visit to the park.

As they drew nearer, Erics heart sank, as no trace of the flower lady could be seen.

"Mum" he said, looking up at his mother "Where's the flower lady"?

"Oh, I don't know darling, I'm sure she'll be there tomorrow" Cassie said as they carried on their way.

Bonnie wasn't there "tomorrow", nor ever again. There was no one to ask what had happened to her or where she went. But it was the first time in that young boy's life that he experienced change, and he remembered that stranger with affection all his life and wished he could have said thank you for the memories, for being there and goodbye.

SOME LIKE IT

Franco stood, naked, in front of the mirror. He really couldn't see why he was still single. Dark hair, dark eyes, good bone structure, great teeth, good body tone, taut butt, twisting slightly round just to check, reasonably packed, athletic legs, though he didn't like his feet, but hey, its not as if he put them on the table when meeting new partners for the first time.

"Hi, my names Franco, nice to meet you, hey, look at my feet".

That didn't happen.

He stood a while longer in front of the long mirror, wishing he could see what other people did that put them off, but he drew a blank.

A big nada.

He checked the clock and realised he had wasted enough time standing naked in his bedroom and, having already shaved and sprayed, walked over to his wardrobe to select this evening's killer outfit.

"What should I wear" he thought to himself, flicking through his shirts and trousers. "Hmm".

He considered himself, as did others, quite a sharp dresser, a real head turner in fact, which made it even more puzzling as to why he failed in his conquests with women, it just made him more and more insecure.

One time back, when things were getting him really down, he even considered that perhaps he was self-sabotaging and that maybe…he was gay. Admittedly that thought didn't stay long as he knew in his heart that wasn't true, but you get rejected time and time again…well…you have to re-evaluate your situation.

Tonight, was going to be purple and black. A deep purple shirt with plain black trousers, well cut and tailored. Now, what about accessories. Eyeing through his belts the orange jumped out, as if shouting "Me, me. Choose me". Pulling the orange belt through his trouser loops he scanned over his shoe selection and found a coordinating pair of shiny bright orange Chelsea's that would do just fine.

He returned to the mirror, brushing himself off, and was pleased with the selection, no need for a jacket tonight, and undid an extra button of his shirt.

"Yup, all good" he said to himself, walking to the door, picking up his keys and slimline wallet. Before closing the door, he turned the little table lamp on and flicked off the ceiling light, leaving the bathroom window open for Tabby to come and go if needed. He hadn't seen her all afternoon, so figured she had figured she had found something interesting or who knows what. That's pets for you. One day they can find entertainment in a scrap of paper for hours, the next day, can't be bothered with anything.

Franco trotted down the stairs of his flat and jumped into his car that was conveniently parked almost outside and drove through the streets to the restaurant, where he was going to meet his blind date for the evening.

They had mutual friends and had been matched accordingly, both having been single for a while and both having similar interests, apparently, but the last time he had been told "Oh, you've got so much in common with so and so" it turned out that she hated his taste in literature and he thought she was a bit of a...monster (though he didn't tell her...not to her face... well...maybe a bit).

"I mean, honestly" he gesticulated to his mate Dave who had set them up "the way she blows her nose, its disgusting" he said grimacing "she checks for treasure" he said heaving, re-membering the final straw when she laughed so loud, she choked on her dessert, blew her nose and he could literally count the seconds she spent inspecting the contents of her tis-sue. "I mean, who would do that".

All he got in return was a "Beggars can't be choosers, man, beg-gars can't be choosers". That was the last time he relied on that friend for a hook-up.

The bistro was your typical Italian fare. Easy lighting, intim-ate tables, raffia covered bottles for decoration and plastic red gingham table cloths, complete with a candle stuck in a used wine bottle for extra mood enhancement, and when he ar-rived, he noticed that she was already sitting there, waiting for him.

He smiled and waved and instantly realised their colour co-ordinates clashed. He had forgotten that she was going to be wearing a red blouse, but she smiled back anyway, so that was a good start.

He strode over and offered his hand.

"Ciao, Franco, pleasure to greet you" he said smiling, not too broadly though, he didn't want to seem desperate or crazy.

"No, my names Camilla" she replied with a stern look on her face, instantly throwing his brain into confusion.

"Sorry, what"? he faltered.

"You called me Franco. My name is Camilla" came the terse reply.

"What? Sorry? Oh, no. I know. My name is Franco" he said falling over his own feet.

Camilla looked at him and laughed "Yeah, I know" she chuckled easily "I'm just messing with you. I know I'm not Franco" she laughed again, smiling at how easy a target he had been, bit cruel, but fun.

"Oh, yes. I see. Franco. Me. Camilla" he said pointing backwards and forwards. "Well, ha. Hi. Night to meece you, I mean nice to meet you". He said quickly correcting himself.

He pulled out a seat and sat down, a waiter appearing instantly for a drinks order.

"I hope you haven't been waiting long" Franco said to his date, while placing his napkin on his lap and admiring how her eyes matched her smile.

"Well, actually, you're late. I've been waiting over an hour" Camilla said checking her watch with noticeable anger in her voice.

"What, no, really?" he flustered, suddenly panicking that he had gotten the time wrong.

"You're an easy target" she said "I'm going to enjoy this".

Franco sat back in his chair and took a deep breath, just as his drink arrived.

"Wooda Sir like a ta order some anti-pasta maybe" the well uniformed waiter enquired.

"That would be lovely, thank you. Just bring a selection of what you think" he said without checking with his guest and suddenly realising his possible error, turned his attention to her.

"I'm sorry, I hope you don't mind, its just that they do great piadinas here, filled with smoked black garlic and ham…" he said excitedly to her, licking his lips "I love garlic" he finalised with great gusto and enthusiasm.

"Hmm" Camilla replied slowly "I noticed". Though he didn't.

The anti-pastas came with a small aperitif and the two on-lookers chatted together easily, swapping horror stories of other blind dates and set-ups, the crazies and the fruit loops, being interspersed by the occasional let downs and hang-ups, while he ate and she drank.

They ordered more wine, which started a stream of criticism of their mutual companions, pointing out their foibles and nuances with much laughter and impressions, all the while growing fonder of each other along the way.

As if seconds had gone the mains arrived. Camilla had opted for a simple and light carbonara with an easy green salad, whereas Franco had opted for the full and robust Tuscan steak. It sat hot and vibrant on his plate defying anyone not to love its glistening charring and moistness.

"I don't mean to be rude," Camilla said twirling some tagliatelle around her fork "but you really do love garlic don't you", trying not to sound too critical.

"Oh, I love it" Franco said exuberantly, already chewing on a piece of steak and cutting in for his next slice.

"You do realise it can be quite…pungent," she continued, trying to be subtle "and some people can find it…a bit of…well… a bit strong" satisfied with her phrasing, without being offensive.

"Oh, that's nonsense," he said waving his knife "that's just a myth" he said, dismissing the mere possibility.

"No." Camilla interjected "It's true. It can be very overpowering to someone who hasn't participated in the eating of said… bulb" still twirling some carbonara.

"Really? I thought it was all just nonsense. You know, like when they say you shouldn't eat food after its best before date."

"Use by date". She pointed out.

"What"?

"Use by date. You shouldn't eat food after its use by date. Best before means just that. It's best before..." she concluded with a little flourish.

Franco sat momentarily open mouthed, thinking of how much of an idiot he was looking now.

"Blimey," he was thinking to himself "what else had he got wrong and why was this beautiful lady the first to correct him".

"So" he nervously and slowly started "this...garlic thing"

"Yes"? she answered, having another sip of wine.

"Are you saying..." he was desperately trying to assess the mess he had made over past mistakes "So, you're saying..."

"Yess" came the reply.

"So, you can tell if someone's eaten garlic"? he gently enquired "When you've not eaten any" he added as an afterthought.

"Of course," Camilla said with a small shrug of her shoulders.

The tidal wave broke and it all started to make sense now.

"So, all those times..." Franco proceeded slowly.

"Probably".

"You mean..."

"Yup" Camilla said emphatically

"That bad..."? he was getting pretty concerned by now.

"Oh...my...,...I can't believe what an eejit I've been" Franco declared putting his knife and fork down, incredulity stopping all functions.

His mind raced back to times of having a sneaky serving of heavy garlic mayonnaise with a chicken salad before meeting a girl for drinks, or crunching on some extra garlicy bread while waiting for a midnight club date, or..., the list, unfortunately, went on.

Camilla could see his mind was racing, so thought she might try and help this lovely chap, who she was growing fond of, something about his naïve charm.

"Why do you like garlic so much"? she asked.

"I dunno," he said "I guess it's my family heritage"

"What? But you're Irish aren't you"?

"Well, yes and…well, yes and no, Italian" confusing even himself.

Camilla looked at him for a moment, deciding to try and make him feel more uncomfortable than he already was. It was quite easy.

The silence hung about like an unwanted guest, shuffling their feet in awkwardness, not knowing whether to ask for another cup of tea or just to run, screaming.

It was Camilla who broke the uneasiness, it was the least she could do, she felt, it was her who put it there and she broke it with a laugh.

The laugh made Franco smile, with relief and nervousness, as nobody had ever put him on the rollercoaster like this before, and, he was enjoying it. A bit like a kid being told at the ice-cream van:

"Right Sammy, which ice-cream would you like"?

"Hmm, chocolate…no, vanilla…no, strawberry…no"

"Why not all three"?

YAY!

They both laughed, the ice had well and truly been broken and underneath lay clear waters and fresh starts.

"Hey, I have an idea" Camilla suggested "Why don't we go an get dessert somewhere else, I know a place, not far".

"That's a great idea" Franco could hear himself saying before the stupid part of him could interject or cause trouble.

They paid and rose, Franco holding the door open as they stepped out into the night, saying their farewells to the restaurant which had brought them together.

They walked apart, then hand in hand, then arm in arm, with Camilla resting her head on his shoulder she softly said:

"Whoever heard of a vampire liking garlic"?

"Nobody's perfect" he smiled.

I SEE YOU!

The shadow flitted across the young girl's bedroom, pausing at the small, plastic dressing table where Annie liked to play with her Barbie dolls, getting them ready for important dates and social functions, such as dinner with Prince Ken (who was actually her brothers Action Man…though he didn't know it).

It heard the sound of footsteps, lightly running up the stairs with a voice calling behind them "I'll be up in a minute. Just get ready for your bath".

The landing light flicked on, illuminating parts of the bedroom, sending the shadow to the back of the room by the curtains where it was nice and dark.

The bedroom door flew open, lighting the room, sending the shadow back where it came from and the little girl rushed in and turned on her bedside light, which her Nanna had given her, and the horses on the carousel started to go round and up and down to the gentle sound of the lullaby.

As every night, she stopped for a moment to admire her birthday present, it was the best thing she had ever been given, she especially like the grey and white horse. Grandad had called it dappled, which sounded a perfect name for it, so she called that one Dapple.

There was also Ping (that was the one she saw first when the music started), Prince (he was very grand), Scarf (because of his neck), John (Mum said she had to let her brother, John, name one, soo original), and finally the last two, Ren and Stimpy (named after daddie's favourite programme, though she didn't like the names much but she loved her daddy).

Annie busied around her bedroom looking for her towel and deciding which Barbie was coming for a bath, explaining to the other toys that they just had to wait their turn and that some of them hadn't eaten their carrots, so no nice treats later.

The toys didn't seem that bothered, they just sat and stared at whatever they were interested in, but Annie knew different.

Her mother shouted up the stairs telling her daughter to put the plug in the bath and start running the cold as she was on the phone to Aunty.

Annie loved her Aunty NooNoo, she was funny, but she had moved a while ago, nearer to Nanna and Grandad actually, with her new boyfriend (who always smelt funny). She realised that Mummy missed Aunty as much she did as she often looked like she had been crying after their phone calls.

Annie looked around her room trying to find her Hawaiian Barbie, who must really be in line for a bath by now, and remembered she had been captured a while ago by the nasty ogre under her dressing table.

She bent down to see if she could see her, but had to lie down on her tummy to reach. An unsettling cold chill creeped its way into her stomach as her hand reached out and touched something unexpectedly as cold as ice though as transparent as cobwebs.

A short sharp scream emitted from the prostrate young girl as she clambered to her feet and stood in horror as she heard silent wisp of a voice "I see you".

She saw the back of her mother dashing into the bathroom, stop and turn, seeing her daughter standing in the middle of her bedroom, shaking, clutching Hanna Barbie in her little, goose bumped arms.

Annie could see her mum had been crying again, her eyes still puffy, but the tears had been driven away by the shock of hearing her daughter in trouble.

Her mother knelt down before her daughter, asking her what the matter was, checking her for signs of injury or harm, while Annie explained what had happened.

Her mother explained that it must have been a spider, or some other creepy crawly, as it was the time of year that they started coming into the house, trying to find a nice warm home for the winter.

Annie looked down to the floor by the dresser, not wanting to see Mr Hairy Scary come out, I hope he's happy with himself, she thought, and imagined the spider waving flags, wearing a party hat and blowing on a party blower at his success...and smiling very triumphantly.

Mother led Annie to the bathroom, turned of the slow running cold tap and turned on the hot, adding a splosh of bubble bath for added comfort and distraction.

The bubbles worked. For the next half hour, mother and daughter were distracted from their troubles in the world, connected in each other's company, playing shops and hair-dressers, with H.B being the most difficult and demanding of customers.

All good things must come to an end, bath time was no exception, the water not staying warm enough for that long and the plug was pulled. That was not quite the end of the fun though, there was still the opportunity to slide up and down the bath as the water emptied, getting faster and faster, trying to add a spin for good measure. The cherry on the cake, so to speak. It's a shame adults can't enjoy things as much as children, her mother was thinking, it's not as if some of them haven't grown up.

Wrapping her daughter and the bubbles up in a towel, she lifted them both out of the bath and set them down on the bath mat and told Annie to get dry while she went and fetched some clean pyjamas.

Annie asked for her unicorn ones and slip slips, not wanting to reach under any surfaces thank you very much, especially as she was now nice and clean.

Her mum returned with smiles and clothes and helped her daughter finishing off getting dry and puffed her body with some talcum powder, a special treat indeed, and hindered her get dressed, putting her legs in her arms holes and arms in her leg holes, back to front and inside out.

After their exhausting few minutes of laughter, Annie's mother suggested a glass of milk and cookie for them both, so Annie hopped into bed with delight as her mum went downstairs to fetch their bedtime snack. Annie stared at her carousel, the horsies still going round and round, up and down, round and round, up and...when she noticed that Dapple was slightly twisted. She didn't remember knocking him. She knew he was loose, looser than the others, that's the problem with favourite things. They get played with.

She straightened him out, just as her mother came into the door with a tray of two small glasses of milk and two cookies... each. Yes!

They sat munching and slurping, each showing each other the contents of their mouths, trying to make the loudest eating and drinking noises possible and seeing if either could get a piece of chocolate chip to come out of their noses.

The scare before was well and truly pushed away as mother suggested teeth wash time, despite remonstrations and lots of huffs and puffings, and Annie shuffled off, back to the bathroom and pretended to brush her little white pegs, she didn't want to lose the flavour of the milk and biscuits, did she.

Bouncing back into the bedroom and straight under the blankets, so her mum couldn't smell the lack of mint, she said her goodnights and asked for her carousel light to be left on.

Her mother leant over the pile of bedding and kissed the duvet goodnight, which wriggled and giggled at the tickles. Then all was quiet. Dad wouldn't be back from work for hours and Stinky John was staying at some friends for the week, so she listened to the sounds of the house, watching the colours of her rotating carousel, now with music off, the hypnotic motion rocking her young mind to a world of endless imagination and possibilities.

Her eyes heavy and body warm and soft, comforted by the security of a full tummy, let her breathing deepen...drifting...

"I SEE YOU" came loud and clear.

The eyes opened wide and full, shocked at the sound, as her heart beat fast, keeping her body as still as possible, trying to sense whether she had just heard what she heard, was her body movement, or was it just a memory echo, recalling what had happened.

The quiet of her bedroom was only interrupted by her pounding chest and the gentle, repetitive squeak of the cogs of her bedside light, so she held her breath for a moment longer.

She called for her mum, the first time too quiet to be heard, who appeared in no time in an unhurried fashion. Annie explained that she was scared and had heard a funny noise, so her mother comforted her and eased her tension, reassuring her that there was nothing really scary to be afraid of, that it was probably just her imagination, she really should get to sleep.

Her mother leant over and clicked off the exhausted horses and left, leaving the bathroom sink light on and the door only slightly ajar...just in case, then went back downstairs, just as the phone rang.

Annie lay in her bed, still comfy, looking up at the ceiling, the darkness black and speckly, some areas looking darker than others, especially when you stare at them, the bits out of view...

She sat up instantly, looking into the darkest corner of the bedroom.

She thought she had seen movement out of the corner of her eye.

Annie stared intently at the spot, unmoving, until her elbows reminded her that they were there. Nothing moved as she stared, but just as she was about to lay back down, a strand of hair fell across her face that caused her to scream.

The landing light clicked on and she saw her mother in the doorway asking what the matter was now. Annie felt stupid to have jumped at her own hair and apologised to her mother for being so silly, but explained that she thought she had seen something and felt even more stupid when she heard herself saying the words.

Again comforted, reassured and told to get to sleep as they had to go out tomorrow, Annie laid down on her side, facing the wall and shut her eyes, tightly.

She drifted quickly into her dreams. Shapes of light and dark danced around her mind as the waves circled and clouds fluttered like butterflies.

The shadow slipped quietly out of the darkest recesses spreading across the floor to the young girl's bed, who lay vulnerable, motionless and unaware. At her side, it reached her.

"I see you" came the long cold noise that emanated from the silent void.

"I SEE YOU" came the louder, second spatial hiss.

Annie was instantly awake, drenched in fear and sweat, cold and shaking, tears drenching her cheeks, her fringe sticking to her forehead.

She called again for her mother, who again arrived promptly though tired. Annie told her mother that something had scared her and woken her up, it hid in the corner but had gone now.

Her mother soothed her, like her mum had done for her when she was a child. She talked about how she sometimes got scared and when younger, imagined all types of things that might be possible or hiding under the bed. Her mother even told her of Nanas childhood, when, in the old days, they used to roll cannonballs under the bed, in case an intruder was hiding there and one day they forgot they had left a full potty under there. She then had to explain what a potty was, which caused a lot of giggling.

Soothed once again, Annie's mother stayed while her daughter drifted back to sleep, hopefully for the last time tonight.

Annie slept, though restless and disturbed as the shadow watched.

Her arm hung down the side of the bed as she dreamt of being in a boat, gliding through icy waters as her hand trailed in the wake, as the edge of the shadow encroached on her skin, hearing the familiar "I…".

She awoke, pulling her hand from the waters freezing clasp and tucked it under her armpit to warm up. She refused to acknowledge whatever it was and remembered the story of the chamber pot and smiled at the warm memory that sent the darkness scurrying, plunging back into the land of nod.

Morning in fits and starts, with little Annie waking to the smell of bacon frying in the pan. Surprised, because she knew it wasn't Sunday, when they normally had something extra, she rubbed her eyes and put on her dressing gown and plodded downstairs.

Arriving in the kitchen, she was surprised to see her daddy up and dressed and not still in bed after his late shift and mum was looking really tired, one hand steadying herself as she stood in front of the hob.

"Morning squirt" her father said affectionately "How'd you sleep?"

Annie sat down at the table next to him after giving him a hug good morning and proceeded to explain about the shadow and the scary crawly thing. He nodded thoughtfully in return, eating his bacon and toast, sipping on his orange juice, with plenty of "Oh's?" and "Ooh's" put in.

"It talked too" Annie said, smiling at her mother as she brought over a bacon sandwich and placed it on the table for her daughter.

"I see you" Annie said as scarily as she could while pointing a finger at her father.

Her dad stopped chewing for a moment and her mother was silent too. Both parents caught each other's eyes at the same time, as the same thought passed between them.

Silence is a bit like snow. There are many types. In the old days, when a certain silence descended into a room with more than two people and at half past the hour, they said that an angel was passing. Now was not that time, but close to it.

"Annie?" her father said reaching out his hand and resting it on hers "Nanna's not well" he explained "We...we thought we might go and visit her today."

The silence returned, not the same, more uncomfortable and filled with the sadness that comes after tears. Annie felt like she wanted to be happy, but the mood of her parents dampened everything inside her, confusing her and slowing her movements, as if walking against a still and quiet, yet almighty wind.

Annie had never experienced anything like this before. No further explanations came from her questions, just the same answers, which only fuelled her concern and anxiety.

As if in her own personal whirlwind, she finished her breakfast and went upstairs to get changed for their outing. She went to reach under her bed for someone to take with her, but instinctively pulled back, selecting a teddy from the middle of the floor instead.

Again, in silence, except for the noises of doors and the routine checks, they got into the car and drove. Annie could tell that her mum was crying and she put her hand on her shoulder from the back seat, as tears started to form in her own eyes.

She watched out of the car window at the world going by, barely registering the people carrying on regardless and unaware of her plight, but soon didn't recognise the route they were taking in the car. "Where are we going?" Annie softly asked, wiping her cheek dry with teddy. "Hospital, darling. Nannas in hospital" her mother replied. Buildings and roads passed by as did the time and eventually they turned in to the large car park of the infirmary, already filling with vehicles.

Annie watched from the window as they parked, at the people getting in and out of their cars, all wrapped up in their own worlds. Perhaps one of them have a sick Nanna, she thought to herself.

Annie watched as her father got out of the car to get a parking ticket.

Something about it filled her with dread and fear, like she was stepping into unknown territory. A place that might be filled with lions and tigers and bears.

Her father returned and put the ticket on the dash, like she had seen him do many times before at many car parks, but this felt different. Everything felt different…scary different. The quiet that could be heard behind the noise of life's activity was getting louder, making her feel odd and alone.

She clasped her mother's hand as they crossed the road, her squeeze being given a squeeze back. She didn't fully understand why, but her eyes were wanting to fill up again, but the warmth of the morning kept them at bay.

All three of them entered the hospital sliding doors and were met with a dizzying selection of arrows and signs pointing to different levels and locations. Her father went over to the receptionist's desk and Annie saw the lady pointing out directions.

She noticed that her heart started beating faster and each step she took made her knees quiver a little more.

They walked down open glass corridors, into the depth of the building, past the day units she had visited and the well-used wards.

Annie became more worried for her Nanna and herself as they entered into the areas that they hadn't visited before, as her gentle tears blurred her vision and she could now hear her heart in her ears. She squeezed hard on teddys paw, who had decided to come, just in case he was needed.

They stopped in front of two large doors and her mother, now aware, knelt down to console her sobbing daughter.

"Don't worry darling," she said cradling the young girls head on her shoulder "everything will be okay."

Sniffing, wiping her eyes with, who wouldn't mind, she saw the sign above the doors.

The letters I.C.U were hanging above the ward.

Then she knew, her mum was right, that she didn't need to be scared anymore.

AND BOB CAME TOO

Bob, as usual, was lying on the floor, hoovering the carpet with his open mouth, one eye vaguely open, unsure whether it could be bothered to focus on anything, though acutely aware that he could see the wall and noticing a stain that it didn't remember seeing before.

He tried moving, but he chair on top of him toppled onto his head and the towel that had hung on the back of it now covered back, which was much more comfortable, despite hearing Larry and Andy having a "discussion".

"Oh Andy, you're such a grump. How can you possibly understand when you're in such a mood?" Larry said happily to his friend.

"Look...*Larry*," Andy said somewhat sarcastically "It's not that I don't understand what you're saying" sardonically "I just don't care what you think."

"Oh Andy, Andy, Andy" Larry cheerfully smiled "I think someone needs to take a few relaxing breaths."

"Fuck off Larry!" Andy said as he stomped off to be angry at something or someone else, anywhere but here "Dick!" he muttered quietly to himself, but unsure about who he was really talking about...but he wasn't going to admit it.

Larry, beaming from ear to ear, stepped over Bob as if he wasn't there and went into the kitchen to find Joe who was getting the picnic ready. Joe looked a mess. He didn't help himself. Larry was sure that if he cleaned himself up a bit it might help. Get a haircut, have a wash and shave, maybe even wear some clean clothes, instead of lounging around in holey sweatpants and stained vest tops that looked two sizes too big for him. The incessant smoking didn't help either, the nicotine-stained fingers and teeth did nothing for his appeal.

Why Joe had been elected to food preparation was beyond Larry, he never cleaned up after himself, the sink was proof of that and the worktops were barely visible, under the pile of debris caused by half attempts of pastry making, half peeled vegetables, but mainly discarded wrappers and boxes of assorted biscuits, cakes and ready meals.

Larry ventured around the kitchen picking up the occasional floor hazard and trying to find a suitable place to put it, the bin was overflowing and looked menacingly unhappy.

"Erm, Joe," Larry said, trying to put a blissfully unaware positive slant on proceedings "anything I can do to help?" knowing full well he was utterly useless at such things, but he did like to offer.

"No thanks Larry" said the ever tired and casual Joe, as ash fell off the cigarette that seemed permanently stuck to his lips and into the bowl of ingredients he was mixing.

Larry delicately picked up some unrecognisable pieces of plastic and briefly inspected it, trying to decide what to do with it next "are you sure?" he enthusiastically asked.

"Yup, everything's under control" Joe said dropping the open packet of butter onto the floor and pushing it under the unit with his flipflopped feet. "Everything's just dandy".

At that moment Andy staggered in, angry at the floor for being in such a stupid place and stared incredulously at his two housemates, unsure who to pick a fight with first. He raised a finger and attempted to point it at Joe, but couldn't think of anything abusive enough to say to him, so averted his attention to Larry instead…who had disappeared.

Shocked at this discovery, he spun round to see where he had gone and finding no clue of his whereabouts, returned to his initial plan of attack. Unfortunately, and frustratingly, for Andy, Joe too had vacated the vicinity, but could be heard at the backdoor, either discussing a curious proposition with a badger or trying to get out of the clutches of the ever-amorous Mandy.

Not wanting to get entangled with the affairs, or in becoming a target, Andy wandered off to vent his aggression elsewhere, hopefully not meeting Sid on his travels, because if he did... Fuelled by the thought, he strode off with purpose, resolute threats uttering from mouth.

Joe shuffled back in from the garden where he had been trying very hard to tell Mandy that, yes, he did love, and no, there was no one else, and yes, he would tell her if there was, and no, he didn't love the girl on the T.V more than her. It seemed to have satisfied for a while, but he really couldn't be bothered, he had much more stuff that he didn't want to do that needed doing.

With perfect timing, to help him procrastinate, the tall broom cupboard at the side of the kitchen creaked open. Sid peered out from behind the door with the chink of glass being heard as he spoke. "Oh, hi Joe" said the quiet, distant voice of Sid and to avoid questioning asked "and, er, what are you up to?"

"You know what I'm doing, Sid. I'm getting the picnic ready. without any help." said the indignant Joe.

"Oh, er, do you need any? Help, that is?" Sid added, pulling himself out of the cupboard, all the while trying to pretend that it was the most normal of places to have been.

Joe declined assistance and was quite frankly getting fed up with all the interruptions, he couldn't remember why they were going on the god forsaken picnic anyway. "Well, er, if you don't need me then, er, I'll just go and er, take a walk." Sid said, scratching his cheek lightly and wondered off while looking over his shoulder as he went...just in case someone was watching.

Joe shuffled over to the fridge that was as full of enthusiasm as he was and stared indignantly at the emptiness as much as it stared at him. With door wide open and both motionless, one of them jumped when Eric came crashing into the room after tripping of the still motionless Bob, though possibly being chased by something or just plain reckless, you could never tell. He might have decided to use his inert friend as a distance marker for a long jump.

"Oi, oi, JoJo me old mukka. How's tricks then?" said the exuberant Eric, sporting a new plaster cast on his arm, already dirty and inked with a chunk taken out of it.

Joe took a huge sigh at the further intrusion and rolled his head back, accidently dropping the knife he had been clutching in the process, which perfectly landed pointy side down just next to his foot.

"Way Ay!" exclaimed the ever enthusiastic, up for anything Eric "That's normally me who does stupid things like that" he said waving his plastered arm in the air and knocking a picture frame. "You ought to be more careful."

"What do you want?" mumbled the unimpressed Joe, rubbing his eyes with his right-hand ringers, the only ones that looked remotely clean (apart from the nicotine stains).

"Just wonderin' what time we were off again?" Eric said looking around for something "you know, if I had time".

Joe stared at Eric for a few seconds, trying to comprehend what had gone wrong in his life, then changing that to what had gone right.

Mandy came strolling in from the garden, all glassy eyed smiles, drifting on her annoyingly, lovey-dovey, ethereal breeze.

"Hello boys," she smiled, head tilting to one side "Oh, aren't you both looking so serious," she said in her poutiest and most condescending voice "yes you are, so serious."

Eric and Joe looked at each other, both knowing what the other was thinking, but not wanting to say it for fear of upsetting her.

"Hello Mandy" they said in unison.

"Isn't it a lovely day for a picnic" she smiled looking wistfully at the grey clouds that lay beyond the bombsite of a garden.

"Has anyone seen Sidney lately?" she enquired looking alternately between the two men "I haven't seen him for ages. I do love Sidney, he's so sweet, I do hope he's coming" she rattled only, mainly to herself.

Joe answered first "He's driving, he's the only one with a licence, so he better be coming."

"I've got a licence" chirped in Eric.

"Eric!" said Joe after having bent down to pick up the knife "A provisional doesn't count and you've had for goodness knows how many years and besides…" Joe said, giving him a disparaging look "do you really think *anyone* would want you to drive? Especially like that." He concluded, pointing the now bent end of the knife towards the broken whatever it was.

"We're going when we're all ready." said Joe.

"Eric, you go and try to motivate Bob over there" another direction point of the knife "and you Mandy. I can hear Andy ranting at someone upstairs. I think he might've found Sid under his bed again."

Mandy smiled in acknowledgement and wandered off in a vague direction of the stairs, while Eric strode over to the still prostrate form of Bob.

"Oi, Bob," shouted Eric down to inert form, prodding it gently but firmly with his foot "you with us mate?" he added, contemplating a harder kick.

Bob groaned and managed to wave his forearm in the air, which was an improvement from earlier. "You going to be ready to go?" Eric asked, as if addressing an elderly patient. Bob groaned again and made a type of slurping noise, followed by a coughing fit, undoubtedly having sucked up some extra air or possibly a passing (and unsuspecting and startled) insect. The spluttering that followed had a fortuitous outcome. Bob rolled onto his back and lurched to a sitting position, hacking up whatever was the cause.

Both Eric and Joe, watching with interest, were disappointed when Bob fell back and ceased to move. All was silent. They stood watching a while longer, trying to see if they could hear any breathing, when suddenly a snore broke the silence and the tension.

Sid's head popped out from behind the sofa, startling the two spectators. "Is Bob still coming with us?" he gently asked.

"I thought you were upstairs?" Joe ventured, still pointing with his kitchen blade.

"Oh, I was. But Andy didn't like me in his bedroom…" which gave Joe a sense of satisfaction "…and I heard mandy…" he whispered carefully "coming upstairs." Everyone knew that Sid was scared of Mandy and her affectionate ways, he was a very private person.

"I think she's coming back down?" said Eric in a loud voice, feigning to look towards the stairs. With a little "ooh", Sid disappeared behind the sofa again and all was quiet.

Joe scoffed at the practical joke, though it had been an easy one to play and returned his attention to Eric who had resumed giving Bob a prod…or two with his foot.

"What do you think Joe? Coffee?" joe scoffed again, though admitted coffee did seem the more sensible idea.

"Tell you what" Joe said "I'll put the kettle on and you get the brandy". A small agreement emanated from the once snoring body.

"Thought might get a response" said Joe to himself, leaving Eric to administer few more physical provocations.

Andy appeared in the doorway looking more harangued than usual "What day is it?" he shouted to no one in particular. A gentle giggle came from the body on the floor causing Andy to storm across the room and bend over the body, wagging his finger as furiously as he could "I don't know what you're laughing at you…you" he really couldn't think of a suitable piece of abuse. He was red scarlet with rage, the bending over wasn't helping, and he'd just about had enough of it all. If one more person…

"Andy, darling," came the soft tones of Mandy.

He turned, glaring, if steam could come out of his ears, it would have,

His eyes bulged, desperately trying to hold back the seething mass, struggling to utter a simple "What?" it came out more like a squawk.

"Could you give me a hand with my bags?" Mandy asked coyly "they're ever so heavy" she smiled, swinging her hips as if embarrassed at her inability.

Andy ranted off, back up the stairs, followed by Mandy and an assortment of crashing's and swearing could be heard…as well as a few squeals from Larry, who sounded like he was provoking and being chased by someone.

The kettle clicked and stopped bubbling and Joe made a large pot of coffee, strong. The body moved, nose first, sensing its time had come.

Eric uncorked the expensive brandy and poured a single glass, placing it near, but further away from the now poured mug of coffee.

"Bobby!" he cooed "Bobby, yum-yums bobby".

Joe and Eric watched. The monster from the deep started to rise.

"It's alive!" Eric yelped with glee as Bob started to try and stand, finding the floor had stopped moving in different directions and the walls and ceiling were still in their rightful place. He didn't so much as to walk to the breakfast bar, but crawling was the next best thing, hauling himself onto a stool he started to look more human than just a pile of something on the sitting room floor,

"Brandy?" his hand searched out for the glass.

"Now, now Bobby" said Eric, enjoying every minute "you know the rules. Coffee first".

"Brandy" came the attempt of assertion.

Joe pushed forward the mug of coffee "I've put some in your coffee" he lied.

Bob rubbed his face and sighed many times, getting used to being upright was a task in itself. He leant forward, the steam flowing over his long greasy hair and inhaled the fumes, raised the mug to his lips and sipped, causing another bout of coughing.

Eric slapped him hardily on the back and easily dodged the back hander, as Joe passed Bob a piece of kitchen paper.

"Welcome back to the living," said Bob.

OH, MR PORTER!

The train whistled as Cyril waved his flag, holding the carriage door open from the platform, as a business gentleman came slowly running down the platform towards him, out of breath and over-weight.

"Thank you, my good man," the gentleman said, putting a hand into his pocket "I don't know what I would have done had I missed this train. Really, I don't" reaching out to press coinage into Cyril's hand.

"Oh, no need for that, thank you Sir. Just doing me job" said Cyril graciously refusing the gratuity, then waved his flag again and blew his whistle while closing the door behind the passenger.

The train let out two sharp toots and the steam hissed, as the heavy load started to be pulled out of the platform, with Cyril keeping a watchful eye on the load, just in case of any stray doors or wayward children. You could never be too careful. You never knew what could happen.

Once the train of carriages had cleared the tracks, he checked his pocket watch and gave it a little wind, with his flag neatly rolled and under his arm.

He had just enough time for a morning cuppa at the station's café, rather than going upstairs to the staff canteen, and besides, he could see Bert on the other platform, so he gave him the signal and the nod.

He walked off the platform, past young Edward in the ticket booth who was looking as eager as ever despite no customers about. He'll learn, thought Cyril as he finger-brushed his bushy, greying moustache.

The door bell rang as he entered and Mavis looked up and waved from behind the counter.

"Usual me duck?" she said in her soft voice.

"Yes please, Mavis" said Cyril "just a quick one though."

"Ooh, saucy." She said, giggling, pouring out a cup of Rosie-Lee.

Cyril sat at his usual table, the one he had been sitting at for thirty years, as Mavis brought out the cup of steaming tea, settling it down with the teaspoon rattling.

He looked up and smiled at her, and she at him.

"Thank you, Mavis, much appreciated." He said with sincere appreciation in his twinkling old eyes.

"You know," he said, adding sugar to his cup and stirring "we've been doing this for over twenty years. Things are changing Mave. And fast."

"I know duck, I know." She sadly replied, walking back to the kitchen "I remember the day you started," she reminisced "seems like only yesterday. Where all those years gone?" she said looking up to the ceiling.

Cyril took some sips of his tea, leaving small beads on the end of his whiskers, only to be licked away in a moment surrounded by memories.

He was about to continue with the conversation when the doorbell rang and a fresh young-faced couple walked in, their long overcoats dampened by the gentle rain outside of the station, and took to seating at a table by the door.

The young gentleman came to the counter and ordered a coffee and poised, turning to his lady friend, saying "Tea or Coffee, Cassie?"

"Oh, Tea please, darling" while she checked her makeup and hair in her compact.

Cyril drained the rest of his cup and took it over to Mavis and placed
a sixpence on the surface.

"Keep the change." He said with a wink and a smile.

"Thank you, duck." Mavis said, gently laying her hand on top of his.

Cyril cleared his throat and turned, pulling his waistcoat down and adjusting his cap, giving it a tug as he passed the young couple as he left the café and onto the platform.

"Yup," he thought to himself, looking around "things is definitely changing.".

The old wooden varnished boards, with brass fixings, that had been used to display the comings and goings of trains, had been replaced by a large black mechanism that clickered and flickered the times, often getting jammed, something the old system never did.

There had been talk of new management coming in. "Stream-lining" and "systems" were the new "buzzwords" and he knew that the steam engines days were numbered, not that he minded that too much. No more sore eyes or coughing fits.

He walked back to the ticket booth only to find young Edward reading a comic of all things. He gently cleared his throat.

Edward jumped a mile "Some kid must've dropped it. I'm surprised you didn't see it when you went for your break" he said, quickly folding it away.

"Just don't let the management catch you reading on the job," Cyril said with a smirk "especially as the way things are going at the moment".

He checked his watch against the large four-sided clock that hung above the ticket office, another ten minutes and the Orpington train would be in, he thought.

He walked back onto the platform to give it a cursory check, making sure spare trolleys were in place, if needed, and everything looked clean and tidy, no rubbish littering up his platform.

He always made sure things were in order before he left, but it didn't hurt to double check.

He was inspecting the area with the sand buckets, in case of fire, though often used as ash trays, when he noticed Bert, now on platform 5, talking to an officious looking type with a clipboard. There was much nodding and pointing going on, plenty of questions, which brought a wry smile onto his face. It quickly disappeared when the two figures turned in uniform and looked in his direction, with Bert pointing.

Cyril's froze and didn't know where to put himself. He never liked bigwigs. Or pencil pushers. Combine the two and...well.

He cleared his throat again and pretended to be looking at

something in the ceiling that had caught his attention. What was that? He couldn't make...it...out. He strained to see and noticing, out of the corner of his eye, that it had also distracted the two on platform 5 (who also were now trying to see), he made a quick dash for the small waiting room that stood on the middle of his platform.

Whilst hiding behind one wall, managing to keep an eye on Clipboard man, he heard the distant whistle of the oncoming train. Relief set in. He really had no time for officials, he just wanted to be left to his work and if he timed it well, he could stretch this busy train for at least twenty minutes. No time management official would want to hang around that long.

The train came billowing into the platform, exhausted and hot from its journey, just as he saw the Clipboard man approach young Edward, who had been watching the whole affair with some amusement.

Doors started opening and people were already stepping onto the platform before the train had come to a full halt. All shapes and sizes in this one, he thought, grabbing a wooden and worn sack truck.

He noticed a largish lady with fancy clothes and a hair net descending from First Class, and attempting, in vain, to re-move two small pieces of hand luggage. She caught his eye and waved for assistance.

As he strode over, he noticed a younger lady with two children,

coming out of 3rd, with a hefty looking trunk. He quickly sig-nalled to First Class that he would attend to the other lady first, which was met with a disapproving look, but by the time he had loaded the trunk onto his cart and made introductions, he was already attending to the large lady, putting her smaller pieces of luggage on top of the large wooden trunk.

With ladies on either side and children walking behind, he escorted them all past young Edward and Clipboard man, who gave a slight shrug and walked off, as Cyril chatted easily be-tween two conversations at the same time.

Luckily for him, they were both requiring a taxi, so, in order to waste a bit more time, because the clipboard was still in the vicinity, he made sure he gave them all his extra special, undivided attention. Making sure they, and luggage, were properly stowed for the next part of their journey and were completely happy with the service that had been provided.

Once the last cab had pulled away, Cyril turned and headed back in, checking around as he went. He saw Bert had moved to platform 3, so quickly walked over for a chat.

"How'd it go, Bert?" Cyril asked.

"Blimey," Bert replied "Ee wanted ta know the ins and out of a cats arsehole did ee." Exclaimed the ruffled old chap."I couldn't remember how long we been here. Said you'd remember". He continued scratching his forehead. "How long has it been Cyril?"

"Since we was demobbed" Cyril replied.

"Blimey." Bert said walking off in bemusement. He stopped and turned "oh, and he was talking about changes, redundancies and such like." The turned again, confused in a world of new possibilities.

Cyril wandered back to his platform thinking about what Bert had said, though checking with young Edward, nothing had been mentioned to him about redundancies.

He perched himself on the small seat behind the ticket booth and rolled up a smoke as it was regarded an off-duty spot. He sat and smoked, the mornings events rolling around in his head, laying out possible futures and thinking of times gone.

He was one of those few who had fought and survived both wars, he thought himself very lucky compared to some that he knew, or used to know. He had always kept himself busy, always worked and always kept his garden. He didn't know what he'd do without coming to work every day. It wasn't the money; he'd been lucky like that. He'd been left a big when younger and had always been careful. His Doris had died years ago and they had never had children. She never could. It would have been nice...he thought, remembering back to his child-hood...

"Ah, Mr..." came the sudden voice, making him drop his rollie. "Sorry, I don't seem to be able to find your surname on this sheet. These records really are appalling..." continued Mr Clipboard Man "...you wouldn't believe what we can't find."

"Tambling-Goggin." Said Cyril quietly.

"Excuse me?"

"My surname. It's Tambling-Goggin. Cyril Tambling-Goggin."

"Oh, well, yes, I see" he said, momentarily unsure of even himself "Well, yes, I, er just need to ask a few details if that's okay. We're updating records and such like, forging ahead, so to speak. Making way for the new..." he said faltering.

Cyril looked from under his cap and took a deep breath. This was going to be a long ten minutes.

The days passed into weeks and the clipboard man had not been seen around the station since. Most of the staff that Cyril talked to had all had their run in, but no news had come down from upstairs, so it was regarded as no news was good news and the speculations and rumours of change were laid to rest. Unfortunately, wheels were in motion and once they start, they seldom stop, until they reach their destination.

The morning started like any other, until about 10:30 when Ernie, from the loading bay was seen leaving the station, hours before his finish time, without his cap on. No one had ever seen Ernie without his cap on. The chatter started and the occasional member of management was seen, though nothing was being confirmed and the tittle-tattle grew and grew.

Cyril wasn't one for waiting around and detested idle talk, so, checking that he had enough time until the 11:15, walked off his platform and up the wrought iron stairs to the offices.

"Morning Gladys," he said with formality and a nod "is George in? I'd like a word".

Gladys looked shocked, over her horn-rimmed glasses. She couldn't remember Cyril ever coming into the office before, well, not without an appointment. She picked up the phone "Mr Braithwaite, so sorry to bother you" she softly said, and then as if announcing a miracle "Cyril's here to see you". Even from where he stood, Cyril could hear the stunned silent response.

"He said to go on through" she signalled with her hand.

Cyril gave a nod of appreciation and went to the wooden framed door, with frosted glass on the top.

As he entered, a nervous George Braithwaite was already standing behind his desk, furrying through a pile of papers and cardboard files.

"Ah, morning Cyril, good of you to come and see me" he said extending his open hand.

Cyril leant forward and briefly shook the softness, clammy with nerves, and sat down as directed.

"Well, I guess you're wondering why I called you here?" George Braithwaite said, light beads of sweat forming on his brow. How he wished he didn't have to do Central Offices bidding. After all, what did they care?

"You didn't call me. I came to see you." Cyril said, slightly amused that he wasn't the only one under duress.

"Oh, er, I see" George said checking a sheet that looked like a roll call. "Ah, yes, well, as you're here, so to speak." He said dreading every moment more and more.

"Well, er, the thing is this…" he carried on "unfortunately, Central want changes, a new look …" he said with a flourish of his hands, "and, well…"

"George," Cyril interrupted "its okay, I understand." He said standing.

"Well, look" George hadn't quite finished, not that he ever really started "the thing is…erm…we can't find your records." At least that was out. "Now, I know you've been here longer than me, in fact, we figure you're our longest running employee, ha," he laughed "we can't even find you on our new payroll system." He said dabbing his forehead with a handkerchief. "So," he continued pulling out the drawer of his desk "We'd like to give you these" Mr Braithwaite said handing Cyril a small box and envelope.

Cyril looked at the two items in his hand.

"We're so sorry to see you go Cyril, you've been a big part of our lives. Almost family." George said, now using his hankie to hide a tear in his eye.

"Thank you for being straight with me George" Cyril said putting out his hand "Thank you for everything." A small lump rose in his throat, but he turned and left, walking slowly down the clonking of the metal staircase.

A train whistled in the distance, the 11:15 "I think I'll leave it for someone else." He thought, and left the station.

He opened the backdoor to his house and went in, putting the envelope and box on the square wooden table in the middle of the kitchen, hung up his cap, for the last time, and went over to the range to pour a fresh cup of tea. He looked at the two parting gifts and walked over to the table. He picked up the envelope and opened, smiling at the cheque that lay inside. He picked up the box and gently took the lid off. Inside was the most exquisite pocket watch, ornate carvings decorated its every golden surface. He turned it in his hand and saw the inscription on the back, causing him to raise an eyebrow.

"To our best, longest serving and most beloved employee Cyril Tambling-Goggin."

He smiled again and laid the watch carefully back in its box and felt a pang of guilt. After all, he had never been an employee there, he just loved playing trains.

ANGEL HEART

Where do you start with a story that has no real beginning but a deciding end? As with most stories of this type, it begins with a man and a woman, for without these two, the third part couldn't happen, and it is the child we are most concerned about.

You see, dear reader, as I am sure you are aware, a stories path twists and turns to ages past. Many parts it will be made of, stone or brick, wood and twig, even dirt and water, but a path will be there, nonetheless.

Some parts, as you will see, are well trodden, but venture away from the hustle and bustle and you will find mere trails, maybe only taken by a rabbit or fox, but paths even so.

So, again, I say, dear reader, where on our path would you like me to begin, because I have seen where all men tread...

Very well, we will begin our journey there...

As with all, a man was born. Nature dealt her hand, as did my lord and the rest was to the parents, to mould and shape as they saw fit, though many don't see what they have or what is required, as sometimes differences lay hidden but need attending nevertheless.

He grew, experiencing hardship, though was hard working and like all mankind, made errors on the way and errors have to be dealt with, otherwise they grow like briar patches around the soul, choking and stifling healthy plants and scratching the skin of innocent travellers.

The complications of man's life spread quickly, branching out like the bough of a tree, one becomes two, two becomes four and so on, and again like the briar, if the buds aren't nipped, they will surely grow.

Not far from where the man came into the world, so too did a woman. She too did not experience the ease of comfort or unwant, but her life was easier in some ways but harder than others, losing her parents at a young age left her without the valued direction that children need.

She too grew with hidden woes, pushed into the depths of her being, while striving to be a better soul, quietly driven by the love of her God, that had been sometimes taught by wrongdoers or peoples whose own lives had been corrupted by injury and possibly failed to grasp the true meanings. Lies and deceits nurture different plants as do loss and want, though all look the same, but behind the mask... This is the way. Though it is to the forecomers we turn to right our wrongs.

As each raised in height, their routes crossed and merged, spiralling together, creating a unison and bond out of which our story truly begins...

The little shack had laid abandoned for many a year when it was come upon by the couple seeking shelter from their woes. Not down hearted and well intention in spirit, they fastened to their new found abound and set to, making it their own.

Life was hard, but hardship was not a stranger, so they delved and span, tilled and chopped, putting their vigour into the clay that lay around, refreshing the earth so as to harvest its fruits.

As they worked, they put their pasts behind them, too hard to bear or too shameful to recount, and forged forward with new strength, determined not to err again or be succumbed by the follies of their youth.

The two years went by with the clouds and seasons, filling the store and fastening their hold, more and more resolute in their determination, until the day of announcement came.

"Father." Said she.

"What, I?" said he.

"Yes, thee." Said she.

And so, it was. A child was born after the summer months had gone and winter claws had not yet clasped on with its icy grip, though distance was in the mother's heart as she knew not how to care for one so reliant. Feed and bathing were the trouble not, more the warmth and tenderness that lay missing from her own bosom, though reveal it she did not, as her companion, at first, put their child on the highest pedestal, as he had done to her when they first met.

/Man has his own freewill, though influenced by many desires and distractions and if he chooses, will allow the self to be led on any route that comes.

The child grew, surrounded by many forms of poverty, as did the other children in the nearby village, for it was not a wealthy one and hardship was a common commodity. The basic needs of any body must be met so as to build upon. Firstly hunger, sleep and water, essential requirements to ascend, but you cannot obtain friendship until security, health and source of structured income has been obtained. And so, as children desire an others toy, so did our child, but she desired more than most, for the lack filled the void that she felt. An emptiness where love and care reside, for her parents often chased their own rainbows, hoping to win eternal security for themselves at the cost of the battles, where their own kin might suffer or perish. They did not see the harm that they inflicted on all, for if they had, they would realise that they had already lost.

As the child grew, so too did her natural hunger. For an infant may be easily amused with clicking sticks and boxes of card, but soon tires when accustomed to their pleasures, for /man has an infinite space inside the limits of the body, ready to explore and understand the working of the world in all its complexities and wonders. It is this undiscovered country that the mind, as a journeyman, has to travel, erring as it crosses the streams of existence and in doing so, knows what footholds to take in future crossings.

But for our youth, experience, of even the mundane, was withheld from her learnings, instead replaced by forced solitude and restrictive thoughts, for fear played a mighty hand, controlling even the most insignificant tasks.

As one starts with the simple purity of life, always dividing in two, the left or the right, the good and the wrong, often, too soon, many wrong paths may be taken and if care is not sought, as walking into the deepest woods, the way may seem lost, with no clear path for escape.

But there are always ways. Even in the densest forest, clues are laid about offering hope and direction, for you will never find yourself totally lost, unless it is your choosing.

And one day, in the deepest of forests the man stood, with his wife to be, lost in the depths of misery, not able to provide for his family, despite the work he did, for one may be wealthy in the goods of the world, yet poor in spirit, the same can be said for when the tables are turned. They had searched and struggled, fervent in approach, but their child, as all children do, especially when great pressure is caused, became into her own, though had been blinded by misguidance, intolerance and a too heavy hand.

Seeing the fruit of their labours, despair and anger stood large, immoveable and resolute, rather than recognising the fault lay in their own hands, where love and understanding would have resolved the years of torment to come.

And in their angst and pain, the angel, visited them, holding a single wish of anything, to cool the fires and wipe away all wrongdoings.

It came to them in the darkest night and burnt a path for them to tread through the flames. The saving grace would protect them for the while, as the wish was thought upon and decided.

"/Man," said the messenger "do you know what it is you need? For on this day, a gift will be bestowed to you. A gift of any doing, but not against accord."

The man and woman shook in the wilds of flaming winds that spun around their heads and rather consider to repair the years or some token for all mankind they uttered instead:

"Your heart."

From the air, a settling of feet onto the ground, that stilled the glowing flames, stepping forward to the mortals new, the herald queried their desire.

"You have my heart with you now, anything I shall give."

But again, they replied "We want your heart for our daughter's body, turned against us she has, wicked and evil, full of spite and goes her separate way. For with your heart, anew she will be and return unto the fold, where glory will shine and honour stand, that will be our gold."

A tear fell from the proclaimer, as his hand placed onto his chest.

"Bring forward your child for the gift, that I may look into her eyes."

A storm of strength erupted all round, yet no sound disturbed the glade, as the very heart of one so pure, was passed and the gift was made.

The man and woman went back to their humble dwelling, child in tow, exhalted in the fortune that had befallen on them and ensured that all would now be right and true.

However, fortune and luck have their own paths to tread and do as they wish, not easily swayed by mans desire or want.

For, in the haste of the moment, woman and man had not seen the folly in the choices that they elected. A heart is but a heart. True, goodness can lie within, but it is not from where it comes. Just as a cup holds water from a stream, it is from the many rivulets and springs, the vast oceans and clouds that deliver the life-giving sustenance.

And so, the same is said. The angel sacrificed its heart in vain, as the couple did not see, nor ever would, that it was they that caused the injuries deep and no matter what could be replaced, the child would be burdened until, when time unfolded, paths would be made clear, the offerings of the forest, and with the burdens of pack horse on her shoulders, would choose the direction to take to take.

The three returned to their house, a waiting for the changes to arrive, but instead frustration called and drove a wedge between young and old, driving out the girl and since she had been pushed away for not meeting the high expectations that could not be met for any one so young, or even aged. And so, she fell into the arms of a waiting boy, who had a deeply troubled pulse and was ready to inflict harm and danger to a young, bereft maiden seeking solace and affection that had been long absent.

Freely she went, eager to sample loves first kiss and warmth of embrace, yearning for tenderness and care and the fulfilment that comes in shared adoration, all things that so distant in the growing years were, instead was schooled in the errors of / man's wantonness.

Kith and kin saw not eye to sight and distance it grew from house to home. Adrift was she, floundering in a sea of confusion, wanting only a safe port to call her own, as the violence flared more often from her beloved and backs turned from the people she craved the most.

It was in these heated times, that a maiden becomes no more and into womanhood she steps, clutching her belly as it swells, to comfort and protect her most treasured gift, but do not forget, that a treasure she already stores.

Nine long months passed on the world, as the still young girl struggled in every step, trying to repair all that she could, but tools for this only come to the most learned of crafters. They are not free to all and many trials and tribulations are costed before hands know how to use their wits. But tried she might. A valiant battle against the struggles of the encroaching tides. Deeper and deeper into despair she plunged until the night of birth.

Again, the heavens opened and watched the story unfold. The lightning struck as the thunder roared and the once maiden felt the pain of labour strike as her man smite her with ferocity enough to shake the logs from the fire. The very ground seemed to shake with anger as blow after blow fell on mother and child, the night sky flashing with fury. The fists and water rained relentlessly down, as the manchild's fury unleashed itself in one final torrent.

The final crack splintered the night as he stood over the still bodies.

He turned and fled. Tried to flee away from his eternal torment, forever to be haunted by his moment of outburst. How it is that a few precious seconds can change so many lives.

They lay unbreathing, connected as one, still sharing the same life, even in death.

And as the ground had become their bed, they rested now in peace.

And I say to you, dearest one, do not despair, for within them beat the heart of an angel, no more shall pain visit at their door, no suffering or want shall they know, eternal in glory and peace will they forever be, with honour as their shield and love as their sword.

DAVE GOES TO A PARTY

Oh, *doo* come on Teddy" Dave said impatiently.
As usual, Teddy was lying on the bed, staring at the ceiling, expecting Dave to do everything for him. Dave, on the other hand, was ready to go and already needing a second wee because of all the excitement.

The present had been wrapped, which looked very enticing, in shiny red paper and lots of sticky tape, which had small bits of purple fur stuck to it, with a big blue ribbon, which finished with a big blue bow. If he had to wait any longer, he would have to open it himself. A card had been written and carefully stuck onto the present, with no help from Little Ted. Some spelling mistakes had been made and the colouring in had gone over the lines, but Teddy said that it didn't matter. Dave didn't know what had gotten into Teddy today.

Looking over to the bed while still hopping around, trying to decide whether to go to the loo or not, Dave asked "Don't you want to go to the party today Teddy"?
Teddy didn't answer, instead, stared into nowhere in particular, obviously trying to ignore Dave.
"Oh, I see" said Dave "you're feeling a bit nervous about meeting all those new people, are you?"
Dave carried on, "Well don't worry, I'll look after you. I always do".
Teddy remembered the last time Dave had said that, it was as they were leaving the house on the way to the zoo, and look how that turned out. It took him ages to get the smell out.

Just then there was a toot-toot from outside and Dave went to the window see. Michael's dad had come to pick them up in his car and take them to the party, doing a round trip picking up a few of Michael's other friends on the way. Dave looked at the size of the car and hoped they'd all fit in, as he did like a bit of space and Teddy did wriggle a lot when he got uncomfortable.

"Gosh this is so exciting" thought Dave, almost bursting, grabbing Teddy in one paw and parcel in the other, rushing down the stairs. "Teddy, when did we last go to a party?" asked Dave as he grabbed a suitable coat, stuffing Ted into the pocket so he couldn't hear the reply and rushed out of the door, down the path and into the car.

"Afternoon Mr. Mihialo" said Dave settling into his seat and trying to do up his seatbelt "Have we got many to pick up"? he asked, deciding whether Ted would prefer to sit by the window, as he did sometimes get car sick, but the middle was much more fun.

"Afternoon young Dave. no" replied Michael's dad "Jason can't come today, he's not feeling well and Susie has already got to the party early, she got the time mixed up. So..." Michaels Dad carried on "...it's just you and Kirsty" Mr. Mihialo finished.

"And Teddy" Dave whispered.

As they drove to Kirsty`s house, Dave had a nagging feeling, something seemed to have been forgotten, something... important. Dave thought and went through a mental checklist. "Teddy, present, card, coat. No. Nothing else was needed".

As they drove on, the worry drifted away, and was replaced by thoughts of which games were going to be played and what food there might be to eat, he hoped for peanut butter and tomato sandwiches and meringues and cream.

His tummy rumbled loudly and blamed it on Little Ted, so thought of something else instead, Kirsty Walsh sharing the car with them. She was a nice enough girl, long curly hair and had lots of friends. The trouble was, thought Dave, carefully undoing his seatbelt and sliding over to the window seat, was that she did like to tickle and prod and play lots of practical joke and could be rather loud. Sometimes, Teddy would get a bit worried that he might get hidden somewhere and forgotten about.

Pulling up outside Kirsty's house, Mr. Mihialo beeped his horn, surprising Ted, said Dave and Kirsty came bounding out.
She was carrying a large, long thin present, much bigger than Dave's (though Teddy had chosen it) and wearing a bright yellow dress and the biggest of smiles. Dave just had to smile back despite the concern he was feeling.

Into the car she bounded, the fresh air billowing in with her, followed by the scent of soap, shampoo and toothpaste.
"Hey Dave, Mr Mihialo and look ... there's Teddy" she said, with a certain amount of mischief in her voice, looking at a pair of feet sticking out of Daves pocket, making Dave (and Teddy) a little uncomfortable.
"Hello Kirsty" both Dave and Mr. Mihalo replied at the same time, both thinking the same thing.

"Dave, look, I got Michael a stunt kite with a picture of Skull and Crossbones on it. What did you get him"? Kirsty enquired entusiastically.

"Oh, that's nice" answered Dave trying to reflect the question, "What colour is it"? he said, thinking that was a good way to change the subject. Dave wanted his present to be kept a secret until it was opened. Dave liked surprises.

"White, *of course*" Kirsty said already getting bored of the conversation.

"Are we picking anyone else up?" she asked, and before anyone could reply, she started chatting on about what she had been doing that morning, how she decided what she *was* going to wear for the party and "Doesn't that lady look really funny?", pointing to across the street.

By the time they got to Michael's house, Dave and Teddy, and Mr. Mihialo were already quite exhausted with Kirsty's chattering. The nagging feeling in the back of his mind was still making Dave feel a little uncomfortable, but thought it wasn't worth thinking too much about (at least, that's what Ted said), besides, there was so much more to do.

The car was parked down the drive at the side of the house and they all got out, walking with Michael's dad to the front door. They could hear the party had started. Lots of noise, lots of children, and lots of running around having fun.

They climbed the eight steps (Little Ted liked counting, said Dave) to the big green door which, when opened, made the noise from indoors, even louder.

Michael saw them straight away and came rushing down the corridor from the kitchen to greet them.

"Wow, hi guys, great to see you. Wow are those for me, thanks" he said with a huge smile, taking the presents away from them and heading back into the kitchen from where he had just come from followed by a throng of other excited bodies, all eagerly cramming into the kitchen, each trying to see if they wanted it as well.

Michael ripped opened Kirsty's present first.

"Wow" exclaimed Michael.

"Wow, seems to be one of Michael's favourite words at the moment" thought Dave, already getting a bit fed up with it.

"Wow, that's a really neat kite Kirst, thanks a bunch," said Michael, eyeing of the picture on the covering and imagining him doing it.

He was just about to plunge onto Dave and Little Ted's present when there was a knock at the door and he rushed off down the corridor again, with his followers in hot pursuit.

Dave followed himself, getting pulled into the excitement, though looked over his shoulder at his present on the table and felt a tinge of disappointment that his present had been left unopened, but Little Ted (who was now holding hands, just in case, since his coat had got thrown off) was thrilled in having the secret of the surprise a little longer.

Michael threw open the door, expecting to see another friend, but instead, all the children gasped. For there before them stood…

"Allow me to introduce myself" the tall dark stranger said, bowing with a swirl of his black cape, the red lining sparkling with mystery, and taking off his top hat at the same time with a dramatic flourish.

"I am The Greatest Magician in the Land. I am The Mighty Caleb. I have come to amaze you all, especially you… Michael" he said pointing directly at Michael.

"Ooh!" was said in unison by the widemouthed children.

"Wow!" said Michael.

Dave looked at Michael.

"Come in Mr. Tim… The Mighty Caleb" said Michael's Mum from behind the group standing in the doorway. "You're a little early, but that doesn't matter. Would you like a cup of tea"? She finished.

"Tea?" The Mighty Caleb answered "No, my good lady. Caleb has no earthly requirements." He said with another flourish of his cape, while holding his case in the other hand. "For The Mighty Caleb travels through the universe on a quest of enlightenment" he replied whilst gesturing and making a bunch of flowers appear from up his sleeve.

"Oh, so you won't want paying then" muttered Michael's Mum under her breath to another parent, causing stifled giggles.

The kids followed Caleb upstairs to the sitting room where he placed his case down and unfolded it to make a table with a big sign hanging down in front of it.

The Greatest Magician in the land told the children that they had to sit down in a semicircle "Otherwise those at the back," making a stuffed dove appear "might not be able to see" he explained.

Some of the guests turned round to see who he was talking about hoping not to miss a thing, but soon realized that there was nothing exciting there.

"I've never seen a magician before Teddy" said Dave to Teddy, but Little Ted was far too absorbed in what was going on than to pay any attention to Dave.

First of all, The Mighty Caleb was showing everyone five, large solid metal hoops, which he kept bashing together, very unnecessarily thought Dave, and which kept linking and unlinking together.

"That's not very clever, even I could do that" said Dave to Teddy. Dave had seen a programme on the telly once about another magician, who told you how all the tricks were done. Dave had to admit that it did spoil the fun a bit, and Little Ted did remind him that he had told him so.

The Great Caleb (as it said on the sign and Dave assumed that he had either been recently promoted (and not bought a new sign yet) or he was borrowing his brothers table…Little Ted said something rude, which Dave ignored) followed his rings trick with some juggling and plate spinning, which was very funny, as the plates kept falling off their sticks. Ted said that wasn't supposed to happen, but Dave enjoyed it anyway.

Afterwards, were some disappearing eggs, which reappeared inside a bag, and Dave wasn't sure if the man was a magician, as he kept dropping the eggs on the floor, even the ones he had hidden in his pockets which made them laugh even louder. Followed by a plastic chicken popping out of his hat, it surprised Ted so much, that Dave remembered he needed the toilet.

As the tricks went on, some of the children were getting a little restless and started poking and prodding each other or falling onto the person sitting next to them. As one such event took place near Dave, Teddy, unoticed slipped away, in the hands of Kirsty, who was sitting right behind them.

Just then Caleb, The Greatest Magician in the World, amidst all the hullabaloo, called out that he needed a volunteer. Suddenly, what seemed like hundreds of hands shot up in the air accompanied by lots of: "Ooh mee, pick me" 's and "Over here, me".

"Hmm"? a great hush fell over the room as The Great Caleb stood, tapping his chin and thought.

He was just about to point to somebody, when Kirsty shouted "Here, use Teddy" and before Dave could react, she had thrown him over the tops of everyone's heads and he landed with a "kerplonk" right inside the upturned top hat.

A great cheer went up and Dave tried to stand up to protest , but was pulled down again, by Kirsty who said with a kind arm around Daves shoulders "Don't worry, he'll be alright". Dave hoped so. He didn't like the look of the saw that the magician was waving about.

"And now, what I am about to perform is not for the feint hearted" Caleb stated "If anyone is of a weak constitution, kindly close you eyes".

Dave couldn't watch, neither could some of the other children. Some covered their eyes with their hands and some peeked out between their fingers. Silence had come back into the room. Everyone watched as Teddy was laid down and had two wooden arches put over his tummy.

"I shall now saw this bear in half". A little girl sitting next to Dave, with a quiet "no" and a few gentle tears caught the attention of Michaels Mum, who came around the back of the group and asked "Would you like to come and see Michaels pet chameleon"?

Dave didn't know where to look. Sitting aghast, mouth still hung open from seeing Teddy volunteer like that, and now he was about to be sawn in half, this party was meant to be fun.

The magician started sawing. Lower and lower went the blade. "I can't watch" Dave said screwing his eyes up very tight and covering ears at the same time. Seconds passed like snails. All of a sudden there was a great cheer and much jostling. Dave looked up and saw Teddy being held up without a scratch on him. "Foods ready" somebody called and everyone was clambering over each other to get out of the room first and into the kitchen downstairs.

"See" said Kirsty "I told you he'd be alright" she said with an affectionate smile and a hand on Daves shoulder. Dave smiled weakly back. Wanting Teddy back and safely in his pocket Dave went forward to The Greatest Magician in the World, who was by now packing up, Teddy could not be seen anywhere.

"Erm, excuse me" said Dave "but" he carried on "have you seen my, erm, have you seen where Little Ted is?" as nonchalantly as he could.

The magician smiled. "Ahh, the volunteer" he said with bravado. With a flourish of his hands over his upended top hat he pulled out...a cabbage. "Oh," he said seeming genuinely confused "this *cannot* be right" and handed the cabbage to Dave.
"Hang on" he mused to himself a while and proceeded to pull lots of colourful hankies out of the hat, some more flowers, a bottle (which he took a sip out of), a small saucepan...which Dave thought was very clever, and, as the proceedings progressed, he even managed to reengage some of the children, which stopped the them in their flight for biscuits and watch the ongoing saga for the search of Teddy.

"Oh dear," said the magician with casual abandon "no Teddy, perhaps..." he smiled, noticing the panic beginning to spread on Dave's face "you try?" he said picking up his wand and passing it to Dave.
"But I can't do magic" replied Dave, putting the cabbage down and now getting a little more than anxious.
"Here we'll all help." The Mightiest of All Magicians said, pointing to the crowd who had now gathered. "We all have to say" he said instructing the growing crowd ""We're all ready, let's see Teddy", okay?"

On the count of three, the large group that had gathered shouted in unison, even some of the adults, and the magician looked inside the hat.

"No, no Teddy" said the magician with a casual shrug of his shoulders.
Terror and panic spun in Dave's mind. "What am I going to do, where could Teddy be, it was all Kirstie's fault" thought Dave in a rush.
The Mighty Caleb leant gently forward, resting his hand on Dave's shoulder "Have you tried looking in your pocket"? enquired Caleb, noticing how soft and cosy Dave's fur felt.

Dave felt the right-hand pocket, the one which Teddy liked the best, but... no Ted.
"Try the other one" came a cry from the crowd.
Dave thought it was a ridiculous idea, as Teddy never sat in the

left hand pocket, "honestly" he said muttering quietly, relenting to the instruction.

And lo behold! Who should be sitting there as big as life (or as little as) "Teddy!?" Dave shouted with happiness and astonishment. "How did you..." and gave him a great big hug, probably the biggest hug he had had for a long time.

Dave thanked the magician (while grasping very firmly onto Little Ted) and followed the rest of the stragglers to the food. "Gosh Teddy, that was close, I'll bet you're hungry after all that excitement." Teddy didn't say anything, he just gave Dave one of his looks, but Dave knew what Teddy was really thinking.

By the time they got into the kitchen, a lot of the food plates looked like a tornado had gone over them and eaten all the best bits. There were still some interesting pieces of sandwich, cake and biscuits left and lots of pineapple, which nobody else seemed to like.

Dave decided it was safer to stay in the kitchen to eat, rather than join everyone else on the floor, as he noticed lots of scattered bodies and debris.

Dave sat on a stool at one end of the table, within easy reach of the pineapple and Michael's mother tipped out a fresh packet of chocolate chip cookies and offered them to Dave with a smile. He smiled back and stuffed three into his mouth. Afterall, they had been through quite an ordeal.

THE CHAT SHOW

Antoine sat in his dressing room eating caviar trying to forget how frustrated he was feeling at the restrictions being placed from the powers that be, he was the star of the show after all, shouldn't he have more say in the matter?

He sat back in his chair and wiped his mouth, looking into the mirror and reflected on his time with the studio. He'd been with them for several years now and just felt, that despite his success and range of celebrity guests, he needed something..., something...more.

A fly buzzed past and he tried to swat it away, knowing full well that it would make no difference, but it gave him an idea. Not a great idea, but an idea, something he could work on, something that could, if the timing was right, rock the industry. Why, it could be him world recognition. Global media attention. Hah, then they'd be sorry.

Damn, pesky fly. He swatted at it again as it fluzzed past.

The bell rang in his dressing room signalling thirty minutes until the brief rehearsal before they went live. That gave him plenty of time.

Admittedly they had done a couple of live performances before, but the stars that you see on the silver screen or cavorting on stage seldom matched up to their off-screen persona. Some were downright boring.

Antoine recalled one action hero that came onto the show, world famous for many a catchphrase, could barely tell a story of a shopping spree without sending the film crew to sleep.

Today though, today was going to be different, ground-breaking. He could barely contain himself.

The door knocked and Terry, the most junior of stagehands, popped his head in through the gap of the door "Thirty minutes Antoine." Then looked sheepish and disappeared again.

Thirty minutes. That meant forty-five until live and until...

He leant back, pleased with his plan and closed his eyes and took his usual short nap before a performance, it calmed his nerves.

Out on stage the activity of preparation was gearing up. Producers were shouting orders, dollies were checking their tracks, gaffers were frantically sticking down the last of the cables, the gantry were checking the bulbs and the guests were very busy in the Green Room, loosening their vocal cords.

"You know darling," said Clive, a camp aficionado to the other, the more, closeted well-known figure of stage and screen "I performed in front of the Queen once, as you know. A great honour." He said, while puffing eloquently on a menthol cigarette on the end of a holder.

"The Queen or A Queen, darling?" came the giggle of a retort from his "friend" Monty (not his real name, but to the ones he knew "better", Pi, as in Python. Yuh.

"Now, now dear. Don't be so catty darling. I know you're only jealous."

"Me? Jealous? Of you?" came the snort of derision "Darling, you couldn't be further from the truth." Pi, I mean, Monty said brushing his hair back.

The two icons had known each other for years, had worked with each other often enough and once...well...we won't go into that...just gossip...supposedly.

"Anyway, my dear boy at least I don't rely on an autocue for my lines or prompts. Just give me my script and I'll have my lines memorised in half an hour" Monty said, pouring another glass of gin.

"Can't be much of a part, can it dear? Half an hour? I've had..." Clive was cut off from his retort by a knock on the door.

"Thirty minutes, gentlemen." Terry said poking his head around the door, smirking.

"Go away, my dear boy. Unless you want to get eaten" Clive shouted out, gnashing his teeth with glee, causing the two luvvies to burst out laughing, leaving the red-faced youth scampering down the corridor towards the extras dressing room.

"Blimey, I've been in some pokey holes," Barry said bumping his shoulders against Cynthia who was bending over a desk, trying to do her make-up, "There's not enough room..." when the knock on their door came.

"Thank you, Terry darling." Cynthia called out, before he had a chance to open the door and say anything.

"Who was that?" asked Barry.

"That was Terry, lovely boy, he's the knocker" Cynthia explained to the gruff northerner.

"Knocker? Bell end, you mean" Barry smiled, finding himself very amusing as normal.

"You getting paid union rates for this job?" he asked Cynthia, who was now adjusting her wig.

"Oh no, darling" she said in surprise "Haven't you heard? This ones on commission only."

Barry went bright red and exploded "Commission only! Like, bloody hell, commission only! I didn't come all the way here for bloody commission only! What the bloody hell were they thinking? Why didn't anyone tell me?" he said breaking into a sweat.

"Well, they told me." Cynthia said gently and confused.

"Oh, did they!" Barry raged, unsure of where to stand and what to do with his arms. "Well, they bloody well didn't tell me! No one ever does. Last to bloody know Barry."

Cynthia smiled and put her hand on his shoulder "Why don't you sit down and have a nice cup of tea, dear." She said, leading him to a small couch in the corner, next to a wooden table where the kettle was.

Barry's mind raced and raged as Cynthia made him a cup of tea.

"Two sugars isn't it darling?" she asked calmly, with Barry nodding his reply.

She passed him his cuppa and his appreciative, shaking hands took the gift.

"I can't believe it." he said.

"Believe what, dear?" Cynthia replied absently, checking in the mirror again.

"Bloody commission" Barry said as if the world had collapsed and he was crushed and exhausted.

"Oh...I was only teasing." she said, smiling at him through the reflection of the mirror.

Barry stared at her in disbelief, laughed and took a sip of his tea.

"You f...".

Antoine stirred from his forty winks and stretched, still congratulating himself with his plan. He got up of his chair and had another stretch and walked about the room, while formulating the finer details of the forthcoming proceedings.

Agnes, the aged tea lady, came in with her trolley "Hello my dear," she said, despite being reminded to call him Antoine on all occasions from the lords above. He couldn't fathom why, he wasn't as precious as "some" others, though they did object to informality of any kind, especially in todays sensitive climate concerning, what he liked to call, the touchy feelies.

"Now my dear," she continued "is there anything I can get you before you go on?" she asked "They told me not to bother you, but Agnes knows best" she said, rummaging around her trolley, looking for that something for everyone.

"No, thank you." Antoine replied, and was about to add, when:

"Ooh," she declared, as if she'd read his mind "your favourite biscuits. I'll leave them over here for you" she said, taking no notice of his remonstrations, and shuffled off, trolley clattering down the corridor.

Antoine eyed the biscuits. He was feeling confident and relaxed about his forthcoming performance, he had natural talent and always handled his guests with ease and professionalism.

He cleared his throat and noticed that perhaps his nerves were building a little bit...in anticipation. He had been trying to watch his weight, because he knew he'd put on a few pounds over the summer break, but, hey ho, the biscuits were there, better not let them go to waste.

"Oh, you can be such a bitch, darling" said Clive to Monty, who was going through the gin like nobody's business.

"Well, you did ask darling." Monty replied, trying to justify his underhandedness, "Besides," he concluded "what's a girl to do?" he said, taking a guilty looking sip.

"Well, I'm ready. How about you?" Clive said, draining the dregs of his glass and brushing his clothes down in front of the wall mirror, checking himself at all angles.

Monty looked at the near empty bottle and calculated that he could, at a push, have it finished before they left for the stage, if they left at the last minute.

"Er, not quite, duckie" Monty replied.

Clive shot him a look. "I think you've had quite enough! You know you only ever call me that when you're drunk." And strode over to rescue the bottle from disappearing.

"Ere, wotcha think you doin'?" screeched Monty as the game of tug of war began.

"Now, behave," Clive warned having firm grasp of the neck of the bottle "...give it to me" he commanded.

"Ohh," squealed the petulant Monty, "you'd like that wouldn't you. Someone might walk in though." He finished, with a elbow to the ribs.

Unfortunately, or fortunately, I can't decide, the bottle of red wine that Clive had been drinking out of wasn't empty and was perched behind Clive in a precarious position as Clive stumbled back from the elbowing he had just received.

A splosh, a crash, followed by a smash and the two darlings stared silently at the scene.

"You hag!" Clive hissed venomously.

Agnes was going to go in and offer her services, "Ah," she thought "it had been a long time since she had given anyone her services", but she heard the commotion inside and decided to move on, to the quieter end of the corridor.

She stopped outside the communal dressing room and changed her mind again. Not today.

"I still don't know why you would say such a thing?" Barry could be heard saying to Cynthia.

"Oh, do stop going on Barry darling," Cynthia replied "I'm sorry, it was a joke, alright?"

"Oh, a joke, was it? I thought a joke was meant to make you laugh" he carried on.

"Do you remember that time we worked in Blackpool together? At that thingy. On the front." Cynthia asked, momentarily putting a spanner in Barry's brain, his cogs seized.

"What?" he said, genuinely confused "What' that got anything to do with anything?"

"Well..." she paused, Barry's face still none the wiser "do you remember that little B&B we all had to cram into?"

"Ooh, that was awful. Bingo (one of the troupe who liked to shout "BINGO" when...well...you know) brought that lad back. Talk about a full house."

They both laughed at the shared memory and eyed each other with affection, they'd both been in this game for too long to hold any serious grudges.

"Well," Cynthia continued "there's something I never told you." She looked at him with slight trepidation. Barry now had the same look.

"You know we all had to chip in £20 each? I collected it all and paid it in when we left." She said still looking cautious.

"Yess." came the low, unsure response.

"Well, the thing is..."

"Yess."

"We never needed to chip in £20 each. I kept it for myself." Cynthia admitted and was met with silence.

Barry sat looking at her, his poker face revealing nothing.

He smiled, saying "We knew, we all knew." Giving a little chuckle.

"What? All of you?" Cynthia said aghast.

"Yeah, we all knew. We knew you were having a tough time of it, so we paid up." He smiled wider.

Cynthia was a bit disconcerted at his broadening smile.

"What?" she asked, "What are you not telling me?"

Barry's smile got bigger and bigger until it erupted into a chuckle.

"You mean you didn't suspect anything?"

"What do you mean "suspect"?"

Barry leant forward in his chair, "Where do you think we would all get crisp £20 notes from at a moments notice. Some of us could barely afford a bag of chips on what we were earning."

Cynthia was looking incredibly confused.

He continued, "That lad Bingo had...he worked at the bank."

"So," she said, "he didn't steal them, did he?" putting her hand over her mouth in shock.

"No, of course not, well…"

"Barry! Tell me he didn't." said the mortified Cynthia.

"They wouldn't have been missed. They were forgeries. Fakes." He sat smiling again.

"But…? What if…? Oh, Barry!" Cynthia sat down heavily onto the small wooden chair, stunned by the revelation.

The bell rang for appearance on set. Both Cynthia and Barry stood, both with sparkling eyes and embraced with the warmth of love and luvvies and left for work.

Out in the corridor they met an unsteady, but relaxed and charming as ever Monty and a Clive, who was having difficulties in buckling up his trousers.

A friendly casual chat was had as they walked towards set, getting themselves prepared for their scene.

Antoine, as ever, was ready and, being the star of the show, certainly didn't need to attend the warm-ups. Instead, he stayed in his dressing room being attended to by make-up. He was sitting in the chair in front of the lit mirror, being preened for his loving audience.

"It looks like a good crowd tonight." Said Fran, brushing his hair back around his ears. "That's about it, I think?" she said, packing he bags up. "Good luck, break a leg."

"Thank you, my dear" Antoine said in his usual casual manner, not wanting to give his excitement of the forthcoming sensation away.

He rose and flexed, stretching out nerves and tension. He was ready. He left his dressing room and took his place onset.

Applause had been done. The stage was set. The audience had been suitably warmed. Everyone knew their place. Everyone knew their marks.

The hush fell.

The red light blinked to signal "Live On Air".

The lights came up and…

"CUE ANTOINE" came the call from the producer's box to the cameraman.

The camera panned round to Antoine's chair...

Only to find him licking his bum, as cats do.

"This'll show them." He thought.

THE BUTLER DID IT!

Thomas had been employed by the family since he had been a young lad. He had started as boot boy, cleaning and polishing the household footwear from dusk to dawn, running quietly through the house as the residents and guests slept, collecting shoes and boots from outside bedroom doors, learning how to make and apply his own polish, make his own brushes and return the needed items before they were needed on rising. As he grew, so did his duties. Taking on a wider range of tasks and responsibilities, he learnt each as well as he could, not letting any failure define him. He became resolute in his desire to achieve a better status for himself and, hopefully, one day, a family, but alas though, the latter never came. His work became all-encompassing as he watched from a distance, through ageing eyes, nieces and nephews fulfil lives, but for him, all was empty, save for a job well done.

The master of the house, now Sir Charles, was a fair and honest gentleman, aware of his servants and their duties, having grown up surrounded by opportunities, but always interested in the lives he didn't see and a thirst of understanding the mechanisms of life. He had a successful life and career in commerce, fortuitous in dealings with some European and Asian countries, enabling him to spread his fortune to the surrounding populace of his country estate and allowed him a good marriage, blessed with fine healthy children, a true blessing in these times, where many succumbed to everyday illnesses, but especially in his family chain who were susceptible to the typhoid and difficulty in conceiving.

The grand house was a modest building, not an ornate or extravagant affair, more utilitarian in design, though adequate and considerate for staff and gentry alike. The architect had been a humble and frugal designer, but dwelled on beauty as a gift and function, allowing even the meagres part of the buildings to give ease to the viewers eye. No formal garden was to be had, save the fruit and vegetable plots, the twisting paths and trees wound across the landscape, unhurried in their destination, taking their time to visit the lake in its secret exquisiteness, where plant and wildlife thrived as if a forgotten part of Eden had been made, but only then, reflected a token of what could have been. Even the rowdiest of children became entranced by its spell, the hushed reverence and soothing calm befell all.

Lady Marjory reflected the beauty of the house with ease. Sir Charles had known her since their younger days and the match was welcomed by both families and was only enhanced by the mutual attraction for each other, as well as each supporting each other's strengths. No weaknesses could be seen in Lady Marjory, her graciousness and generosity were well known, so much so as none would consider to take advantage of the charity often issued, instead many would offer up assistance in repayment of gratitude. Lady Marjory could be seen on many occasions visiting local vendors and interacting with tradesmen of the local village, and if any bystander unaware of who she might be and slant her good name, they would be quickly admonished and corrected, with a slap across the back of the head for good measure.

"...and don't let me hear you say that again!" might be added.

As the children of the house grew, so too did the wealth of the household. Good fortune was distributed to all, ensuring no one was left out of the fortuitous situation, as each was considered a valuable cog in the small and precious mechanism.

"I don't know how master managed to have such healthy and lovely children such as them three." said Mrs Paget, the head housekeeper, known as Fanny to her more personal friends, as she sat at the kitchen table looking over her books and budgeting for the next month.

"They've such a healthy glow about them and ever so well behaved," she continued, as Thomas sat before the fire reading his daily paper, "not like master when he was young. Ooh, what a little scoundrel he was. Same as his father when he was young."

Mrs Paget stared momentarily into the open fire and reminisced about when she first started, about the same time as Thomas, though their paths seldom crossed; her being a kitchen maid in learning and him being the boot boy. The only time that they rubbed shoulders, so to speak, and not like that I'll have you mind, was when he retired to the cupboard by the stairs, outside the kitchen, for sleep and would often pinch some extra scraps of meat from the pantry.

Thomas dropped the top of his paper, enough to look over, an eyed Fanny with a smile. "You're right there," he said "the lord and master both were right little scamps." He remembered one night, when the house was full, a shooting party weekend, they had to bring in extra help from the village. He was up almost 48 hours straight, washing the muck off from the fields and polishing and laying out the shoes, when some young rascal decided to go down the corridors of the west wing rooms and mix up all the shoes. If it hadn't been for Old George, the head butler then, vouching for his diligence and servitude, well, goodness knows where he'd be now.

The bell rang from the master's study, so Thomas folded his paper, placed it on his chair, put on his coat, giving Fanny a wink, and walked steadily up the stairs, brushing his arms as he went and flattening his hair.

As a mark of respect, despite Sir Charles insisting otherwise, Thomas knocked twice on the door and entered.

"Ah, Thomas, good of you to come so quickly." Said Sir Charles standing over a pile of papers on his desk. He seemed somewhat more distracted than normal, more agitated, preoccupied.

"Thank you, Sir." Thomas replied "How may I assist?"

"Thomas...we've known each other...well, all my life" Sir Charles said, walking to the fireplace and leaning on the mantlepiece looking at the clock that had ticked time as long as he had been on the earth. "You've...always been there for me," he continued, turning and looking directly at Thomas "helped me through many...a situation."

Thomas gave the slightest of nods, acknowledging his aid, as well as signalling compliance and gratitude at the same time.

"You've never asked for anything in return for your tireless efforts, Thomas. You've been invaluable to this household, through all its ups and downs." Sir Charles paused, again looking at the clock. The intricate engravings, subtle and understated, yet of the highest craftsmanship, the hand obviously loved his craft and was adept at its performance. He was eternally grateful for being given such a position in life and he didn't want to let anyone to suffer due to errors on his behalf. They had all supported his family over the years, it was the least he could do, to show them how much he cared in return.

As Sir Charles turned to his trusted and long-standing man-servant, even in the dimness of the study, Thomas was sure he could see a glistening in his master's eye.

"Thomas..." said Sir Charles, softly and directly "...we've discussed...things...at length...I need you to do something for me."

The Old Bull and Duck sat on the edge of the green in the village, used years ago by smugglers, who, avoiding the taxmen and local constabularies, would hide their barrels of brandy and rum, and the occasional bundle of silk, in the depths of the ducking pond, only to be hooked out when the coast was clear. The magistrates thought the practice of raking at the water by the yokels, on the nights when the moon was at its fullest, a sign of madness and left them well enough alone, not realising that their booty was merely being retrieved. The illness spread and people infected by it became known as Moonrakers.

Inside the inn, talk was being had, the latest sensational gossip, the like of which had not ignited tongues since...ever.

"Who'd have thought it?" said old Jim, the gnarly old farmer, hat pushed back off his red-cheeked face as he sank his fourth cider of the evening.

"I heard," said Frank the landlord, leaning a little closer to the crowd, though no difference would it make as he was still behind the bar and they sat communing in the window seats. "I heard, there had been trouble."

"Yah, don't talk daft." Said Bezzum, the local shadow of the group. He was well tolerated and called a shadow for his flitting about in the darkness. If something was needed, then turn to Bezzum, but ask no questions, for one day things might disappear from your shed or barn.

"True." Said Frank leaning back and standing upright "Right mischief, so I'm told."

Old Jim spluttered into his flagon, laughing "Only thing you're told is stop eyeing the maids or you'll get a slap." Which produced a round of raucous guffaws and Frank throwing his cloth down on the bar in disgust.

"What's all this noise." Came the demanding tones of Maisy, the landlord's wife and real ruler of the roost, as she appeared from outback, looking as threatening and gentle as ever.

"The lads was just talking about the goings on up at the house." Frank informed her, while quickly trying to look busy.

"Were they now?" she said, crossing her arms and making the men cower. "You should know better Jim, starting a run of gossip like that." Knowing full well that was probably where it started from.

"I didn't say nothing." Said Old Jim earnestly, burrowing himself back into his drink.

"Well, mind it stays that way." Maisy said, directing her threat to all present, "You know how much they've done for all of us over the years, 'specially you Gordon," who looked the guiltiest of them all, but hadn't said anything "Where would we be? Just because a one little upset…well…I think you should be more grateful, that's all." Maisy finished with a turn, heading back and leaving the subject done.

"Could be a spot of rain coming." Said Gordon breaking the silence, which was met with a round of approving coughs and general relief.

Apparently, as rumour goes, not that you're interested in anything as vulgar as hearsay, was that there had been some thinning of staff at the big house, following some business irregularities up in the city, where Sir Charles had many expensive concerns and a fire had broken out at one of his ventures, destroying part of the docks and a couple of ships that were too slow to avoid the damage. In themselves they were of little concern, compared to the size of his wealth and the insurers would undoubtedly pay in time, but inconvenience and speculation can be more damaging and the ripples could be felt almost instantly.

Sir Charles would need to spend time away, healing business wounds and reassuring contacts, while his wife and still relatively young family tended house and calmed the waves.

To add insult to injury, there were tales that dissatisfaction had been brewing in some of the more... mature employees, unaccepting of the changes being made and requests being given, resulting in petty larceny, following the drinking of some of the finest port and spirits stored under lock and key, and held by only one person. Never had the likes been heard of before, nothing so shocking had crossed the threshold of the house in all its many years. The man responsible had tainted the good name and brought shame upon the house, after all those years how could Thomas had done such a thing.

Time moved and as the hours grew bigger, so too did the theories. The largest of them all was that Thomas himself was responsible for all the misfortune. He was the one who started the fires and destroyed the lives that depended on the trade.

Investigations spiralled and branched as Thomas's whereabouts became unknown; staff were questioned about any changes in his character or any sightings of dealings with persons of a disputable nature, not even his distant family had seen their uncle or knew whereof.

Intrigue and speculation make good bedfellows, but the truth can be mightier than fiction.

I shall let you in what on the real occurrences, as I'm sure you know that Thomas was not a bad or spiteful man. I will have no besmirchment of his goodwill either, as you will find in his loyalty.

It is right to say that Thomas was dismissed from service, but it was for good cause and for the interest in others. It is also true that drink was consumed, but in a secret farewell union between master and servant, each mourning the others journey to be had.

Sadly, it can also be said that Thomas embarked on a venture, with Sir Charles's knowledge, to bring ruin, not total destruction though, to the profitable business, in order to boost productivity and commence new contracts, while still being paid handsomely by the brokers for the loss.

There had been theft as well, something less talked about, kept more within the confines of the house, done more to discredit the once valued servant and in doing so, ensure no return to the area would be possible.

Sadness wrecked both men's souls. They had relied upon each other for years, but in both of their hearts, knew this day would come.

My dearest reader, have you guessed now why these events unfolded the way they did?

It was done with love. For beauty and grace.

For as the children grow, surely some resemblance might show itself.

Thomas had returned to the house after the night of the fire. An autumn dawn, dew heavy, but his tracks concealed by the paths and beds and other wild animals that roamed the estate.

He stood, with his heavy overcoat by the bank of the lake, a gentle fog rolling over the cool and fresh waters with the house set back in the distance, with fresh wisps of smoke rising from the hearths of newly lit fires.

The only trace of any disturbance in this beauty of the morning, was a line of parted duckweed from the edge of the lake and gentle ripples that made the lilies bob. Then all was still.

BORED GAMES

When writing, it can be hard to attribute the correct name to the right character, otherwise the flow can be stopped and you're left feeling awkward and kicking your heels in embarrassment.

This next story is case in point. I have decided to call them John and Jeff, though even now, knowing more than you do, do not feel the names...appropriate. I just thought you might like to know.

Jeff was bored.

The type of bored you get to when you know there's thing to do, if you could only think of them, but he really couldn't be bothered. I know that sounds a terrible thing to say, but sometimes its true. Sometimes, you just can't be bothered, especially when you've been busy for a while, weeding out the little jobs, completing all the bigger ones, ignoring the mundane ones and it just gets to the point...when...you say to yourself "you know what?... I just can't be bothered."

Jeff was having one of those days.

He wandered around his house trying to find things not to do and succeeding quite well, though it was starting to get the better of him. He realised that, even though he felt like it, the effort to make a cup of tea was beyond him. He sat down with a thud into his favourite, deep, square, leather armchair, that admittedly had seen better days, and that was before he found it discarded while out on a stroll one day.

He looked at a crack in the upholstery on one of the arms, the flattened stuffing starting to show through and absent-mindedly, picked at a little bit of fluff. He wanted to do something, he was feeling a bit fed up with working so hard lately, but he wanted a rest.

He looked at the phone. The phone tried to ignore him. Perhaps he'll go away. Jeff looked at the phone some more and then it came to him.

He lurched forward and dialled.

The phone rang...and rang...and rang...

"Hello?" came the voice from the other end, sounding like he'd been disturbed doing something and confused who might be calling at this time of day, at the same time.

"Barry! Hi, it's Jeff!" said Jeff with enthusiasm, which surprised even him.

"Oh, er, hi Jeff," said Barry, definitely being interrupted "Er, how's you? Not talked for a while."

"I'm bored Barry" said Jeff, finding the phrase funny whilst ignoring pleasantries and not being too good at social inter-action.

"Thanks for that. Nice to know who you can turn to when you feel...bored" Barry replied, trying not to sound interrupted... or hurt.

"Bazza, look, come on over, lets have a game of something. We haven't played Monopoly in ages."

Barry was silent for a moment, remembering "And why haven't we played in ages?" he asked.

It was Jeff's turn to be silent. "Ah, Steve can't help it." He replied.

"Jeff, he cheats at every game we play, what do you mean "He can't help it?""

Jeff thought, then said "Okay, I won't invite Steve."

"Really? You won't ask Steve to come?"

"Nah, it'll be fine, we can play something else, Mastermind or something. Ooh, Battleships." Jeff said, trying to make Barry happy, which was always a task in itself. Jeff always felt like the middle man.

"But Steve'll find out, then he'll get pissed with us."

"Oh, you're such a worrier Baz. It'll be fine. Trust me."

The thought hung in the air as Barry recalled the last time Jeff had told him to "trust" him. It turned out to be a very expen-sive weekend and it took him ages to get the stains out of his clothes.

"You promise you're not goin' to tell Steve?" Barry reiterated.

"C'mon Bazza, leave what you're doing and get your arse over here." Jeff was getting excited now, he was wondering what game to play first.

"All right then. I'll just finish off then I'll be over" Barry said hanging up the phone. Admittedly, it had been a while since they just kicked back and had a bit fun.

Jeff was feeling energised, not so bored, but energised. He went into the kitchen to see what snacks he could find for them both. Ooh, he felt like Twiglets...and some mint Aero...ooh, and something to drink. He rummaged around the cupboards and fridge but nothing excited him. Rubbery cucumber, some tins of sausages and beans and a packet of opened roasted peanuts...that didn't smell too good. Hmm...

A while later, not too long but long enough for Jeff to get fidgety and impatient, the door-bell rang. Jeff dashed to the door to find Barry with a plastic carrier bag, from a well-known supermarket, of something, so dragged him in eager to start playing.

Barry took his coat of and chucked it on the floor, which annoyed jeff a bit because...well...it was untidy, he could at least put it on the chair. The coat was followed by the bag and Jeff was eager to see what his mate Barry had brought; it must've been good because he wasn't saying anything about it.

"Right," said Barry, clapping his hands in anticipation and looking around "where's the Battleships?"

"Here," Said Jeff holding out a piece of paper and a pencil "what's in the bag?"

"Oh, nothing. You don't play Battleships with pen and paper," Barry said perplexed "It's that fold out game, with pegs and batteries and exploding sounds." He made some very good impersonations of explosions.

"Oh no, this is original Battleships, here, look." Jeff showed Barry the little shapes you had to draw, it actually looked quite fun.

"You must have something in the bag," Jeff continued "I mean, it's obviously got something in it."

"Oh yeah, nothing really." Barry replied "This does look like fun though," diverting attention "we could add our own explosions" he said carrying on his impressions of grenades and mortars. Barry liked explosions.

"Do you want a cup of tea or coffee before we start or a bit of toast maybe?" Which was pointless saying because he didn't have any bread for toast, but was hoping that perhaps Barry had some in his bag. Jeff liked toast.

"No, I'm fine thanks, for the moment, maybe in a while." Jeff was relieved as he didn't have any milk either. That wasn't strictly true. He did have milk, though it was a bit lumpy and only had a slight smell of milk.

They sat down on adjacent sofas and started filling in the positions of their fleet and aircraft, each trying their hardest to conceal pencil movement, not wanting to give the game away, and occasionally adding fake strokes...just in case.

The game commenced and Jeff was the first to strike a hit, much to the annoyance of Barry, whose splashes and misses weren't up to the same sound effects standards as explosions.

Tiddles, Jeffs cat, wandered in, jumped up and decided to start paying attention to the new visitor, any chance to get extra attention and the pencil looked like an effective face rubbing tool. Much to the annoyance of the holder.

Jeff was winning.

"Aw, c'mon, Jeff," Barry sighed "give us a break. I've gotta get one hit in." he said feeling furloughed.

"Try B6." Suggested Jeff.

"B6?" Barry said, scrutinising his sheet, wondering what possibly could be hidden in the area. "Okay, B6."

"Miss!" shouted an ecstatic Jeff.

"Dick" came a mumble from the other side of the room.

Barry wasn't enjoying the game, until things turned about two moves later with "Hit".

"BOOMMM!" said the elated Barry, at last, just as he was almost ready to chuck the game in. it was always the same when playing with Jeff. Barry seldom won when playing against Jeff or Steve, though he prided himself at being the better player of the games, they were just luckier.

"Ping pong" went the doorbell, or was it "Ding dong?" Barry

couldn't quite tell.

Barry didn't like the way Jeff smiled at him.

"I'll get it" said Jeff rising from the couch and trotting to the door out in the hallway.

Tiddles wouldn't stop rubbing herself against Barry's hand, no matter how much he tried to gently nudge her away, so, checking that Jeff was still at the door, gave her a bit more than a gentle nudge, that did it.

"Hi, Bazza me old fruit!"

Barry's heart sunk. Which was ironic. It was Steve.

"Oh, er, hi Steve." Barry waved a half-hearted wave "really glad" to see Steve. Great.

"Jeff said to bring milk" Steve lifted up a bag which obviously held a two-pint plastic container with milk in it. Barry wondered why he couldn't've just carried the bottle was beyond him.

"What we playing then? Risk, Monopoly, ooh I know, Escape from Colditz, bagsies the Germans" Steve said sitting down in Jeffs spot.

"Get the kettle on Jeff" Steve turned to say, but Jeff could be heard in the kitchen doing exactly that.

"What you got there?" Steve asked, already standing up and snatching Barry's piece of paper out of his hand.

"You're not doing very well, are you?" Steve mocked, handing the paper back "What we going to play?"

Barry was just about to say he had to be going when Jeff came in.

"Kettles on. Look, I found some chocolate Digestives" Jeff said triumphantly, excluding the information about being under the sink and already opened. Funnily, he couldn't remember having chocolate Digestives or putting them there, but he had picked off the worst bits.

"Barry said Colditz, as long as I could be the Germans" Steve winked at Barry, who sat there open mouthed and flabbergasted. He remembered more and more why he didn't like Steve.

"Fine by me" Jeff said going over to the sideboard and pulling out the well-used, but cherished box.

"You two get it set up while I make the coffees." Jeff announced striding off back into the kitchen.

"Jeff!" shouted Barry "Can I have tea please?" he hated Jeffs coffee, he was always tight with the spoonful measures and put too much milk in.

"Sorry, Bazza, I've only got a couple of bags left" Jeff replied, looking into the caddy at the last four bags, "I'm saving them for a special occasion."

Steve was organising the board and getting himself in the zone, already imagining patrols on the watchtowers, manning the searchlights and sharpening his bayonet. That was Steve, adding those little touches which were totally unnecessary.

Jeff came in with a tray of coffees and set them down on the table by the board.

"Help yourself...they're all the same"

Barry hesitated "Do you have any sugar?" he asked.

"Ah, no, sorry, ran out" Jeff replied while picking up his favourite mug before Steve got his hands on it.

"Off you go Bazza, you go first," smiled Steve "though you might as well give in now because you're not going to win" with an even broader smile.

Colditz can be quite a long game, prisoners escaping over walls, getting recaptured, the goons finding equipment caches are all parts of the unfolding saga. It is advisable to set a time limit on the game, especially for new comers or limiting the number of escapees or killed, rather than your entire number of pieces.

Four hours later and they were still playing and nerves were beginning to get fraught.

"Steve! Really? That was so blatant." Said an infuriated Barry, who had just caught his opponent swapping a card to enable him to hold a roll call of prisoners.

"What?" said Steve gesturing his open palms "I didn't do nothing" he said smiling. Steve also liked to smile.

"But I saw you, plain as day" Barry insisted.

"C'mon Barry, it's your turn" Jeff pointed out, getting a bit fidgety himself.

"But he cheated! I saw him. He always cheats! Barry was unhappy, not just because of Steve's cheating, but because two of his men would get caught and he'd only just started doing okay.

"Barry, leave it, just take your turn, we all know Steve cheats."

"I do not! I object!" said Steve, now continually grinning, incredulous that anyone should think such a thing.

"C'mon Steve, don't aggravate Bazza, you know how sensitive he can be."

"Me sensitive?" Baz exclaimed "What about the time Steve lost in Scrabble. We didn't hear the end of it for weeks."

"I still don't think you should be allowed to spell doughnut as D.O.N.U.T. its just not right" Steve said sulkily.

"Oh, I wondered when you'd bring that up again," Barry said standing "I've had enough, I'm going home."

"Aw, don't be like that Bazza, come on, lets finish first" Steve suggested, but only because he was winning, despite Barry only noticing Steve cheating for the first time today, when it was actually the third. A little joke between him and Steve.

"No, I'm tired anyway, big day tomorrow." Barry said picking up his coat and bag, "Here Jeff, you can have these." He passed the bag to Jeff who peered inside.

"Ooh, thank you." Jeff appreciatingly replied.

"I was going to drop them off at Steve's" he sneered a convincing "so there" look at Steve "But I guess I changed my mind" Barry ended with a satirical smile of his own. "Bye!" he waved, exiting, giving Tiddles a gentle kick as he left through the door, leaving Steve Satan and his counterpart to haggle over his newly acquired bag of souls. He had seen all those secret winks and grins. No one could cheat Death.

BOB'S GONE!

Joe stood at the bottom of the stairs in the hallway and shouted up "Anyone seen Bob?". He'd woken up a short while ago, under his upturned bed and had staggered out of his room, down to the (what was once looked like a) kitchen and tried to make himself a cup of tea. He was joined a short while afterwards by Mandy, who seemed unphased by their surroundings and looking as if she had just stepped out of a crumpled catalogue (though obviously had already restarted on the gin). After their tea and conversation, Joe had a nagging feeling of disconcert about Bob, but nothing solid came (that had all been emptied during the night he recalled) as he looked at the land of destruction that lay about.

Joe surveyed the open kitchen sitting room, last night had been a doozy, as far as parties went, it was pretty way up there in the leader board judging by the small flashes of memory that popped up. He even had a snippet of Sid dancing on the coffee table, wildly waving his shirt in the air and gyrating, something he never thought possible of Sid, he was such a quiet and elusive chap.

He looked over to the doorway to the hall and there was something about gate crashers and remembered seeing Mandy smooching up to a couple, freaking them out with her over attendance, while Andy stood over them being his usual aggressive self, the perfect good cop bad cop routine.

"Mandy?" Joe asked "Do you remember those gate crashers last night?"

"Gate crashers? No, darling. Why, did you fancy one of them, hmm?" she smiled with her eyes over her tea.

"What? No!" said Joe, more than a little taken aback by her comment "No," he grimaced "It's just...I don't know...something about Bob." He looked vaguely into the air and wished he could remember.

At that moment Larry came gingerly in, even he seemed to be nurturing a hangover, though was as upbeat as ever.

"Hi guys, tea in the pot? I heard movement." He said as he tentatively approached the teapot with caution, expecting it to strike out at any moment.

"Ooh," crooned Mandy "did we drink that much last night?" she said as her eyes surveyed the array of discarded bottles and an impressive large pile of beer cans in the corner of the room, a good place to chuck them thought Joe, self-congratulating himself as he remembered being the first to start the pile.

"Larry dear," Mandy sighed, leaning on the breakfast bar, in case it fell over "have you seen Bobby bunny anywhere? Little Joey's worried."

Larry went into a gaze like trance, the mental cogs visibly working hard as a trace of memory yearned to be discovered, yet refused to come in from play. "I remember..." uttered Larry as if quietly locating the whereabouts of a lost and used tissue, that had been inadvertently stuck down the side of the sofa, "I remember...Andy, shouting at someone in the garden, something about the pond and a lemon". he concluded as if the voice from the ether had gone. "Ohh, hang on...didn't he leave with those gatecrashers?"

He looked at Mandy and Joe as if he had just delivered the crown jewels who stared back with unimpressed faces with bits of things still attached from the night before.

Joe walked over to the kitchen window and looked out to the pond, sighed, then returned back to join the pack.

"Well?" Mandy demanded.

Joe looked at her in shock, it was the first time he had ever heard her be abrupt.

"I saw a lemon," he said "but no Bob bobbing." He smiled but mainly to himself.

"Have you checked all the rooms?" asked Larry, hopeful in the idea that it was a stupid question.

Mandy looked at Joe "Well, have you?"

"Er, no, not yet, he's usually crashed somewhere in a heap near the sideboard" where, this morning, the bottles weren't.

"Well...lets take a look, shall we?" said the sarcastic tones of Mandy, which frightened Joe even more, what was wrong with the world this morning.

They agreed on a plan of execution, Mandy would take Andy's

room, Larry Eric's and Joe would check on Bob's and Sid's.

Trying not to seem like children playing hide and seek they split up on their prospective targets.

Mandy knocked gently on Andy's bedroom door, only to hear a mumbled expletive of where she should go and how to do it. She opened the door instead and entered.

Even from downstairs, as Andy lived in the top of the house (the senior position, he liked to think) they could hear the explosive shouting, swearing and threats being issued. "Damn," thought Joe, "Mandy's really giving it to him" as he heard a door slam and saw Mandy appear smiling and calm at the top of the stairs "I've been wanting to say that to him for ages. Now, is there any gin left?" as she walked back down to the kitchen, leaving Joe impressed and unnerved, but with the conclusion that Andy didn't know where Bob was.

Before he could do anything else a Larry shout was heard "Hey, Joe, come here." Which he did.

"You found him?" asked Joe in the doorway of Eric's room and marvelled. "Blimey!"

Joe realised he had never been in Eric's room before and it wasn't how he expected it to be. It was tidy. Not like his hovel. Organised and tidy. He walked in and marvelled some more, like entering a cave of wonders. A clean made bed, which he brushed his hand over, pictures, with glass, unbroken, on the wall, a clean floor, with no litter... a totally normal room...well, he had seen everything now.

Larry signalled with a wave, while saying "Here, come here, look." As if he too had discovered something wonderous. Joe saw he was holding a piece of paper with writing on it.

"Hey Guys, thought I'd leave a note. Just in case. Left it in here. Safest place. Put Bob in his room. Didn't want him trampled on. Wild party. Gone off with Sue and Teri. See you later. Oi, Oi."

"Who the fuck is Sue and Teri" Joe asked Larry who looked none the wiser.

"You checked his room yet?" Larry asked Joe.

"No, was just about to when you called." Joe replied.

"Come on then, lets go!" Larry jumped out of the room hoping Robin might follow, which he didn't.

"Should we knock?" suggested Joe, to which Larry smirked and said "Why bother, Eric said he was already hammered, he probably left him with a bottle, just in case."

They opened the door and Joe gasped.

What was going on today.

If he hadn't known better, which he was having doubts about, he could have sworn he walked back into Eric's room, tidy, clean…how was it possible. But no Bob.

They checked under the bed, in the wardrobe and just to be ridiculous, behind the curtains, but, no Bob.

"I don't understand?" Joe said to Larry, who was now checking the draws. "Bob's not here."

"Well observed." Said Larry in a patronising manner that only fuelled to disconcert Joe even more. "What was wrong with everyone today?" he thought.

"Perhaps we should check on Sid, see if he knows anything." Larry suggested, walking out onto the landing and knocking on Sid's door.

Nothing happened. He knocked louder, three times, but still no answer. Larry tried to turn the handle.

"No point in doing that," Joe pointed out "he keeps it locked all the time." Realising that he had never fully seen the inside of Sid's bedroom either. Sid had lived here longer than anyone, in fact, he had been part of the original house crew when Joe arrived. Joe had once caught a glimpse of Sid's bedroom, when he first arrived and the door was left unlocked and ajar and recollected it being very spartan, bare and no thrills so to speak.

"He's obviously not in there otherwise he would've answered. You know what Sid's like." Joe said to an uncertain Larry.

"Well, what next?" Larry asked, perplexed at the situation.

"Not sure" Bob replied "Guess we could go and start tidying up (he couldn't believe he just said that) and see what happens." After all, Bob was old enough to look after himself, he had to take responsibility for himself…sometime. He snorted a small grunt of amusement.

Larry and Joe made their way back down the stairs and found Mands in the kitchen with a cup and saucer, saved for those special occasions, filled with collected dregs of various bottles.

"No luck?" she enquired smiling with her natural ease, now resuming normality.

"Well, Eric's out," Joe started to list "Sid...well we don't know about Sid..."

"hmm? what?"

A gentle clatter of cans tumbling caused the three housemates to turn their attention to the pile in the corner of the room which was now revealing itself to be a camouflaged Sid.

"Sid?" Larry called over "What the hell you doing there?" which, even he, thought was a bit of a stupid question.

"Oh, er...not really sure." Said the damp looking crumpled mess which was slowly rising to full height. He stretched, yawned and ruffled his hair, making Joe realise it seemed a long time since Joe had seen Sid in entire human form.

Sid stood, bare chested, tattooed with lipstick and splotchy damp trousers, trying to revisit the previous night events, but it was so hard to see due to the thumping on his head.

"Have you seen Bob anywhere?" Larry asked, immediately feeling very foolish as the three other people in the room looked at him incredulously.

"Larry!" Joe said first "He's been piled up in a mound of beer cans, I don't think we'll find Bob in there as well...oh, no, hang on...". Larry looked, then felt even more stupid.

Joe turned to ask Sid whether he had any ideas of anything that might lend itself to Bob's whereabouts, only to discover him gone.

He quickly looked about him in all directions, in case he was hiding behind him.

"Not there darling," smoothed Mandy "he went upstairs." She pointed with her almost empty cup.

"I guess we're back to square one then." Said Joe, starting to lose enthusiasm for anything, especially tidying up.

"Well," Larry piped up "I can't hang about deals to see and people to do." He said smiling "See you guys later."

"But what about the mess, what about Bob, what about…?" Joe was trying to find something else to add and was annoyed that he didn't have anything to distract him from the task ahead.

"Hmm, me too sweetie," Mandy cooed "I've got to go to work." She said draining her refill.

"Work? You don't work Mandy!" Joe said emphatically.

"Of course, I do darling, where do you think the money comes from to pay for all this?" she waved her hands over the disarray.

Joe stood, open mouthed, he'd heard it all now.

"What do you do?" he said, the words falling out of his mouth.

Mandy stared at him in disbelief "How did we meet Joe?" she asked him softly, leaning forward on the breakfast bar and making eye contact directly.

He couldn't remember. Nothing. No memory. He must've been drunk. So, he concentrated harder, this was becoming a horrible day, he was going to have to give up the booze. He tried to wring his brain.

He…something about…lights, yes…flashing lights, no, no that was…before. Yes, that's right, flashing lights then…darkness. Hmm.

"You're a solicitor!" he triumphantly exploded.

"Barrister, darling" Mandy corrected him.

"What's the difference?" he asked.

"Oh, in your case about 10 years." Mandy grinned, leaving her stool walking around to Joes side and giving him a kiss and tap on the cheek "See you later sweetie." She smiled and left.

Joe was none the wiser about anything today, he was feeling very lost and thought about his blanket he had when he was a child.

The next hour Joe spent attempting to get the downstairs back in some kind of order, only once being interrupted by an Andy going out the front door.

"Oh, hi Andy, could you…" was cut off with a very sincere and heartfelt threat and what might occur if a fish were to be passing at the time. Joe didn't fully understand the context of the said sentence, but fully grasped the "…not today thank you I'm frightfully busy, ta ta." Or words to that effect.

As Andy was ploughing out, Eric was coming in and also received a gracious good morning.

"oh, its you." Said Eric to Joe coldly.

"Er…" stumbled Joe's speech, just not knowing what the hell was going on. had it always been this weird or was the world just trying to mess with his head today. "Yes," he said in that confirmation type of way "Its me." Just making sure.

"Alright then, see you." Eric said sulkily, while heading upstairs.

"Hang on Eric, hang on." Joe said following after him.

"Eric, have you seen Bob anywhere?" Joe asked "He wasn't in his room like you said he was in your note."

Eric looked at Joe as if he was…a plank, a scaffolding plank.

"I didn't say he was in his room." Sneered Eric.

"Yes, yes you did…wait a minute…what's up with you today, why are you being like this?" asked Joe, really worried that he really could be losing the plot.

"I think you know all too well." Eric convincingly said.

"I don't, I don't know at all." Joe really didn't.

"Last night? We had an argument…remember?" Eric declared, much to Joe's befuddlement.

"No, we didn't" replied Joe, totally confused now.

"Yes, we did," Eric insisted "in the dining room, about what's her name."

"But we don't have a dining room."

Eric turned around to look where he thought it was and it was true, it wasn't there.

"Oh." Said Eric "Hmm." And "Well."

"Ah, well, that note might have been misunderstood then, I

see." Eric admitted, though failed to help Joe understand. "You see, when I said <u>his</u>, I meant yours, I was being facetious, I was a bit annoyed with you...or someone." He smiled apologetically and shrugged his shoulders.

"You mean you put Bob in my room? Why? Where?" so many questions were running through Bobs head it hurt.

"Well, it seemed the safest place, I mean" he laughed "no ones going to go in there are they" Bob was a little offended but then realised that Eric was probably right. "I put him in the wardrobe." Eric finished and went up to his room.

Joe stood in the hallway for a long, few seconds, those cogs just weren't working fast today and he tentatively started up the stairs to his room.

He slowly opened the door and stepped in and walked up to the wardrobe. He placed his ear against the door to see if he could hear anything and to his amazement could hear the slightest breathing sounds coming through the wood.

He creaked open the door to see a wide mouthed, sleeping Bob stuffed in the bottom of the wardrobe in an uncomfortable sitting position with an almost empty bottle of whisky in his clutches and the unmistakable eau de urine mixing with Joe's trainers.

Relieved, Joe slowly closed the door and thought to himself "Well, it could have been worse, he could have been..." the retching sounds stopped him there.

UG

Ug sat by his fire feeling a bit down, staring into the flames that flickered and danced, lighting up his cave as he hit the soft earth of the ground with a rock he had found that fitted his hand nicely.

He had been aimlessly thumping the ground for a while, but a wisp of a memory came to visit and he remembered how he had seen a poster once, about becoming a Mountie in the Rockies. It looked like a very nice valley in the background as the Mountie struck a heroic and important pose, lots of trees, and a big river running through it. He thought of all the hunting and fishing he could do there and big fires he could have to dance around, while calling up to the blue yonder, dressed up in all types of imaginary skins and furs.

But, it all seemed so far away. Not many trees around here, plenty of caves and boulders with lots of sand and snakes. He shivered. He didn't like the snakes. They always tried to bite him, even if he was minding his own business. The spiders were just as bad. Sometimes, like when he got up in the morning, he had to check his hide shoes, just in case someone put another spider in there like before. His big toe swelled up as big as a…well…big swollen toe and he couldn't wear his shoes for lots of time.

Ug was getting bored of the thudding so swapped hands.

The fire still crackled and popped.

Ug sat staring deep into the flames, as a small idea was trying to make itself heard amongst the noise of emptiness in his brain, battling with decisions of food or…well, actually it was only food on his mind at the moment, though even he didn't realise it yet. It would be quite a few thousand years until mankind had decision making sorted a bit better, but even then, some still wouldn't be able to tell their arse from their elbow (not literally of course, no one is that stupid…are they?).

So, Ug kept on staring, thumping the ground with his rock, thinking of food and doing nothing else, apart from the idea growing, demanding to be heard.

Veronica came waltzing into the cave, stroking her hair looking as beautiful as ever (Cro Magnons, like all animals, follow the belief that beauty is in the eye of the beholder…to us though…).

"Hi Ug, what ya doing?" surprisingly she had an American accent.

Ug looked at her, the thought of food leaving his mind "Uh" he grunted.

Veronica laughed "Oh Ug, you're so funny." She swayed her hips some more and walked over to the fire, the other side of Ug.

Ug watched and rubbed himself between the legs, though quickly stopped as he had forgotten he was still holding the rock. It wasn't comfortable.

"Some of the guys are going hunting. Are you going to go with them? Maybe bring something back for Veronica?" she smiled an almost toothless smile.

Ug's head jolted upright and he looked around "Ug?" he said.

"I said some of the guys are going hunting?" Veronica repeated as requested.

Ug's eyes widened, that small brewing thought had just exploded into view. It was so big Ug didn't know what to do with it or where to put it. He had never had a thought like this before. It was really quite odd.

He suddenly stood, erect and proud, startling Veronica and causing her to take a step back.

"Ooh ah" Ug stated, striking a charismatic pose.

"You're going to do what?" Veronica squawked.

"Ah, ah OOH AH!" he said triumphantly, proud to have realised his destiny and capabilities in one fail swoop (though he wasn't sure about the capability part).

Just as Ug was starting to feel really good and positive about things, Tarquin came in.

"oh, hey guys" Tarquin said as he entered, brushing the fancy piece of leather that was hanging off his left shoulder, "inadvertently" showing off the string of pebbles that wrapped around his wrist.

"We're just off for a spot of huntin' and fishin'," Tarquers said, trying to sound more down with the people.

"Ooh ah ah ah oooh" Ug said, trying to hide his contempt.

Veronica sidled up to Tarquin and put her hand onto his shoulder "Now, now Ug, let's not get ahead of ourselves. I'm sure Tarquin was just trying to be helpful."

Ug remembered the last time Tarquin was "helpful". Ug spent days stuck in a hole in the ground after they told him he had to defend it from a group of monkeys that were apparently terrorising the area. The only time he saw a monkey was when a baboon came by, looked, threw down some unwanted bodily material and left seeming very happy with itself.

"Besides," Veronica continued "Ug says he going to become a Mountie."

Tarquin burst out laughing, sending out a flush of embarrassment across Ug's body, making him grit his teeth with resolve.

"How on earth are you going to become a Mountie?" Tarquin spluttered between laughs. "There's no mountains around here and besides, what are you going to ride?" he clutched his chest as if it was the best joke he had heard in ages.

Veronica felt bad for Ug, though she did find the amusement infectious and was soon laughing too, especially as Ug was now pulling that silly pouting face of his. Oh, it was simply too much.

Ug growled "Grr." picked up his spear and stomped off, out of HIS cave, off to find a bit of undisturbed peace and quiet, so decided to go back to that hole in the ground, but hopefully, this time, with no visitors.

As Ug left the noise of the tribe behind him, his thoughts turned back to being a Mountie and considered whether it really was that bad an idea. He mumbled to himself a bit and mimicked Tarquin's laugh, but with some added sarcasm for effect, and prodded the air with his spear, roughly the same height as "Tarquers" backside, which made him chuckle.

Suddenly, something caught his attention out of the corner of his eye and turning quickly in a crouch, found that it had gone, so paying no attention he carried on his way, kicking the occasional innocent stone and stamping on the frequent bug, though minding they weren't the spiky type.

A large pair of amber eyes watched him go, then turned and headed off in the direction where Ug had come from.

The further Ug went, the greater the distance was from his upset, until he decided not to bother with the hole, but wander instead, especially as he was determined to catch the butterfly that had been fluttering around him the last few moments.

As he hopped and jumped, trying to snatch or catch it out of the air, it was joined by another and then another. Soon Ug was surrounded by the yellow and purple winged flying insects landing on a bush of brightly coloured flours. With one mighty, if over enthusiastic, swipe, he managed to swot one with a satisfying squelch. Lifting his hand to carefully inspect his victory, he marvelled at the pulpy mess of wings and goo which now made a vibrant red colour that stuck on his hand. He tentatively wiped his hand on his scrap of clothing and became excited by what he saw, firing his imagination and the possibilities it offered. He looked at all the other butterflies for a moment, happily flapping about their business and he licked his lips.

After many exhausting minutes of pirouettes, arabesques and jetes, Ug stood panting, surrounded by a littered battlefield of fallen coloured splotches, which he proceeded to scoop up and rub over his bits of clothing, staining everything a bright, yet sometimes mottled red.

When completed, he looked about him to see if any had been left unutilised and when he saw that all was complete, he dashed off in the direction of a stream so he could admire his handiwork.

He reached the little brook in no time and carefully leaning over the water, not wanting to wash away his efforts, peered into the ripples and was more than pleased at his now red outfit. He whooped with happiness and gave a couple of victorious jumps, landed on a stone and almost fell in to the water. He quickly steadied himself and decided to rush back and show everyone his labours.

Ug strode off, feeling very proud of himself and imagined himself doing heroic deeds, like saving kittens from trees or stopping a bank robber, not that they had any banks, nor would do for millennia, but if they had…well…that's what he would do.

As he neared to his cave, Ug heard the terrified screams of women and children and realised his tribe must be in trouble. His grip tightened onto his spear as he started to run and as he got closer, he could also hear the roars of sabretooth tigers terrorising his people. His run turned into a mighty sprint until, with one giant leap he bound onto a rock and stepped into the air, spear raised above his head, his battle cry shouting out as he landed on the back of a sabretooth and plunged his spear deep in its neck.

The animal fell, instantly dead, though the screaming continued as Ug saw other animals circling and attacking the defenceless, who had been left behind as the men hunted.

Ug rolled off the dead animal as it crashed to the ground and instantly picked his next target. In one smooth movement he pulled his spear from the still body and lunged toward his nearest foe and thrust with all his might into the hindquarters of the unsuspecting animal. Mortally wounded, the creature turned to lash out at the culprit, but Ug had already leapt back out of harms way, as the claws slashed the air in front of him.

Unfortunately for Ug, a third tiger of the pack lunged at the same time, its razor claws shredding his shoulder, causing him to yell in pain. Though Ug was a brave, fearsome and experienced warrior and rolled to the ground to avoid the second strike, as the third cat leapt for him.

Ug times it well. Through mid-flight, Ug managed to secure his footing and as the sabretooth landed, Ug spun and plowed his spear into the shoulder of the largest of cats and straddled it on its back as it ran off in pain and terror, trying to push the spear in further.

It was the last that was seen of Ug. Though when the men returned to a devastated tribe, they told them of Ug's courage and how he fought 3 sabretooth tigers on his own and saved many lives. They spoke in mystery of how he appeared out of the blue sky, clothed in red and ready for battle.

Some believed him dead, while others heard rumours of a caveman riding a sabretooth and dressed in red coming to peoples' aid. Long may he rest in the great hunting ground in the sky.

JOEY'S

The rain was dropping like a corrupted vicar's trousers, fast and loose, splattering against the fire escapes of the tall buildings that stood next to each other, the proverbial neighbours never seeing eye to eye.

The dark alley smelt of corruption and cheap wine, with

plenty of corners to hide the dealings of two-bit bags and two-bit punks, trying to make an existence in their sorry world, though were going nowhere fast.

The dumpsters overflowed from a lack of neglect, spewing out their contents like a stuffed fat pig who has eaten too much at some fancy restaurant, trying to impress a discounted dame with jewellery and promises, promises he could never keep.

The rain wasn't going to end anytime soon, so I stood, huddling to the wall for protection, my collar turned up against my neck as my hat took the brunt of it.

"What a lousy way to make a living." I thought to myself getting soaked, as I watched the darkened apartment across the street, the one above Joeys Deli, the one which served the best salmon rye bagels in town. Some town.

I knew Joey, he was a good man, the honest type, always pleased to see his customers and went to church regular, though his kid hadn't turned out so good and almost wound up feeding the fishes. Had to step in and put things right, help iron out the creases if you know what I mean.

I hadn't worked this part of the town for a while, left it to Mickey Bianco mostly, it was his turf after all, I was just helping out, but it was good to get back out on the streets sometimes, puts you back in touch…back in touch with the lowlifes and scum who fought among themselves for any scrap that was going.

I'd been put on the trail of Cindy. She was a doll who played patter cake with any Charlie who came along…for a price, though this time her prince handsome was a possessive type, didn't like the thought of his property being rented out by any other Tom and pardon my French, Dick or Harry.

Cindy had been a clean-cut and attractive kid, a real looker. Came from a good hard-working background too. Her folks had been real conscientious types, until the depression hit and like everyone else, they were left struggling, counting their nickels and dimes to pay the rent.,

That's when they got bit.

Sharks always smell blood, no matter how far away the bleeding is and pretty soon, like so many others, they came to prey on the drowning and the victims.

Repayments always started easy and friendly like, but like the sun in the morning, they go up. Cindy's folks got deeper and deeper into debt, the kind of debt where it'll never get paid, no matter how many hours of grease work you do, that's when Cindy got the bright idea of helping out, lending a hand, if you catch my drift.

Sure, things started easy enough, plenty of takers for fresh produce, but like any cabbage, over time, the leaves start to wilt.

That's when the trouble really started.

Some Joe got happy with Bobby the Blade one night, thought he'd cut himself a fresh piece rather than pay his dues and Cindy spent a two week stretch at Ward 10, trying to put herself and her face back together.

Lucky for her, a local mobster, Charming Sam, saw something in the way she walked and took her under his wing, but as time went on he started getting twitchy, nervous like, always looking over his shoulder at the next guy.

Some perp reckoned it was Ricky the Riot spreading bad rumours about Sam, something to do with business gone wrong back east. Who knows? Let's just say that Sam started getting real protective like, so protective that he had to wear two pairs of socks, just in case.

The rain hadn't let off any when the light in Cindy's apartment flicked on. I only saw a shadow move behind the drawn blind, reach down and turn on the table lamp. I couldn't tell whether it was Cinders or not, I ain't no fairy Godmother. They bent over, to sit down most probably, rearranging some fancy cushions, like the ones my feet could do with about now, but then went and turned the overhead off instead. That's when I knew it wasn't Cindy and we were in for trouble. That's with a capital T.

Whoever it was, took the seat by the lamp and lit up a smoke as I checked my pocket to reassure myself. I didn't like to use heat, but when a broad is in distress, someone's gotta take it off.

I walked, quiet like, to the end of the alley and scoured the street for any tailers. You never knew, they might've come in pairs, like Noah said, most things do.

It was quiet, except for the water falling from sky and the thunder it left behind. It was late, what d'ya expect. Only the occasional cab drove by and a few bums were taking advantage of Joeys late night openings. Couldn't blame 'em. I had a hankering for a cup of hot java right now, somewhere nice'n' dry, anywhere but this godforsaken part of town.

I had been one of the lucky few that managed to escape the fate that these poor schmucks had been dealt. Since then, I counted my blessings, but only on my left hand, my right was for other work, things I didn't think a maker might like to see.

I remembered the night clearly. Me and the kids were up to no good on the roof tops. We were young and easily led. This one guy, Stan, Little Stanley, we called him, though little was ironic see. We were looking into some breaking and entering, so me being smart and wanting to make a name for myself took it literal. I fell through a skylight and almost broke my back. Landed on some old dames' poodle. Saved my like though, otherwise I woulda smacked my head on a concrete slab.

After that Father Mahoney took me in and put me back on the right path. Made sure I had a roof over my head and warm food in my belly. Got me some work down at the mill, didn't pay great, but hey, I was a kid and became grateful for what he did. Never wanted anything in return, not like some other folk. I'm sure he would have given his last teeth if it helped someone.

That's how I ended up here. Wet through in a stinkin' alley, looking out for a dame. If only she knew.

The table lamp clicked off. Guess whoever it was knew Cindy's schedule better than me. I could have saved myself some time and damp clothes.

I moved back into the darkness of the alley, cloaking myself in its protection and waited, listening to the beat of my blood course through my veins. Getting ready for action and come what may.

I didn't have to wait too long. I heard her before I smelt her. The cheap cologne was carried by the clicking of her heels on the wet street, dodging puddles and the things that they may hide. I never understood how some broads, whatever weather, wear pointy shoes that are fit for nothing. Snow, sun and beach, there yo'll find 'em.

Now, I'm the first in line when it comes to trying to better yourself, but for the love of Mary it makes no practical sense to me. Guess it's the way of the birds and de bees. Me? I'm just glad I'm a bee.

I tilted my hat up so as not to spoil the view and put my hand in my right coat pocket, watching her start to climb the steps to her door. I'll follow when she gets three quarters up and I get ready to run.

I figure whoever is in the flat is ready as well, got themselves in some position. Poor old Cinders just don't know what's about to happen. I'll have to act smart and fast. It's a dog-eat-dog world.

I time my run just right. I see her reaching into her bag for her key and start to run. Stupid me didn't check the street and met a cab full on, sending me over its bonnet and letting the road say hello to my head.

By the time I got up, she was gone. Probably already making her way up the stairs. I had to move. And fast. I ran hard, leaving my hat behind, I figured I'd get it later, on the way out, I knew what that might mean.

I pushed through the locked door first time, thinking that the janitor should've bought better locks and took to the stairs.

I couldn't hear her steps on the wood so figured she must already be at her door, key about to go in. But then I heard her talk. Even at this time of night, nosy neighbours can be a blessing.

I carried on climbing though slowed my pace, listening carefully to their talk, as no doubt was her would be attacker.

I was almost there when I heard a gasp and a turn of heel and was almost knocked over as Cinders flew down the stairs, escaping her brush with death.

I carried on my way, the coast now clear and the pressure off.

I turned the handle of her apartment door and two shots rang out, the flashes lighting up the room.

I wished I had seen Cinders face as she entered the street and heard what was meant for her. Hopefully she'll have more sense next time and get herself back on the right track, find herself a job or some respect.

The bullets hit me in the chest, nice grouping I thought.

If the light had been on, he would have seen me smile as I fell to the ground. There for the grace of God go I...

FOR WILL

Tues 4TH Sept

Dads so funny, he cracks me up all the time. Mum tells him off for being so silly, but me and Martina can't stop laughing, like today at tea he showed us how to blow milk out of his nose. Ben is too young to realise what's going on but he laughs anyway.

5th Sept

Back to School. New term, new year and some new faces. Nice to see Terry again, he hasn't changed, feels like it's been a long summer. Gordy and me had to go and see Miss Robins about being put in the wrong class.

6th Sept

Got a new sports teacher, Mr Hooper, we accidently called him Cooper and he got really mad. Saw Miss Samuels today, schwing! Told Dad about her and we laughed. Only second day back and got loads of homework.

7th Sept

Mum forgot my packed lunch so had to go down shops to get food, saw John BarCOCK down there. What a dick! Saw him shoplifting and showing off. He thinks he's so tough. He's trying to grow a moustache. Glad it Saturday tomorrow.

8th Sept

Thank goodness it's Saturday. Going to cinema later with Tel and Gordy. Got to wash Dad's car. Yay, Mum said I didn't need to wash Dad's car. Went and saw Karate Kid, hi ya! Wax on, wax off. Wish I knew Karate, kick Barcock's arse.

9th Sept

I DO have to wash Dad's car. I'll practice my wax on and wax off. Homework done. Roast for lunch. Mum's a great cook. Dad was flicking peas at me and wouldn't stop until Mum clonked him one. He's making a new squeezebox.

10th Sept

I hate Monday's. Double Maths first thing. Man, it sucks. Got a new girl in our class Susan Miller, she's got a nice smile. Terry and Gordy think she's stuck up but I don't think so. Got to go down the shops for Mum later.

11th Sept

Swimming. Dad swapped my lunchbox around. Gave me a jar of apple sauce, bag of raisins and a yoghurt...all of Ben's fave stuff. Martina blanked me today, she was hanging out with some of her friends, I've hidden her shoes.

12th Sept

School, blah, blah, blah, and its only just started. Terry, me and Johnno had a competition to see who could roll the biggest bogey. Tel won. Not surprised, he's always blowing his nose.

13th Sept

School sucks. John Barcott is a big twat of a bully. I wish he would drop dead and leave me alone, and his mates.

14th Sept

Hand hurts. Tried hitting JB back. Dick. Saw Susan walking across the playground. The other boys make fun of her, but I think she's nice. I like the way she smiles at me, friendly like. She's smart as well, perhaps that's why the other boys don't like her. Mum and Dad say it's because they're jealous.

15th Sept

Dad's taking me to a footie match today. It was great. We won. Dad bought me a Wimpy on the way home and played me a tape of a gig they did a couple of weeks ago. I don't really see the point of Irish Folk Music.

16th Sept

Sunday, Sunday, Sunday. Me and Mart went for a bike ride. Cycled over to the bird reservation. Really peaceful. Nice place.

17th Sept

Why did they invent Maths? Made a new mate. Brian, we call him Bugs. He's got big eyes (and teeth) and ginger hair but he seems okay. He's new to the school so doesn't know anyone.

18th Sept

Footie practice tonight. Dad came and watched. Dads a really loud spectator, kind of embarrassing but funny because he swears so much.

19th Sept

In assembly, Mr P said we're going to do a play or something at the end of term. The younger kids are going to do nativity, but the rest of us are going to do something different. Sounds silly to me.

20th Sept

Drama lesson was fun. Bobby said that the nativity was going to be for parents to come and see, but the rest of us were going to do a variety show. Anyone can do anything they want...if they want. A lot said they didn't want to do anything. Its for years 4,5 and 6. Should be great.

21st Sept

Gordy, Tel, Johnno and Bugs are coming over later. Mum said we could watch tv and stay up late as tomorrows Saturday. Martina's off out with some of her mates.

22nd Sept

We came up with a great idea for the show last night. We're going to all be Mr Gumby and do flower arranging. I might do the Idiot song as well; I've got my bald head mask with hair on the sides. Bugs said he thinks Susan Miller fancies me and Terry and Gordon took the piss for the rest of the night.

23rd Sept

Marty didn't come home until lunchtime and Mum got really mad at her. Ben started crying and then made a really bad smell. Dad said he's taking us all out for a treat tonight. Going to that new steak place.

24th Sept

Great time last night. Dad let me and Marty drink some of his wine when Mum wasn't looking. She wondered why we kept giggling. Even Ben found it funny. Had Black Forest Gateau for pudding, really yummy, and Dad ordered another one for me. Stuffed.

25th Sept

Susan Miller wasn't in school today, kind of missed not seeing her. Mr Cooper is taking us for Maths as well as P.E. he really helps you understand from different angles if you don't get it at first, though I don't think Gordy understands anything. It's not that he's thick, he just sees things differently. Some people give him a hard time over it. Normally the really dumb ones. Footie practice.

26th Sept

Susan was back at school today. I went to go to try and talk to her but got distracted by Johnno and Terry. Got told off by Miss

Robins for kicking a chair over in Class 5, didn't see her walk in behind me. Got a clip over the head as well. Everyone laughed. Except Susan, she just smiled at me.

27th Sept

John BarCOCK got in trouble today. Not only did he get caught smoking, but he hit a 3rd year kid who went and reported him. He's such a dick. Glad I only have a couple of classes with him.

28th Sept

Dads got a gig with the band tomorrow night, we've all got to go. Boring. But it will be nice to see everyone, they're all quite fun in their own way, especially Manny. Its really funny when Dad starts winding him up for being a communist. Manny gets really heated, even when he knows Dad is just pulling his leg.

29th Sept

Glad that week was over with. We've started copying our script for the show from one of Monty Pythons records, its going to be great. I already know the lines to the Idiot Song, just need to find something to wear. Got trousers and boots, need something like a tailcoat.

30th Sept

That was a great night last night. The band and punters were really lively, everyone in a good mood. Manny let me have a pint of cider. He bought it and pretended it was his, but let me drink it instead. I felt really spinny by the time we got home. I went straight to bed and the room wouldn't stop turning. It was so funny.

1st Oct

New week, new month. Wow, where's the year gone. Not long until Halloween and Bonfire night. Going to have to organise something for Halloween this year, see if anyone's up for it. We normally go over to Aunty M's for bonfire night and fireworks.

2nd Oct

I plucked up the courage and went and talked to Susan Miller. She's so sweet. I didn't realise what nice eyes she's got as well. Its not nice that people treat her differently, she just really nice and friendly, but I forget what to say when I'm near her and then I feel pretty stupid afterwards.

3rd Oct

Forgot to go to Footie practice after school yesterday. Got told off for it. I was talking to Susan after school, walking to our bus, got on and didn't realise my mistake until we were already half way home. Got to remember to go and see Cooper tomorrow.

4th Oct

Blimey! What a fuss! I miss one practice and get told I'm not committed enough. I've being doing footie at school longer than he's been teaching here. Got extra Maths's homework, but it doesn't matter, I'll get Mart to do it. She likes Maths.

5th Oct

Mum told me off for getting Martina to do my homework. Dad said it was good thinking. We did some practicing for Mr Gumby and it was really funny. Terry was the best, then Bug, Gordy was funny but in the wrong way which made it even funnier.

6th Oct

Spent the day in town with Bugs and Gordy. What a pair. Mucking around and got pushed in none other than Susan Miller. She smelt fantastic, all fresh and softly clean, with a hint of summer and something warm and nice in the background. I think she likes me.

7th Oct

Why do I always have to wash Dad's car? Its just so unfair. Mum told me to stop complaining. Martina never has to do it. Mum made fruit salad and Ben pinched all the grapes, got caught putting them in his pocket. It was priceless.

8th Oct

JB is a knob. Saw Susan at break time and we went for a walk around the school field together...alone! I really like her but I don't know what to do. We chat great but then I get stupid and nervous and dash off to see my mates. Man, what a donkey!

9th Oct

Talked to Dad about Susan. He said I should ignore what the others say and do what feels right. He says you only live once and got to make the most out of it, otherwise you can regret it later on, then he farted (which was really funny). I'm still none the wise though, still don't know what I'm meant to do.

10th Oct

Got teased at Footy tonight. Susan Miller came and watched. I got embarrassed, tried not to look and ignore her but she kept giving me a smile, even a little wave. Felt really stupid. Martina took the mick out of me at tea time, Mum told her off and dad did his kissy kissy routine. Man! What are they like?

11th Oct

Chatting with Tel, Gordy and Bugs about Gumby, deciding that we've got to wear shorts and wellies otherwise it wouldn't be right. Tel told me his sister fancies me and wants to go out sometime. I said I'll see.

12th Oct

Dads finished another one of his musical instruments he's been making. It looks great, bit like a bagpipe but you stick it under your arm. Ben doesn't like the noise it makes, it made him cry. Got told off for squeezing it and upsetting Benny.

13th Oct

Met up with the boys in town at the café. Had a milkshake. Showed them what dad taught me about blowing it out of your nose. Laughed so hard it went everywhere. Got chucked out, but the guys were impressed. Thanks dad, you're the best.

14th Oct

Non-stop rain. Nothing to do. No-one about. Homework done. Stared at ceiling. That fun.

15th Oct

School sucks! Almost half-term. Can't wait. Seems like I've been at school for ages. Losing interest in Diary.

16th Oct

Blah, blah, blah.

17th Oct

Footy. Yay. Great game tonight. We won. Saw Miss Samuels at lunchbreak. Ouch. Got teased by Bugs and Gordy saying that Miss Samuels and me were getting married.

18th Oct

Found out today that The Monkees aren't a new group at all. They were around years ago. Martina and me have been watching them on telly and thought they were really cool and funny. Who knew?

19th Oct

Half-Term starts tomorrow. A whole week off. Mum and Dad said we're going to take a trip to Alton Towers. AWEsome! I'm not going to write any diary all half-term, so there!

22nd Oct

Saw Susan in town with her family, she smiled and waved.

24th Oct

Spending the night at Bugs, the others are coming over as well. Should be great fun.

28th Oct

Home. Knackered.

29th Oct

Back at school, again. Half-term didn't last long enough. We had a great time at Alton Towers, stayed at the hotel there for 3 days. Fantastic fun, even Toby enjoyed it. Got to go on every ride there at least twice, took some funny photos of us and we all agreed we ought to back sometime. Maybe next year. Dad had lots of work to do, but managed to spend time with him and helped him start a new instrument, which was fun. Terry's sister, Mandy asked me out. Said yes.

30th Oct

Met up with Mandy at break time and lunch, went down to The Gap to get away from everyone, its normally where the smokers go but it was quiet today.

31st Oct

Halloween...ooh...spooky. Dads pretended to be choking on mums scrambled eggs at breakfast, fell on the floor and lay still, he winked at me and mum thought he'd collapsed. It was great, she really fell for it. He even bought a fake knife that looked like it stuck in his head. Met with Mandy again.

1st Nov

Lads told me off for missing play practice. I think they're just jealous but Dad says I shouldn't let love come between friends. Its not love, just...whatever it's called.

2nd Nov

Dad said we could go and choose some fireworks tomorrow and have them on Sunday. Mum and Dad said we could invite whoever we wanted over dad gave me a wink and a nudge, idiot. Marty said she's going to invite Judy and Smelly Sammy, I hope she doesn't come. I told the boys but only Bugs can come, the others are off doing something else.

3rd Nov

We all went into town with dad to get fireworks. Mum and Ben went off to the park and Martina, dad and me went shopping. Marty and me chose some excellent looking ones and dad chose the rockets. Really looking forward to it. Saw Susan in town. She still smiled and waved. I felt kind of bad. I still really like her. I don't know what it is. Mandy's okay, she's really nice and everything, like her a lot, but, well, I don't know, I don't know what it is. Hey ho.

4th Nov

Got to build a small bonfire in the back garden of Aunty M's and make a mini-Guy to go on top. Bugs couldn't make it, nor could Judy, but Smelly Sammy did. Guess what? Still smells. Fireworks were great, though Ben didn't like the louder ones so mum took him indoors. Dad let me light some fireworks for the first time ever. Cool.

5th Nov

Dad messed up my packed lunch again. Cheers dad. Gave me peanut butter and tuna sandwiches, sprinkled cornflakes over everything and topped it off with yoghurt. What a mess! Didn't taste that bad though.

8th Nov

9th Nov

10th Nov

11th Nov

We were all sitting up to the table eating supper and dad went face down into his curry. We thought he was messing about. Dad had died.

12th November

Thompson Twins. Hold Me Now.

(a time that touched my heart and left its mark)

THE FOREST

The squiffling grunts of a pygmy gnu echoed through the tugly woods as it snuffled in the undergrowth of the bardock tree, as tall elm and yew watched on.

The crack of foot on branch startled the smiglebumps, who scurried into their hidey-holes in the banks of sandy loam, which stood above long forgotten streams, now mossy and brockly in nature.

Cribbets flickered up from the ground, all a whirlypoos, as the figure clad in thickly suede and softy fur clodded its way across the forest floor.

It stood, half in crouch, and snaffled at the heady air, nostrils twitching of smellygogs and bungshufflers, looking to see which way its quarried hope had gone.

The big thick hat, made of many a yangun grew, got pushed back to wipe the sweat from the brow of smurt.

The nassal was shuffered and cloth put back from time it came, direction setted on, despite the clowdy spots that dampened the leaf and yew.

On they traipsed, checking under booder and crock, many of which broken hence gone, finding morsel few to nourish away the while.

A dincall flapped up from perch up mamat shub, all a jittery and loike, though danswankle, it naint be erd, such squawking made, tis none work can be done around.

Big thick hat, for that the name for which was seen, reckoned on not more long spent shuffin and teps as already day be spend and camp nedded.

BeTeeAj, shortened type, checkin arms of branch and see if some had bin fall or knockem by what was serched for. Some little gorders twirlied and fudged, not wanting to leave a fuss and some minkers hooped their funny tell, macking and hooing at very tospy tops, as if it made no sense.

Seeing that none could soon be seen, branchy bits pulled and strappered for timby frame, all be covered, wit and dye, with tree and shubby flats, making it nice and hoesome.

A large hoopy set of flames now danced infront of B t snug, hoesome some, scaring away the main'n'nancy crodmongers and sharpy teeth pipips and tother werst of the nigit. For out here, in the depthsys of the tudge, the nigits were lengthy long and could get mightly bad and cary, ooh cary cary.

For in the toime of no shine, the crods and pips were the lest of tour woes. For in the lackest, darkes were the olihooks.

The olihooks. Big and flappishus they were, ooh scary deed. Meek meek were they cry, sharpy bit to cut any would so be. And nailsies. Ooh, the nailsies bad as be. They spot thee from distance far far and whoop, gone, all sudden loike, leavin onl terror screech, though biggy and whoge, silent as shuffler be. So, mind keep back safe and eyseys pen wide.

B t chumped at sum dried berry and stripes o'puffyroom, all wisheyed down with aliantha splosh, a drinksy so good, nort else cood be a wanting.

After such splendid feasting, special for traipsies long, weariness was quickly to follow and soon, eysies heavy, B t noggled into slumby, though heart ever watched for the olihook.

Gentle plips were the wakening call, the plip-plaps not yet falling fast, but B t was drysy hansum in his snuggle burroe of tree an shub.

Lookin out on day of wit, around his tended of the nigit, two piny eye starey look roight back from under a shubby shub neary to.

No want for startle sudden, B t tended no note, feign to eyesy, but all toime areach for net in backyback to sling an catsure so.

But, fore net could be got, all a flutter do go. Out boundy bound came Tiddy, lost no more, but closer back came nassy n'cru a pipip, all a gernashers an chompin, rorin summit fearce, galumphing wantin bite for food itsel.

B t stood fast, pickin up little Tids, scooping up ta safety, and with miteyest leap ever saw, jumped clear over pipips head, leavin ol pipip to chomper and tent instead.

My, how B t ran, jumpin brook and shub, takin no heed of snag or tear case that pipip was still in chase. Run did run, Tids tuck safely in arm til omey place was seen at foot of mighty haycorn and door firmy shut behind 'em.

Out came Tids and put front of hearth, new flame being built and bowl o' thick put down for lappin.

"By words Tids," who purred and purred with delight "don't the ever high tail that again." B t said collapsing, exhausted though happiness back in the rockety rock by the flames.

BERT AND ETHEL

Bert and Ethel lived in a quiet street in a small house. It was the same house that Ethel had been born in, grown-up in and even gave birth in. Her parents moved there when they were first married at the front end of the century, brought up their family, all seven in total, stacked up on each other, each wanting more space, so finding it in the freedom of the streets outside, which, in those days, were safe to play in, mainly due to the number of watchful eyes around, everyone looking out for each other, and the Mrs Jones's of the world gossiping the day away. Not like these days. Nowadays your neighbours live behind net curtains and locked doors, keeping the world out and fearfully guarding what is theirs, and talking on their thingys in the internet.

Ethel was in the kitchen, busying around the sink with her back to Bert, who was sitting in his chair reading his morning paper, mouth open, head back, face turned to the ceiling and snoring. Her hair still tied up in a net, not yet ready to take her curlers out and her clean apron was already damp from washing up from breakfast.

She looked out of the window above the sink into the small garden and saw a robin perching on the handle of a garden fork that had been left sticking into the soil. Ethel smiled to herself thinking of when the garden was nothing but slabs, remembering cutting her knee on the corner by the back gate, having been pushed by Arthur, her older brother, in a hurry to catch up with his mates.

Dear Arthur. He was such a lovely boy. He used to let her sit on his shoulders when they walked down the alley so she could see into the backs of everyone's houses. Ooh, Mrs Sloane used to shout something rotten if she caught you peering over the fence into her garden. She would send her Harold out with a rolled-up newspaper, waving it about like trying to swat an angry wasp. They would laugh like anything which only seemed to make him more irate. Then, when he went back inside, you could hear Mrs Sloane giving him what for and him trying to stand up for his self.

Arthur bought it in the Mid-Atlantic during the war. She only learned the full story some years back and it made her cry even more than the first time.

Ethel finished off her drying and putting away and went into the front room to check on her Bert.

As she entered, the photographs on top of the well-used piano, of days gone by, caught her eye, as they always did, of their wedding day, Bert looking so handsome and happy and of the children when they were young. There was one of their Brian, looking very grumpy, eating an ice cream down by the beach, while wearing his favourite striped shorts which he got wet later on. Annie, showing the world her frilly knickers, nothing much changed there and Michael...taken too early.

Bert made a smacking sound with his chops and Ethel turned, wondering whether he was waking, ready for his mid-morning cup of tea. She stood next to him, looking down at the once youthful man that she had married and considered either waking him or dropping something into his toothless mouth. How somebody could sleep so much having not long been up never ceased to amaze her, but it didn't matter, it gave her time to potter and tidy up and reminisce over the golden days.

The old clock chimed ten as Ethel left the room and her slumbering husband and made her way upstairs to clean the bath and make the bed.

More pictures lined the stairs, as well as the fading wallpaper and well-trodden carpet, one of these days...

She straightened each one as she went, looking deep into the scenes and reliving each precious moment where was life was so full of comings and goings, up and downs. She wished that she had a magic lamp to rub that could take her back to all the happy times of their lives, before they had gotten too old to do anything or be of any use to anyone. Times that maybe they had underappreciated or had not cared for enough or even when they thought they had been doing the right thing at the time, for themselves, but didn't realise how it might affect someone years down the line.

As she straightened one picture, she saw a stain under it on the wallpaper and remembered when their Annie, in a fit of anger when coming down the stairs, putting on her lipstick to go out, was told by her father that "No, girl of mine is going out looking like that!".

Ooh, a face like thunder she had. She banged on the wall so hard the neighbours came round and she left a big smudge of lipstick that never came out, no matter how hard Ethel tried to clean it.

Ethel tried to cover the stain with the now upright picture, but it didn't quite work, so she left that one slightly crooked.

"Ethel? I'm putting the kettle on" came the shouted hint from downstairs.

Bless him. He must've swallowed a fly or something.

"Down in a minute love." Ethel shouted back.

It would probably be more like quarter or an hour by the time she got back down, but knowing Bert he'd overfill the kettle, put it on very low, or not at all. That's even if he actually did make it in to the kitchen.

Ethel went into the bathroom, deciding that she would start in their first.

She went to the cupboard under the sink but couldn't find any powder that she usually used to scour the bath with. She couldn't remember using it all up but knew that a new can was under the sink downstairs, so would get it later, probably after lunch, and bring it up with her, when she had her afternoon nap. She sat on the edge of the bath wondering how she had forgotten to bring up a new can. She seemed to be forgetting a lot of little things lately. Just silly little things, nothing important.

Yesterday she forgot to turn the hallway light off, she thought they had intruders, scared her to death it did. Then, the day before that she was resting on the bed, feeling a bit tired and out of sorts, when the phone rang. She figured she must've been asleep because it gave her such a start and she didn't realise where she was or what the phone was doing ringing. She felt all confused and worried, like that she had forgotten something very important, it put her out for the rest of the day. She didn't want to worry Bert with it. Its probably just one of those things about getting old.

Ethel got up and walked into the bedroom instead, suddenly feeling very tired. She lay down on the bed, on Bert's side, feeling exhausted.

The doorbell rang...

Ethel, head on the pillow looked blankly beyond the open bedroom door.

The doorbell rang again...

"Ethel, someone at the door!" Bert called up

Someone knocked on the door...

Ethel heard someone enter their house and heard talking coming from the front room, so assumed it must be Pat, nice girl, drops in everyday to make sure everything is okay and whether they needed anything.

"Ethel? Pat's here" came another shout up the stairs.

She was too tired to answer and her head was too comfortable being supported by Bert's pillow. She heard Pat go into the kitchen, probably to make Bert his morning cuppa as she was taking so long doing her morning routine upstairs, hopefully there would be one for her on the side when she got down, if she was lucky.

Ethel was suddenly startled when she heard the front door close, and realising that she must have nodded off for a moment, cursed herself for her lackadaisical behaviour, especially as there was so much work to do. Ethel sat up, swinging her feet unsteadily onto the floor and felt a tug of embarrassment as she did so, knowing that Pat must have come up to check on her while slumbering and left without saying goodbye.

Standing, Ethel went through the process of making the bed and collecting Bert's strewn clothing that he had gotten in the habit of leaving laying about of late. She stood holding one of his socks thinking how he never used to be so untidy, but she had noticed little changes in him lately, subtle differences in his behaviour and as for his hearing, well.

Ethel decided that the next time Pat came she might mention something to her about Bert or perhaps she could ring the doctor herself, if only she could remember where she'd left her phone book. It had all her numbers in it and birthday dates. She felt lost without it. Ethel remembered, quite a while back, when she hadn't been feeling very well, Bert had, for some reason, found her little black book, something she liked to call it, even though it was red, he found it in the oven of all places. What on earth possessed him to put it in the oven, heaven only knows.

The phone rang.

"Ethel? The phones ringing. Ethel?" Bert shouted up from his chair.

"Honestly," thought Ethel, tutting to herself "can't that man do anything?"

By the time she reached the top of the stairs the phone had been answered. "Will wonders never cease?" she said quietly to herself, as she made her way down the creaky steps.

Ethel looked into the front room from the hallway.

Bert had his back to her as he chatted on the phone. He stood hunched and looked old...weak...no, frail. She could see the young man she married though, hidden under the layer of years.

Oh, he was so handsome back then. Many a girl was chasing after him, but she won, she won. What a lovely day their wedding was. The whole street turned out to cheer them off...and back.

Gerty and Mavis were her bridesmaid and Mrs Bridges from round the corner made the cake, she was so clever with potatoes. Oh, how they danced all night. Grandad was on the piano and old Mrs Fairfax did the singing. Oh, it was so funny. The more she drunk the more she forgot the words so started making it up as she went along. By the time midnight came even she was blushing from what came out of her mouth.

By the time Ethel had stopped recollecting the good old days, Bert had finished his phone call and gone back to his paper.

"Who was that then dear?" Ethel asked her engrossed husband and getting no reply. "I said," Ethel said louder, knowing that he really must get his hearing checked "WHO WAS ON THE PHONE? Bert? You're not still mad at me for burning your bacon, are you? Bert? I'm talking! Honestly!" said Eth walking back into the kitchen with a bit of a swagger.

As she went past, Bert looked over the top of his newspaper with raised eyebrows.

Ethel sat down at the small square kitchen table and pulled out a hankie from her sleeve. She felt like having a really good cry, things just seem to be getting so difficult lately, but every time she felt the tears coming...she just didn't feel like she could. Felt wrong somehow. She couldn't explain it. No point talking to mopey face about anything, doubt he would understand, just give her a pat on the shoulder and say there, there.

Ethel looked into the sugar bowl that sat before and decided to have a lump.

When the five of them were kids, they used to creep into the kitchen sometimes and steal a couple of lumps...to share mind. They could only pinch two, five would have given the game away. Get called "thieving monkeys" by mother or "cheeky beggars" by father. They would run out the back door and into the yard to share the loot, their ill-gotten gains, giggling, not too loud though, wouldn't want to get caught. Not that anything bad would happen. Just a telling off and no milk at bedtime. Not like Henry down the street. Poor Henry. Used to get beaten black and blue did Henry, head to toe. One day, even the police were called the screams were that bad.

"Ethel? You there?"

"Daft sod" thought Ethel "Forgotten already. Where else would I be?"

"Eth...I'm not feeling too good..."

"I'll be there in a min, just putting the kettle on" Ethel said absentmindedly, more to herself as she was still thinking of sad young Henry and the other boys she used to know.

Before she had met Bert there had been Charlie. Charlie Swatton. And he was a right Charlie alright. Always mucking about and making a fool of himself. He fancied himself as a bit of an acrobat, always said he'd run off to the circus one day. Daft bugger got himself shot fighting the Germans. Such a waste of youth.

"Eth..."

Ethel looked around the kitchen, waiting for the kettle to boil, feeling lost and all out of sorts. She really must make an appointment for the doctor sometime, she really hadn't been feeling herself lately, kept forgetting to do silly little things or started on job, like cleaning the bath and get side tracked half way through, remembering that she left the tap dripping in the kitchen sink and as she went down to turn it off, found that the stair carpet needed brushing. Before you knew it, umpteen different jobs had been started and left and Bert would just sit there, snoring his days away without a care in the world.

That's what it was.

Bread.

They'd run out of bread. Better nip down to the shop and pick some up, while its still fresh and they hadn't run out.

Ethel put on her coat and picked up her purse. She saw Bert sitting in his chair, head back, mouth wide open, as ever, so left by the back door so as not to disturb him.

Entering into the back yard, she wasn't surprised to see the slabs of grey rather than the pretty little abundance of plants that Bert had created for her. There was Toby's old dog shed as well, thought that went years ago, must remember to get some bones from the butcher for him. Ethel left the back gate open and walked down the alley way into her forgotten land of memories.

Due to a last-minute staff juggling, because one carer had left, fed up with the demands of the job and how inefficient and uncaring the care company was and another's car had broken down, Bert wasn't found for two days. It's a common occurrence for visits to be missed, notification not given or forgotten, sometimes leaving an individual, who is unable to cope for themselves, more vulnerable or confused, sometimes leading to dramatic instances.

Pat knocked on the door and rang the bell, a new recruit by her side being introduced to the area and clients. No answer came, so she let herself in, using the emergency key stored in the combination safe by the side of the door.

"Bert?" Pat called as they entered "Bert? It's Pat."

No answer came from the quiet and untidy house or the still body that sat in the armchair by the unlit gas fire.

The new recruit gasped, but Pat went over and checked for a pulse, first gently putting her hand on his shoulder and calling his name clearly and firmly. No breath could be felt or heard, so Pat advised the newcomer to call the emergency services.

Pat checked the rest of the downstairs, then sat and waited for the phone call to finish.

"They said they won't be long, not very busy at the moment."

"Good," said Pat "poor chap, at least he can rest now. He had vascular dementia the love. Not bad, but its progressive. He was ever so lonely, lost his wife a couple of years ago."

They went into the kitchen and made a pot of tea and waited for the services to arrive, smelling a hint of bacon in the air.

DAVE GOES TO THE ZOO

Dave didn't know what to do.

A tower of building blocks had been quite masterfully built, paws had been stuck together whilst, unsuccessfully, trying to build a snowman out of cotton wool and pipe cleaners and fairy cakes had even been made, not decorated and eaten, so Dave sat on window seat, staring out at the beautiful clear blue sky, where he would be drifting with the clouds…if there had been any. It was a truly a wonderful blue and it was so big, all that space above the rooftops and trees.

As Dave sat day dreaming, high in the sky, he noticed a single bird sail and glide, then joined by another and that's what gave

Dave the idea.

"I know!" thought Dave, hitting on an idea "Teddy," he called out "we're going to the zoo". He felt very triumphant in his decision making.

Dave liked that word, triumphant, it always made him feel as big as a trumpet playing elephant, "Gosh, it must have been a happy elephant" thought Dave.

Dave had only been to the Zoo once before and that was by bus, but today was special and he knew just how to get there.

"First things first." Dave said to Teddy, whilst walking into the kitchen and opening up the rucksack.

Little Ted always packed too much food whenever they went on journeys, especially cakes, biscuits and sweets, but Dave reminded him that they should at least take some fruit and plenty of water to drink, because "drinking is much more important than eating".

As Dave rummaged through the cupboards (with Ted laying on the table) he came across a large bag of crisps and some popcorn. "We better take these as well," said Dave looking over to the inert Ted "you never know who we might bump into".

Dave did like to be prepared and food tasted so much better when you shared it with someone, sometimes.

Rucksack full and securely tied and Teddy sticking out of the top (his favorite place to be when traveling, he could see everything from there), it was time to go.

"Oops" thought Dave "almost forgot something Teddy" Dave said "Loo".

After Dave checked that Little Ted didn't need to go as well, he closed the front door firmly and set off down the path.

"This was an excellent idea of yours Teddy" Dave said to Teddy "and my, what a wonderful day it is" Dave said with a big breath in and a little bounce of happiness as they walked.

And truly felt like a wonderful day to Dave. It seemed as if everything had only just been made for the first time, and who ever had made it, well, their happiness was certainly rubbing off onto everything. "I hope this lasts forever" Dave said to Teddy, who obviously hadn't been listening to a word being said, as it appeared that Teddy had already fallen asleep.

"Never mind," thought Dave "I'll wake Teddy when we get their".

They seemed to walk for ages, until they rounded the last corner, and there they were, not at the Zoo, but how they were going to get there, the canal.

"Teddy, wake up, its time for our boat ride."

Dave thought Teddy was startled, even though he didn't say anything. Dave had been told about this way of getting to the Zoo, but had never let on to Teddy, who by now, Dave could tell, was really excited.

Down a gentle sloping leafy path, they walked and before them rested the long water boat called a barge. It was beautifully decorated, green and red and bursts of painted flowers by every curtained window. The engine sat quietly chugging to whoever listened to it, and an old man who looked like he had just come off the high seas was gently puffing on a pipe whilst leaning on the tiller.

Dave might seem simple but he knew some things.

They said good morning to the old man and paid the fare then got comfy on a seat by a window.

It was all wood and brass in the cabin and the warmth of the sun shone through the windows, and above the noise of the engine you could hear the gentle slosh of water plopping against the side of the boat. It seemed to have a voice all of its own.

"Listened Teddy" Dave whispered "we're about to get going."

And as soon as that had been said, the engine belched out a puff of smoke and off thy glided.

Ted had never been in a boat before, so Dave took him out of the rucksack and held him by the window so to see the water life go past.

Moorhens, ducks and swans and other boats drifted aimlessly past as well as an array of rowing boats, boats that looked like houses, little speed boats and even a couple of canoes. Dave fancied trying canoeing, thinking that it would be an excellent way to splash around in the water.

All this excitement and activity made Teddy hungry, so Dave got out a fairy cake, to share, knowing that Ted would never eat a whole one by himself.

Dave munched on the ⅞ of fairy cake, whilst explaining to Teddy why ducks were ducks and why canoes were canoes and why manners were always very important and why fish blew bubbles, they all seemed to connect somewhere but he couldn't quite remember where. Just then, as they came round a bend in the water, a few crumbs fell out of Dave's open and stationary mouth.

For there, in front, in the distance, towering above the tree tops, was a gigantic curved metal cage.

"Wow" said Dave to anyone and no-one "that must hold a huge animal" he said silently to Little Ted who was currently in a prostrate position on the table enjoying staring at the ceiling.

The old man steering the barge chuckled.

"Dar, be for the birds tha' be" he gruffled through his pipe.

Dave looked amazed at Teddy and quietly asked "Do you think he's a pirate?"

The Saucy Sue, for that was the name of the barge, pulled to the side, where a small group of people were waiting for their return journey. Dave thanked the man for the trip and apologized for any crumbs that Teddy might have spilt and hoped that he would "Have a nice day" as it did seem that surely everyone should have such a nice day as he was having.

Dave decided not to put Ted back in the rucksack, but held him by his hand instead, just so Ted didn't get nervous, going somewhere he had never been before.

Up the ramp (which was very much like the one they had walked down) they went, up to the main road to the busy traffic lights, where on the opposite side stood large black metal railings, a large black metal gate and four large black metal turnstiles, with a kiosk at one side, this was the entrance to the Zoo, it even looked like a zoo, and it even said ZOO in large black metal letters.

Dave and Little Ted carefully crossed the road and went to the ticket counter, where a very kind lady explained that teddies got in free as long as they behaved themselves and that you shouldn't feed the animals any fairy cakes. Dave was rather startled by this comment but as they walked away he glanced down at Teddy, who was glancing up, pointing out the crumbs all over Dave's T-Shirt.

"Teddy" said Dave sternly "you really must try to be more careful"

With that, Dave brushed the crumbs off (with Teddy, who really didn't mind that much) and looked around where they should start first.

"Hmm," said Dave.

There were signposts everywhere, pointing in all directions, monkeys, giraffes, hippopotamouses (whatever they were), reptiles...

"Aah," Dave said to Teddy "Here's a good start."

So off they went, time for a cup of tea at the cafeteria.

As Dave and Teddy were queuing for their cup of tea, and possibly a biscuit (biscuits bought with a cup of tea always tasted different from your own, well, that's what Ted had once told Dave), he noticed a free map of the zoo, so Dave took two, one each, in case they got separated and put them on the tray next to Teddy who was sitting patiently, enjoying watching all the food go by.

Dave paid for the tray of refreshments and sat at a large table by the window so they could spread the map out and see where things were, and try to sort a route out around the Zoo.

Between them, they decided they wanted to see the elephants, reptiles, penguins and monkeys most all, and guessed that Teddy would like the pandas and polar bears and ants, so that took them round the whole zoo and they might get to see pretty much everything in-between.

Finishing the tea, Teddy said that they should get going, but Dave just put that down to excitement. First, they made sure they left the table tidy and swept up the sugar that Teddy had sprayed everywhere trying to open a sachet and put the cup and saucer back onto the tray for someone to collect.

Dave got up and headed for the exit door, when a voice called out.

"Excuse me" it was the till lady "you've left your friend behind".

Dave half turned then realized that she was pointing back at the table.

"Honestly Teddy, do come on, we haven't got all day" Dave called, as went back and grabbed Teddy from the window sill.

"Really Teddy, you must concentrate more" which was said with affection.

Once outside the sun seemed warmer than ever and the day was filled with excitement and expectation.

"Right Teddy, lets go" and off strode Dave, Teddy in hand, in the completely opposite direction they were meant to be going in.

The noises and smells of the zoo were bewildering. They walked past cages of little birds hopping around, big colourful parrots, very chirpy blue and yellow things, and some fabulous looking peacocks that were just walking around screeching a lot and showing off their big tail feathers, it reminded Dave of a multicoloured fan he had once made.

Much as they both liked looking at these birds and realised what a great job the zoo was doing and how the birds looked happy enough, it just didn't feel right having birds in cages.

As they walked on, they saw some really big cages, and noticed a lioness pacing backwards and forwards inside. On either side there were bored looking lions and some tigers that were fast asleep. Dave held Teddy's hand firmer. Just in case.

"Good day, Mrs Lion" said Dave. But she didn't answer, she just kept pacing, looking very worried about nothing.

"Oh, er, good day Mr Lion". Tried Dave again. "Hrum?" lowly growled the lion.

"Ees na gud speking tu thim" said the asleep Tiger with now one eye open. "theys too boord , tork ta me, I'll eet yu".

Dave stood staring for one second, suddenly shocked by what the tiger had just said. Turning and leaving very quickly Dave called out "Goodbye, er, nice to meet you too, bye. Sorry, haven't got time to stay and chat. Penguins you know".

"Oh, dear Teddy" Dave gasped when they were a safe enough distance away, glancing over his shoulder "I hope we don't meet too many more animals like that, I'm quite shaky now".

"That's a good idea Ted; a biscuit would calm my nerves".

So, Dave ruffled through the bag, with Teds help, and found a chocolate chip cookie to nibble on, though Teddy didn't want any, apparently, he was still full from their last snack, who ever heard such nonsense.

As they strolled along Dave stared up at the trees whose leaves were letting through the dappled light and rustling gently to themselves even though Dave could feel no breeze, their minds began to wander.

Just as Dave was letting out a big sigh, he noticed a keeper giving people rides on the back of a camel. That did look like fun. There was a ladder nearby, like a small flight of stairs, made of metal with a couple of people standing by them and a sign saying "Camel Rides".

After standing in the queue for a while and watching the other people on the camels back, Dave started to feel a bit worried as the camel started coming towards them. It looked bigger and bigger. So just to make sure Teddy didn't get too worried (Dave could feel him trembling), Teddy decided to give Dave a big hug just before hiding in Dave's jacket pocket.

The Zoo Keeper helped the children down from the camel, which was slobbering a lot and even smelt quite odd, then looked at Dave.

"Well, what do we 'ave 'ere, someone else wants a ride on yer back Nelly. What d'ya think. Eh girl"? enquired the keeper, Dave presumed he was talking to the Camel.

"Well, climb aboard me hearty, can't be standin' around all day. Got things to do." said the keeper again, as he led Dave (and Teddy) up the steps and onto the hairy back of the camel between its two humps.

"Hold tight" the keeper called out and off they went.

It was a bumpty, clip, clonk, smooth sort of ride. At first Dave thought he was going to fall off, but then he got the hang of it. He didn't know what the camel used for soap, but the hair up there could certainly have a better wash.

As they walked around, Dave got a really good view of more of the zoo.

He could see some chimpanzees being taken for a walk, in the distance some large cages and funny whooping noises were coming from that direction, he could also see the childrens farm where you could pet rabbits, goats and guinea pigs. He... could... even ...see...

Dave was stretching up out of his seat to try and get a better view of...something..., when the camel caught its foot on a stone and made Dave sit firmly back onto his seat with a jolt.

From that moment on he sat and held on firmly, but still enjoying the view and telling Teddy everything.

The ride was over and the Keeper helped Dave down from the saddle.

"Teddy?" Dave instantly thought, putting his hand in his pocket.

"TEDDY"? Dave said in a terrified voice.

"**TEDDY**"!? with increasing alarm, Dave frantically searching his coat.

"TEDDY WHERE ARE YOU !??"

Dave searched and searched, the keeper helped as well, so did a couple of passing children, but no sign of Teddy could be found. The keeper said it must have happened when Dave was standing up out of his seat. "Someone would 'ave found 'im" reassured the Keeper. But Dave was not reassured. What would Teddy do? He'd never been on his own before. The Keeper suggested to Dave "Why don't you check at lost property on your way home? Someone might've 'anded 'im in."

So, with a tear in his eye and a sniff or three, Dave, very sadly, walked off, feeling lonely, scared and worried.

Dave walked in a daze. His head down, his chin quivering, occasionally looking up just in case Teddy was there. But no. No Ted.

He walked right past the large gorillas, which were incidentally, sitting around, picking their noses and other unpleasant things. Past the cage where the funny whooping noises were coming from. Past the Ring-tail Limas that had been on T.V. Past a very large empty cage. Past the Chimps Tea Party.

"At least they look like they're having fun" thought Dave sadly.

"Tea and sandwiches and..." Very glumly Dave remembered how he and...

"TEDDY?!"

"TEDDY!!" called Dave.

There on the table, surrounded by mugs and tea pots, and chimps, sat Teddy.

Before anyone knew what was happening, Dave rushed up to the table and snatched Teddy from the middle of the party. Everyone was so surprised.

Even the chimpanzees looked startled.

"Here, you can't do that" called a voice.

But it was too late, it had been done.

As swift as anything Dave had a firm grip on Teddy and was already running for the exit. As he ran, he ran right past the lion cages and the lions gave an enormous **"ROAR"!!**

Well, that was enough for Dave. Having never been a great runner, those little legs took off and ran as fast as ever before, his heart pounded and everything became a blur. Hardly even a breath seemed to be taken as he left the zoo and ran all the way home.

With a slam of the front door, Dave and Teddy were safely back inside.

"...oh...my..." gasped Dave.

Teddy just seemed to stare up with that expression of his, that type of "What? Something the matter? One minute I'm sitting down, having a nice cup of tea with my new friends (who very kindly picked me up after you dropped me on the ground) and the next minute I'm yanked off the table and rushed home as if I've done something wrong." look.

Dave couldn't believe it. "Well Teddy" he said with exasperation.

"If that's the way you feel". He was just about to walk away when he realized that Teddy was probably quite shaken up and needed a hug. A BIG hug.

"I'm so sorry" said Dave quietly "perhaps we shouldn't go back to the zoo"

"Well not for a while" thought Teddy.

WHERE'S GAVIN?

The party was getting bigger by the moment. Nigel knew he had invited some of his mates and, invariably, those mates would have mentioned it to a few others, but the buzz must have got around, because now that Nige walked around the crowded rooms, different music playing in each room, depending on the vibe, he realised that he recognised fewer and fewer faces.

The throng of heads, bodies, colours, noise and smells, not all legal, all packed in (pre-Covid, of course) to his three-bedroom house, made it difficult to manoeuvre around and despite that people were obviously enjoying themselves, he couldn't help feeling a bit concerned. He had been to other parties himself and had seen the fallout afterwards.

At that moment he bumped into Tom who was drunkenly chatting to a very non interested person of the opposite sex and gender from which he had been born with (in future we'll just say women).

"Tom?" shouted Nigel to his friend, who tried to ignore him, convinced that he was making progress with the now back of the head of forementioned female.

(I should like to point out at this point, a bit late in the day I know, but the male is essentially a genetic mutation of the female form, so, ergo, the word male is a lesser form of female the same as man is a lesser form of woman and not the other way round, ie "erm, I know, lets add a Wo to Man". Just though I'd mention it.)

"Tom!" Nigel shouted louder.

"Aw, look what you've done," slurred Tom, turning around "you've scared her away." He added, immediately looking around the room for another possible target.

"You seen Gav?" laughed Nigel unsurely (he wasn't very good at relaxing, even when unsober, as he was now), showing his friend a picture, he had just taken on his phone.

Tom gave Nigel an incredulous look "Why would I want to see Gavin, relax, this is a party..." he said, gesticulating, pointing out the obvious and suddenly walking off, excusing himself through the crowd, his sonar having been alerted on his next target.

Nigel knew they had done the right thing, the party, it was Gav's idea after all, but, so many people, something might get broken and the clean up was going to be terrible and, unfortunately, Nigel had literally picked the short straw when they were deciding where to have the party. He also picked the shortest straw when it came to who was going to buy the booze and who was going to keep an eye on party boy Gav. He was notoriously problematic and mischievous.

In fact, Nigel remembered one time, at another party, when...

The flashback was broken, possibly thankfully, when shouting came from the kitchen and Nigel made an effort to dash to see what was going on, just in case, no one else seemed to want to take responsibility for the unfolding events. He had always found it hard, letting go, even on his birthdays and holidays, feeling the need to be in control at all times, though often failing, perhaps that's why a big bash was suggested, try and shake a few leaves from the tree.

Nigel pushed his way into the kitchen to see a drinking game in full swing, the uproar being caused by removal of various articles of clothing and the use of some of the fridge's contents. Doesn't look like Nigel with be having his usual yoghurt and muesli for breakfast tomorrow, he wasn't a fancier of hairy yoghurt, though he did think it was considerate of someone to decide to put it back in the fridge.

Gavin sat in the corner of the kitchen, in the armchair, the party hat still on and a red lipstick kiss on his face, bottle firmly clutched in his hand, soaked in alcohol and well and truly out for the count.

Grabbing a bottle beer from the table, Nigel popped the cap and took a swig of the warm liquid and decided to throw caution to the wind and try his luck at some male to female conversation (I'm really not being sexist it was just the way it was going to go), besides, if Tom could have such luck, then why not him.

Nigel pushed and bumped his way through the happy party-goer's bodies and occasionally felt an unattached hand grab certain parts of his anatomy, which disappointed him a little, because it had been that rather attractive brunette which seemed to ignore him, he would have liked to know.

The jostling became more intense as he neared the dancy part of the downstairs and an errant elbow knocked his newly acquired bottle flying and he heard it skittering across the floor.

There seemed little point in attempting to retrieve it, besides, he didn't want to be accused of being a pervert, crawling around people's ankles looking for a, probably now, empty bottle, so decided it would be easier to return to the kitchen and get another. It would also give him chance to possibly make eye contact with the brunette and, who knows, maybe feel another wandering hand.

Sadly, he made it back into the kitchen unmolested and unsuccessful in relocating his quarry but did manage to grab the last beer from the table.

He took a swig and sat down in the armchair in the corner and immediately felt very low down and separated from the ongoings.

That's when it hit.

Nigel very quickly (and relatively stupidly) looked down to his left and then down to his right trying to check under his chair for Gavin (you see, I said stupidly, under an arm chair? Really?). Obviously, Gavin wasn't there. He had definitely been sitting there only moments before, the damp patch could be felt through his trousers, but now he was gone.

Startled by the prompt disappearance of his supposedly dead to the world chum, he leapt up from his sitting position, knocking a couple who had decided to start to get to know each other by swapping, no, not telephone numbers, saliva. They seemed unperturbed by the push and reconnected quickly, which reminded Nigel of the toilet plungers you used to be able to buy.

Before Nigel stumbled, with purpose out of the kitchen to find Tom.

He found him in the corridor of the hall, chatting to Nigel's brunette.

"Tom, Tom, you seen Gav?" Nigel asked Tom while shaking his shoulder.

"What is it with you and Gav today, Nigel? Can't you see I'm... bollocks!" Tom said, noticing that the brunette had taken advantage of the moments distraction and disappeared into the mass.

"Thanks Nige, thanks a lot. Me and Samantha..."

"Jinny," said a voice next to him "her name is Jinny."

Tom looked at the unwanted interruption and wondered what

his chances were.

"Tom, Gavin's not in the kitchen." Nigel said while getting an enthusiastic elbow in the back of the head.

"Well, he's got to be somewhere, he's a big boy, he can look after himself." Tom said while getting distracted by a tinge of smoke wafting its way across the room, nostrils alerted the blood-hound in him sprang in to action.

Left standing, he felt a bit of a pudding, though he was keen to find where Gav had got to, after all...

The brunette stood in front of him, looking him straight in the eyes. For Nigel, in that instance, there was only the two of them in the universe, all else ceased to exist, he saw her lips start to form a word.

"You Nigel?" Jinny asked, as heavenly choirs sang above his head.

With the mustering of all his expectations and yearnings, the years of seeking his only soulmate, the beauty of the poetry of love and wisdom he uttered "Er...".

"You're wanted in the kitchen."

And with that...she was gone...again.

Amazed at his own ineptness he turned and pushed his way back the through tight confines of his once lovely decorated hall, not that you could notice at the moment, nor probably later, and into the kitchen. A hairy would-be biker type chap approached him "You looking for your mate, what's his name, Gavin?"

Nigel nodded and answered "Yeah". "Wow," he thought to himself "I'm really burning with scintillating conversation to-night."

"Yeah, well, I saw him go out into the back garden, didn't look too good though." Hairy biker thing said.

"What? Gavin?"

"Yeah, that's what I said. Your mate Gavin. Blimey, you thick or something?" and walked off.

Nigel's bottom lip stuck out and his eyes looked about the room and he realised he must be looking pretty odd, standing there, alone, pulling faces, so walked out the back door of the kitchen and looked out into the open back garden.

Feeling very self-conscious he called quietly "Gav?"

All was quiet. But then he saw, lying on the grass, about twelve feet in front of him, Gavin's bottle.

"Gavin? You out here?" he shouted, just as the party sounded like it had stepped up a notch behind him.

Admittedly, he felt like he should've been inside enjoying himself instead of worrying about his elected tasks for this evening, though he was convinced someone cheated when they were pulling lots, but he was an excellent worrier and figured that's why his so-called friends chose him to host a party.

Now that Nigel was standing in the coolness of the night garden, he realised that a conspiracy might be afoot, he had, after all, held the last two parties as well and...

A soft rustling in some shrubs at the end of the garden focused Nigel's attention.

He looked back at the house, yearning to for someone to call him in, instead here he was, babysitting a full-grown man.

A louder, definite rustle was followed by a lot of cracking, which sounded like Nigel's rickety spindle fence getting broken by someone clambering over it.

"Gavin? Is that you? Gav?" in a way, hoping it was and not a badger or fox or any wild creature come to that. He was terrified of wild creatures, always hairy and sharp little teeth. Hamsters were the worst. Those mean, beady eyes. He shivered at the thought.

Nigel could now hear definite movement and was that a chuckle? moving away from him, into the distance, which worried him somewhat, especially as beyond his garden lay the open countryside and now, he stood motionless, craning his ears to decide which direction he could give chase on one hand and on the other, pretty convinced it wasn't Gavin, because the last time he saw him, he wasn't going anywhere.

"Aw, come on Gavin, don't mess about." he said reluctantly, more to himself and knowing that the game was afoot, gave chase.

Nigel pulled out his phone from his pocket and turned on his torch, though cursed that his battery was below 50%, realising he better work quick.

A snap to his right and a definite snigger made him turn in crouch mode, "...badgers don't snigger," he suddenly reassured himself.

"Gavin, come back Gav, come on." he shouted. What else could he say?

Another muffled guffaw and sudden movement between some trees in the distance were caught in his torches light.

Thinking that he might pander to Gavin's known tendencies he tried a different approach.

"Ooh, Gavin, what have I got here?" Nigel said, feeling really stupid now "I've got a nice, fresh bottle of vodka." He lied, but it might work and then they could all go back to normal...yeah, right!

Nigel stood staring at the spot where he had seen the sudden movement but nothing stirred, silent and still, the enticement obviously failing. He yearned to be back indoors, the party sounding a million miles away, all that fun he could be having, then he remembered all the mess.

"Gav!" he shouted abruptly "This isn't funny! Get back here this instant!" Nigel had decided the authoritative approach might work. It didn't. Instead, he just heard a faint giggle from some distance off.

"C'mon Gav, please?" he shouted out, imploring for some resolution.

"Well, stuff you, I'm going in!" Nigel shouted into the silent night.

He made his way back towards his house, mumbling to himself, getting angry with sticks and the possibility that he had totally lost his chance with that nice brunette, "Blast!" he berated himself, he couldn't even remember her name, "oh, yeah, great party" he added under his breath suddenly turning as he heard a laugh in the distance.

He threw his hands up in the air, giving up in disgust, and decided to return to the house and drown his sorrows.

Behind Nigel's back, the woods stayed quiet, save the occasional rustle of foliage or snapping twig and if you listened hard enough, maybe a muffled giggle.

Weeks passed, as did Gavin's funeral, that was held without the body, even though friends and relatives of had checked with the local hospitals and police, just in case, but no trace was ever found of him. They all came to the same conclusion, that someone, with a particularly warped sense of humour, had decided to steal Gavin's body from his own pre-funeral wake and neglected to return him. But, as so many times in life, or death, the truth can be stranger than fiction, because, this time, Gavin had joined the ranks of the undead and now, somewhere out there, maybe deep in the woods or bushes near you, the body of Gavin can been seen shuffling about on his own playing hide and seek with the wildlife.

THE LAST LAUGH.

Summer had gone. So too had the flocks of tourists who had swarmed over the sand and shingle marking out their territory with towels, blankets and bags of all shapes, colours and sizes.

The beach huts and kiosks had now been boarded up for the winter and the air was filled with the saltiness of the sea from the waves that were collapsing onto the beach, spraying up their foam and dragging the shingle and sand back with their watery grasp with loud shushes coming from the tumbling pebbles. The light wind buffeted the seagulls, who screeched and turned looking for any left-over tasty morsel that might be had, that they had become so used to, and the fine rain fell, mixing with the aquatic spray that had travelled just as far as its airborne relative.

Both sea and rain landed on the old wooden planks of the pier that not long since had been covered in footfall instead and the buttresses were still sturdy and defiant after all these years having withstood far more hardy challenges than a mere smattering of dampness, though the human visitors would've scampered for shelter and retreat to safety, forgetting that once they too would have thought nothing of such weather and would instead continue in their daily tasks shrugging off a gentle soaking.

The pier itself was not overly long, but it had been an attraction from its day of opening, a certain charm in design had made it even more appealing and it offered interesting vantage points for dramatic sunsets and rises alike as well as housing a small theatre and Salty Sally's Café at its far end (with its bright red metallic lettering ending with an embossed metal image of the buxom smiling lass) and this is where our story lives.

We will not be troubled by the pillars and awnings that offer light protection from above, nor the stanchions that have supported such weight through the seasons and often have been disregarded by the comers, neither shall we talk to the myriad of curved metal and wooden benches that have offered comfort and rest and listened to all that had been said. Instead, we take a small stroll, behind the theatre, to the last walkway that looks out onto the vastness of the waters itself. For there, sitting with its the back to the building, looking out across the last few boards of the pier and railings, stands the wooden and glass kiosk that hold the mechanical upper half of Jolly Jack, the laughing sailor.

He sits, ever ready for coinage to be deposited and when activated, his torso and head will roll with laughter coming from the antiquated speakers, as his eyes, fixed with eerie merriment and beaming mouth, with bright red lips that never seem to fade having always been enclosed in his protective case away from the elements, though his arms, never moving, give him the support that all his jollity needs.

He has sat there entertaining guests, young and old alike, for almost 100 years staring out at the wide-open watery space, yet few would consider his age, instead they would deposit their money and wait to be amused. Some would smile or laugh, some may well be repulsed and some, normally the youngest and most innocent would cry and become frightened of this careering spectacle.

But regardless of all the visits and days that had passed, Jack would be left alone, alone to stare with empty eyes, either with head tilted back looking up into the depths of the sky or out across the waters or eyes down to watch the feet of passing strangers. On the very rare occasion, when his head was tilted to his far-right side, reflected in his glass he could see the smiling, welcoming face who brought warmth into his cold and hard mechanisms.

If he could have, he would have often thought of the friendly smile and wonder whether she knew of his existence just feet away and if she did, were her feelings for him the same as his for hers?

He could only dream, but he was glad that they now shared the same view, at least they could share that.

He had not always been located at the remotest part of the pier...

The van pulled up and stopped and daylight shone in to the back as the tarpaulin flaps were pulled aside and the wooden flap of the back lowered to drag the machine out.

"Blimey Bill, wonder wha e's bin drinkin to make 'im look so jolly?"

"Ha, ha, either that or e's bin thinkin' of your Gladys"

"Ere, what you mean by that, you cheeky sod?"

"Ha, ha, ha. Blimey, bit 'eavy, innit?"

The two men heaved and hauled the Jolly Jack out of the back of the truck and put him in his new home, prime position, in the middle of the entrance to the pier and wired him up.

From that day on he greeted all visitors with his penny activated rolls of loud, raucous laughter (being forced to perform whether he was happy or not) that would set the mood for the time people spent on the pier, in the days when holidaying was new and attractions were varied.

But, over the years, trends changed and the demand for new technologies came, though seldom people realised how the simpler things could be more rewarding, and Jolly Jack, in his cabinet of laughter was slowly moved, from location to location, until he sat where he was now, distant and removed from the daily activities, side-lined for something younger and more colourful.

He didn't mind. How could he? He was just a machine. But his eyes did see some wonderful sunsets, which made his cogs hum sometimes, with, want for a better word, sadness. Such beauty at the end of the day as the burning globe sank behind the sea, a farewell few bothered to witness, yet as spectacular and colourful than any manmade creation and all delivered with natural ease and grace.

Yet he had none to share these events with, but sometimes, on those nights when the sun had gone, yet was replaced by the fullness of the moon, bright enough to clearly see the planks and bolts, he might witness a pair of lovers stare out across the sparkling blackness of the waters, where even the stars are being reflected on its surface, so the sea and sky become one giant and endless void and the three of them share an instant that will be lost to time and shared with no other. But mostly he stands alone, with only his dreams and wishes and a reflection of beauty for company.

Time marches to its own rhythm, with the world of humans often out of step and out of tune of its own achievements, with many never recognising the change or advancements that life has put in front of them. Corrosion eats away like neglect, as backs are turned chasing their own faulty dreams caused by misinformed childhoods and as time moves on, we pass a time when the pier becomes run down, disregarded, and unrepaired.

The storm brews beyond the horizon, far out to sea, building strength and impending destruction that little suspect or, at the moment, care for.

The night sky was starless and bible black, yet silent distant flashes of dimmed light could be seen on the horizon, signalling the vastness of the angry storm as it moved to meet the land.

Jack did not feel the winds brush his face as Sally did, but he felt the quivering and buffeting shake of his casing and saw the swirling movements of raindrops on his glass cabinet.

The thunder rumbled closer, waves could be seen being whipped up in the flashes from the animosity of the sky as the rain became a heavy downpour and cried down, determined to penetrate any heart or crevice available.

This was to be no normal storm. The crescendo and cacophony grew with ferocity, buffeting Jack who was only being saved by the weight of his archaic gears and cogs, not like the lightness of his circuit board compadres.

He felt the structure and boardwalk of the pier buckling and straining under the torrent of the winds and abuse of the waves, pulling and crashing at the old rusted and unkempt stanchions and saw Sally quivering as the unseen fingers try and pry her from the side of the building.

Panic would have risen in his body as an almighty crack shook his world. The metal pillars screamed and groaning, sensing their fate and the long wooden boards splintered and popped from their lifelong moorings feeling unwanted freedom for the first time and were cast into the waters like some unwanted debris.

Jacks casing lurched forward and toppled forward on its front, eschewing his view from the surrounding events.

He was sure he heard a distant scream of terror that belonged to his distant and unacquainted figure of love as the world about him collapsed and sent him tumbling in the rage and plummeting into the watery depths.

This was no safe haven. For even below the water's surface the turmoil continued. The tides, ever working, relentlessly twisted and pulled at their quarry, having little regard for the fleeting enormity of a storm and its attempts to control all.

Jolly Jack sank hard, water filling through the broken glass and frame and he became settled on the bed wedged between heavy fallen girders. He lay on his tilted back looking up to the surface his arms now floating helplessly upwards before his eyes.

Even from this depth he could've told that the hurricane abated, exhausting itself now that it had made landfall and tired and spent, slowly dissipated.

In the darkness of the night and depth, his vision became blocked by a large, twisted object slowly spiralling down from above in his direction. His arms were pushed in the surge of the current, as if waving, signalling, and the broken and warped metal sheet turned in the waters and landed softly between his arms causing them to fold, as if, from a passing fish might see, in his embrace.

The morning came and so did still and light. People ventured out of damaged properties and inspected the destruction and gasped at the tangled mess that had once been a local attraction and beauty spot.

A shredded display was all that was left. The years had been torn apart and only sadness and memories stayed.

But, if they could have seen, maybe gladness would have been shared. For, far below there lies a machine, broken and never to be used again, true. But after all that he has given, he now lies, with his arms wrapped around a metal sign, the two sets of eyes looking into each other's with constant smiles of happiness on their faces and in their hearts.

MR CELLEOPHANE

The thin, old man stood at his small, first floor flat window looking out onto the quiet and cold street of yuletide shoppers, dipping in and out below in their quest to find unwanted presents at the cost of their happiness and the park with the bench where they liked to sit, feed the birds and watch the world go by together as a freshly made mug of tea, in his wrinkled, nicotine stained and cracked hands, wisped thin trails of steam.

He could feel the bitterness growing inside as the coldness of early winter crept through the glass, knowing that a harder cold was yet to come which would call for scarves and extra blankets to keep him warm and as he watched, the now bare treetops swayed mindless in wind and though the chill was only surface deep, for, like so many things, his soul was beyond touching as it lay hidden and lost from all that he saw.

Turning his back to the window and outside world, like he had first done many years ago, he walked into the compact, dilapidated, and tired kitchen to find a biscuit to go with his drink.

All was silent in his small collection of rooms, stillness had entered even the shelves of his cupboards leaving even the most mundane items like a statue frozen in time, though, once, when they had first moved there, life had seemed vibrant and full, life in abundance, but now. Sometimes, to prove a point to himself, he would just stand, or sit, motionless and inert, not even allowing thoughts to enter his mind, only stopping when the full force of futility took over and the sadness of his loneliness came too much to bear.

There would be no one to come to his rescue, there would be none to mourn his passing, he could sit for as long as he wanted in his old and decrepit world, and none would know or remember. He had been an uncle by marriage. Which had been fun when the children were young and full of vitality and learning, he smiled. Mary always loved children, especially so as...the smile dropped from his face.

He hated this time of year, most of all.

He resumed his position by the window, custard cream in hand, and continued to watch the bag laden folks pursue their fruitless goals of trying to appease each other, all the while increasing their debt and personal misery by buying plastic gifts and rubbish at inflated prices for acquaintances and loved ones, who, forcibly reciprocate, all the while forgetting and not even caring about the true message and reasons for the celebration, instead are happy to fuel a system of making the wealthy richer and the poor more desperate, an ever increasing divide that grows in size while the earth and most needy suffer from the widespread impact.

His disdain for his fellow man saddened him to his core. He wished goodwill, peace and love to all, though was often faced by threats of violence and ignorance and a lack of understanding and stupidity.

What a curse it was to be able to see and understand. To have your blinkers removed, even for a moment to glimpse into the reality of the world. Sights you can never unsee, understandings you can never forget. They lie within and only grow, expanding your awareness, which, if you fight it, only cause conflict and dilemmas which lead to sorrow and confusion. The only thing that can be done is to remove the curtains altogether and learn how to live within the spiral of lies.

Standing by his cold window and ragged curtains that had seen better days, he took another sip of his tea and coughed.

He missed his Mary. She had been the only thing that kept him grounded sometimes. Always had a kind word, always knew what to say, so full of love and life. He was sorry that he wasn't able to give her what she had always wanted, she would have made a great Mother. He watched as a couple of kids on bikes ride between the pedestrians, aggravating some and swearing at others, but laughing all the while at their own exploits and achievements.

"What's wrong with people today?" he thought to himself, wishing that he could just...

But it would be no good. People don't listen. They don't want to, or don't know how to. They don't want to hear that they might be looking at things the wrong way round, they just want to carry on in their own mislearnt existence, shielded or protected from realities to make it easier to control them.

He spluttered on a sip of tea.

This wasn't how his life was meant to have been. Not that he had given it much thought at the time about his future, but he had once known that he had wanted love, contentment, and happiness until his dying day. He had assumed it would just happen. He would learn about life as he grew and everything else would grow in proportion, but no one told him of the snares and traps that lay hidden, or of the bandits and outlaws waiting to rob you blind...or the pitfalls and pain of love.

He grunted to himself and recalled old scars, long healed, but learning curves nonetheless, he hoped he had learnt from them and not stored them up in a closet of pain, to come back and haunt him when most vulnerable.

He turned away from the window and sat in his worn arm-chair, resting his mug with its cooling remnants of tea on the arm rest.

Joe looked out across the floor of his sitting room with its threadbare carpet and tired wallpaper and his chin slowly sank onto his chest as his eyes closed and he passed into a sleep of dreams filled with laughter, colour and warmth.

The loud bang and muffled crying woke him with a start. The young mother in the flat below hard returned and her baby and young child were in obvious need of comfort and nourishment, both of which he knew were sparse for her and hard to come by. Her "partner" had left her with the two infants after finding distraction elsewhere, leaving a heartbroken, naïve young girl to fend for herself in a sea where she didn't know how to swim in.

She always seemed pleasant enough, stressed but pleasant, and guessed that her family had either turned their back on her or were too far away to offer assistance, either way...she struggled.

He rose from his sunken chair and walked into their bedroom and opened Marys dressing table drawer and took out the box and opened the lid.

"Still there." he thought as he gently ran his finger over the pieces of fine jewellery.

He remembered every piece. Each had its own memory. Where or who he had bought them from, how he had given them to Mary, her reaction to each, always surprise or delight, that beautiful sparkle in her eye...his eyes watered.

Every wedding anniversary was marked here. Every special year of the fifty that they shared, each passing year more magnificent from the last as his appreciation for her grew ever deeper. Here, in this old cigar box, lay his world of times gone. Early morning espresso at the Piazza Navona, a picnic, years later, while hiking through the South Pass or even a romantic and intimate dinner at their new flat (the same day the diagnosis came through).

At one time they were special, now, painful reminders of happiness and loss, meaningless pieces of metal and stone that he wished he could trade for a second to be with her again.

He closed the lid but didn't put it back in the drawer, leaving it on the side instead as he heard the distraught noises rise up through the floorboards once again.

He sat down heavily on the end of the bed with a sigh, staring at the box with no thoughts going through his head.

"There's nothing left anymore, nothing real..." he contemplated to himself "only memories."

Joe was surprised at his own rational thinking and clarity, but he couldn't find fault no matter how he looked at it.

He stood with some discomfort and walked back into the sitting room and sat down on the simple wooden chair in front of the roll top writing desk. Pulling out the drawer opened the roll of veneered wood exposing the trays and drawers with ornate decoration and enabled the felt covered work top to be folded out.

He smiled to himself as he picked out his pen, thinking of how fitting it was to be using the one he instinctively went to. He thought he could smell Mary's perfume as he began to write and could see her as if it was only yesterday keeping up with her correspondence, which she was so fond of.

Pausing while writing, he wondered whether he was doing the right thing, but then imagined his wife's hand gently rest on his shoulder with encouragement.

Placing the completed note into an envelope he hoped that what he had written made sense and would be taken in the right way but was tempted to open it and reread what he had attempted to say, then decided against it.

Sitting still at the desk he wondered when he ought to deliver the note. The afternoon was wearing on and he wasn't prepared, but then...

He looked around at his surroundings and decided that now was indeed as good as time as any. Pulling out a small roll of brown paper and some Sellotape, he picked up the note and walked back into the bedroom.

The young, struggling mum of two was summoned to her door by a sudden, startling and unexpected knock. Startling and unexpected because she knew no one in the area, except for the landlord (bloodsucker and parasite, like so many of them were, for the western world is designed for "man's" greed and not "man's" good) and maybe the bailiff, but she was sure she was up on her payments.

The tentatively opened the door, hoping she wouldn't be attacked and found to her surprise no one there, instead a small parcel lay at her feet by the doorway.

Somewhat confused she picked up the package and closed the door behind her as she returned to her spartan life and sat on her small sofa in front of her means of warmth. Her T.V.

She turned the parcel over in her hands and heard the contents move as she read the writing: For you, the young Mum with the two children.

Still confused, Jessica opened the wrapping and a note fell out. She opened it and read:

My dear girl,

You don't know me and I'm sorry I don't know you or your name, but you would have been old enough to be my...our granddaughter. We never had children.

My wife, Mary, died some years back and I miss her terribly, I'm not cut out for this world, not on my own.

We spent many years together, each treasured, as you will see.

I hope these gifts will help you find a better life and you put them to good use, because each one is filled with precious love and meaning that once flowed in the hearts and veins of two people who cared for all and everything.

Merry Christmas my dear x

Jess opened the box at the same time as she opened her mouth with unbelief.

Tears burst forth from her eyes and a softened stuttered sound touched her throat.

Unbelieving, her hand reached out and touched the obviously expensive collection of jewellery and the tip of one of her fingers slipped into a band of clean white metal.

She raised her trembling hand and slipped the ring further onto her finger, fitting it comfortably onto her hand.

Putting the box quickly down by her side, she rushed to the door to make sure she had not accidentally missed the deliverer. Of course, no one was there.

Her mind raced as she reread the note, all the while rechecking the box and its contents and looking at the ring on her finger. The tears of shock and gratitude still flowed, but now were interspersed with moments of incredulous laughter of relief and happiness.

The darkness of early winter had already lit the streetlights and sent shoppers scurrying home for the warmth of their houses, but Joe sat on their bench in the cold evening, warmth in his heart, knowing that Mary would be pleased with what he had done.

He sat alone, uninterrupted, no one would be out tonight, too cold be trouble making outdoors, so he leant back and relaxed, feeling at peace at long last.

Jessica struggled the stairs with her two children as she descended her way, taking young Charlie to toddlers and then to a jewellers with her excited trove, but had decided to keep the ring on her finger so she never forgot the moment.

Struggling down the last few steps outside her place, she saw an ambulance by the park gates and paused.

"Found some old tramp on a bench," said a largish lady watching the proceedings "poor old bugger must've froze to death last night."

Jess suddenly felt a pang of guilt and sorrow. How fortunate she had been to have been chosen for rescue.

DOWN BY THE STREAM

Arnie was small for 8 months old, curled up in the corner of his cage shaking with cold, fear, and hunger as his sister, asleep and oblivious, was caged next to him, the metal bars apparently protecting them from the other, more aggressive, and dominant dogs in the household.

They were rarely let out of their prison and would often be admonished (mainly for soiling their confines) by shouting, hitting (with what was ever at hand, a recent burn to the forehead was inflicted by a hot iron) or even kicking, but shouting was the most common and could be just as terrifying.

But on this particular day all that he knew in his life changed.

He watched as other people came to his house and there was a lot of angry shouting, more than normal but gladly not directed at him, which was a relief but just as frightening, then followed by crying and silence. He and his sister were gently lifted from their sheets of paper by strangers who had good smells and soft words and placed into other, dark cages in a van.

The larger dogs were more confused, agitated, and angry than him and his sister (who, as always, seemed to take everything in her stride and was settling down for another nap) as they were led into a different section behind them. Doors closed, shutting out the light, and Arnie felt the vehicle move, the start of a long and distant journey.

He woke from the dream and stretched, legs and paws pushing his owner's legs out of the way, though feeling the comfort of their warmth and closeness. He grunted with contentment.

His old though reliable stomach told him it wasn't quite time for anything yet, so returned to slumber, surrounded by security and companionship, and his dreams.

The distant memory seeped it way back through the cracks of time, the long darkness of the night's sleep reminding him of the long and sickening journey, filled with fear, thirst and hunger to his new temporary home. The vehicle stopped, and the doors opened to the sound of many voices all barking and yapping, some afraid, some excited, some barking just to join in.

Each one was unloaded from their transport cages, one by one, and led to a room with a hard table, where they were thoroughly examined by caring hands and a firm touch, but unfamiliar with smells of chemicals and traces other animals.

A dog barked in a distant property setting off a chain reaction of responses in the surrounding houses where other canines resided. Arnie joined in, woken again from his slumber, though tying in nicely with the noises from his kennel dreams.

"Oi, Arnie." a half sleep voice commanded, as a foot reached out and softly prodded their dog to be quiet, but also to re-assure the old boy that nothing was wrong. It worked. Silence resumed in the house despite the continued far-off noise from outside.

Arnie stretched again and shuffled his way across the bed and slid onto the step that helped him get up and flopped onto the floor. He lay there for a while, until his stomach and bladder told him that it was about time someone took notice of him.

He gave a little whine hoping someone would respond. When no one stirred he stood, stretched again making a small squeak emitted from somewhere behind him, and walked over to his leader of the packs side of the bed. Whining again still gave no movement, so the wet nose flipped the bottom corner of the duvet and nudged a shin.

A hand waved at the side of the bed signalling for him to get closer, but he knew to stay his distance to get what he wanted and soon enough, with another nudge and whine, the day started.

Arnie waited diligently at the top of the stairs waiting to be carried down. His legs and hip had been getting more sore and stairs were a difficult manoeuvre, though much as he would prefer to do it himself, his boss had commanded him to stay, so...

Eventually the wait was over. The long process of getting dressed was complete. Why they bothered Arnie never under-stood.

Scooped up in arms, he was carried and deposited by the back door so he could go out for his morning sniff around and de-posits while his breakfast and fresh water was prepared for him.

He stood momentarily by the back door taking in the February air and looking where to go first. He gruffed at the birds at the bird table causing them to flap away, so, contented with his first act, he trotted off into the garden to inspect any new scents and all the old ones.

The garden had changed a bit since he first came here. The

pond was a nice addition, the frogs were fun to chase or watch and it also attracted hedgehogs, which was great, but he did get a very sore nose, mouth and paw after every encounter, but it did mean less grass to tear around on. Going past one of the oldest shrubs in the garden, he briefly remembered being taught how to play with a ball. His idea of fun was to crazily around the entire garden, he had known such space and freedom, and then throw himself at whoever had the ball. It was great to see them almost fall over.

Arnie could hear the biscuits being put into his bowl and decided he needed to hurry up, so, finishing his morning business he kicked at the ground and trotted indoors just in time to witness his bowl being placed down for him.

He sniffed at it, ate fast, licked the bowl clean (just in case), stretched, then decided that a nap was needed. Too much exertion had already been expended this morning.

He had been banned from the sitting room on his own for some (unknown to him) reason, so part of his bed had been put outside the kitchen door in the hallway. A good spot, he thought, but a bit drafty.

He laid on his bed, waiting for 11 o'clock (treat time), knowing that morning walks were now a thing of the past. He didn't care that his legs hurt, he still wanted to chase birds, rabbits and cats...especially cats. He smiled in his journey to slumber town, imaginings of large wiggling balls of warm fur being shaken in his mouth.

He dreamt of his first time of real freedom. Boss and Boss jnr. took him for a drive to go for a walk. They parked by a little bridge and got out, the three of them heading into some woods with a river running through it. Lots of new and exciting smells met Arnies year old nose, and it twitched and sniffled at every piece of ground and plant.

The dirt track was dry and plants were in full growth and the area was quiet and peaceful. Nature was in its full beauty mode and things were good in this world.

"Right, this looks like a good spot."

"But Dad, he's never been off his lead before."

"I know, but it's got to happen sometime."

"But he'll run off."

"I'm sure he'll be fine."

"Mum won't like it."

"It'll be fine."

He bent down and unclipped the lead.

Whoosh! Gone!

"Told you. Mum's going to be mad."

"Arnie? Come here Arnie. Arnie?"

Searching went on for about twenty minutes with no result, the older of the two being regularly reminded of their plight and situation. Having to admit defeat they turned around and headed back to the vehicle to return home empty handed, apart from a bowl full of "told you so's".

Stepping out of the last path in the woods and back onto the small road, both father and son couldn't believe their eyes. Sitting happily by the front wheel of the car, little tail thumping the ground and tongue lollygagging with joy sat Arnie.

"Ooh, you are so lucky. Mums going to hear about all of this."

Between mid-morning scratches, tummy rubs and the postman at the door, time dragged until his elevenses treat and no sooner had that been devoured it was thoughts onto the next item on his agenda; the two o'clock walk.

The daily, if he was lucky, routine was now a brief stroll around the block, going past the old people's bungalows, across the road and around the back of the garages that sat by the lane that led out towards open country, where he used to enjoy the long field excursions.

While living in the countryside has its advantages, many a time one is limited on where to roam, often restricted to poorly maintained signed footpaths.

However, some paths, the more secret and hidden ones, not known to many newcomers lead across open farm land, where, if you keep your eyes open, allow you total field access away from the ever-watchful eyes of the farmer. Obviously, respect is given to the property and care is paramount so as not to ruin it for others who might be privy to the rural routes. As long as no one damages gates or fences and ensures animal welfare at all times where necessary, the farmer won't be too unkind to your excursions. Keep to the edges and don't assume your rights. Ever.

Two o'clock came round quick enough and Arnie had already strategically positioned himself, for maximum effect, for the whines to be clearly heard in the house and to anyone in earshot. Shoes on, coat on and lead in hand meant only one thing in his eyes.

The first half of the walk was about getting his aches and pains moving, checking out the competition odours and emptying that extra weight he was carrying.

By the time they had cleared the old people's bungalows set back on the small green, expectation was always peeked as the lane for easy access to the open pastures began here.

Arnie's ears raised in hope, remembering the variety of possible routes that used to be taken, each offering their own particular reward.

The first part of the lane was wooded, but narrow, secured on either side by thick bushes and hedges that gave way to a wire fence on one side when opening up into the field. A good field of vision was had, so he was always allowed off the lead to walk at his own pace inspecting any patch he desired.

Coming to the first gate he always hoped to turn left. Right would take them across a small, but still, open field, but led back to paths and roads, but with a bonus of the long alley way, where there was always a guarantee to accost another dog and show who was really top dog, regardless of what anyone said.

But left turn, ah. After a short stroll through the first non-descript patch of ground lay his first love.

When he first came to live with his pack it was this short-grassed area where they came to learn how to really play and run. The large expanse of green had a gate on each side of its square, though only two were used by walkers and their companions and one could clearly see off in the distance any need to take care.

And so it was, Arnie and his thrower would spend a happy time, running for all he was worth, collapsing in the heat of the summer sun, panting for all he was worth, but never wanting the fun to end.

One day, in the middle of a serious session, games stopped. Curious as to what was happening, Arnie noticed his friend walk off in a direction they hadn't been before. Following calls, he tailed tentatively, preferring to want to stay and catch a few more frisbees.

Walking down the gentle slope they came to a small iron gate, which was dutifully opened for him, and they entered into another world.

Immediately before them was a narrow wooden structure that didn't look at all save or reliable to walk over. The human crossed confidently, unaware of the possible hazard, but Arnie was having none of it, instead he took a move secure route.

He headed down the bank only to meet another obstacle blocking his way. The little stream ran over the rocks and stones with its own bobbling voice, chatting incessantly about where it had been, what it was doing and where it was off to.

Arnie had never come across such a hurdle as this and was quite taken aback, so decided a different route was called for. He clambered easily back up the bank only to be instantly reminded of why he had gone down there in the first place.

He looked, then whined.

"C'mon boy, you can do it"

He understood the "c'mon" part and the hand signal, but... what was he to do. He whined again and sat.

"C'mon Arnie, ooh, look, pusscat!"

Arnie's ears and body instantly went up.

"Puss..!"

Before the word could be finished, Arnie dashed across the makeshift bridge in search for his quarry, forgetting all about his nerves (fierce dog indeed), only to find that it must have escaped.

Instead, to his delight, he saw the ball being thrown into the longer grass, so dashed off to destroy it and see if any long-eared friends might be waiting to be discovered and played with.

The sun shone for all to see, and the cloudless sky, big and blue, was just as high. Arnie liked this new field. He would, in the years to come, get to know the long walk, where this would make a great half way point.

Never ceasing amounts of energy were released as her tore around, only stopping, spread eagled and panting, when his body decided that enough was enough.

The human called him back over to the wooden bridge which he had forgotten about, and reluctantly went over as instructed.

"C'm 'ere Arnie, come on boy."

Arnie rather he didn't, but knew he had to.

He trotted over, still panting and noticeably getting distracted on the way, desperate for any chance to avoid the obstacle again.

"Down here boy."

Arnie looked at the madness of the situation.

"Come here." came the more direct tone.

With a body of reluctance, Arnie edged forward into the running water.

Nature took over.

Sudden realisation that this stuff was the same as what was in his bowl filled him with glee.

Before any could pass his lips, he laid, again spread eagled, in the babbling brook. Oh, the pleasured look of delight on his face. He lay there until his panting's ceased and he had rehydrated himself and then he had to be coerced to get out of his new found pleasure.

This was his summer heaven.

Any chance he got, he would try and head towards this spot, but now...the spirit was willing, oh so willing, but the legs said "No".

Instead, now, he had to make do with a walk around a block, long sleeps on the sofa, pills every few hours, lots of strokes and tummy scratches (which hadn't changed) and dreams of when he was young and times down by the stream.

ACT 3

WHAT HO!

WHAT HO!

The racing green Riley 9 pulled into the turning for the house, wheels lightly skidding as it took the corner with the hand-brake, and speeded up the gravel drive, not yet ready to halt its journey.

The car stopped with the usual satisfying scrunch of loose stone under the wheels and Teddy jumped out, refreshed yet thirsty after the invigorating journey. He removed his hat, goggles and scarf and took a deep breath of the fresh, still, morning country air, dew still damp on the lawn with a thin layer of mist drifting over the grass tops, as the sun and residents, only just stirring, would shine in their summer clothes later in the day.

A small bird sang and flew up from a clump of bushes, happy with its task, as two black, large birds flew high overhead, crowing a meeting to the morning.

Teddy noticed a spot on one of his shoes, rubbed it with the heel of the other, then on the back of his trouser leg, satisfied, turned and grabbed his bag from the passenger seat of his car, the leather handles comfortably worn, but the canvas still looking as strong as ever, and strode to the front door.

He turned the large black knob but the door was locked, unsurprising, as he wasn't expected until tomorrow, so rapped the dolphin shaped knocker rather than use the bell.

He didn't have to wait long until he saw the silhouetted form of Mrs Magtree, the house maid, busily shuffling down the corridor towards him, tying up her morning coat and adjusting her hair to greet the early guest.

"Well, bless me. Master Teddy. I thought I heard a vehicle on the drive." She exclaimed opening the door, letting the morning coolness wrap itself around her ankles.

"Morning Maggie, how are you my dear." He said leaning forward to kiss her on the cheek.

"Ooh, very well thank you, mustn't grumble." she smiled "Come in, come in, I've got the kettle on for everyone else." Maggie Magtree stood back from the door to allow Master Teddy entry and led the way back up the corridor with a little shiver and round the corner to the kitchen.

On the side, by the breakfast bar, two trays sat ready with cups, saucers, spoons and plates just waiting to be filled with tea and toast, an appertiser before the main event to be delivered forthwith.

The night cold of the kitchen was already being driven away by the awakening Aga and Maggie had resumed her tea making duties and called out "Well, you might as well make yourself busy, Master Teddy, if you would. Be so kind and butter that toast for me would you, me dear." Signalling to the butter dish.

Teddy obliged and cut off the crusts, as he knew the family well, and placed the right amount on each tray.

"Good. That's grand." Mrs Magtree said as she poured out the cups of tea "You take young Bunty's and I'll take the Masters and Mrs. Go on then. Be quick. Before it gets cold." She said picking up the appropriate tray and heading off.

Teddy followed behind, up the stairs and around the bend on

the small landing, until they separated, their own ways, to either end of the corridor. He walked along the old creaky floorboards covered with luxuriant red and gold runners towards his Bunty's bedroom and knocked on the door, slowly turned the handle with his spare hand and entered.

In the dim morning light, dampened by the heavy tapestry curtains that hung in the tall windows, he could see his fiancé to be lying still asleep in the middle of the old four poster bed.

Teddy walked over to the bedside and lay the tray on the large oak table by the bedside and stared down at the recumbent body, the outline not hidden by the covers or darkness. He leant slightly over and softly trailed the back of his hand along her sleeping form, like he had done before, to the others, and tenderly moved her hair away from her forehead, exposing the full beauty of her face.

Bunty's breath was momentarily interrupted by a quiet sigh, so he leant over further and kissed her brow, whispering her name and sitting beside her, waiting for the information to filter through.

He sat a while in thought on the previous night movements and smiled at his good fortune, looking around the room and inhaling the air of the old house that must have witnessed countless events, mundane and thrilling, in its centuries of existence.

Noticing that Bunty had resumed her deep slumber, his efforts obviously not effective, he considered his possibilities. He knew what he desired, but the house was awakening, so he stood and walked to the window and pulled open the heavy curtains letting light fill the room with a burst while saying with gusto "What Ho Bunty! Beautiful morning!" in an extravagant flourish.

"Teddy?" came the soft, waking confused voice from the bed, followed quickly by an enthusiastic and surprised "Teddy! Darling! It's you!"

"In the flesh, my dearest Bunty. And with Tea and Toast." He said pointing to the tray.

"Oh, Teddy darling, how lovely to see you. But you're not meant to be here until tomorrow" Bunty said, sitting up and propping herself up with pillows.

"Come here and pass me my tea, darling" she said patting the bed.

Teddy walked over and dutifully did as he was told and received a kiss for his obedience.

"Oh Teddy, this is a lovely surprise. I thought you were busy though."

"Well," he said, brushing his floppy locks back "I managed to..." he thought how could he put it "get it done earlier than expected. Even a little extra." He cheerfully smiled.

"Oh, this really is too wonderful." Bunty said biting into her cold toast, Teddy watching where the crumbs fell. "Dolly and Sedders are coming over today too. We could go down to the courts and play doubles. Oh, won't that be just divine." She smiled brushing the remnants off her silk night blouse.

Waving with her hand she commanded to Teddy, saying "Now run along sweetie and let Bunty get up and dressed. I'll see you downstairs in a mo. X."

Teddy briefly paused, the feeling rose, but remembering where he was, his smile and demeanour stayed fixed, intact, as he vacated, returning to Mrs Magtree, downstairs, in the kitchen and her morning delights.

Breakfast was a welcome affair, refuelling energies spent and catching up with Bunty's gruff father about the latest trends in the city's financial markets to take advantage of, while a simultaneous and diverse conversement was being had with Joanna, Bunty's mother.

"Tell me Teddy," Joanna said resting her hand on his wrist "I hear you've moved to Earls Court."

Bunty missed the freeze that passed over Teddys body as he inadvertently flashed her a miniscule look of surprised horror.

"I thought you were going up in the world?" Joanna added.

Quickly, so as not to expose his truths and desires Teddy replied "Well, to be honest Joanna," stalling for time as a myriad of thoughts tumbled, like a collapsing brick wall, through his being, feeling beads of sweat forming on his body "...to be honest, I'm having the flat overhauled and I thought it would be fun to see how the other half lived" he tacked on to the end...at least that part was partly true.

"But Earls Court my dear, isn't it...somewhat...louche?" Bunty's mother said, trying to hide her disdain and make her words sound more palatable.

"Oh Mother," Bunty interrupted, not wanting the day, breakfast or life to get so serious "not all of E.C is like that, some parts are divine, just like anywhere." She concluded, returning to eggs, satisfied that the issue had been laid to rest, even though, in her dreams, she would never be seen dead in "that" part of town.

Mr Chadwick came out from behind his morning paper, his balding head and large moustache leading the way. "I knew a chap from Earls Court once, served in the battalion, decent type, rum chap, if you know what I mean..." he laughed as the memories came back to him, "He had one of those confounded contraptions. You know. Those things that you shake." He performed a shaking action to all present around the table, who were none the wiser of what he was talking about or where the conversation might be leading to. "The blighter almost took the captains head off with it..." he paused again in thought, not entirely sure himself if he wasn't getting some memories mixed up with sometime else. "Anyway, the point was that it happened on a Thursday. Ha! And Nanny could always see if you hadn't washed your hands...or was it Edgware?" then sipped his morning coffee and returned behind broadsheet, mumbling a pesky bees and blasted butterflies.

The table sat quiet for a moment, apart from Mr Mumbles, until Teddy broke the awkward silence with "How is Mr Magtree? Is he still gardening for you?"

Unfortunately, this did nothing to stifle the hush, rather, prolong it, and even Mr Mumbles stopped chittering and emitted a couple of gruff coughs.

"No, sadly he passed away some months back." Joanna informed Teddy while dabbing the corners of her mouth with the napkin, ridding herself of the morning's takings and conversation stains.

"Oh, I told you Teddy, don't you remember. Apparently…" while looking at her father "he shot himself while cleaning the hunting guns. Terrible mess. Absolutely ghastly."

Mrs Chadwick rose from the table, not remembering any time that her breakfast had been ruined so, and departed with cordiality and excuses of a busy morning ahead.

No sooner as she had left, Mrs Magtree came bustling in to start removing the repast and make way for the next mealtime.

Teddy was unsure whether to broach the subject of her husband's passing, but was saved by Bunty's interjection.

"Thank you for the lovely breakfast, Maggie; the eggs especially." She said as she stood up and pushed her chair back under the table.

Teddy took the queue to do the same and soon left Mrs Magtree circumnavigating around Mr Chadwick who would probably still be there in an hour, only to find that he had been left alone, though unsure if anyone had been there in the first place.

At about the same time Johnathan Chadwick left the table for a walk to the potting shed, another body was being pulled from the River Thames on the banks of Hammersmith. Inspector Poole had already been called and was already on his way, having only been home a short while since into the night, trying to shed light on the latest string of possibly connected crimes.

A local bobby had been patrolling along the northside of the river when little Timmy Tomkins, a known waif of the area, normally up to no good with his bulldog, Boxer, both came running up, out of breath.

"Oi Charlie," little Timmy blurted in excitement between breaths "there's another dead 'un down the ways. Not all bloated like the last one. Looks right fresh!" he said, dashing on to go and get the rest of his tearaway gang.

P.C 9062 Charles Bankworth pulled out his whistle and blew, running to the area Timmy had come from, eyes searching the water and shoreline for the possible victim. In the near distance he could make out a large shape of either a boulder or small boat, but knew no large rocks lay on this side of the river and no jetties were nearby.

As he drew closer, he observed two sets of small footprints, one four legged, emerging from the mound. His whistle blowing had garnered the attention of two other P. C's, as well as some locals, who were all also convening to the same destination.

"Come on, keep back please. Keep back" P.C Charlie authoritatively said while replacing his whistle into his breast pocket.

Charlie and Old George, the longest serving copper from his station, went to inspect their discovery, while John Peters, a more delicate soul, stayed back to keep the spectators at bay.

"Same as before wouldn't you say?" Old George said observing the visible knife marks and cord around the neck. "They say they were done after strangulation," he said tipping his helmet back to wipe some sweat from his brow, but also to wipe his eye at the same time. "She be about the same age as me Tabitha." He pointed out, more to himself than to any listener.

"Should I cover her with my coat?" asked Charlie.

"No. I think leave things alone until Inspector gets here. You know what he can be like."

George turned his back on the latest victim, but not before quietly uttering a prayer of rest for the tormented soul.

———

"What Ho! Snorkers!" yelped the ever-enthusiastic Sedders, as he sat down at the kitchen table for a veritable feast, all lovingly prepared by his absolutely adorable (and aloof) darling of a peach, Dolly.

He tucked into his tea, toast and sausages with gusto (and a good helping of Gentleman's Relish) and his delicious Dolly sat at the other end of the small table with a cup of java and a woodbine in her kimono.

"Not eating dearest?" piped the ever-cheerful Sedders.

Dolly glowered a disdaining and withering look from behind her smoke and steam.

"All the more for me then!" Sedders yodelled triumphantly.

To say that they were an odd couple is an understatement.

All their friends, and even some of their family, couldn't fathom how they stayed together.

Sedders, or Cedric Fortescue-ffrench-Hodges III (not forgetting the two small f's) as he was correctly known, was, what is colloquially known as a bon viveur. He was, not so much as a man about town, but certainly a chap around town. Seen at all the best parties, restaurants, theatres and events. Party at the Palace? He was there. Any exclusive event that might be had and you would hear the ever-effervescent tones and see the rather large nose of Sedders in the background and he didn't seem to have a bad bone in his body.

Whereas...

Dolly Price.

Dolly Price. Sultry maiden, sleek and svelte like, stunningly and effortlessly good looking, though you wouldn't be surprised to find a gun and poison in her purse, ready to dispatch anyone on a whim.

She was an heir to colossal wealth, more so than Cedric, but they resided in modest accommodation for their status and were truly committed to each other, through thick and thin.

"I say Dolly dearest, these are frightfully good." Cedric pointed out about the sausages, buttering another piece of toast.

"Have you packed everything you need for the weekend darling?" Dolly dryly asked as if she hadn't heard anything about the sausages.

"Er, no, no yet." He admitted, as Dolly rolled her eyes in disbelief, standing and heading off in the direction of his bedroom.

"Why don't we get you a manservant?" she called while rummaging through the various cupboards and drawers, pulling out assorted items of clothing. "It would much easier and we have plenty of space."

Cedric did like the sound of a "manservant", quite fun actually, they had talked about one a while ago, but decided against it for some reason, but now Pongo had one…well…seems only fitting, what.

"Where would we find one?" Cedric called out, while he inspected the frying pan to see if any lone resident might have been left behind and unattended.

"Leave it to me." Called back Dolores as she leaned over, pushing down onto Cedric's portmanteau travel bag.

"I say," said Sedders entering the room "Looks like I arrived just in time." As he started unshouldering his braces.

Dolly looked over her shoulder and smiled "Really Sedders darling, there's just no stopping you is there?"

Bunty and Teddy were taking a constitutional around the grounds, knowing that it wouldn't be until after lunch when Dolly and Sedders would arrive to stay, so she had organised with Maggie to get some sandwiches and cake prepared for tea down by the pavilion.

As they walked in the still fresh morning air, Teddy tried to put his arm around Bunty's waist, once clear from view of the house, but was promptly rebuffed and had to settle instead for arm in arm contact instead.

As they walked, talk turned to their future plans of engagement, though his mind kept wandering back to the night before. It all seemed like a million miles away, another time, yet here he was just a few hours later...

"Teddy! Honestly! I don't think you've been listening to a word I've said." Bunty nudged him gently in the ribs.

"What? Oh. Sorry, darling. Work you know. Just been so busy lately. What with the move as well?" Teddy replied, trying his best to make a good enough excuse.

"Poor Teddy." Bunty said, pouting and stroking his iddy biddy face. "I know what Teddy needs." Though she didn't.

"Come on, I'll race you back to the house and get Magtree to make us some cocoa. Come on, don't be last."

Bunty ran off, excited with the game and Teddy followed, suddenly exhausted with life and the pretence of it all. If only everyone could stop pretending, he was sure a lot more problems could be solved.

He suddenly realised that Bunty had a fair head start on him, so putting his thoughts away, locked and chained until he had time to savour them, he gave chase.

Inspector Poole sat at his desk, staring down at the pile of papers in front of him. Now that he had stopped, tiredness was creeping up on him and his thoughts were beginning to stray. He had spent the morning down by the river and had left some men combing the area, knocking on the right doors, asking questions, though felt sure that the body had probably drifted down from Chiswick.

With no clues to go by, he had to assume that these girls were all working girls, at least that was a starting point, and someone either wanted to make identification difficult, which was very unlikely or…it was the "or" he didn't like.

Picking up the files for the tenth time, he hoped the answer might fall out. All five had been garrotted first, with a red sash of all things, and then had suffered the horrendous knife injuries, subsequently being dumped in the river. No one sees nothing, hears nothing, knows nothing. He lightly tapped his pencil.

They'd checked all the local pubs and haunts and known hangouts, but nothing. No one knew these girls, so they must come from further afield.

Whoever was committing these acts was doing them elsewhere, then taking their bodies as far as east of Kew or the other side of Hammersmith, meaning he knows the area, well enough not to be discovered, and has his own transport.

The last part just didn't make sense to the Inspector. This wasn't any low-class vagrant or hardworking tradesman, they rarely went that far afield, not for pleasure anyway, besides, it would be too time consuming and get easily noticed, their comings and goings.

Whoever they were, they were trying to be clever at covering their tracks, but if anything, when the time came, they would stand out in the crowd, bit like a shilling in a handful of pennies.

There was a knock on the door and the Desk Sergeant came in, carrying a fresh cup of tea.

"Thanks Bob, I need that" Edward Poole said to his colleague.

"Nothing like a cup of Rosie to get brain cells working." Bob said, placing the metal mug down on the desk.

"It's a rum one alright, isn't it?" he continued, looking at the blackboard with Edward Poole's scribblings across it. "Any ideas yet?"

Ed Poole sat back in his creaky chair and sighed.

"Got some ideas, don't understand them mind, got a feeling we're on the trail but I can't see it." Inspector Poole said, reaching for his mug of tea, blowing on it and taking a sip.

"Well, the way I see it" Bob started, on one of his insights that his long career had garnered, "this fellow has fled away from what he does, change of scenery so to speak. Different lives and all that. Can't live like that way all the time. It'll lose flavour for him. Though, he'll be getting used to the routine and will start either making mistakes, come complacent like or...up his game."

Edward looked amazed at the Desk Sergeant and wondered why he had never been promoted. He had asked him once, but was given a cock'n'bull story about how he'd miss his garden too much.

But he had to admit it, Bob was right, things don't stay the same forever, something was going to change. Hopefully something in their favour.

Bob was still looking at the blackboard.

"You know," he started observing "these murders, very specific, only started a short while ago. Bit odd don't you think?"

"Odd?" Edward asked, getting up from his chair and wandering over to the board as well.

"Well, things don't just start...fully mature like. They grow, like my garden. Plants take a lot of work and care, trial and error sometimes, to get them growing properly, in the right place so to speak." Bob pointed out, while thinking how he could improve his latest batch of begonias.

Edward Poole was astounded by Bob's insight, but realised that it was a possibility, movement, out of the area, locations, accessibility...

————

Cedric and Dolly had boarded the 2:10 and settled into their First-Class carriage. The train pulled out of the station on time and proceeded on its journey into the awaiting countryside where they were to spend the weekend with Bunty and her family.

Dolly eyed her beau from opposite giving him an unseen incorrigible grin, as his attentions were already being taken by the latest novel of Agatha Christie. She sighed, loudly, but garnered no reaction, so delved into her handbag to find her cigarettes. As she rummaged for her lighter, she was certain it was in there somewhere, the door to their compartment slid open and a stout, bespectacled gentleman, with a hat, ridiculously too small for him, perching at a jaunty angle on his head, entered and sat down.

Dolly watched as he made himself comfortable, without saying a word, and pulled a paper from under his arm and started reading.

She looked at Cedric who was oblivious to the events, so had to be kicked firmly on the shin.

"Oh!" he squealed as he sat upright from his slouch, protesting at the injury.

Dolly glared at him, that kept him quiet, confused but quiet, and then she turned her head in direction of the newcomer.

"Oh." Cedric said now understanding, "Oh, I say, good afternoon my dear sir, I think you've got the wrong carriage." He conveyed to the newcomer.

"What? What?" came the spluttering response, suddenly being disturbed from the confines of his world. "Wrong carriage?" he said fumbling his newspaper, looking for his ticket in his waistcoat pocket.

He produced the small cardboard strip and scrutinised the writing and markings of the glass panel on the door.

"No, no, right carriage." He said, returning to his reading.

Dolly kicked Cedric's shin again as he looked at her with help-less eyes.

"Erm, the thing is my dear fellow," Cedric pursued "We've booked the cabin for ourselves you see."

The gentleman peered out over his glasses and surveyed the couple, gave a little cough and puff. "Sorry dear boy, but orders is orders. This is where I'm meant to sit, so sit I shall." and returned again to his broadsheet.

Cedric shrugged to his beloved who sent daggers in return, along with rolling eyes and a large exasperated sigh…just for good measure and to ensure he understood that she wasn't happy. Point taken.

Time and train rattled along on the tracks they were fixed to, until the silence was broken from behind the paper.

"Nasty business…murder."

Cedric and Dolly looked at each other, unsure whether they were being addressed or the gentleman was talking to himself.

"Five of 'em now they say, five. What's this world coming to? That's what I want to know?"

Cedric looked dumbfounded, so Dolly answered for him. "Yes terrible, no one's safe really." She said, evoking a surprised reaction from their guest.

"What? No one?" he said, sounding genuinely shocked.

There was a lot of pluff and bluster exuded, as the gentleman tried to put himself right, the last comment obviously having put him out of sorts, much to the amusement of Dolly, though totally lost on Cedric who had already been reabsorbed into his little book.

Dolly looked out of the window, watching the trees, hills and fields go by, letting her mind wander with the scenery and feeling the rhythmic rocking of the train and the sounds of the engine and wheels on the tracks. She closed her eyes and drifted...drifted into a nightmare...where the steams whistle was heard as the screams of victims.

———

The murderer sat at the table reading about the recent discovery of the fourth, well...actually sixth, victim, the first two didn't really count as they were never discovered, nor were they meant to be, they were regarded as practice for the main event. Honing one's skills some might say. Ironing out the creases. Sharpening the knives...that brought a smile across the lips.

They stood and walked over to the window, leaving the paper on the table, and looked out onto the passing world, each busy with their lot, unaware with whom they were rubbing shoulders with, knowing that, that even a smallest piece of information couldn't be shared, for it would spoil the whole game and take way any pleasure that had been acquired so far.

The murders, such an insignificant word for something so profound and important, seemed so far away, and the need for another was building too quickly, so the urge had to be forced down and distractions put in place, but knowing that more was to come was only wood for the fire.

The thought turned to the strangulation, the necessity of the ritual, the foreplay so to speak, the frantic grabbing, limbs thrashing, the amusing gurgling, though the voiding could sometimes be extreme and unpleasant, but once the blade came out to play, everything was swept away in a thunderous heat of pleasure. In those few moments, red focus was all there was, nothing else was heard or seen, that doorway into the other world opened and welcomed them in, the feelings of completeness, warmth, fulfilment became one. They were one. It was one.

Sadly, as now, all good things come to an end. Sated for the now, yet returning was so disappointing, never fully satisfied, maybe the last one will do, maybe the last one will reveal, but for that, things will have to be different. Things will have to change.

The heart started beating faster at the mere thought of changing routine. The excitement of trying something different, but also of the dangers that it may pose. The potential of exposure. Planning would have to be careful and precise. Perhaps small steps to see if anyone notices the changes

A horse and cart clattered by with the driver smoking a pipe, small plumes of blue smoke puffing out as they went.

What was he thinking while drawing on his pipe as his eyes watched the road ahead? Was he feeling the jolt of the road? The weight of his dray? The hardships that his life affords? Would he like to feel the lack of constraints that bind him to his daily toil?

The slayer turned their back on the window to the world and returned to the confines and limitations of the room, staring down at the paper that still lay upon the table.

They would start the changes with number 5 (7), leave a little clue and see if they notice, that would be an extra bit of sport. But what if they missed? They're fault, not theirs.

The feeling began to rise again, this time relief would be had.

––––––––

The handsome cab pulled up outside Chadwick Manor in time for late luncheon, with Cedric being famished and Dolly feeling the chill from such a frightful journey.

They were greeted by Mrs Chadwick, as Bunty and Teddy had driven in to town to fetch some joints of meat, as Percy, the local...supplier, had not arrived with his promised catch. Such a shame, as the trout and game were always of remarkable quality.

Joanna ordered the inundated Mrs Magtree to take the cases up to the prepared rooms, despite the remonstrations from Cedric, as she led the way to the drawing room with its burning log fire already warming any coolness Dolly might have felt, and the promise of a very dry Martini...or two.

Mr Chadwick was sound asleep in his chair, taking his daily after lunch nap before being revived with a whisky with ice, the ice only there to try and freshen him up before the onslaught.

"Johnny dear? Visitors." Johanna called out as they entered.

The reply was more heavy breathing.

"Johnathan!" came the effective sharp rebuke, causing immediate awakeness and sitting up to attention, like a berated schoolboy.

"Ah, visitors, yes my dear." Mr Chadwick said, blinking rapidly, realigning himself with the world about him.

"Whiskey, darling?" Joanna enquired and not needing an answer turned to Cedric and said "Do the honours would you my darling, so good of you" and took a seat, waiting to be served on and signalled for her Dolly to join her.

Cedric went to the drinks table to perform his duties as Dolly ventured over to sit by "Mrs" Chadwick and perform hers.

Joanna effortlessly offered the opened cigarette case to Dolores with a gracious smile while looking directly into her eyes to see if the sparkle and acknowledgement was there.

Dolly traced her fingers over the thin white tobacco sticks and selected one, putting it to her lips, the clink of ice being dropped into a glass behind her as Joanna now offered her a lit lighter.

Dolly leant forward to the naked flame and gently held the lighter and hand still, feeling the slight tremoring of the skin. She fed the recipients answer with the briefest of prolonged touch, and the removal of the cigarette from her lips, an exhale of smoke, followed by the slightest protuberance of her eager tongue, dampening the edges of her dry mouth.

Joanna flushed and was grateful for the dimness of the room and the lack of a strong afternoon sun as she stood to assist Cedric with the delivery of drinks and to compose herself, though wishing the night would come sooner than it would.

As if a spell was lifted, Bunty and Teddy could be heard outside in the hall as they came in full of the freshness of the day, bursting the doors into the drawing room to greet the newcomers and welcomed guests.

"Sedders, Dolly, how lovely you could make it." hollered Bunty at her friends, as she rushed over to Dols to give hugs.

"How'd you do old man?" said Teddy extending a friendly handshake to Cedric, who was just about to get his first much needed sip in.

"What Ho! Old boy. Good to see you after so long, what." Cedric replied, though quite frankly couldn't stand the chap.

Both shared similar feelings and some of the same clubs in town and were aware of each other's dealings and reputations.

The sudden new outburst of conversation re-awakened Johnathan Chadwick from his drifting's, causing him to jolt once again in his chair, rattling his whisky on the rocks, though not causing a drop to be spilt, fine practice.

"What? What have I missed?" he said looking about him "I'll show them" he sounded, preparing himself to gauge all borders.

"Johnathan!" the raised voice of Joanna cut the air sternly "Behave! We have guests."

"Guests? Guests?" he said in a somewhat confused manner, looking about himself "Who did I invite this time? Better go see to the radishes." Mr Chadwick started trying to raise himself from his chair, but discovered a glass clutched in his hand that looked like it needed company, so settled back to enjoy a few moments of intimacy.

"Bunty dear, did you get what Maggie wanted?" her mother enquired.

Bunty, momentarily frozen in time, looked at her mother until the penny quickly dropped. "My heavens, how silly, we've left them in the car." she said turning to retrieve the goods.

"Don't worry, I'll go, you stay." Teddy volunteered, quickly leaving the room with relief.

"Come on you two" Bunty enthusiastically said, addressing her friends, lets go and get ready for tennis, it'll be a hoot." She grabbed Dolly's hand and forcibly pulling her up and out of her seat, much to the look of regret from her mother, and made for the open door that Cedric was already standing by, having already downed his drink and ready for action.

The life and vibrancy left the room as suddenly as it had entered, only to leave disdain, bitterness and resentment and the tangible taste of loss and sorrow.

Joanna stood and walked to the window and yanked the curtain fully open, wanting to be bathed in cleansing light, purged from the pain and the snoring old man in the chair. She looked softly at him. Once handsome and valiant, the offer of so much until…until…

She turned again her attentions to outside and failed to see the beauty of the day, thinking only of the pleasures of the night to come.

———

The four walked together across the lawns to the tennis court in their whites, chatting idly about the nothings in their worlds, with the occasional practice swing of a racquet and a ripple of laughter through the air.

Teddy, ever galante, held the wire meshed gate open for the friends, breathing in as Dolores passed to catch her scent. He found something particularly exhilarating and fascinating with her, a heady combination, but couldn't tell what it exactly was that attracted him to her.

"Right," Bunty said immediately taking command, in response to the awareness she felt. "Sedders and Dolly, you take the tree end and Teddy and I will serve first from this end."

Sedders immediately did as he was told and assumed position, leaving Dolores and Teddy paused in motion, their natural instincts not being so used to being ordered about.

Teddy smiled at Dolores by way of recognition of a kindred spirit, though was quickly shot down in flames by a blank rebuttal, so joined Bunty for war.

The game started friendly and easily enough, though as each body warmed up with the exercise, so did the competition.

"I say, steady on old chap," Sedders piped, after receiving a well, if unintentional, aimed shot between his legs.

Teddy laughed and waved his racquet in the air while walking back to line after scoring the point. "Sorry old man, no harm done."

"Cedric!" Dolly said in a hushed but firm tone "Pull yourself together. We can beat them you know."

Cedric gave her a forlorn look, "I thought we'd come for a spot of fun, not Murder on the Orient Express" he said pitifully, only to garner a fiercer glare in return.

The dance of rivalry continued. The music of the thwack and bounce of the ball played harmoniously with the grunts of exertion, the light taps of wood on tarmacadam and the under-breath cursing.

The sun was enjoying the spectacle when Mrs Magree arrived, pushing the outdoor trolley laden with all that was required for a civilised afternoon tea.

Weapons were put to the side and a momentary truce was called as the opposing forces met on the neutral ground of the pavilion, to replenish and fortify and find a possible course of repatriation and peace,

"Here you are my dears, a nice cup of tea." Maggie Magtree said, pouring out the ready brew and removing the cloth coverings from the sandwiches, cakes and biscuits.

With grateful aplomb, the group tucked into to the supplied feast, not realising how their stores had been depleted, with many a "By George" from Sedders and "yummy" from Bunty and Dolores.

As the food and drink took effect, conversation too returned, driving back the primal urges that had come to the forefront and the grudges that had been building were also neatly put away.

As crumbs and empty cups were left on the trolley for Mrs Magtree to take back to the house, the four decided not to re-turn to the battlefield, it was a too nicer day, instead electing on a leisurely stroll around the garden and discuss their latest interests or happenings.

"Did anyone see this morning's paper?" Dolly asked as they parted company from Maggie. "Another one of those murders apparently, found further downstream than the last."

"Ooh, ghastly," Bunty said giving a shiver "it gives me night-mares just thinking about it."

"I'm sure they'll catch him soon enough," Cedric postulated "someone must know who he is."

A silence fell for a few seconds as they reflected on events.

"Suppose you were the murderer?" Dolly addressed them all "How would you keep from getting caught?" she asked.

"I wouldn't do it to start with" said Bunty, keeping her head down, wanting to avoid the subject altogether.

"Well, if it was me," Sedders started, going first "I would mix things up a bit. You know? Not keep doing the same thing."

"Why so Cedric?" asked Teddy, interested in his point of view.

"Well, if you wanted to…to carry on, so to speak. If you change your pattern, they might think it was someone else. Throw them off the scent, what."

"Cedric, that's awful." Bunty exclaimed, horrified of such a proposition coming so readily to mind.

"No, Sedders has got a point, haven't you darling." Dolores backing up her partner said. "Quite a good one as well."

"I agree," joined in Teddy "nothing like stirring the pot." He said, smiling at Dolores again, hoping to acquire a more favourable reaction.

"I think you're all ghastly. I'm going in. Dolly?" Bunty turned a started back for the house and was shortly followed by Dolores, out of duty for her friend, though once the two men were left together the balance had been tipped and they resided to follow as well.

Edward Poole sat asleep in his chair in the corner of his office, the one he used for such occasions as these. Long hours, difficult cases, not worth the bother going home, Deirdre would understand bless her. He was leaning back, mouth agape and feet up, dreaming of cabbages when the phone rang.

It jolted him from his sleep so much that it threw him off balance and almost out of his chair, only to be stopped by his hands on his knees.

The phone kept ringing, knowing that with each ring it would send the message of importance until it was answered.

Inspector Poole stood and walked to the phone on his desk, buttoning his waistcoat back up and hand combing back his hair into place.

"Inspector Poole." He commanded, though his voice broke somewhat, still clearing out his slumber.

"Inspector?" came the noticeable Welsh twang down the phone "Peter Phillips, down at the mortuary. Got an interesting development on the cadaver you gave us. I don't think the victim was killed by the same person."

"What? What do you mean?" Edward Poole spluttered out his sip of cold tea he had just taken a drink of, "Course it's the same person, don't be ridiculous man!"

"Ooh, I'm not so sure," Peter Phillips continued as the unseen Inspector Poole wiped the dribbles of liquid from his lips with his handkerchief, "you see, the knife wounds are left-handed. All the others have been right."

"Well, couldn't the culprit have just swapped hands?" Edward Poole enquired, still not thinking clearly from his slumber.

"They could have I suppose, but we could tell the difference see...tell which is the dominant hand. I'm not in any doubt, but there is something strange. Got me worried really."

Inspector Poole waited for the information to continue, but could clearly see Peter Phillips sitting at his desk waiting as well. Waiting for to be asked. As if he didn't have enough cat and mouse games to play. Yielding to the silence, he relented "What's got you worried Peter?" he asked.

"Well, the thing is...the knots are the same. Different make of cord mind. Same colour, true, but different make and same knot. Very odd, hmm" he finished, drifting off in thought.

Edward Poole was silent as he put down the phone on the cradle, his mind too going off into thought.

"Not the same killer...but same knot..." something wasn't sitting right, something...niggled at him.

He walked slightly absent-mindedly to his door opened it and called "Tea!" then added "Sweet!" someone would get the message, knowing that if "sweet" was added, things were afoot.

He turned, walked back to his comfy chair and slipped his shoes back on and rested his foot on the wooden chair, there for guests, to tie his laces.

A knock came on the door, not a Bob knock though.

"Yes" he snapped "Who is it?"

The door creaked nervously open with the sound of a rattling tea cup. A head followed the cup and saucer, a fresh-faced P.C, Archibald Jones. "Your tea Sir." Came the nervous remark.

"Thank you, Jones, put it on my desk" issued Inspector Poole, trying not to sound too severe, but severe enough to keep him on his toes.

P.C Archibald Jones, the newest recruit in the station, carefully delivered the crown jewels to their rightful place, flushing red and hot under his collar.

"Er, Sir?" Archibald Jones said.

"What is it now lad?" Edward Poole loudly questioned, wanting to get on with his thinking without interruptions.

"Er, well, its your shirt tails Sir. They're hanging out at the back."

It was Ed Pooles turn to flush. "Oh, erm, thank you lad. Thanks for the tea. On your way." He said in a smoother tone, tucking in his shirt as young Jones left, closing the door behind him.

The Inspector, now properly attired, resumed his place behind his desk and took a sip of the hot, sweet tea.

He sat thinking, pencil in hand looking down at his blotting pad, then had another drink. "Perhaps…" he thought to himself, hoping that something would come. He leant back, closed his eyes and let all thoughts go, until there was just blackness.

The thought grew. "Perhaps…change…somethings changed… perhaps this wasn't the first change?" He opened his eyes, leaning forward and took another slurp.

He could have been looking too hard in the wrong place. Change is constant after all. Perhaps things had changed, definitely they had, but perhaps…things had changed in the killer's life as well…

Outside of his office, life was continuing in its normal routine in the station.

Old Mrs Langford was complaining to Sergeant Bob Matthews about litter being left in her passage way, as Stan, the local drunk, was sleeping it off on the bench.

"It's really too bad," said the diminutive Mrs Langford "no matter how many times I tidy it up, when I come back out, more. There's more!" Bob Matthews smiled at her knowing that she hadn't quite finished, "Yesterday, and after 5 o'clock, disgraceful behaviour, I found a scrumpled up cigarette paper, oh, the shock…" Bob was thinking of the stew and dumplings his Deidre was making for his tea…she made excellent dumplings, always light and fluffy…"and then he pushed me out of the way, how rude can you get."

"Sorry Ma'am, what did you say?" Bob suddenly acknowledging a change of routine.

"The man. The one with the blood stain on his jacket. Just pushed me out of his way like nobodies' business." she said with a degree of irritation, as the shout of "More tea!" came from Inspector Pooles' office.

———

Timmy was as proud as punch at finding the body. The event had quickly become a real cause celebre in his world (not that anyone knew the French saying), news travelling fast and his reputation grew throughout his peers, attracting new envies, jealousies and admiration.

Boxer was enjoying the extra attention as well. After all, it was he who had actually found the body and was being regaled with extra scraps of meat, plenty of head scratches and the occasional bone from the local community.

Timmy and Boxer sat on an upturned row boat, watching life go by and kicking his heels, while thinking of how he could keep the recognition going. Next time, he thought, he might get a reward, might be rich. He looked down at Boxer the bulldog who licked his lips and snorted, as if in agreement, probably imagining a mound of fresh bones to call his own.

It was then that Timmy struck upon an idea.

All the bodies found so far, had washed up along the river nearby and hadn't been in the water long. You could tell by the bloating. He had seen one body once, looked like a balloon, all puffed up it was, ready to burst. He was sure that if he had been allowed to prod it with a sharp stick it would have shot of like a motor boat.

He chuckled to himself gently, causing Boxer to look around and see what all the fuss was about.

Timmy needed a plan. Some idea. That's when he saw Stevie walking along the footpath, closely inspecting something in his hands.

"Oi Stevie!" shouted Timmy, adding in a wave to make sure Stevie saw him. Stevie didn't have too good of eyesight.

Stevie stopped what he was doing and looked around and ran towards Timmy was sitting, Boxer standing up, little stub of the tail wagging, ready for more attention.

"Hey Stevie, what you got there?" he asked his chum.

"An old cutthroat by the looks of it." he said opening it up to show the flat ended blade. "Bit rusty, wooden handle though, found it in the mud further down. Must've been there for ages. Took some doing to open it."

"Cor!" exclaimed Timmy, marvelling at the find. "Perhaps someone got done in with it, years ago, evidence got thrown away." He said all fired up with excitement.

"Nah," relpied Stevie, "some boatmen probably cutting lines and lost it overboard."

Timmy sat back down, deflated, unimpressed with the explanation.

The friends both sat in silence, both sets of heels now kicking the upturned boat beneath them.

"Was it horrid?" Stevie asked

"Nah, seen worse." Said Timmy casually, feeling a renewed sense of importance.

"We ought to get a gang together, there's enough of us you know." Stevie suggested.

Timmy looked at him, not quite sure what he was getting at.

"To watch for when the next body gets dumped. We could find it first. Like you did. We could be like Dick Tracy." Stevie was talking up his ideas, while his examination of his newly found cutthroat resumed.

"That's it. That's great Stevie. We'll form a gang." Timmy's brain started exploding with ideas, possibilities and scenarios. "We gotta get to work fast. We've got a lot of ground to cover. I know a few upstream, how about you?"

Stevie looked at him, surprised at the reaction his idea had received. No-one ever liked his ideas. He could be Marshall Steve, head of the posse. "I know a few too, they probably know others as well."

Timmy's mind was racing now, they could catch the killer dumping the body, they would be heroes. Why hadn't anyone else thought of it.

————

Evening Dinner came around soon enough, though Joanna had excused herself, feeling unwell and with a headache, so had retired early to her room for the night, leaving Johnathan Chadwick no excuse but to forgo solid nourishment and focus solely on his friends, the shorts, no doubt leaving himself paralytic by 10:30 and would probably be found in his study or at the bottom of the stairs come morning.

The four had suitably dressed for the evening meal and convened in the drawing room for aperitifs.

Teddy was on cocktail duty, mixing a host of Maidens Prayers, hoping it might entice some good fortune to come his way, as Bunty, the last to arrive, walked in with a cloud still hanging over her head from earlier, showing that her immaturity in years still affected her behaviour and decision making.

Dolly took a newly poured glass from Teddys hand and walked it over to her friend and host.

"Here we go darling, something to lift the spirits." She said while drawing from her cigarette holder, blowing the smoke innocently, yet purposely to annoy.

"Thank you." said Bunty gloomily, waving the cloud away as she stood in front of the roaring fire of the hearth.

Cedric stood the other side of the fireplace, staring deeply into its depths as an arm slipped itself around his waist, bringing him back into the room, just as a kind and reassuring kiss brushed his cheek.

"Sedders old man. Time for a refill?" Teddy called over happy with his mixology.

Cedric drained the last drops of liquid from his glass and brought the empty glass over, relieved for some distraction of his thoughts.

Sensing the subduedness of the room Teddy carried on the conversation. "Well, I thought today was going to be a livelier affair, but didn't expect this." Realising that it wasn't the most tactful way of breaking the ice and not receiving any retort, decided to change tack. "Anyone got any plans for a getaway?"

For some reason, Teddy thought Dolores looked suddenly uncomfortable, but Cedric quickly piped up.

"I've always fancied a trip on the Orient Express. I hear Istanbul is full of mystery and intrigue, really exotic."

Dolly sidled over to again him and placed her hand discreetly on his left buttock "Hmm, we all know about your exotic tastes, don't we darling." She said giving him a little squeeze.

"I think it sounds very romantic," Bunty said "the Orient Express. I think it would be divine, going through France and Italy, I think it goes all the way to Bucharest now."

"Just give me a month on the Riviera darlings, and I would be happy." Dolores inclined "Laying on the beach or by a pool of the hotel, drinks brought every half hour, massages, then casino in the evening. What more could a girl need."

"Well, actually," Teddy started to declare "an uncle of mine has a large private villa on some little Greek island. Says I can go anytime, just wondering if anyone would like to come for a jaunt?"

He had made the room go quiet again.

"That's awfully sporting of you." Cedric said, genuinely taken aback.

Though Dolly was more reserved "Yes, lovely." Being as elusive as ever.

"Are you inviting me to go away with you?" Bunty asked in a deeply moved manner.

"Well, yes, I suppose so. It's an open invitation to all really." Teddy replied.

"Oh, darling." Bunty rushed towards Teddy and flung her arms around his neck, causing him to be rather startled at her reaction and for Dolores to give one of her "honestly!" sighs.

"When can we go?" said Bunty enthusiastically, eagerness building quickly. "Perhaps I should go and tell mother. Should I start packing now? What's the weather like at this time of year?"

Teddy was starting to regret the whole thing. In fact, he wasn't even sure if Bunty really was the girl for him after all. The money was appealing, but even that was starting to lose its allure, now he had found a new passion.

Just then the dinner gong sounded. "Saved by the gong" Teddy thought, as did the other, rather sympathetic two.

They finished their cocktails and Dolly and Bunty led the way into the dining room, conversation having been ignited and stomachs suitably primed.

The meal was a fine affair, as always. Maggie Magtrees skills in the kitchen seemed to know no bounds and every course was as satisfying as the last, well balanced with each mouthful complementing the other.

The talk had been as varied as the food and wines and by the time the meal was over, each was satisfied and complete, glasses and plates emptied, as were the topics of humour and forthcoming adventures.

They retired once again to the drawing room for coffee, cigars and brandy, but the conversation had once again become muted and tired.

It was Dolores who elected herself to retire first from the group, kissing her Cedric a goodnight and wishing all a goodnight and left for her prospective room.

Bunty was the next to leave, still heady with excitement and ready for bed and a pillow of dreams and shortly followed too by Cedric, wanting the flatness of his bed to ease his over imbibing.

Teddy was left alone with just his thoughts for company, the fire too almost dimming and coldness of the night approaching fast. He heard Maggie finishing off tidying up and what he assumed to be Johnathan Chadwick stumbling about in the direction of his study, obviously out to catch the fuzzy-wuzzies.

He looked about the room and decided to pour himself another Brandy, at least that would keep him company for a while longer and hopefully subdue any urges he might have. He considered calling on Bunty then thought better of it. He placed a couple more logs onto the dying fire and settled down into the armchair near by and let his thoughts take them where they chose.

The house became quiet and settled down for the night.

If one had been standing in the hall, straining to ascertain the slightest noise, you might've heard a door softly and ever so quietly, slowly creak open and close.

Joanna left her room and walked down the dark corridor, her nightdress and hair suitably arranged.

She stood outside the door and gently knocked.

The door opened and the light from the small fireplace danced with shadows across the walls, as Dolores smiled, eyes catching the flames.

"Well," she said leaning evocatively on the open door "I thought you'd never come."

She turned and hips swaying, walked back into the room, leaving Joanna to follow, closing the door behind her, senses and heart pounding as she slipped her clothing off her shoulders.

Dolly turned to suddenly face her as Joanna realised, they were not alone. In the darkened corner of the room, the light of a cigarette grew and faded, alarm and shock ran through her as she attempted to cover her nakedness.

Dolores took one of Joanna's hands away from her breast and placed it behind Dolores's back, bringing them closer.

"Oh, don't worry about Cedric," she said softly into Joanna's ear, "we do everything together these days."

————

Sarah Guppy had been an attractive young lady at one time, though now her skin, hair and clothing were almost the same darkened colour, having been forced out of moderate accommodation with her family, into their new found position of despair.

The three breadwinners of the household, Sarah, her father and brother, all losing their employment in the slump and being forced to seek handouts and assistance where available, but with so many other needy mouths, drastic and sudden changes had to be made.

They now found themselves living in the slums, another face lining up with no hope in their pockets and only chance to help them out of the pit of despair.

They had been used as oil for the wheels of the mighty engine that turned and when the building of the machine had become too big, refinement was needed. Excess was stripped away, new methods were implemented, like the modern-day equivalent of replacing old valves with circuit boards, but the antiquated thrown on the discarded pile of humanity. Backs turned as the wealthy carried on in their feasting, readying themselves for another couple of decades of gluttony, until the next drop, where again, they will find another pile to clamber over to sate their wantonness and lack of care.

It is no longer seen as survival of the fittest in this era, but survival of the wealthiest, yet, this is the trap that many have fallen.

Sarah and her family had fallen from their unrealised fragile existence and now, she was already scarred, mentally and physically, from trying to put bread into the mouths that she loved.

It was a dark and cold night. The blackness drawing in quicker and some of the November eves could seem colder and harsher than a February one, probably due to being closer to the recent summer and autumn and their memories still keeping you warm.

Regardless, weather doesn't make allowances for empty stomachs, so Sarah put her finest shawl on and walked the streets, frequenting known haunts of gentlemen seeking cheap company, while trying to avoid the darker lanes of danger.

Their paths crossed on a green as she was making her way from the lit, still bustling busy quarter where the pubs were warm and secure to a quieter and more tentative part of town, where it paid to go with company, so at least one watchful eye could be had.

Tonight, though was not the case. Sarah almost bumped into the man, darkness being so close, but the cold also causing her to keep her head down.

"Oh, I'm sorry Sir." she said, startled by the sudden impact and when no reply came, she knew then she should have kept walking, instead she continued in query. "You looking for some warmth this cold night?"

Even though it was impossible to see, she could feel his eyes staring into her soul, heard his heavy breath and felt him take hold of her arm.

"Come. This way." were the only words he spoke to her as he led her away from the path a deeper into the green, towards the small woods that lay on the edge.

They walked a brisk pace, with Sarah being pulled, as if in a hurry and she was uncertain on whether she ought to flee, but thought she saw a flicker of a light in the direction they went so felt some sense of reassurance.

As soon as they arrived at the edge of the trees she was pushed to the ground, skirt hoisted, and taken violently from behind. A cord was suddenly placed around her neck and started choking her. Sarah thrashed and reached into the air to grasp for anything. She was sure that someone else was there, but saw or heard nothing, just felt a presence nearby. Within seconds she felt herself passing out, choking for air as the blackness and stars of the night filled her head.

As she came too, her world seemed slow, she could feel the man standing over her, straddling her, lowering himself down. Silently, without wanting to reveal her awareness, she instinctively clawed at where she thought his face might be, missing contact with her perpetrators face, but feeling a heat to her hand and wetness follow down her arm. She clawed more, twisting and contorting her body, trying to free itself from her captor. Her face and arms felt pain and for the first time screamed out for help.

Instantly she could hear assistance from afar. Shouts of concern and alertness that made her assailant disappear as instantly as he had arrived.

Sarah got to her shaking legs and was met by warm, friendly and concerned arms. Little did she know that she had been the first victim. Others, unfortunately, would not be so lucky, as her escape only honed the killer's skill and determination.

———

The breakfast gong sounded and was proceeded by the opening and closing of doors and footsteps on stairs making their way to break their nights fast in the dining room.

Mr John Chadwick sat at one end of the table, suitable engrossed in the mornings paper having already said good morning to a strong Bloody Mary, a punchy little number, the celery freshly picked by Mrs Magtree this very morning on her early stroll around the garden, checking the bushes and greenhouse for tell-tale signs of visitors, by which we mean a prostrate Mr Chadwick from the night before.

Thankfully, for Maggie Magtree, this morning he was found at the feet of the stuffed bear in the hall, something that had become commonplace of late, and she surmised that Mr Chadwick felt a compelling urge to confide in his new found friend of late, knowing that unconditional love was a one-way street and sooner or later John Chadwick would move on to find a new comrade in arms, having fallen out with its predecessor.

Maggie found the whole affair quite intriguing and she had a little bet with Wendy, the "occasional", to see which inanimate object would be the receptor of John Chadwick's attention.

There didn't seem to be any set pattern or direction around the house involved, as anything from the old grandfather clock to a paperweight could be found in flagrante delicto and in any room.

One particularly disturbing morning a while back, was finding John Chadwick, behind the curtains in the drawing room. He was still asleep, but somehow had managed to keep himself vertical, in a semi undressed condition, with an onion in one hand and a porcelain bust of a horse in the other.

At the other end of the table sat Joanna Chadwick, sipping her morning coffee, looking more relaxed than normal yet tentative at the same time. Maggie often saw this behaviour in the morning when they had guests staying and put down to her wanting for her guests to be accommodated in every way they needed. Little did she know how true her words were.

Teddy was the first to arrive, having already had a good walk around the grounds, something he missed doing while living in the city. He breezed in through the door open with gusto, bringing the freshness of the outside in, causing Joanna to breath in the morning and remind her of days gone.

"Morning Teddy, did you sleep well dear?" she asked her guest.

"Like a log, thank you Joanna. Always do when I'm here." Teddy replied helping himself to some kippers.

Joanna was just about to continue the conversation but was cut short by the arrival of Bunty, Dolores and Cedric, Joanna's latest new "acquaintance". She blushed momentarily and adjusted her seating position and with a light cough and dabbed the corners of her mouth with her napkin "Good morning' everybody. I hope you all…slept well?" she enquired smiling.

Bunty and Dolores whispered something to each other and laughed.

"Very well thank you Joanna," Sedders said, offering a slight bow "All thanks for your wonderful accommodation" he smiled, with the girls giggling behind him again.

Joanna flushed again, but this time out of uncomfortable embarrassment, feeling that somehow, she was being ridiculed.

"Honestly girls," she exclaimed "do behave, it is the morning and your father was up all night."

"I was up quite a bit of it as well" Cedric wryly and cruelly implied and got the response he desired from Dolores and Bunty who burst out laughing again.

"Honestly, this is too much." said Joanna shaking her head and rose gracefully from the table. "I'll see you children later…" and looking directly into Dolly's eyes as she passed added "and if you need anything, well, you know where to find me."

Joanna left the room and silence behind her.

Teddy, who still hadn't started eating his kippers, had watched the whole show with a certain widemouthed disbelief, though resumed buttering his toast with an uncertain thought in his head.

John Chadwick turned a page and looked over the top of his paper.

"The harpies gone then?" he asked "Blessed relief. Well, I'm off to water me melons." He said folding his paper carefully and tossing it onto the floor as he got up from his chair. "Like to make her work for her money. Can't make life easy for the char you know."

Mr Chadwick walked past his guests and out of the dining room, mumbling a conversation with an invisible comrade in arms about the time he spent at a camp, 100 miles north east of Bombay.

"Well, that was a pleasant way to start the morning." Bunty chirped up, easing the path of conversation. "Who's for eggs?"

———

Timmy and Stevie had set about their recruitment of The Watch Gang with great passion and seriousness. The word spread rapidly, garnering great interest from the urchins and would be detectives of the north bank of the river, with each new connection adding a novel piece of information to the story and tasks ahead.

What had started as a watchful eye, discreet and cunning downstream, had now turned into rumours of funding by Scotland Yard itself and a reward so large it would have to be delivered by van.

This latest addition of news rippled its way inland and up the age groups, round the narrow-cobbled streets where talk was even bantered around adult folks in ramshackle drinking dens, where talk was as cheap as the drink. Though quickly squashed as hearsay, it left some still pondering the authenticity and dark plans were hatched, where, one way or another, a price would be extracted for themselves.

The grimy pile of clothes that sat next to the fire of an excuse for a pub, was the locally known, though locally unliked figure of Wilbur Curtain, with his cap pulled down as always, minding his own business but paying keen attention to others. His trade, if you could call it that and like his father and his father before that, was the opening of anything closed and his tools ranged from a jimmy to a knife.

Many a night work was had, stealthily visiting wealthier folk when they were tucked up in bed, finding a business who were lax in locks or to return to his waterside haunts, collecting unpaid debts with heavy handed severity.

Wilbur Curtains reputation certainly preceded him, though few knew him by his looks, only by dealings would you know him and then probably wished that you did not.

Hearing of the young ruffians and scallywags venture, he took it upon himself to earn the monies offered, but, if for some strike of luck, the other party was apprehended, well, perhaps they might pay more to be allowed to continue in their work. Besides, business is business.

He had spent his entire life along the river, born in Canvey Island working his way along into the heart of the city, when it was easier to make a living with the waters help, especially around the wharfs and jetties of Puddle Dock, where barges were easy pickings and people were too busy to ask questions.

Wilbur finished his tankard of ale and slipped out into the night, joining his friends of dark alleys and shadows as he made his way to the waters edge.

He set off on foot along the towpath, being wary of anyone who might take him for a stranger, competition could be fierce, but was confident enough to know that his very appearance would more than likely deter any foe.

As he walked in the night of the moon, the occasional boat still moving on the Thames, he figured at least a quarter of an hour's fast pace until he slowed and started to pay real attention.

Despite the years of living by the water, he had never needed to find a place to dispose of a body from. Any confrontation that had involved his hand was normally...well...he had never killed anyone, intentionally. Sometimes a beating had not gone as expected, or a robbery had gotten out of hand, but Wilbur Curtain was no murderer and he prided himself in that.

As he walked, he lit his pipe and gently sang The Cruel Mother to himself, a song his mother used to sing to him when a lad, sitting by the hearth of their cottage, waiting for his father to return with his belt. He was surprised to hear again after so long, remembering the words clearly and wondered why it should come back to him now.

A coldness came about him and he looked nervously over his shoulder, something he wasn't used to doing, though felt sure someone was watching him on his journey of discovery and possible fortune.

He tapped and put away his pipe and fastened his pace, wanting to find some suitable spots to mark and keep an eye on for himself before any morning light came, wanting to be back in his room before the light arose.

Wilbur watched and looked. He was glad of the full moon and clear night, the darkest patches stood out clearly for him, some he knew were areas frequented by other nightly customs, some led to inaccessible areas and he was surprised how few leant themselves to what he was looking for.

A couple he marked by chalk from his pocket, but he wasn't convinced that those places would take the bodies where they had ended up, due to tides and pull of the undercurrents. All things you learnt about fast while living on the river.

The further he walked the more disappointed he became, doubting his skills at finding "that" spot, until.

In the distance he noted a large patch of dark, but the way the trees stood, suggested a footpath or trail leading away and judging by the way the bend in the river was, a boat would undoubtedly take the south bank for navigation purposes.

The closer he got, the happier he was. He would stay here until almost dawn then head back, giving him plenty of time to explore the area more thoroughly and get acquainted with possible scenarios.

He felt his blood pumping and he knew he had found the spot. All he had to do now was wait.

The small red bricked terraced house sat behind a low red bricked wall with a small patch of garden separating the two. The quiet street was once a hustle and bustle of community lives, children playing in the streets, knocking on people's doors for bowls of sugar and pulling tongues at the debt and rent collectors, but since the wounds of the Great War, fewer children were being born and the gap was noticed and felt by the older citizens, especially poignant to those who had lost their children in conflict.

For Sergeant Bob Matthews, being home was like being stuck between a rock and a hard place. He enjoyed his work and had strived to be a conscientious member of the force, unlike some of his up-and-coming recruits, who, to him, seemed to be getting recruited from any walk of life, merely to fill the ever-growing gap of need.

So, while desk duties now replaced being on-the beat, which, admittedly, he was thankful for, his legs not being able to chase the ruffians of the day, he did find the level of crimes, or moreover, the level of inhumanity disturbing, but hardly surprising, considering what some of the chaps had probably been through. Everything has a consequence.

Home life gave little respite. Once a happy vibrant house, his Doris took the loss badly and had never fully recovered and there would always be that slight, distant look in her eyes, of an unknown field, across the channel, where, God willing, they might visit one day to tell them that they were loved and thought of and how they wished beyond anything else that they could change places with them. Maybe one day, as long as nothing else bad happens.

Bob sat and the kitchen table waiting for his cup of tea that Doris was making for him, having been out in the back garden talking to his begonias. He pulled out his pouch and took out his papers and cabbage leaf which held his tobacco, keeping it fresh.

"I don't know, you talk to your begonias more than me these days." Doris said as she poured a bit of hot kettle water into the empty teapot to warm it up. "First it was marigolds, then your pansies..."

"They were lovely those pansies, very pretty, reminded me of you." smiled Bob as he puffed on his newly lit roll-up.

"Ooh, you cheeky beggar." Doris said, noticeably embarrassed.

Bob missed his wife's smile, he was glad to see it, she must be having one of her better days he thought.

"What it is with you and your flowers, I don't know?" she carried on saying, while putting the leafed tea into the now empty pot and filling it from the kettle.

"They remind me of your beauty and of innocence" said Bob with honesty and poignance.

The kitchen went still and silent and Doris gripped the side of the sink to keep herself steady.

Bob put his cigarette down and stood. He walked behind Doris and rested his compassionate hands on her aching shoulders. "C'mon lass, take a seat, I'll finish this off."

"Oh, Bob." Doris uttered as she turned and burrowed her weeping eyes into his shoulder, the never-ending waterfall of grief spilling over the precipice, ever falling. "When will it be over?" she cried.

Bob had no answer for her, just his love and support, though knew that many a time even that wasn't enough to help them through it.

"There, there, c'mon deary, you'll curdle the milk if you carry on like this." Bob said while gently patting her back.

"Ooh, you beast." Doris replied with humour in her tears, giving him an imploring, desperate look of lostness.

"I'm going to try growing some orchids again next year, it's been a while." said Bob, wanting to change the subject and not get stuck in the going nowhere conversation. It wasn't that he didn't care, he just didn't know what else to do, the past was the past, no matter how much you grieve for it.

Doris wiped her eyes with the bottom of her apron and sat down in Bob's seat, feeling it's warmth underneath her as he finished off making the now two cups of tea and picked up his rollie and took a couple of drags, the first helping it to relight.

"The orchids you grew last time did nothing but fail" Doris said, pulling a bit of loose baccy from her lip.

"Well, I thought it might be nice to try again, you never know." he said, sitting in the chair opposite.

They both sat in silence for a few moments and sipped the brewed and made cups of tea.

The quiet was broken with Doris nonchalantly saying "I suppose," having had the thought tumble around inside for a while "I guess if you don't succeed at first, you've got to go back to the drawing board, figure out where it went wrong. You got to keep trying, don't you?" she said working through her own dilemmas more than anything else. "Once you practice some more you can do it real, proper, get it right." She said abstractedly taking another puff.

Bob smiled at his Doris, he did love her so and he only wished things had turned out different for them and taking a sip of his tea he realised that she was right.

———

As Teddy drove back to London, the heaviness came over him, leaving an exhaustion that felt like it would never leave, despite the gentle warmth of the sun and the air washing over his face. It felt ironic to him that his early departure from the city to the weekend in the countryside had been such an occasion of elation and exhilaration, yet now, here he was, refreshed and renewed, yet feeling trepidation from an unwanted scenario and despair for the unknowingness of how he was going to resolve his situation, or if he was ever going to be free from such heavy constraints and burdens.

He mentally castigated himself for the proposal of holidaying at his uncle's villa, though suspected that Cedric's response to the suggestion mirrored his awareness of the flaws in the pitch. He was surprised and intrigued at how much Cedric was possibly aware of and how much he would divulge to Dolores or perhaps he would just pass it off as nothing, or even, perhaps, thought Teddy, that he was making too much out of nothing himself.

His head spun at the abundance of potentials his mind was conjuring up and all of them supposition, mainly due to the web of lies he was spinning for himself, but what else was he to do.

It was true that he had painted himself into a corner, but some of which had not been by his own design. The confusion that life had offered and the lack of security instilled from an early age had been complicated enough and now, as an adult, being constantly told that one was in control of one's destiny when it was difficult enough to face the daily demands of a routine existence.

[PK1]

Printed in Great Britain
by Amazon